The Line of Duty

Part one of
The Bremmand Chronicles

Cate Caruth

The Line of Duty
Part one of the Bremmand Chronicles

ISBN: 978-1-4116-8588-8

Originally printed by Lulu.com

Second Edition

For Kif

Who gave me the impetus I needed to do this

Map 1: Southern Bremmand

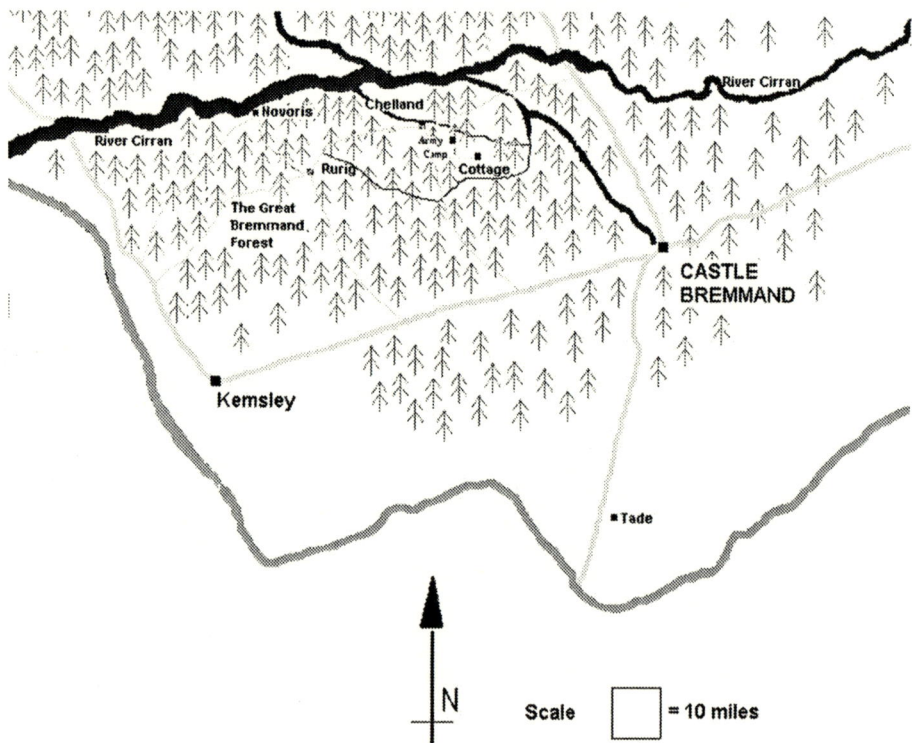

River Cirran

Novoris

Chelland

Army Camp

Rurig

Cottage

River Cirran

The Great Bremmand Forest

CASTLE BREMMAND

Kemsley

Tade

N

Scale [ ] = 10 miles

Map 2: Passant and Arias

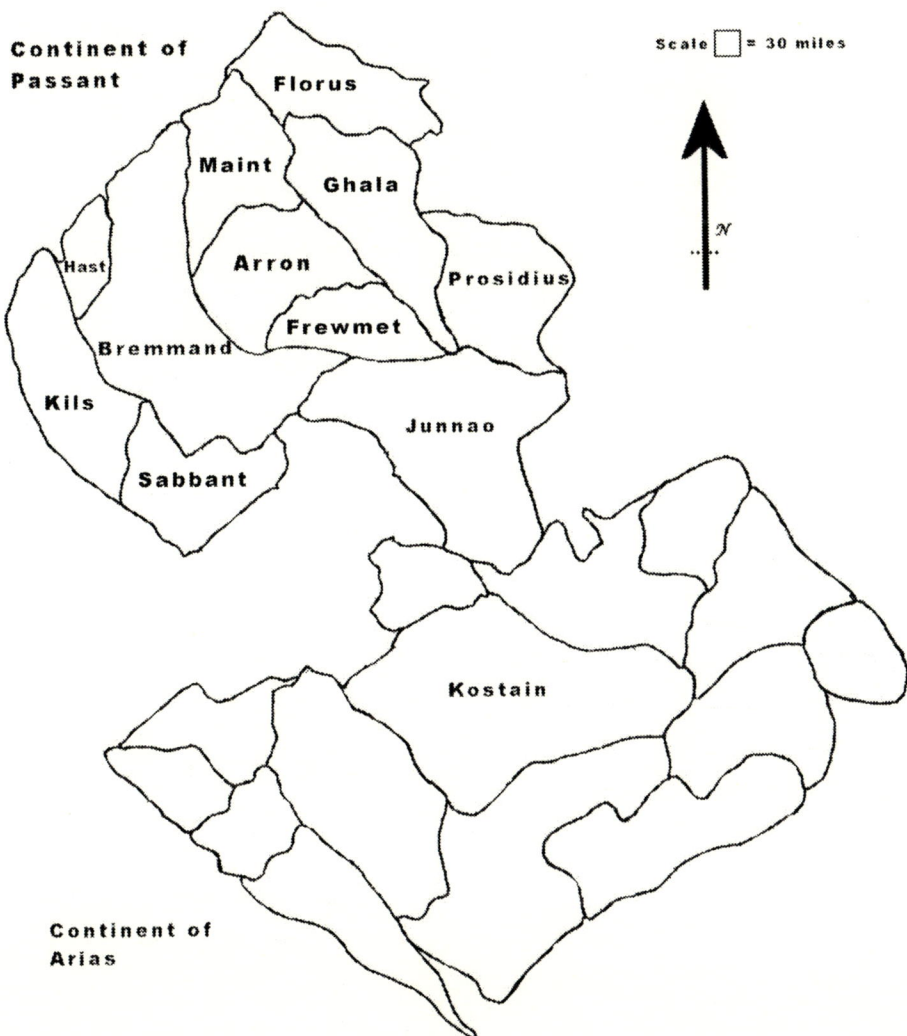

Continent of Passant

Florus

Maint

Ghala

Hast

Arron

Prosidius

Bremmand

Frewmet

Kils

Junnao

Sabbant

Kostain

Continent of Arias

Scale ☐ = 30 miles

N

1154 marked the 500th anniversary of the Rometh dynasty, which ruled Kostain. In the autumn of that year, Emperor Darvett decided to mark the rise to power of his ancestors by leading a campaign to take Junao. Junao was a rich nation, having a large supply of several precious metals, and Darvett, new to the throne and eager to prove himself, could not resist this prize. His advisors warned him that attack in the autumn was unwise, but he insisted. His venerable ancestor had taken control of Kostain in the autumn, so why shouldn't he, Darvett, do the same with Junao? Besides, Junao was almost defenceless.

This much was true. Junao and Prosidius had been at war for the last 50 years, on and off, over the ownership of the mountain passes between them. As a result Junao was exhausted and depleted of most of its fighting force and, with all its young men lost to war, their wealth remained firmly buried in the ground.

When the Kostinian army arrived at its borders, Junao, unable to stave off the mighty army from the empire, did the only thing it could think of. It appealed to the Bremmand Alliance for aid. Who could resist such an appeal? If Junao joined the alliance, their gold would allow them to defend from Kostain forever.

The Alliance mobilised – the different kingdoms each bringing their particular skills to the combined army. Thus with the great military thinking of Hast, the fearless troops of Kils and the bold leadership of Bremmand, Darvett was met with a resistance he had not expected. He was forced to retreat and, with the winter setting in, there was no opportunity for a second attack until the spring.

Darvett was determined not to let the Junao gold end up in the hands of the Bremmand Alliance, so he spent the winter moving troops north and equipping them for a second assault. He moved as soon as the weather improved with a massive force behind him. It proved unnecessary since the first attempt to ward off Darvett's troops had exhausted much of the alliance reserve and Junao was unprotected against this second wave of Kostinian troops. By the summer of 1155 Junao was occupied by the Kostain Empire.

For Darvett, however, the eventual victory was not enough. The earlier defeat was the first that the Empire of Kostain had suffered for more than two hundred years and for Darvett it was a political disaster. There were whispers that Darvett did not have the abilities of his Father, and that he would soon lead the Empire into ruin. One of those who was most eager to whip up discontent was Sallent, Darvett's younger half-brother, ever eager to grab power.

Darvett was no fool. If he wanted to make more moves to expand the Empire (and thus build his reputation) he would have to eliminate the resistance which the Bremmand Alliance was offering. He began to build his forces into a mighty army which would be able to tear out the heart of the alliance by taking control of Bremmand itself.

Two years later, in the Spring of 1157, Darvett led a vast army towards Bremmand. The Alliance, with King Jorvis of Bremmand and his four eldest sons in the vanguard, met them on the southern border at Kantora.

The Line of Duty

Flight

Captain Dale Ronas lifted his head above the shelter of the undergrowth and took a long careful look about. All appeared to be quiet but he wasn't taking any chances - not when he was responsible for such a precious company.

He was still adjusting to how fast everything had changed. A week ago he was Captain of the Palace guard, seething with frustration at being left at the castle when the rest of the troops had marched off to war. Then, in the night, a fast rider bringing bad news from one of the watch posts on the Southern borders of Bremmand. Empire troops had been seen penetrating northwards, taking up positions well beyond the Alliance lines. Darvett was marching north to take Castle Bremmand.

It had not taken long to gather the queen and her five youngest children, along with an entourage of other palace dignitaries and essential staff, to start the flight north under the protection of the four dozen palace guards designated for the task. The journey to the safety of the northern country of Hast would be long and arduous and the small company of soldiers had done everything in their power to keep the family safe but with the children so young they had been unable to move as fast as was needed. Darvett's men had been upon them within the week.

Verdin, Lord of Langate, commander of the guard, having realised that Empire troops were on their trail and getting close, had been forced to make some hard decisions and had split the party into three groups. The main bulk of the troops would continue along the North road he ordered, to lead their pursuers off the scent while smaller groups, consisting of the royal family, divided up into two parties would leave the road and go in opposite directions, taking a circuitous route towards Hast. They would rendezvous there - beyond Darvett's clutches.

It had seemed like the best compromise in a bad situation but the Queen had added an improvement of her own. She would, she insisted, ride with the main party, taking the obvious and fastest route to Hast. Verdin had argued, quietly pointing out that this was the decoy, most likely to be caught.

"Which is exactly why I should travel with you," Queen Isolde had remarked serenely. "Judging by the speed with which these men are pursuing us, they are determined to catch us and bring us back to Castle Bremmand. That means, if they catch the decoy party, there needs to be someone there to make them feel they have achieved their goal, or they will simply continue to hunt those who have gone in other directions. I am the most expendable member of the family but probably the most useful hostage for the invaders. If Darvett holds me, he can be assured of Hast's co-operation. They'd have to stop for long enough to ensure I was held captive."

Verdin had begun to argue again, protesting his duty to protect her but she cut him short. "My Lord Verdin, I know exactly what I am doing in this decision. I am giving myself to Darvett's men willingly, so that my children stand a chance of survival. Can you not understand that they are of far greater importance than I, both to the future of Bremmand, and to me? If I am right, and I am intended as a hostage, then I will be able to slow our pursuers down and force at least some of them to abandon the chase and return to Castle Bremmand."

"But then Hast will be tied. Your importance to Darvett is also your importance to us."

"They won't be able to use me. I'll delay them as much as I can and then I'll kill myself. If I die, nothing will prevent my father from assisting Bremmand in any way necessary." Isolde said this in such a cool and calculating way that Verdin had gasped.

"You can't be serious, Isolde?"

"I am absolutely serious. I'm going with you. I'll be the decoy that is needed to ensure my children have every chance of survival and then I'll take my own life."

"No!" Verdin had said, horrified. "I won't allow it!"

"You don't understand, Verdin. Darvett is here, in Bremmand. That can only mean that Jorvis is dead. My life is less than nothing to me without him, and all that I have left to do is ensure that at least some of my sons live to succeed their father. This is the best way to do it - and you cannot dispute it."

They had argued back and forth for a while longer but the Queen had been adamant and Verdin was forced to agree. Thus it was that the five children of the Marchand house had been divided into two groups. The eldest, Prince Corist, and the youngest, the princess Josanna, with the middle boy, Allinaias had been put in one group while the other two, Princes Davys and Andred would travel a different way. Verdin had assigned as few soldiers as he dared to each group - he didn't want the Kostinians to work out what they had done, so the decoy party had to look convincing - but had picked them with care for their fighting ability and, in Dale's case, his skills as a woodsman. Added to Dale's party, along with three other soldiers was the princes' tutor. He was Trystin of Dracia, one of the scholars engaged by the King to educate his many sons in the more civilised skills. As far as Dale recalled, Master Trystin taught History and Politics and had escorted the Princes in order to help the Queen and her ladies manage the children on the flight north.

Everyone else was to travel with the main party, Verdin declared, having allocated people to the other royal group of children as well, and would continue on their journey up the North Road. This largest group would have to take all the horses, he explained a trifle regretfully. He knew that leaving the side parties on foot would slow them down but if the pursuing enemy saw that the numbers in their quarry had fallen they would guess what had happened and they would lose their advantage. Besides, Dale had agreed consolingly, they were going to be travelling through the depths of the forest and horses would be in their way in that terrain.

Dale Ronas was a big man, well built and strong. His rust-coloured hair and beard betrayed him as a man of the woods, from central Bremmand, where all men were similarly coloured. But, despite his size, and the reputation of his people for being slow and clumsy, he was fast on his feet and as agile as a cat. Verdin knew he was one of the strongest and most intelligent of the small troop and also one of the most loyal, so had not hesitated in choosing him to safeguard the children of the fallen King. The big Captain had served Lord Verdin for several years, and as far as it was possible and appropriate, they had become friends. They trusted each other and understood each other well. It was this as much as anything that made Verdin ask him to take command of one of the escape parties.

"The priority is to get your party safely to Hast. Don't worry about how long it takes, just make sure they get there," Verdin had instructed. "They must reach their Grandfather alive. Your first and only priority is to protect The Royal Family. You are to do whatever is necessary to achieve that."

Dale had nodded. "It might be safest to hole up for a bit. They won't expect us to stay in the country."

"Whatever your judgement tells you, Captain, but don't tell me, or indeed anyone, what you are planning. It's safest if no-one knows." Verdin had looked suddenly grief stricken, knowing that he was almost certain to die on this journey north. "When you have completed that mission, Dale, I have another task for you. A favour for me." Dale already knew what this would be.

"Your son?"

Verdin nodded. "I had to leave him behind with one of the women who lives in The Castle; A seamstress…" Dale nodded - it wasn't public knowledge, but it wasn't exactly a secret either that Verdin had relations with the woman. He'd lost his wife several years before and every man needed someone to alleviate his loneliness. "When it's safe, come back to Bremmand and collect him. Take him, and the woman if she'll come, to Hast and see that he is made known to the King. His bloodline is as old as the Marchand's and I want him to be raised to serve the King as my family always has." Without ceremony, Verdin pulled a fine gold chain from about his neck, on which hung a medallion. On one side was an interwoven pattern, the insignia of Verdin's family and on the other the royal herald, indicating the bond between the two houses of Langate and Marchand that had lasted for over 500 years. He dropped it into Dale's hand. "Take this. Sela should know you by it. She'll know it's from me and that she can trust you. I…" he hesitated, before explaining "I never take it off, and it's been a bit of a joke between us - that I always wear it. It should go to my son now. I suspect I'll not need it where I'm going, and I don't much care for the idea that some scavenging soldier should take it with no understanding of its meaning."

Dale nodded, as he stared at the golden token in his hand. "If the need arises, then I shall ensure he is cared for as you have commanded but let us pray that you'll be able to collect him yourself."

Dale had stood to one side, waiting while the Queen had said goodbye to her children and had been impressed and amazed by the composed way she had parted for the last time with her offspring. She had acted exactly as if this was an everyday thing; that they would soon be together again and, to keep them from fretting, had ensured that each had some little duty to perform on the trip. Prince Allinaias had been charged with minding his sister and making sure she was looked after, and the little princess was asked to make sure everyone was happy. Only Prince Corist did she not patronise with the idea that all was as it should be. Out of the hearing of the others she had spoken a few quiet words to him which had seen him first wince and then fling his arms emotionally about her neck. They had clung to each other for a few moments and then she had disentangled herself from him gently and, after a few more brief words, had made him turn and join the rest of his family.

Dale had got them all moving quickly after that. He didn't want the children dwelling on this parting and had realised that the sooner they had their minds on something else the better things would be. He wanted them under cover and gone to ground just as soon as he could.

They hadn't been lucky. Dale had tracked westward through the forest for a while, leading his party up an incline heading for the high ground of the forest, but as they had crossed one of the minor paths that littered the dense woods, a handful of Empire soldiers had come upon them. There weren't many of them and they were far less determined than the King's guard, but four soldiers were not really a match for eight and as he fought grimly on Dale could hear the voice of Verdin, Earl of Langate ringing in his ears.

Your first and only priority is to protect the Royal Family. Protect the Royal family … Your first and only Priority…

With a sick feeling of despair he knew that he had to abandon his men in order to fulfil his mission for Verdin. He bawled at Master Trystin to run and saw, as he cut down one of the enemy troops, that the slender scholar had had the wits to grab hold of Prince Corist, who had the young Princess by his side, and haul him deep into the undergrowth, snatching up the girl as he did so.

With a sharp thrust he cut down another Empire soldier, issued a hasty command to his men to stand their ground and then turned and grabbed up the ten-year-old Prince Allinaias, standing dazed in the middle of all the carnage, and dived for cover in the trees.

Despite being only a few moments behind the Tutor and the two children in his care, Dale was unable to find them in the thick undergrowth. There was no time to hunt for them now, he realised with frustration. He'd been born in these forest and knew that even experienced woodsmen could blunder about in the trees for days without finding another soul. He simply had to keep moving and hope that the tutor had the sense to do the same with the others.

Dale had instinctively headed north, still carrying the Prince in his arms - barely aware that he was there. His mind was reeling at what had happened - his men were almost certainly dead, Prince Corist and the Princess were lost in the forest, the Lord only knew where and he was now the only soldier left to protect his three charges, always assuming he ever found them again. In his guts was the churning shame of having run away and left his troops to be cut down, but still, running over the top of all this horror, were the orders he had been given as they had prepared to separate from the main party.

Your first and only priority is to protect the Royal Family. Do whatever is necessary... Your first and only Priority... Protect the boy...

They had travelled randomly through the forest for a while, putting as much distance between them and Darvett's troops as they could. Through this first, wild run, the young prince had clung frantically to the soldier, eyes wide and panting, still unable to speak from shock. Finally, when Dale was sure they were not being pursued, he carried his young charge under cover of a dense thicket, and put him down. He fought to regain his breath, and started to consider options, but for the first time, Prince Allinaias spoke to him.

"Who were those men?" he asked somewhat breathlessly, his face white with shock.

"Darvett's troops," came the grim reply.

"But my father took an army to stop him. The whole Bremmand Alliance marched south to put an end to Darvett for good."

Dale looked down at the earnest face of the Prince and felt a wave of pity flood over him. Poor little wretch! He was still young enough to believe totally in the might of his father, and could not comprehend the possibility that Jorvis might have failed. So, unable to break that belief just yet, and wanting to keep the boy's spirits up, he lied as best he could.

"There are always little groups of enemy soldiers who don't get sorted out in the first battle. This lot must have been separated from the main fighting, fled north and just came across us by chance. I guess they thought it better to die in a blaze of glory than to surrender to the enemy."

"But shouldn't we go back? I mean Cori might want some help, and they'll be worried about me going off like that..." Dale looked at the boy carefully. The chances were the whole of this child's family had been wiped out today, his brother included, but for now the Prince seemed to want to pretend that wasn't a possibility. He was behaving as though there had been some minor confusion and the party had merely been split up.

They were heading for topics which Dale did not want to get into now, but he had to say something to get the child off this line of questioning. He shrank away from the idea of lying to the boy, but to tell him the truth and have him go to pieces there and then, with Darvett's men sweeping the forest around them... He settled for a half lie and evasion.

"We have strict orders on how to proceed when a group is split up like this, Your Highness. Hunting around for each other just means that everyone wastes time playing tag in the woods, so what we have to do is make our position secure, and take cover, and then when we are sure it's safe, continue our journey. Everyone else will do the same, so we'll meet up in Hast."

The Prince nodded uncertainly, and shrank down into the brush that was their only protection. In his heart he knew it was a lie, that the situation was far worse than he was being told but he desperately wanted to believe that everything was going to be all right soon, that this nightmare would be quickly over, so that everything could go back to normal.

Dale knew that was not going to happen - the speed and savagery with which they had been caught made it clear. This was no skirmish on the edges of the battle, but a full invasion party, under orders to capture or kill anyone with loyalty to Jorvis and the Alliance. Darvett was right here, right now, and he was going to take Bremmand as fast and as ruthlessly as possible. And all the time, the captain could hear Verdin's voice,

Your first and only priority is to protect the Royal family...

"Your Highness, we are not safe here. We should move to somewhere that gives us more protection as soon as possible. I want to make sure you are hidden away safely until all this is over." Until this is over - as if it wasn't all over already! "We need to move quickly and carefully, so you are going to need to trust me and do exactly what I say for now." He looked down at the white face and wide eyes and tried to stay as calm and assured as possible. The boy had to believe that they were going to get out alive, or he might go to pieces completely. But he had underestimated the child. This wasn't Jorvis's son for nothing!

"Where are we going to hide?" His voice was small, but totally calm - he knew he had no choice but to follow Ronas' lead and attempted to do so with as much dignity as possible.

"I don't know yet," the Captain admitted, "but we are a bit too close to the fighting here and I'd rather get as much distance between us and them as possible." Seeing the boy nod again, he decided to share his immediate plans with the lad now, so that when he tried to carry them out they would not be met with as much resistance. As casually as he could manage he said, "We might need to hide out in the woods for a few days; until things settle down again." No response, so he continued, "I'd rather avoid too much moving about until nightfall though, so for now we have to find somewhere which gives us cover until it gets dark. Then we can find somewhere a bit safer."

He thought for a moment, getting his bearings and trying to figure out the best place to find shelter. After considering several options he finally decided, and then turned to his charge.

"I know of somewhere quite close to here, which might be a good place to hide. There is the ruin of an old castle. It hasn't been occupied for two hundred years I should think, and most of the walls are gone, but my friends and I came across it when we were travelling the forest for our proving." *Proving* was a woodsman tradition. Life in the depths of the forest was harsh and young men were expected to show themselves able to survive by heading off with only the barest of equipment to learn the hard way how to survive. It was during his own proving at fifteen, along with two other woodsmen's sons, that Dale had discovered the ancient ruin he was now describing to the Prince.

"There used to be a couple of decent hiding places in what must have once been the gardens." As he spoke, he sketched out a map in the dust from where they were now to the old ruin. He wanted the boy to be able to find the place alone, if the need arose. The prince studied the makeshift map, and looked hopefully up, but Dale didn't want to mislead him into believing this would be simple, so he felt obliged to add, "It's not easy to get to, though, Your Highness. It originally had a moat, so it's a stiff clamber up to the castle, and there are no paths to reach it. We are going to have to go back on ourselves for a bit too, so it's a bit of a walk, and not an easy one. We'll have to cut a path through the undergrowth. Think you can manage it?"

The prince nodded positively. Dale could see that the lad was drawing strength from the confidence of the Captain, and trusted him implicitly. With an encouraging smile, Dale patted him on the shoulder.

"Good for you!" His Royal Highness, Prince Allinaias looked faintly startled at such an informal attitude, but after a second, the look of astonishment was replaced by the slightest sketch of a grin. He met Dale's eyes, indicating his readiness to go.

Dale replied with a reassuring smile, and a few final words of instruction. "Keep close to me, and if you see any trouble, leave it to me to deal with. You run as fast as you can to that hiding place. I'll come and find you there. Understood?" His reply was a wide-eyed look, followed by a tiny nod. The idea of another direct attack upon them obviously hadn't occurred to the boy, and he suddenly looked very small. Impulsively, the big man took his hand, and folded it within his own. Allinaias found the warmth of the huge fist immensely comforting, and after a second or two, found the strength to say,

"I'll be all right. Let's go."

Hand in hand they trekked through the forest, keeping low and moving fast. Dale was all but dragging the young prince through some very rough terrain, and his clothing was already looking the worse for wear, as brambles and mud both did their bit to ruin his finery. But the prince did not complain. He kept pace with Dale all the way to the edge of a steep ditch which marked the start of the old castle moat. Only then did he cry halt.

"I need a minute," he panted, "before I do *that,*" and he indicated the gully at their feet with his head. Dale breathlessly nodded his agreement and they both sank to their feet at the very edge of the precipice. As they recovered their breath Dale surveyed the next stage of their journey.

The ditch was deep and both sides steep with determined looking gorse and bramble clinging in random clumps on both sides. The few remains of the castle were barely visible on the opposite bank, overgrown and choked as they were with the forest undergrowth. The Captain gazed at it in dismay.

"It... it's steeper than I remembered it," he said a little hesitantly, but the Prince looked undaunted.

"Its not that bad," he said diffidently. "I can do it all right, I just needed a rest first."

Dale raised an amused eyebrow. "It wasn't you I was worried about, Your Highness! I may have been able to race up and down there once, but I'm getting a bit old for such things now."

The look his young charge gave him spoke more clearly than the words. "You won't make me go alone, will you?"

"No Sire," was Dale's gentle reply, "we'll go together."

The scramble up the bank proved to be not as bad as Dale had expected. The short, tufty grass which had taken hold on the banks made good handholds, and while the captain did not manage to swarm down the one bank and back up the other with quite the alacrity of his young companion, he did manage to arrive in the castle keep with a minimum of bumps and bruises and almost all of his dignity.

The castle ruins looked even less inviting from closer inspection and Dale felt the Prince slide his hand back into that of his only protector as they explored the plateau together. After a short while Dale began to remember some of the broken walls and collapsed pillars. The more he walked, the more confident he became that he knew where he was. With a cheerful tug at the princes hand he said positively,

"It's this way. Come on." He was so relieved to be close to getting his charge under cover and into relative safely, that he abandoned all formality and became almost like a small boy himself. Prince Allinaias mirrored this upswing in mood and quickened his pace, until they were both almost running across the ruined landscape, racing each other to get to their destination first.

Finally they reached it - the remains of a wall, once tall, but now pulled down by the suffocating growth of the forest. However, stubbornly, between the ivy and mistletoe, the odd rose bloom could be seen. Dale tracked along the wall until he found what he was looking for and then pushed through the ivy curtain and vanished.

A few seconds later he poked his head back through the barrier and grinned at the surprised-looking prince.

"Good, eh?" he asked jovially. In silence, the young royal nodded, and then moved timidly to follow through the hidden entrance.

As they walked silently through the time-ravaged scene behind the wall, the prince gazed about him in awe. It was overgrown and weed-infested like the rest of the castle grounds, but dotted here and there were plants that most certainly did not belong in a forest. Tall, cultivated trees, pretty shrubs with leaves of many different colours, and long tall blooms, hanging like grapes from trees and shrubs alike. This had clearly once been a garden of some beauty. Stranger still: in that long forgotten sanctuary, the horrors of the world on the other side of the wall seemed to vanish. Almost idly the Prince and his protector gazed at the plants and flowers, inhaling the fragrances and enjoying the colours so long unappreciated. Dale pointed some plants out as they walked, adding commentary here and there.

"Jasmine – those white blooms are used for perfume; hyssop - butterflies love them; always good to have in a garden if you want wildlife in the garden; that stuff climbing over the wall is Humulus. It can be used to make a brew that helps you sleep. Good for making beer too...:

"How do you know so much about plants?" Allinaias was obliged to ask finally, his curiosity piqued by finding this unlikely interest in a soldier. Dale grinned.

"I'm friends with a fellow who's a gardener at the palace. When I'm off duty I go and see him and he'll walk me round the garden like this, pointing stuff out. I suppose it's rubbed off on me."

The Captain led his young charge down what had once been a long walk. The slabs which made up the path still remained in places, but they were cracked and pushed out of place by roots from the untrained and out of control trees which lined the walkway. Dale guided the Prince to a large dense collection of shrubs. They grew against the northern most wall, and lined one side of the moss-smothered pathways of the walk for about thirty feet, growing thickly all the way to the outer wall, some ten feet back. The ground rose slightly towards the wall, making the bushes seem taller than they actually were, and causing the branches to lean forward, folding layer upon layer of leaves over the front of the shrubbery. Low ground-cover plants lined the front of the bigger bushes, closing off any gap that lay between the lower branches and the ground.

Without hesitation, Captain Ronas slipped between two of the largest bushes, and when he was up against the wall, pushed his way into the heart of the vegetation, guiding the young prince with him. Once through the thick leaf cover, the prince gave a little gasp, for the inside of the shrubbery was hollow, apart from the branches, which sprouted from a central trunk. The outer foliage was dense, and grew thickly all the way to the wall, both along the sides, and overhead, providing a complete canopy of leaf cover. From the outside, you could only see the leaves, and anything inside was totally obscured. Dale privately congratulated himself on his choice - it was indeed a good place to hide. This had been made even more so by some fairly effective earth workings inside the bush. Dale recalled the summer during which he and his two companions had hollowed out the ground inside the bush, pushing the spoil up into a wall, which built up a soil barrier between the hiding space and the front of the pathway and over which the branches were supported. This created more space both by lowering the floor, and by forcing the tree to grow further out from the centre. The leaf lined room was, by dint of this work, at least eight foot square, and four foot high, but only two feet above ground level in the rest of the garden. Dale never remembered that they had made it so big. *You could hide a small army in here* he thought almost idly.

They sat in the dim light for a while, saying nothing and enjoying the feeling of relative safety. As they sat there, Dale regarded the young boy in his care for the first time.

He'd served in the palace guard for a little over two years now, first as a lieutenant and now as Captain, reporting directly to Lord Verdin, Lord Protector, but despite the title (it was always called the 'Palace Guard', but the official title was *The first regiment, protectorate to the King, and loyal guard to the Queen and all the Royal Family*) he had very little to do with the members of royalty. He knew them all by sight of course. He saw them on state occasions, with the troops surrounding them in an impractical and uncomfortable formal uniform, or when he was asked to provide escort for one member of the family or another while on a state visit to one of their allies. He was occasionally asked by the Weapons Master to assist as a sword partner for one of the older Princes to provide practice with an unfamiliar opponent, but he had not had occasion to hold conversations and develop friendships with any of his charges. Other than one exceptional circumstance when he'd come to know one of the older princes more closely, his relationship with the Royal Family was remote and formal.

He had had one chance encounter with young Prince Allinaias quite recently, however, which he thought about now, comparing the bad-tempered and arrogant child of that afternoon, with his frightened charge of today.

The atmosphere in the Castle had been tense. It hung in the air all morning, and made everyone nervous. The King and the army had ridden out three days before, and so far there had been no news from the battlefield, but everyone knew that Darvett's army was vast, and he was determined not to be defeated a second time. Everyone was waiting for the news they knew must come: hoping it would be good, but knowing how unlikely that must be.

It was a bright sunny day, and the light from the mid-afternoon sun was streaming through the high palace windows across the long gallery, catching every speck of dust as it danced in the warm air. The Gallery was some 200 feet in length, with the great staircase at one end and the nursery at the other. At the far end, a pair of guards were always posted. That day Lord Verdin had instructed his Captain that he wanted him to take the nursery watch personally from now on, along with at least one of his three trusted lieutenants. The Earl wanted to be sure that, if there was a need to evacuate the royal family and other essential staff, Captain Ronas and at least one other officer were close at hand to ensure the protection of the Queen and her children.

So Ronas had found himself back on guard duty, some years after he had believed that he had finally been promoted beyond such tasks, with Verdin's instructions ringing in his ears. "If bad news should come, you have one priority only - to escort the Queen and her children out of here and convey them safely to Hast. Nothing else matters." In that quiet castle it seemed almost absurd that this warning was necessary and it made the two men standing on duty even more edgy.

With a bang, the nursery door was flung open, making the guards jump nervously. Once it was clear that the "danger" was from the wrong end of the corridor there was a quick exchange of nervous grins, and embarrassed looks. With interest, they turned to see what was causing the commotion.

From the royal rooms raced a dark-haired boy of about ten years of age. He was finely dressed in a blue tunic and hose, with a gold belt. The combination of the fine clothes, expressive blue eyes and handsome features made for a very pleasing sight, which was sadly ruined by the angry scowl on his face. He turned briefly and stated furiously into the open doorway, "I don't care. I'm going out!" and he began to race down the gallery towards the guards.

A nurse also appeared at the nursery entrance. "Your Highness, come back here at once!"

"No! I'm sick of being held prisoner in my own home. Everyone treats me like I'm a baby. I want to go outside," and with this he continued his flight down the corridor.

As the nurse had begun to pursue the boy, Captain Ronas called out,

"I've got him," and stepped in to intercept the child. He caught hold of the young prince as he tried to pass "And where do you thing you're off to, Sire?" His reply was a bellow of rage.

"Take your hands off me! You have no right to even speak to me!" It was then that the Captain recognised that this was Prince Allinaias, as he held on to the now fiercely struggling child. *Needs a good hiding* he thought grimly to himself, but at that moment the prince had twisted suddenly, managed to wrench himself free and sped off down the gallery.

"Bloody Hell!" swore the captain, and said to his lieutenant "Stay here. I'd better go and get him back."

The other officer stared in horror for a second and then protested, "You can't. If you leave here, Verdin'll have your head on a plate."

"And if I don't get that boy back, the Queen'll have my balls. Which would you choose?" Without waiting for an answer, he turned and hurried after the fast disappearing child.

He finally caught up with the boy at the far side of the courtyard. The youngster was so enraged at the temerity of this guard to have followed him, that he stopped to allow the captain to approach him and proceeded to lambaste the man for his audacity and lack of respect toward a member of the royal family. The captain bore the furious tirade with patience and then politely pointed out to his young master that he answered to the King.

"The King has commanded that I protect you, Sire. You cannot expect me to do that, if you are wandering about all over the palace, now can you?"

"Well, I shall speak to the King, and tell him that you are the rudest, most disrespectful guard I've ever met, and that I won't have you protecting me ever again. You'll be lucky if he doesn't cut your head off." This was not a particularly alarming threat. It was hardly likely that King Jorvis would take his son's part in such a matter, if he took any interest in it at all. Domestic concerns were hardly something that the King had time for these days. The Captain recognised the prince's words as the idle brag that any boy of this age might make when trying to get his own way, and was mildly amused by it. However, in deference to the lad's pride he did his best to conceal the fact. He kept his face as dispassionate as possible and replied with all the respect afforded to a crown Prince,

"That is your prerogative Sire, but until you father returns, I must ask you to return to the nursery," and he stood aside, bowing slightly, to allow the boy to turn and pass back into the building. The young prince stared angrily at him for a moment, debating whether to argue the matter further, and took in his pursuer for the first time. The Captain was a big man, broad of beam and tall, which Prince Allinaias found a trifle intimidating. His own height was a constant subject for ridicule by his older brothers, for he was slight and fine-boned. This man could knock him over in a single blow if he so wished - if he dared! But it was his manner which spoke the loudest message - the Prince's glare was met by a stony look that was entirely unafraid of his superior rank and station and it was as clear as day that he would have his own way, by one means or another.

Recognising that he had lost this particular battle, and not wishing to be physically carried back into the building - he had no doubt that this man would do it either – the Prince said icily

"I shall not forget this," and then as an afterthought, "What is your name? My father will wish to know who to have arrested."

"Captain Dale Ronas, Sire. Palace Guard."

"Well Captain Ronas, on this occasion I will return to the nursery. Not because you tell me to, but because I choose to."

"That is most gracious of you, your Royal Highness." The Captain's voice was a flat monotone of courtesy. The young prince searched the guard's face, searching for the irony he knew must be behind the remark but his look was met by a steady pair of brown eyes, calm and impassive, so with as much dignity as he could muster, the royal child began to cross the courtyard back to the entrance to the royal apartments. They had returned to the nursery without another word passing between them but, when Dale had brought the Prince to the door of the nursery, and reached up to knock he was stopped.

"Thank you Captain, I can manage from here." It wasn't said with any anger, but instead was the polite and formal dismissal of a subject. It was as if the whole ugly little scene of earlier had never happened. Then the boy had turned and entered the nursery without another word.

Ronas had found that he couldn't help liking the boy that day, despite his arrogance and abuse of power. So what if he had tried to threaten his appointed protector into getting his own way? When it was clear that this would not work, he had accepted his lot without further complaint. If there was one thing that the Captain couldn't stand, it was children who grizzled on and on when they failed to get their own way.

After a while, the prince said in a small voice,

"I didn't mean it you know - about telling my father, and getting you arrested." The Captain stared at him in astonishment for a moment, too surprised by the child's echo of his own thoughts to speak. Misunderstanding the silence, the boy continued, "I couldn't anyway - I can't remember your name." This provoked a short laugh from the Officer.

"Then it's just as well you didn't mean it, isn't it? But for the record, it's Captain Ronas." After a moment's thought, the Captain added, "Call me Dale."

"I'm glad you didn't intend to speak to your father. In truth, I think it might have got you into rather a lot of hot water, don't you?" The big man could just about make out the shamefaced look which told him he was right. The King would have been far more put out by his disobedient son, than the guard who attempted to return him to a place of safety. He grinned into the half-light waiting for some reply to this, but it never came. It only then occurred to him, that since he had taken it on the castle plateau, the young prince had not once let go of his hand.

They sat in silence for a while longer, and then Dale cleared his throat carefully.

"I should go and see what is going on out there. You'll be quite safe here," and he moved to crawl out of the shrub. The boy's hand gripped him slightly tighter, arresting his movement.

"You will come back won't you?" Dale looked at the prince, and could see the fear in his eyes, even inside the dense shrubbery. The lad had managed very well up until now, but the idea of being left alone was too much for him.

Your first and only priority…

A part of him was burning to go back and see what remained of the party he was charged to protect. He had to be sure that there was no-one else who had survived, had to know what had happened to the other royal children before he made his plans for the protection of Prince Allinaias. Further, he hated the fact that the men under his command were fighting and dying for their country, while he was cowering in a bush. And yet, if anything happened to him, who would look after the boy?

Your first and only priority…

"Would you rather I stayed here, Your Highness?"

The Prince considered this for a moment. "Yes!" He took a deep breath, "but you have your job to do. If you go, I shall be all right here. But please come back. I… I… command it." It was clear that the young royal was not at all familiar with issuing commands, but also that this was his last desperate attempt to ensure that he wasn't abandoned there for too long. Dale gently squeezed his young master's hand and responded to the command with all the formality he would have afforded his King.

"As you command, Sire," and he did his best to bow in the cramped surroundings. Then, more informally, "I won't be long. I'll see if I can find any sign of your brother then I'll be right back," and with that he crawled out from the hiding place and back into the garden.

The return journey to the place where they had been ambushed took far less time than it had taken on the outward leg. Before he left the castle plateau, he shucked off his military armour and left it in a bush - he could move faster and in the open without it. He kept his sword though.

This time he knew exactly where he was going, and he took an almost direct line from the Castle ruins to the side road along which they had been travelling when the attack had befallen them. He crossed it a mile or so north of the ambush site and then began to track back south, just off the road, keeping sheltered in the trees which lined the road. After about half a mile, something made him stop. Coming towards him, moving stealthily, also using the trees as a shield was the sound of two, maybe three, men. As silently as possible he began to draw back into the forest. But as luck would have it, just as he thought he was out of sight, he trod on a dry stick and the snap reverberated loudly around the wood. The approaching footsteps stopped abruptly, and then Dale heard them start again, but now heading in his direction. He drew his sword carefully and stood, bracing himself to strike as soon as the enemy was in range.

To the end of his days, Dale never knew what caused him to hesitate before he brought the sword down, but in the heartbeat while he paused he was able to take in the two figures who stood before him. The first was a thin, un-athletic looking young man, with dark hair and pale blue eyes, armed with a sword held in a way certain to result in a broken wrist at the first contact with another weapon. He was shielding a youth, who Dale recognised at the same moment that the lad cried out,

"Captain Ronas!"

The startled Captain brought his sword to an abrupt halt in mid-air inches short of the other man's blade, and then let it slide harmlessly away to one side. He gazed at the younger man with a mixture of shock and relief. It was Prince Corist, and in his arms, Princess Josanna, both alive and well. Without further hesitation, Dale pulled him and Master Trystin at his side down low so that they were out of sight of the road and spoke without ceremony, directly to the Prince.

"We need to get you under better cover and quickly, Sire. These woods aren't safe at the moment. I know of a place, a few miles from here, but we need to move quickly and quietly. Follow close behind me and keep low. Understood?"

Prince Corist nodded silently, but then he said one more thing before obeying the Captain's command. "Allin...?"

"Is safe. Now we need to move."

The Prince tried to resist when Dale took his sister from his arms but with one look, Dale over-ruled him. The Captain turned to Master Trystin, took the sword curtly from his hand and replaced it with the Princess then he passed the sword to the young prince, dryly remarking, "At least I know you've been taught how to hold it properly. I've not seen any troops coming this way so far, so you shouldn't need it but, if you do, stick to defence. You stay alive and he," nodding again at the tutor, "can come round the back and brain them with a rock. Think you can manage that?"

The Prince seemed slightly cheered by this contemptuous reflection on the scholar's abilities, and nodded more positively.

The second trek to the castle ruin was, if anything, more harrowing than the first. Prince Allinaias had been young enough that, if needs be, Dale could have picked him up bodily and run with him to safety. This time he had to protect two royal youngsters and the tutor, who was clearly not in the least bit adept at trekking through the forest. Of them all, Master Trystin found the fast pace and rough terrain hardest to manage and stumbled several times, only saved by Dale supporting him. Dale had soon realised that the scholar couldn't move as fast as either the fit and well-trained Captain or the young Prince, especially not when carrying the extra burden of the Princess, so he took the girl from the man. He chafed at the difficulty he would face in defending them all if they did hit trouble, but he knew that the sooner they got to the castle ruins the safer they would all be. Ronas began to wonder if, should they come into contact with more Empire troops, he could save them all.

Their luck held, and without sight of another human soul, they were safely back at the hideout in the long walk. Dale put the Princess down and pushed his way past the thick branches and into the hollow where Allinaias was huddled close to the entry point and had clearly been watching out for his protector. He took a firm grip on the Captain's arm before Dale was even fully into the bush and all but pulled him in. Dale smiled at him and quietly repeated his parting words to the boy

"As you command, Sire." The relieved half grin he received in reply showed that the prince understood his meaning but his face lost all sign of anxiety as soon as Dale turned and ushered in first Prince Corist and then Master Trystin and the little Princess. The reunion of the three royal children was emotional to say the least. For the first few minutes they clung to each other, and then they each recounted their own tales of how they came to be there. It gave Dale the chance to discover how Master Trystin and the two royals had come to be hiding in the woods where he had almost attacked them.

At the first shock of the Kostinians attack, and hearing Dale's shouted commands to everyone to get under cover and protect the royal children, Master Trystin had grabbed hold of Prince Corist, and the Princess and hauled them, in Corist's case unwillingly, into the shelter of the trees.

The Prince had wanted to return to the battle and had all but fought his tutor who was forced to restrain him in order to protect his life. Master Trystin had confiscated the Prince's sword and dragged him further away from the fighting. Corist described this sequence of events fairly briefly but, sitting next to Dale, Master Trystin added comments of his own quietly to the Captain. It was clear to Dale how eager the lad had been to fight, both from Master Trystin's remarks and the cool way in which the Prince looked at his tutor when describing how he had been forced to run and hide.

When King Jorvis had gone into battle taking his elder sons with him, Dale knew that Corist had been angry and disappointed to be left behind. At fifteen he felt himself ready to go to war, but the King had not agreed, and the young man had been forced, with poor grace, to remain behind in order to complete his education. Now he had again been denied his first battle, and Dale was somewhat amazed that Master Trystin, who to his eyes seemed mild and fastidious about proper observances of rank, had somehow managed to keep the boy from returning to what would most certainly have been his death.

Once they were sure of their escape, Master Trystin and his two charges had waited until the sounds of the battle had ended and had cautiously returned to the ambush point. Everyone there was dead, he explained, although it looked as if one of the Bremmand soldiers had lived a little while after the fighting had ended, having managed to drag himself part way into the undergrowth. At Dale's careful questioning, Trystin was able to confirm that all the Empire troops were accounted for - until they failed to report, no-one would even search for them let alone find out that they had come across part of the fleeing royal group.

With no guide and no protection, Master Trystin had been at a loss to know what to do next. He was no woodsman but knew enough of Bremmand terrain to realise that he would never find Dale again, except by a stroke of amazing good fortune, so they had decided not to try. The tutor had figured their best bet was to return to the road they had crossed and then follow it north towards Hast. It was as they had travelled, parallel to the road that they had come across Dale.

Once all the stories had been told, everyone sat for a few moments, reflecting upon the chance that had saved them, when fate had placed such peril in their path.

Dale watched for a few moments, marvelling at how well the children were managing to cope with the trauma that had ripped their lives apart. Since the party had been divided that morning, neither Prince Corist or Prince Allinaias had shown anything but courage or maturity. They had both followed his instructions, putting their faith in him from the moment he had established his authority in the matter of their safety, and allowing him to do his job.

Into the silence, Master Trystin looked at Ronas for a moment, and then asked,

"And now what, Captain? We can't stay here forever."

"I know a few places in the forest where we can hide out for a few days, until we have a chance to find out what is going on. We must keep these children safe until we can get them to Hast, and I'd rather it was thought they had perished in the attack back there, than have Empire troops sending out a full-scale search for them. With a bit of luck, no-one will think to count the dead for a while yet, so they won't be missed." He felt Allinaias' grip on his arm tighten at the mention of the dead, so he pulled his arm free in order to wrap it round the boy's shoulders. He continued to instruct the boys in what he now had in mind.

"It's best if we travel by night for now. The chances of evading any enemy troops is a lot easier in the dark, and we have the advantage of knowing the lie of the land. The best thing we can do for now is get some sleep. We'll need to be alert tonight to travel, and we're pretty safe here for now, as long as we keep quiet. There'll be plenty of warning if anyone comes near here, and we'd be very unlucky for them to do a really thorough search of this old ruin today." He looked down at the younger prince, now sheltered in the crook of his arm. "This is going to be a bit of an adventure for you, Your Highness. Think you can manage it?" Corist spoke up for his brother and himself.

"We both can, Captain. We place ourselves entirely in your hands for as long as it takes for order to be restored. You have our complete trust."

"Thank you, Sire. This may not be an easy few days, but I'll see you all to safety," *Or die trying.* Dale completed the sentence to himself. He had no idea how he was going to do this. Gods, the surrounding area could be crawling with Darvett's men by now!

He had to get three children, and an untrained scholar out of the Castle ruins, and a good sixty miles deeper into the forest, without crossing the path of anyone. He could feel the children's eyes on him, and he managed a smile, hoping that he looked confident. "Now, you all try and get some rest. I'll keep a watch until it's time to go."

For a few moments no-one moved and Dale glanced at Master Trystin, looking for support. The slim man was sitting, staring blankly in to the middle distance, his thoughts clearly miles away.

Dale sighed to himself, stifling the traditional soldiers' contempt for non-fighting men. He'd hoped that he was going to be able to look to the tutor for support and assistance, but that clearly wasn't to be. In fact, while the children were coping extraordinarily well with the trauma of their changed circumstances, the scholar seemed to be managing extraordinarily badly. Instead of being a help to him, Master Trystin looked as if he was going to be a positive hindrance. It would be up to Dale to make the decisions and manage their progress from this point onwards, he decided. However, he didn't want the man to fall entirely to pieces and he knew the best way to avoid this was to keep the fellow busy, so Dale leaned over and gave him a sharp nudge in the ribs.

"You can settle Their Highnesses down to get some sleep, can't you, Sir?" he suggested in a tone that would brook no refusal.

The thin man started, looked irritated at being prodded in such a familiar way, but then pulled himself together and, with a nod to the Captain, took command of the young royals as requested. He instructed his charges to make themselves as comfortable as possible in order to rest, and, familiar with deferring to their tutor, they obediently lay down, with the little princess on the ground between them, where she would be warm.

Master Trystin was hoping that they would all sleep, so that he could discuss with the Captain more about what was really going on. He knew that this was not the brief skirmish that Prince Allinaias mentioned Ronas had described - it was altogether too efficient and ruthless, and as he, the Princess and Prince had fled from the attack on the road, he had seen the flash of scarlet on the North Road down below them, as another Legion of Darvett's men began to establish themselves in the forest. He could already guess that Jorvis had been defeated and that Bremmand was lost, but he was not a military expert, and wanted to pick Ronas's brains about the likely outcome on the battlefield.

The opportunity for the two men to talk never came. Neither of the two boys could sleep in these uncomfortable and unfamiliar surroundings. The best either could manage was to snooze, but the slightest sound or movement had them both sitting up to see what was coming.

Finally, as it crept towards midnight, Dale quietly spoke.

"It'll soon be time for us to go. We're going to go over the wall right here, behind where this bush is. This wall backs directly onto forest, so we'll have plenty of cover, and puts us in the right direction for where we are going. Master Trystin, I'll need to go first to make sure it is safe, then you hand the girl over to me. Prince Corist, you'll be next, then your brother and Master Trystin will come over last. We need to do this quickly, and you'll need to be a quiet as possible, but if you do as I say, we'll all be fine. Understood?"

Out of the darkness, Dale heard the two princes and Master Trystin each indicate their agreement, but then, for the first time, Dale heard another voice, small and timid, but determined not to be outdone.

"Ess." It was Princess Josanna, now sitting close to Master Trystin, to whom she seemed to have taken a fancy. Dale stifled the urge to laugh, and by his side he felt Josanna's brother squirm with a similar amusement. Prince Allinaias couldn't resist the urge to say, delightedly,

"She's just a baby, Dale. She doesn't really underst...." He was cut short by Prince Corist who slammed into him rapidly, clamped one hand across his brother's mouth and the other firmly round the back of his head, and hissed furiously into the younger boy's ear, shaking his head violently as he spoke each word.

"The Captain said we were to be absolutely silent, and you're just about yelling your head off. Do you want to get us all killed?" For a second everyone sat stunned by the vicious savagery of Prince Corist's attack on his younger brother but as Prince Allinaias shook his head in alarm, Dale reached out to Prince Corist, put a firm hand on the youth's arm and gently removed it from the boy's face. He looked kindly at the older lad and said, as reassuringly as possible,

"No-one is going to get killed, Your Highness. I'll make sure of that." Corist looked at him angrily for a second and then his face changed. He suddenly looked very small and afraid and for a second Dale wondered if he was going to cry. Then he pulled rapidly away and sank back into the corner of the pit where he'd been sitting, wrapping his arms about himself tightly and doing his best to avoid eye contact with any of them. They all sat in silence for a few minutes, shocked by the incident. Prince Allinaias, already keeping as close to Dale as possible, now re-established his firm grip on the soldier's arm.

Dale cursed himself for a fool. He had spent the last few hours doing his best to ensure that the little Princess and Prince Allinaias were reassured and confident, and they had all but ignored young Corist. At nearly sixteen he had assumed that the lad would be much more able to keep his head. Dale now realised that this was a mistake. Prince Corist was far less likely to be taken in by the trite lies that Dale had been telling his brother, and was almost certainly aware that this was no small attack, no group of stragglers from the battle. Of all of them, Dale now feared, the elder Prince was the one closest to the brink as he struggled to come to terms with the inevitable elimination of the rest of his kinsmen and his sudden promotion to head of the family.

"*God's teeth,*" thought Dale in sudden horror, "*that makes him the King!*" As this awesome possibility struck him, he found himself staring at the young man. This was his monarch, cowering in a bush, looking as if he was about ten years old. Despite his growing impatience to get moving again, he knew he was going to have to take the time, here and now, to reassure the youth. Dale gently shook off the grip of Prince Allinaias and slid over to be next to Prince Corist.

"We're all afraid, Your Highness" he said quietly. "There's nothing to be ashamed of in that - but you can trust me to protect you." Corist looked at him, and said in a broken voice, so low that Dale could barely hear it,

"I keep thinking about what happens if there are hundreds of soldiers waiting on the other side of the wall, or if they find us in here, or... " Dale put a comforting arm on the lad.

".. or a thousand and one other things that probably won't happen. The biggest risk we face right now is our own fear. I know I'm asking a lot of you, but I need you to keep it together right now - for the children's sake. They'll take a lead from you, and if you can keep going, so will they. We'll be out of here pretty soon now, and I know somewhere we can go where we'll be well hidden. Then we can take the time to find out what's really happening, and make some decisions from there."

"This isn't a minor skirmish, like you told Allin, is it?" Dale thought for a second before answering.

"No, Sire. There are too many of them, and it was too well organised."

"Then..."

"I don't know," Dale cut across him hastily. "For now I have to assume the worst, so we aren't going to take any chances but don't give up all hope just yet. The men seen in South Bremmand and those we've met today got a long way north really quickly and with such speed that there can't be many of them. Darvett could have sent a small force to scout north and establish a presence – maybe take Castle Bremmand - while he tackled the main army. Once we fled from the Castle, he'd want to try and stop us before we got North and reached reinforcements. For all we know alliance troops are chasing them here."

"Why do that? Why try to attack Castle Bremmand?" Prince Allinaias had crept closer, and was now listening in to this discussion. His brother looked at him and then said distantly, as if quoting from something else,

"To kill a lion, all you have to do is cut out his heart."

Dale nodded slowly in agreement and explained to the younger boy,

"Bremmand holds the Alliance together, and to take control of the Alliance, all Darvett needs to do is take Bremmand. The centre of Bremmand is Castle Bremmand. So once he's broken through the enemy lines, if Darvett can get north, enter the city, take the castle, eliminate everyone of importance from within it and be sitting on the throne before Alliance forces can catch up with them, everything else will come down like a pile of sticks."

As Dale spoke both boys' eyes widened in horror, and for a second the Captain couldn't work out why they were both staring at him. Then Prince Corist said slowly,

"Eliminate…" and Dale realised his mistake. He had allowed his guard to drop and his tongue had run away with him. He mentally kicked himself for his stupidity. He was no great diplomat, but he should have been able at least to shield these young men from the harsh reality of what they were facing. Now his careless mouth had confirmed for them what they were both fearing, and instead of boosting their confidence he'd slapped them in the face with more than they were able to manage. Allinaias looked at him, hardly daring to ask, but still he had to know.

"Then they wanted us dead, those men? And they'll be after the others too? Mamma? And Dav and...?" Corist cut across him hurriedly.

"Don't, Allin," Prince Corist said abruptly, desperate to stop his brother from listing every possible member of their family who might now be dead. He shut his eyes briefly, swallowed hard and then said more reasonably, "They wouldn't kill women and children. Not even Darvett would stoop to that, would he Captain?" He looked hopefully at the soldier.

"We'll hope not Your Highness. They make good hostages, so it is often worth the effort of keeping them alive." Prince Corist nodded. Strangely comforted by Dale's honesty, he squared his shoulders and looked back at his brother.

"Right now, it is our duty to stay alive and represent the crown until our father returns. We have a responsibility to the whole kingdom to safeguard the throne. Captain Ronas can help us do that, so we must do everything he says from now on. Are we agreed, brother?"

At the mention of the word *duty* the young Prince Allinaias underwent an indefinable but perceptible change in attitude. The word acted like a clarion call to him. Duty - the fundamental principle that underpinned the life of this child. His whole upbringing was structured to educate him in the idea that duty was all-powerful. Dale found himself reassessing the royal family significantly. Like most commoners, he had always assumed that royalty didn't really do much, except in times of great conflict. The King was a figurehead who appealed to the simple minded, and who made up the rules on a whim but it was clear from the three noble children in front of him that their whole existence was preoccupied with the guiding principles of responsibility and duty. What was more their training started early. The little girl, barely three years old, had also responded to that word *duty*. Her understanding was scant but, as Dale was to discover over the next few days, she followed along in the spirit of the word as best she could. In the years that followed, Dale never forgot that extraordinary moment when he first came face to face with the value that was at the very core of this family and in all the times he saw it after that day, he never ceased to marvel at it.

Nocturne

The exit from the castle ruin was trouble free and, once they had all cleared the wall, and slid down and back up the steep moat banks, Dale led them quickly south, deep into the forest in which the castle was seated. With some regret the solider had decided to leave his armour behind. It would help if they were attacked again but it drew attention to him and hampered his movements. Therefore he had hauled the hard leather chest plate, shield and helmet in to the overgrown garden and left them there until such time as he could return and retrieve them.

It was dark, and there was thankfully little moon, making it all the harder for them to be seen. It also meant, however, that they could barely see where they were going and the young princes both fell foul of thorns and brambles as they struggled to put as much distance between themselves and their home as possible. Both boys carried on without complaining but after the first two miles, Dale could see that they were flagging. Master Trystin, carrying the half sleeping Princess Josanna was also looking tired, his head rolling slightly as he kept up the killing pace.

Dale called a halt and lifted Josanna from Master Trystin's arms with a quiet, "My turn, I think," ignoring the man's brief resistance at being relieved of the responsibility. Then he spoke to the boys.

"We can slow a little, now. We are clear of the immediate danger, but we are going to have to keep going. I know you are both tired, but we're going to have to travel by night for the next few days, which means we'll have to carry on until dawn. All right?"

Allinaias, looking very worn and dishevelled, eyed him mournfully, but Corist, at his side, put a supporting hand on his brother's shoulder.

"We'll be fine Captain. We can manage, can't we Allin?" and looked at the younger lad expectantly.

Prince Allinaias bit his lip and looked beseechingly at his brother and then, as their eyes met for a second, he straightened and said as bravely as he could manage, "Yes, we can keep going as long as you want."

Dale nodded perfunctorily, not wanting to say anything, but in his heart he was incredibly impressed with the courage and determination of these children. He looked at the two boys, walking wearily ahead of him. Prince Corist, tall and beginning to fill out as he moved from boy to man, with his light brown, almost golden, hair and eyes like sapphires, and Allinaias, still very much a child and small of frame, with his father's dark colouring, but eyes that were every bit a match for his brother in clarity and hue. In Dale's arms, the little Princess shifted. She too had the same dark copper hair that marked her as a Marchand but the deep brown eyes of her mother which, when open and alert, were large and engaging. As Dale watched, he saw Corist move his hand from his younger brother's shoulder and slide it comfortably round the back of his neck. They weren't talking but Dale could see that they were keeping each other going through that single point of contact. As he gazed at them he reflected upon what great men they would make - *if they survive the next 24 hours.*

It was at that precise moment that Dale Ronas experienced a fundamental shift in his attitude to his current situation. Up until this point, he had seen his current role as a part of his job, something he was paid to do as a soldier. He protected these three youngsters because, well, that was what he did. He followed his training, and that decided everything else. But now... now it had become a mission, something to be carried out with a passion. He was not a very emotional man and didn't easily get excited but he found himself swelling with a kind of pride and affection for these children that he never would have believed possible based on such a brief acquaintance. He spoke quietly to Master Trystin but with a ferocity and passion that surprised the tutor at his side.

"We're going to get these children to a place of safety and we're going to see them out of Bremmand and under Hastian protection. You have my word on that." Master Trystin raised an eyebrow, looking faintly puzzled.

"Your word? Why? Is there suddenly a need to declare yourself? Ahh!" this as he saw Dale's fierce gaze fixed on the backs of the two princes "You've become enamoured of these young men as well, have you?"

"Enamoured? I... what do you mean?" Dale looked puzzled, and slightly alarmed by the implication he thought the scholar might be making.

"Oh, nothing sinister or unsavoury, I assure you, but they are the most engaging of families, these Marchands. There's a spirit of bravery and resolve that burns like a lantern in the dark. It lights up their very souls and keeps them going in the face of hopeless odds, even in the youngest of them." He nodded slightly towards Prince Allinaias. "He won't give up, or complain, or refuse to accept what is happening. None of them will, even the little girl here, if she's anything like the rest of her family. There's strength of character there and an underlying sense of right so that you cannot possibly resent them for driving everyone to their limits. Rather the reverse in fact. You find yourself so swayed by it that you are ready to die for them. Oh not like the normal military rhetoric suggests" - this as Dale had been about to protest his willingness to lay down his life before now - "but for each one of them personally, for even the smallest of reasons. If it makes you feel better, I've seen this golden quality in every one of them, and there is nothing I wouldn't do for them. For any one of them." The regret in Master Trystin's voice was obvious, something Dale couldn't really understand. All the same, they were going to have to work together to get the princes to safety, so the Captain decided he should try and show an interest.

"You taught them all?"

"Yes - except the little ones of course. Andred and the princess were too young. I was hired to teach history to Prince Herest when he was nine, and I carried on teaching them all in turn. They were all fine young men." He smiled, regretfully. "Not that any of them had much of a passion for history. Richol thought it was vaguely interesting but for the rest it was just a necessary evil. I suppose it's only reasonable that they'd find the politics going on around them more interesting than that of long dead ancestors. Except Jorvis of course, Prince Jorvis that is, not the King. He always seemed to hate everything about politics and court intrigue. If he couldn't fight it, he didn't want to know about it. I'll bet Darvett would have had a shock if he'd come up against that one!"

"You talk about them as if you'd already given them up for dead," said Dale sharply.

"No." Master Trystin answered slowly. "But for a teacher, you tend to use the past tense once they pass out of your hands and into adulthood. Somehow, you find yourself always thinking of the boy you knew, rather than the man now before you. The character you see in childhood is often a good indication of the kind of man a boy will become." He paused before going on to explain. "You could always tell that Richol would be the one to break hearts, while Jorvis was breaking heads and that Perrold was going to get himself into some kind of scandal or other, if something wasn't done. We were right about that anyway." Master Trystin was referring to the furore at court two summers before, when Prince Perrold, then fifteen, along with a few other young bloods from the castle, had "borrowed" some horses, ridden into the town of Castle Bremmand, which nestled in the shadow of the royal palace, got roaring drunk and made a nuisance of themselves with a number of local women. The town watch had arrested them and, when Perrold had threatened them with execution for treason, had been obliged to call in the palace guard to have them escorted home. Most people assumed that royalty could do pretty much as they liked but one of those who didn't agree with this was the King himself. As soon as the lad had been returned to him, the King had dismissed the court and thrashed his wayward son in the hastily emptied throne room - an unusual occurrence for a monarch who generally kept his domestic affairs very separate from matters of state - and then packed Perrold off to Hast for a year, to stay with his grandfather, "to see if they can teach him manners," as the King had been grimly heard to say. It had worked. Prince Perrold had come back a good deal more sober and sensible than he had been when he left.

"What about Prince Corist?" Dale asked, innocently "What's he like as a student?"

"A reasonable scholar, I suppose. He's got a good mind and he understands people." Master Trystin looked sideways at Dale, not misunderstanding the real reason for the question. He added slowly, in a low voice "He'll make a good King."

"Then you do think…?"

"Don't you?" He sounded vaguely irritated. "I'm not just some dim, inscrutable scholar, who doesn't take his nose out of a book long enough to see what is going on. History is littered with the bodies of kings, and their families." Here he looked at Prince - *King* - Corist, and continued, "Of all of them, Corist is probably the best candidate for the throne anyway. He's not inherited his father's temper, along with all the more loveable qualities, and he's easy to get along with. Most of the court find him approachable and easy to talk to - we'll need that if we are to drum up support from the common people."

Dale nodded. He had undergone a change in attitude since leaving the confines of the castle ruin and he could tell that Master Trystin had done so too. While still in the mouth of the enemy, they had only been thinking about when this could be over, and hoping against hope that the King and his troops would ride to the rescue. Now they had escaped from the immediate danger, both were thinking more long term, and a great deal more realistically.

"I think it's probably better, Master Trystin, if we don't discuss this until we reach our destination. We need to keep these youngsters going and that means keeping things positive. We'll talk about the future once we are safe."

"Where *are* we going, Captain? You seem to have somewhere specific in mind."

"I do. My father was a woodcutter." He smiled ruefully. "Who isn't in this part of Bremmand? I grew up about sixty miles from here, in a godforsaken little house miles from anywhere. It isn't even close to a road, so no-one visits there from one year to the next. I don't think most people even remember it's there most of the time. Small wonder I joined the army at the first opportunity - anything to get closer to a few more human beings.

"After my Da died, it came to me and when I married we lived there for a while. I left the army to take up a safer trade - take up my Da's trade." He smiled at the memories of his wife. "My two girls were born there, and it was a good place to live 'till we were fever-hit about six years ago. I went back to the military after that." He moved on hastily, not wishing to dwell on this painful memory.

"It's a good place to stay though. It's dry and warm, it's mine and I know the area like the back of my hand. It's on rising ground as luck would have it, so it's hard to spot from anywhere around it and I reckon I could defend it against a small army if I had to.

"I still keep a lot of my stuff there. I come up about twice a year, check it's all right, collect stuff I'll need for the next season - that kind of thing. I was there about a moon-cycle ago. There's clothes, supplies, all sorts."

"It sounds suitable," Master Trystin agreed. "Sixty miles is a long way though."

"Two days' march," Dale shrugged.

"Two days' forced march for a trained soldier, Captain'" Master Trystin pointed out coolly. "These boys are brave and strong but they are not indestructible. You'll not be able to drive them as hard as your regular troops."

"I know. I wasn't planning to. I've done it with my son, before. He was about nine the last time, and we made it from home to Castle Bremmand, which is about the same distance, in just under five days. These boys are a little older, but not as used to the conditions and we'll have to do it mostly in the dark and off the paths, so I expect it'll take about a week."

Master Trystin smiled faintly to himself in the darkness. "Not quite two days then."

"Always set hard targets, and then you'll stretch to reach them."

"Verdin of Langate's book of wisdom, lesson sixteen," Master Trystin remarked with a tone of disapproval. He clearly didn't agree with the Lord Protector's philosophies but Dale merely laughed.

"Yes, all right, it's one of the Earl's theories. But he's no fool, and an excellent commander."

Now, three days later, they were still travelling, but were less than a day from their final target. After the first desperate night, the children had adapted to their strange new world, and were managing a decent pace - in fact it was Master Trystin, with his added burden of the Princess, which was the main factor in the speed they could manage. Dale did his best to assist with the task of carrying young Josanna but she seemed strangely shy of him, and far more taken with the young tutor, so whenever she was in the big man's arms she tended to squirm and wriggled until she was handed back to her favourite. The two Princes also attempted to assist, but that didn't please her at all, and in the end it was easier and quicker to leave the task to Master Trystin as much as he could bear.

The hardest part had been crossing the Cirran River. It was deep and wide in that part of the forest, and there were no good fording points for a long way. Dale was not prepared to have them walk so far out of their way, or risk coming into contact with more Empire troops, so the only choice was to find another way across.

Deep water and darkness was far too dangerous a combination so when they arrived at the north bank, some hours before dawn, Dale instructed the rest of the party to sleep and, while they did so, he applied his woodman's skills to providing a boat. By the time Master Trystin and the royal children awoke at sunset, the Captain had constructed a makeshift raft from branches and strips of bark. Using a vertical paddle, the big man rowed the five of them across the stretch of fast flowing water to the south bank.

It wasn't a bad vessel considering the tools and materials available, but it was only just seaworthy and everyone got miserably wet on the crossing. To make matters worse, the current carried the craft someway downstream making the distance to their final destination even further.

"Never mind," Dale had consoled them briskly. "We need something to get us all dry and warm again, and the walk will do that for us nicely. Even better if we run the first bit."

No-one had argued, but it wasn't hard for Dale to tell that Darvett wasn't those children's greatest enemy that night!

The night after the drenching, during which it had been necessary for Master Trystin to call across sharply to Prince Allinaias from the other side of the leaky raft to prevent him falling in, the scholar made a somewhat reluctant observation to the Captain.

"It would seem that the use of royal titles may present a risk to us all for the duration of this journey. If anyone heard…"

"Yes, quite," Dale had agreed promptly, always a hater of formal titles, even before the necessity of the current situation. "Call me Dale."

The scholar looked a little startled. "I was thinking of the princes."

"It should apply to us all," was the blunt reply. "There's not really any place for formality now and it's about time we relaxed things for the youngsters a little. Forcing them to observe court behaviour is pointless when things are so rough for them."

Master Trystin tried to argue that it was better not to allow standards to slip with the royal children, but Dale took no notice. The Captain knew enough of the royal tutor by this time to know that he liked formality, and was likely to be the least willing to relinquish it. If Dale didn't force the matter, the easy friendship he was trying to establish with the children to get them to trust and obey him, was going to be constantly hampered by the tutor's insistence on a more 'proper' relationship. Trystin himself had provided Dale with the opening and he wasn't about to waste the opportunity.

When they came to a halt the following morning, Dale announced that it had been decided and over their supper, in the chill of the dawn, he led the way by insisting on being called Dale and suggesting the scholar, with no consultation, should be just Trystin. Now, in the growing light, it was only the children who needed to give them a simple name to use.

"Cori," Prince Corist had said a little shyly. "At least that's what my family all call me." He hesitated at the reminder of a family he knew in his heart probably no longer existed. Quelling the thought, he gestured to his dark-headed brother, "And Allin."

"And she's 'Sannah," Allin added after shooting a quick scowl at his older brother for speaking on his behalf.

"Hmm," Dale said thoughtfully, rubbing his beard. "I think that might be a problem."

"A problem? Why?" Allin looked startled.

"Cori and Allin are both fairly ordinary names. Cori is usually short for Korim, and Allin's a name in itself. But Sannah's unusual - distinctive."

"It's Hastian." Cori said, a little defensively. "Josanna was a fairy or something."

"A wood spirit," Trystin murmured quietly.

"Mother wanted to call her something magical," Cori went on, ignoring his tutor's correction. "On account of finally having a girl."

"Well, I think we are going to have to find something a little more common-place, I'm afraid."

"But you can't go and change her name," Allin protested stubbornly. "She wouldn't understand it."

"Oh, I think you under-estimate her. She won't mind a different name, will you little flower?" And he poked gently at the little girl's nose. She smiled timidly at him, and then hid her face behind Trystin, suddenly shy, but she watched him with her bright little eyes, intrigued by this big man.

"What about Joss?" Cori suggested. "It's like her name, and it's common enough. One of the footmen was called Joss, and that groom who got stepped on by Pallis."

"It's a boy's name," Allin snorted. "You can't giver her a boy's name!"

"Why not? All Lady Bessander's friends call her Bes, and that's a boy's name too. Besides, I rather like it."

"It will do," Trystin said firmly, to prevent further argument, although his face did seem to suggest that he thought the name inappropriate. "It isn't for very long and we don't have time for a lengthy debate. 'Sannah isn't suitable so Joss it will have to be. Don't you agree Capt... err.. Dale?" Trystin glanced at the big man, and was astonished to see a stricken look on his face.

With an effort, Dale seemed to pull himself together. "Yes. Yes. Joss is fine. Cori, Allin and Joss. Now, you children should all get some rest. I want to get moving again just as soon as it's dark tonight."

Allin looked as if he was about to protest - he wasn't at all sleepy and he was sick of not seeing daylight from one day to the next. He had been hoping to stay awake for once but Cori hadn't missed that expression on Dale's face, or the sudden change of mood. With the bossy authority at which all teenage brothers seem adept, he took his sister's hand and placed a single sharp finger in Allin's back, firmly steering his protesting sibling off to the area that had been previously cleared for sleep.

Despite Allin's desire to remain awake, he was tired and it didn't take long for all three youngsters to be asleep. Trystin kept a watching eye on them for a while, as he always did, making sure they were all settled and still, before he turned back to Dale.

The big soldier had not spoken again since sending the children to bed and was idly cleaning his sword blade as he sat, staring distantly into the fire. Trystin watched him for a little while, knowing something was amiss but not sure how to get the big man to tell him what had changed so suddenly. Dale however was aware he was being observed and knew why, so it was he who spoke first.

"Do you believe in fate?" he asked quietly.

A little puzzled by the question, Trystin answered cautiously. "I don't know. I can't say I think about it much."

"I do. I think most soldiers do to some degree or another - we're a superstitious bunch as a rule. I've always believed that some things are meant to be; pre-ordained by God and Brem. It helps sometimes, when you have to face up to something awful, to hold on to the idea that it was meant to be and is happening for some greater purpose that you can't see or understand. You know what I mean?"

"I do. It isn't something I personally hold any great store by, but I'll allow that some do." There was a long pause, so Trystin added, "I'm presuming there is a reason for you telling me this, not just a sudden desire to discuss personal beliefs."

Dale nodded. "If you believe in fate sometimes, long after things happen, you see patterns that tell you it was destined to take place."

"Go on." Trystin was beginning to be impatient. "I take it you've seen one of these patterns, to make sense of something."

Another nod. "My son, who died of spring fever," - Trystin bobbed his head to show he remembered - "he was born in the same moon-cycle of the same year as Cori there. Had he lived, he'd have been the same age. When he died, he was the same age as young Allin - again, to the very moon." He stopped for a minute.

"It's an interesting coincidence, Dale," Trystin began, "but..."

"His name was Joss." Dale said it quietly, not even looking at the young scholar, as though it was a thing of no importance but even Trystin could see the significance of the remark to the soldier.

"My goodness," he said faintly. "It is remarkable that pure chance should provide a link such as that." Then more briskly, "I can't say I believe it as being fate taking a hand, however. Since you clearly think so, I imagine you also have an idea of what it might mean?"

With a firm shake of his head, Dale smiled. "Who knows? Maybe everything that's happened here in Bremmand was supposed to happen - that my destiny and yours, and that of those three children has been entwined together for hundreds of years. Maybe it's just a kindly God telling me that my son is at peace. It may be exactly what it seems to be - an incredible coincidence. But there is one thing I know for sure. It never pays to try and interpret the fates. If you try to guess what the meaning is, you can end up following a path that is so far away from the one God planned for you that you stand no chance of happiness in this life or the next. All we can do is take comfort in the fact that He is trying to tell us something and trust that we're following the right path."

"But if He's trying to tell us something...?"

"Then if we haven't got the message, He'll just say it louder. If there is something we are meant to do, He'll make sure we know about it. God is with us, Trystin. He's watching our footsteps for us."

"He's certainly looked after the weather for us, anyway," the scholar remarked quietly.

This was true enough. The weather had been warm and dry for the entire journey to date, making travel easy and, with the ground beneath their feet as hard as iron, keeping their trail as hard to follow as possible.

Dale grinned at him. "Even if that's all He's done for us, it's more than enough. Now," he got to his feet and slid his blade back into its scabbard, "I'm going to scout around and see what I can find to feed our hungry young troops on when they wake up." And with a nod of farewell, he vanished silently into the forest.

Food was abundant in these parts of the Great Forest. The remote and sheltered lands were teeming with wildlife - none of which Dale dared to catch, fearful that the fire required to cook it would be seen - but all manner of edible plants grew in abundance and for the duration of the journey they had lived on nuts, fruit and berries. It wasn't an ideal diet, but Dale had been insistent that, unless they were prepared to eat their rabbits raw, it was the best he could do. He wasn't all that keen on the monotonous fare, any more than the young royals and knew it was another hardship that they could all do without but, until they had reached the relative safety of his cottage, he wasn't prepared to take any chances. All he could do was try and make the daily food offerings as varied as possible.

Today he was in luck. Less than ten minutes walk from where they had set up their camp was a large pear tree. How it had come to be there, Dale had no idea, but it was healthy and well-laden despite it being early in the year. Dale was able to gather a good crop of the soft ripe fruit, which he knew would cheer the whole party, before collecting the usual array of red currants and blackberries which grew everywhere in this part of the forest.

As he headed back to the camp, he offered up a silent prayer of thanks to whatever God was watching over them. *Now*, he added at the end, *just be protecting King Jorvis as well, so that we can bring these three children back to a place of safety and their family before too long.*

The change of diet, if only the exchange of one fruit for another, did a lot to lift the mood of children and men alike and somehow it carried them through the last night of their journey in far better spirits than any of the previous parts. It was helped, too, by the fact that the moon, still in its first quarter, was now beginning to shed enough light by which to see. The seemingly endless walking was somehow less miserable when they weren't all constantly tripping over things and getting tangled up in briars, unseen in the darkness.

As dawn approached, Dale called the little party to a halt. "If we are planning to stop, we should start to look for somewhere to bed down soon but I reckon we are only a half day's walk from the cottage now. If you want to, if you feel up to it, we can carry on walking and see if we can get there today. What do you think boys?" He looked first to the two Princes, determined that Trystin would follow whatever lead Dale gave.

Allin looked at Dale wearily but his eyes full of hope. "We're really almost there?"

"Yes, though it's still a goodish walk away. It will still be there tomorrow too, so don't feel we must go on today, if you'd rather rest up."

Cori rubbed his forehead - the exhaustion creeping up on him from the last few days of exertion, irregular sleep and the constant haunting fear that this was all that was left of his family was making his brain sluggish and he couldn't think. "Once we get there, we'll be able to stop properly for a bit won't we?" he asked slowly.

"Yes. We'll be quite safe to stay there for a while."

Cori didn't look as if he wanted to continue but he said bravely, "Then we should go on if we can. The sooner we get to somewhere we can stop the better it must be. What about you Allin? Do you think you'll be able to manage another half day?"

The young boy nodded. "Let's keep going."

"Good for you," Dale said encouragingly.

They stopped for a short while, to eat the last of the pears Dale had thoughtfully remembered to bring along with him, raising sprits once more with the simple but delicious fruit and then they continued. Weariness made progress slower than Dale had estimated and in the end they were obliged to stop for an hour or two as the sun reached its zenith, too tired to complete the journey without some rest. As a result it was late afternoon when Dale led them finally along the narrow, wooded pathway which led to their destination.

The Cottage in the Woods

"Here we are then - home sweet home! Not much, I know, but it should serve us well enough."

The cottage, and the clearing in which it stood, were indeed not much. The wooden building itself was small, and looked pretty run down. The roof was choked with moss and the one small window, covered by a wooden shutter, was overgrown and looked as if it would never open. On the ground around the simple dwelling the grass grew long and straggly, waist high in places, with bindweed and thistles scattered around. The clearing itself showed that it hadn't been used in a long time - the grasses stood high and the forest undergrowth was starting to encroach upon the clear ground which must have once made up the woodcutter's working area. Dale could almost feel the dismay emanating from the others - they were all tired and had been keeping themselves going with the incentive of reaching this place and he knew it was a great disappointment. It seemed that his role as the raiser of spirits wasn't yet complete. Briskly he began to hand out tasks to keep everyone busy.

"Right then! Let's start getting this place tidied up, shall we? Allin, I want to get a fire going as soon as possible, so can you and Joss gather up some of the wood that's lying around and pile them up here." He pointed to a patch just outside the cottage door. "Cori, you and Trystin can help me open up the cottage and get some daylight in. Then you can get some of the blankets out and air them so we'll have something to sleep in tonight. All right?" He looked challengingly at them and was given a look of weary agreement in reply. He knew that none of them was in the least bit keen to start working now - they had all been expecting to stop when they reached here and to find that there was more to do was clearly unpopular. But Dale's show of energy did at least stir them into movement.

Only Trystin didn't start to head for his appointed task, instead looking as if he wanted to argue with the big man. As the scholar opened his mouth, however, Dale fixed him with a firm look and said bluntly,

"Don't argue. This isn't the time. We need to keep those lads going for a bit longer and you bellyaching won't help that. I want to keep their spirits up and it will help if they make the place look a bit less scruffy." He paused and then added, "Besides, it will keep them occupied for a while. There's no fresh food, and no means to cook it, even if there were, so if they're busy they won't think about it yet and it'll give me time to go out and forage for something." Trystin looked rebelliously at the Captain for a moment, offended by the abrupt way he'd been handled, but there was a certain logic to Dale's reasoning and he knew that the children's well-being had to be their first concern. So he nodded slightly and then headed for the cottage door, managing to pull his drooping shoulders up and walk more briskly.

Dale allowed himself a moment of relief that the scholar was willing to do what was needed of him, despite the fact that he disliked it. It was clear that, of all of them, Trystin was still finding it hardest to adapt to this sudden change in his lifestyle. The princes, while raised in comfort and safety, were both young and full of energy, the princess had been carried a fair degree of the way and Dale was used to the soldiers' life of hard work, outdoor action and making do in poor conditions. Trystin, however, must be used to very little physical exertion, there not being much call for it when teaching History, and he was not that much younger than Dale, so wouldn't be blessed with the energy of the young and fit. He didn't care for the rough life that was necessary in order to ensure the survival of the young princes and he was already questioning Dale's decisions, although he hadn't yet given any show of defiance to the officer. He had no experience of forest ways and even less of military matters, so his criticism of Dale's authority was beginning to be wearing but the big man wasn't prepared to hammer home his authority until forced. While Trystin continued to do as he was told and supported Dale's efforts to protect and reassure the royal children, then Dale was willing to work around the inexperience and complaints of the Scholar.

Noticing that Cori was struggling to open the door, Dale crossed over to the cottage and showed him the catch which held it fast and how to push the peg free to unlock it. Then, with a shove of his shoulder, he pushed the door open, to let the evening sunshine flood in.

It was dim and damp smelling in the cottage and there was a layer of dust over most things but it was tidy inside, with a simple table and four chairs in the main living area. There was a partition wall to the right, behind which, Dale showed, was the sleeping area. Room for them all, he said cheerfully, as he pointed at the three beds which stood there, stripped down to bare wood but big enough to accommodate them all. Then he showed Cori and Trystin the wooden settle in the corner where the bedding was kept and left them to get on with the task of pulling out the blankets and bringing them outside to rid them of the musty smell of years in storage.

Back in the main living area, he lifted from the shelves beside the fireplace an axe-head and a whetstone. He picked up a bucket from beside the door, shook out an indignant spider which had been living there and went back outside.

He glanced briefly round the clearing and watched Allin pulling sticks grumpily into his arms from the ground, followed by Joss, holding a handful of pathetic looking twigs. Allin was clearly not amused at having to do this and was stamping from place to place muttering under his breath as he did so. He headed to the edge of the clearing and as he put a foot onto the path which led towards the stream that provided fresh water to the cottage, Dale felt obliged to call out,

"Don't leave the clearing please, Allin. There's plenty of fire wood here and I don't want you getting lost or falling down a pit." He got a scowl in return but the boy did turn back into the clearing. Joss walked up to the big man and shyly handed her bundle of twigs to Dale.

"Sticks," she said shyly. Dale smiled, thanked her politely, and took her hand to show her where to put them.

"That won't make much of a fire," Allin commented sarcastically but Dale merely said mildly,

"I need kindling though, to get the fire started. It will do nicely for that."

Allin stamped over and dumped an armful of larger branches beside Joss's little pile. Then he looked challengingly up at Dale. "Why won't you let me go into the forest - there's bound to be some big stuff there, and it would save loads of time if I didn't have to pick up all these stupid little sticks but got one big one instead?"

"Well it would," Dale agreed, walking to the side of the cottage, picking up an axe handle and fitting the axe head to it, "but I need the smaller stuff to get the fire going and it gets the area cleared up at the same time, so it does twice as much good. Besides, I need you to keep an eye on your sister and she's a little young to go wandering in the forest."

"It's all anyone wants me to do, be a nursemaid to Joss. It's like you all think I can't do anything else, or that I'll mess things up." Allin sounded hurt, so Dale put a supportive hand on his shoulder.

"It's not much fun, I know, but we'll all have to pitch in and do some of the rotten jobs I'm afraid."

"It doesn't look like you're doing anything rotten at all" Allin said bitterly, eyeing the axe. "Why don't you let me take that, and you can watch Joss."

Dale grinned - to a ten-year-old, the chance to use something as lethal as an axe must be pretty appealing but he replied politely, "It's kind of you to offer, Your Highness, but perhaps another time." Then, changing from mock formal to a more friendly tone he added, "Look, if you'll do as I ask you for the moment, as soon as we have a bit of time, I'll teach you how to use an axe. How's that?"

"How to fight with it?" Allin asked eagerly, surprising Dale somewhat.

"Well, this isn't really a fighting axe; you need something with a different balance for that. All this is really good for is chopping wood but I can show you how that's done if you want." This clearly disappointed the boy, so Dale added, "If it's fighting you're interested in, I'd stick to a sword if I were you. It's easier to pick up the basics, and you've already made a start." The King's sons all started training with the Weapons Master when they were about eight, so Dale knew Allin already had a good deal of practice. Allin gave him a disgusted look.

"Swords are boring - practice, practice, practice, and we never do anything exciting."

"Well, I hate to have to tell you this, but it's no different with a fighting axe. The technique is a lot harder, so you spend a lot more time practising moves and balance than with a sword. You'd find it a lot more boring; and much harder work too. An axe is a lot heavier you know. You need the shoulders of a bear to wield one well."

Allin gazed at Dale, taking in his broad shoulders "You could use one."

"I could." Dale agreed with a smile. This wasn't the first small boy who had remarked on his stature, which seemed immense to a slender little creature like young Allin. "But size isn't all it takes. I know how to use an axe to fight but I'm not very good at it and personally I don't care for them. I know what I'm doing with this" - he touched his sword hilt lightly, the blade still hanging at his side - "and it's never failed me yet."

"Have you killed many people?" the boy asked, curiously.

"Allin! You don't ask people questions like that." Cori rebuked him sharply, having heard as he came out from the cottage with a bundle of blankets in his arms. "It's not polite, and you know it."

The boy shot a rebellious look at his brother and protested, "I was only asking?"

"Well don't," was the flat response. "Just because we aren't at home doesn't mean you can forget your manners. Now, stop asking impertinent questions, apologise to Dale and get on with whatever it is you are *supposed* to be doing."

Allin opened his mouth to argue once more and then shut it again and, with a look that clearly communicated what he thought of older brothers, muttered an apology which was mostly insincere and stamped off to pick up more of the loose sticks that were strewn about the clearing.

Cori watched him with an exasperated eye and then turned to Dale. "I'm sorry about him. He does know better than that, really. He just does it to annoy."

"Or maybe to find out the answers," Dale suggested mildly. Cori gave him a quizzical look, so the Captain went on, "Don't be too quick to assume that he's being deliberately disobedient. He's ten years old. It's natural for him to be curious, especially about things like war and fighting with all that's going on about you at the moment but he won't always understand what one can and can't ask of people."

"You don't know him. Allin's always determined to do exactly what he pleases, regardless of what he's been taught. He's been told again and again that it isn't good manners to ask personal questions but he still does it." Cori was looking determined about this - positive that he was in the right about his troublesome brother.

"Does he know why?"

"What?" Cori gaped at him.

"Or what is meant by a 'personal question'?"

"Well," Cori began to splutter, suddenly feeling less secure in his point of view. "Of course he knows. Everyone knows what a personal question is."

"You'd ask a blacksmith how many swords he's made," Dale pointed out. "Simple interest in what he does for a living and a perfectly reasonable question to ask. I'm a soldier - when you come down to it, what I do for a living is kill people. So, to a ten-year-old, is it so different to ask me about my job? The question didn't offend me, if that's worrying you."

Cori scowled. "You're just defending him because he's little and looks like he's sweet and innocent but he isn't and if you let him get away with it once he'll carry on behaving badly until he's impossible. You don't have to live with him all the time."

Dale sighed, seeing the natural sibling rivalry and age gap showing its face. "All right. Let's drop it for now. I can see we aren't getting anywhere. But try and be patient with him, son. He's only a child and he's done pretty well to come this far with so little complaint. I suspect things are going to get tougher for him before they get better."

Cori gave him a hollow look. *So he does know*, Dale reflected. *He's aware that this is probably all that's left of his family.* The light brown head dropped for a second and then came back up. "Isn't that all the more reason to keep things as normal as possible? If he starts getting treated differently and can get away with things that my parents wouldn't allow, then he's going to guess...."

Dale put a comforting hand on the lad's shoulder. "He's going to work it out for himself, Cori, if we don't tell him. He's clever and old enough to have some idea of what happens in a war. In fact I'd suspect he's already got a pretty good idea but is trying to pretend it isn't so." He gazed across at the boy, now holding his little sister's hand and helping her increase her little collection of kindling by pointing out more places where twigs were lying in the long grass. "He needs the people around him to be his friends. He especially needs to know that his brother is on his side."

Cori was also staring at the remaining members of his family. "I am. I just..." His face twisted in pain. "I don't know how I'm going to tell him. Joss is so little that she won't really understand but Allin..."

Dale looked at him for a moment and then said gently, "You don't have to do this alone, Cori. I'll be here to help you."

"Will you?" the lad asked as though he almost didn't dare to believe it.

Dale nodded. "Whatever we do, from now until this is all over, we do it together."

Dale urged Cori to keep himself busy rather than dwell on his troubles so the lad started to shake out the blankets he'd been carrying. He was not used to domestic chores so he got rather tangled up in the grey cloth. He turned and his eye fell on his younger brother who was starting to run out of sticks to collect so he called "Come and give me a hand with this, Allin, will you."

Allin didn't look keen but he came obediently enough, Joss following at his heels contentedly. "What do you want?"

"You hold that end so that I can stretch this blanket out."

"Why?"

Cori looked at him blankly. The mysteries of airing bedding was lost on him and he eventually said helplessly, "I don't know. Because Trystin asked me to, I suppose. I don't know anything about these things."

Allin looked equally puzzled but gave his assistance to his brother. They took the four corners between them and hurled the blanket up into the air. Not expecting Cori to use such a sharp flick and being considerably smaller than his brother, Allin's end was snatched out of his hands and the whole blanket came flying down on Cori's head. As the older boy struggled out of the enveloping fabric his younger brother couldn't help but grin while Joss giggled in delight at the sight. Cori scowled, feeling ridiculous.

"Don't fool about Allin. This isn't a game."

"I wasn't fooling," came the injured reply. "You pulled too hard."

"Well hang on properly next time," Cori retorted irritably as he handed the two corners back to his brother.

Now the blanket was twisted, and it took another moment or two, with both brothers untwisting their ends and thus creating another rotation in the material before the blanket was pulled out flat. Cori tutted, getting more cross with every moment at this seemingly deliberate attempt on his little brother's part to make a simple task as difficult as possible.

Finally they had the substantial square of grey wool held out flat once more and this time when they gave it a shake, all four corners stayed in the boys' grasp and, as the centre reached its apogee, a cloud of dust flew up and out of the blanket. A couple more shakes saw the blanket free of the worst of the dust of moon-cycles in a chest and they moved on to the next one.

Joss had watched the blanket flying up and down with great interest but as the process was repeated with a second she decided that the view would be far better from beneath the canopy. She ran underneath and stood gurgling with pleasure as the fabric rose and fell above her. After two or three throws, Allin, unable to resist the entertainment, allowed his ends to drop as the blanket descended once more so that the woollen cloth enveloped the little girl.

For a second, Cori looked like he might explode and then he suddenly took in the delighted giggling of the amorphous lump that was his sister and Allin's amused grinning and all at once he was laughing with them. He too dropped his ends and strode in on his sister, bundling her up in the blanket, rolling her gently off her feet and on to the ground. Allin quickly joined them, dragging the other three blankets with him and attempted to bury the older lad in the woollens.

By the time Dale returned from the stream with a bucket of fresh drawn water, the three children were totally tangled up in the grey cloth, in fits of helpless giggles.

"Well, I suppose that's one way to air the blankets," he observed dryly to the wriggling mass as he dumped the bucket down.

Cori poked his head up abruptly, looking worried. "I'm sorry," he apologised contritely. "We were shaking them out but then Joss wanted to play and…" he trailed off, knowing this was no excuse for failing to follow instructions. "We'll get back to work," and he began to tug at the blankets trying to disentangle the two youngsters writhing around in the covers.

Dale began to grin but said soberly enough, "Here let me help you. Why don't I take this blanket back to Trystin?" and he reached down, took a good handful of blanket and at least one small body in his arms and began to carry it across the clearing towards the scholar, who had stopped at the doorway to watch the fun. By the shrieks of laughter from beneath the rough fabric it was clearly Joss he had bundled in his arms but he pretended not to notice. He looked back at Cori with a mock expression of concern and said in an artificially loud voice. "This blanket still seems to have some bugs in it. I think you can't have shaken it out well enough." The giggling grew louder under the grey wool, and Cori, who had been staring in astonishment at the soldier's sudden geniality when he had been mostly serious and grim, began to laugh once more. From behind him, Allin rose up like a monster from a lake and threw another blanket high over his brother's head, dragging him back into the romp.

Dale burrowed into the wriggling bundle in his arms, until he could push back the folds and uncover Joss's face. Her eyes were wide and sparkling with light and her whole face was lit up by a bright little smile that was entirely infectious. "Well now," Dale declared, as he handed the whole bundle over to Trystin, "what do we do with this little creature I've found living in the blankets, Trystin? Do we throw it out do you think?"

Joss laughed. "No! More! More!" to the big man and reached out to try and grab on to him.

"All right then," he grinned and swung the child up on to his shoulders so she could see the whole clearing. She seemed quite content to sit there, still giggling, watching as her two brothers continued to roll in the other blankets. Trystin,

Dale and Joss all stood there, just by the little cottage, watching the two boys play just like any other children the world over.

The play was getting rougher now that the boys didn't have to be mindful of their sister and they began to wrestle. Cori had all the advantages of size and superior strength but Allin was quick and agile and had a seemingly inexhaustible energy, so every time Cori managed to get grip on him and tried to pin him down, the smaller boy could wriggle away and come around to envelop the light brown head in blinding cloth once more.

Eventually, Cori had to admit defeat. "Enough Allin," he gasped, fighting for breath. "No more. I concede. Stop before I die of exhaustion!"

Allin immediately pulled away, fell to the floor and lay flat out in the grass as he too inhaled deeply, to bring more air in to his heaving lungs. For a few minutes the boys just lay there, recovering and then Cori sat up and gazed at the messy tangle of blankets. Somewhat dismayed at the mess, he patted his brother's ankle, the part closest to him at the time and said regretfully. "We still have to get these shaken out."

Allin rolled his head around to look in disgust at his brother. He groaned, but Cori was already getting to his feet, all business.

"Come on, Pup. It won't take all that long and it was what we were supposed to be doing after all."

Led by his brother's brisk tones and move to action, Allin began to get to his feet and together they began to pull the blankets apart and once more shake the dust and grass from them.

Dale took this cue as well and handed Joss back to Trystin. "Can you keep her with you for a bit? I need to chop some wood and I want to be sure she's out of the way. I don't imagine she's got any idea of the dangers of an axe and I'd hate for something to happen to her."

"Of course," Trystin said and then looked rather awkwardly at the child. He didn't have much to do with infants and was never quite sure how to talk to them. But he had to make an effort so he put on a smile and said, "Do you want to come and help me open up the cottage then little one?" Then he carried her in to the cottage, closing the door to prevent her from slipping away from him.

Dale picked up the blanket from which he had unwrapped Joss and carried it over to Cori and Allin. They were working quite happily together, their spirits lifted by the few minutes of foolishness. As he walked past Allin, Dale scrubbed the top of his head jovially. "All right then?" The boy nodded and watched as the big man collected his abandoned bucket, which had miraculously remained un-spilled, and crossed to the side of the cottage where the axe sat waiting to be sharpened.

"Are you sure you don't want me to do that?" Allin called after him hopefully but now teasing rather than annoyed.

Dale flashed a grin back at the boy over his shoulder. "Quite sure, thanks. Some other time perhaps. When we don't need a fire so badly."

"I'll hold you to that, Captain."

"I make it a habit of always keeping promises made to princes," Dale replied with a smile.

By the time Dale had put an edge back on the blade and chopped enough firewood to keep them going until the following day, the two young princes had finished shaking out the blankets, had returned them to the cottage and were now assisting Trystin with some rudimentary cleaning. Although the chores they were doing were mostly menial, they were not tasks to which Princes were accustomed so they were entertained by the novelty of what they were doing. It kept spirits raised through the drudgery.

As Dale began to carry the sticks and twigs that Joss and Allin had gathered in to the cottage to lay up in the fireplace, Cori said suddenly,

"You know what? I'm starving."

"So am I," Allin agreed promptly.

Trystin crossed the room and took the armful of kindling from Dale. "I can do this, if you'll lend me your tinder box."

Dale handed it over willingly and then turned with a smile to the two boys.

"Well then, if you gentlemen will excuse me, I'll go and get us all something to eat," and he shouldered his hunting bag as he prepared to head out of the clearing.

Allin gave Dale a long gloomy look and said dismally, "More berries?"

Dale gave him a sidelong look and said soberly, "Well, I was planning on rabbit but if course if you prefer berries…" and he grinned at the boy before heading out.

Their first meat in almost a week tasted like a banquet to both children and adults alike and it left them full and content so that they were able to ignore the meagre state of their surroundings. The cottage was still gloomy and dust smeared and there was no light save for that thrown out by the fire. They were all tired, the short break they had taken during the afternoon the only sleep that they had taken in almost a day, so no-one argued when Dale suggested shortly after the sun had set, that the children go to bed.

It didn't take more than a few moments for the three to peel themselves out of their filthy garments for the first time since they had left the castle and to get into one of the wide beds now made up with the blankets aired earlier. Within half an hour all three were still and quiet but even so Trystin sat with them until he was sure they were all sleeping soundly. He was now so used to them being restless and needing his presence for reassurance that he was unsettled when they seemed to need him no longer.

Dale was at the fireplace when Trystin finally returned.

"More brew?" he offered but Trystin shook his head. Dale shrugged and poured himself another mug of the steaming leaf infusion that was popular amongst the troops and common folk. Most homes had a couple of bushes that produced the sweet leaves growing nearby, and Dale's cottage had been no exception. It had been almost the first thing for which he had used the fire when he returned with the rabbit and wild mushrooms for their supper.

Trystin watched as Dale returned to his seat, and then spoke, "And now what?"

"We sit tight," was the simple reply. "The one thing we can be sure of is that Darvett's troops will be looking for someone who seems to be fleeing. So that's just what we don't do. We make ourselves comfortable here and melt in to the background. If we put a bit of effort into it, we can make this place look like we've been living here for years in no time at all. If anyone happens by they'd find a simple woodcutter, his three children and his wife's brother. They wouldn't suspect a thing."

"You sound pretty sure of that. Can you be so certain? The Marchand children are rather conspicuous," Trystin said, thinking of the three exceptional personalities that they were now protecting.

"Get rid of the fine clothing, replace it with something more common, and cover the whole thing with a few days' worth of good old peasant grime, and they'll blend in easily enough." Dale smiled and the tutor's doubtful look and reminded him. "They looked remarkably ordinary this afternoon."

"They are hardly ordinary." Trystin returned tartly but then he recalled that afternoon and said more thoughtfully, "Still, it was good to see that they are still able to play, after all this."

"And with all that's ahead of them too. I don't think the news is going to get any better."

There was a pause and then Trystin cleared his throat. "Well, you are a better judge than me, I suppose. I'm no military expert." There was a bitterness to Trystin's tone for reasons that defeated Dale entirely. The man seemed to find fault in everything and it was beginning to be very tiresome. What was becoming apparent was that Trystin thought as little of Dale as the Captain thought of him. Still, Dale consoled himself, you don't have to like people, just get them to do as they are told. If Trystin wanted to be pig-headed then he would learn soon enough that the Captain could be at least as stubborn and was quite prepared to back up his authority with a fist if he had to.

"And I take it you have already decided that there is no chance of the others getting through to Hast?"

"The side party might, with the other two boys but Verdin and the Queen? Not a hope." Dale sighed, as he cast his mind briefly over the men, several his friends, many who served under his own command, who had most certainly died on the north road. "Darvett's dogs were baying at our heels pretty closely when Verdin split the party. He made his group a deliberate decoy to draw attention away from us and he knew they were all going to be slaughtered. So did Isolde at a guess. She gave herself up to save her children."

"Do you think they know that?" Trystin tilted his head towards the back room where the three royal children lay sleeping.

"Cori does - I think the Queen told him as much before she left them - and Allin isn't stupid. He must have some understanding of what's going on around him, even if he doesn't want to believe it right now. His whole way of life has changed overnight with very little warning. He must be asking himself what would cause that to happen."

"Poor little wretch," Trystin mused sympathetically. "He's going to find this very hard. To lose both his parents so young and to be ripped away from everything he's ever known…"

"They all will, but they'll survive. They're strong and they know how to support each other."

"Golden children." Trystin murmured.

"Right. Well it's now that they are going to need that golden quality the most. It'll get them through these hard times and hopefully bring them out the other side."

"Is there an 'other side'? Darvett's men in Bremmand means the news from the battle must be bad - that was why we all fled the Castle as we did. It means that Jorvis is dead…"

"The King is dead, long live the King." Dale spoke softly, but with intense feeling.

"A King without a kingdom?"

Dale felt a stab of irritation. "Shall we go and surrender right now, since you're so convinced that all is lost?"

"Captain," Trystin replied icily, "I have no intention of giving up but I believe it is better to deal with a problem by facing it head on."

As if the man has ever had to face a problem much greater than whether to have lamb or venison for dinner, Dale thought bitterly. It wasn't as if the scholar with his sheltered upbringing and cloistered life would have the faintest idea what to do if he did understand the situation as fully as he claimed to desire. The man had all but fallen to pieces after the first skirmish so what he'd do now was anybody's guess. And for precisely that reason, Dale wasn't about to share his plans with the tutor. Still, Trystin had claimed that he wanted the truth, so Dale gave him a little of it.

"The situation doesn't look good and our three youngsters back there are probably all that's left of the holy bloodline, but let's not hand Bremmand over to Darvett until we know there's no other choice and don't assume that he'll find the people of Brem so willing to allow this usurper to rule their promised land when his blood is as common as yours and mine. Don't forget the sacred bond that exists between the people and the bloodline and the faith they have that these lands will forever belong to them so long as the bloodline of Holy Brem remains. They'll do anything to keep the descendants of Brem in power and will fight tooth and nail to restore the true king, if Darvett tries to hold sway here. He's going to find this a much harder kingdom to hold than any of the others he's bullied his way into."

Trystin bowed his head, looking almost grief stricken. "I'd love to believe that by keeping these children here we are saving the land from invasion but I think it's too late. Darvett's here; he's already won."

"Not while there are still Marchands alive, Trystin." Dale stared into the fire and said fiercely, "There is still something to fight for. The way he pursued us, the effort he put into tracking down Jorvis's family, means Darvett knows how important they are. He's proved it by his determination to murder innocent children. He wants to eliminate every last drop of Brem's blood because he knows what it represents. Their very existence threatens him. So, we make sure that threat remains and we do that by hiding our three young ones well and keeping them safe until they are ready to reclaim their kingdom. Even if we have to lead these children away and put them under Hast's protection; even if the bloodline *does* leave the land, while the common people know it's still flowing in Marchand veins, that the true King is waiting on the border to reclaim his birthright, Darvett will never truly command them. He knows that and he's afraid of it. He may sit in the chair at Castle Bremmand but right now the throne is right here, in this little cottage, because *this* is where the Marchand bloodline is."

Trystin nodded. "How long do we stay here then, before we start out for Hast?"

"I'm not sure." Dale shifted uneasily and then got to his feet to pour another cup of brew from the stove pot.

"Dale?" Trystin said suspiciously. "What are you thinking? You've got something else in mind haven't you?"

For a second Dale hesitated. Perhaps he could give the scholar an idea... but then, with an innocent look on his face he replied, "I've got nothing planned. We just have to wait it out here until things are safer. Then we'll go to Hast."

Trystin looked as if he wanted to argue again but then, as they sat there with only the light of the fire illuminating the room, the scholar became aware of a faint whispering from the trees outside. As it grew more persistent he threw a slightly worried glance at Dale, unfamiliar with the ways of the deep forest.

"Is that the wind?" and indeed it did sound a little like leaves rustling in the breeze but Dale shook his head.

"Rain," he explained briefly, unperturbed. "Sounds like it's going to chuck it down." Even as he said this, the whispering became a hiss and then dropped down a few tones, the sound of the raindrops drumming on the ground becoming audible. The two men sat in silence for a few minutes listening to the downpour before Trystin spoke once more.

"It sounds like we were lucky to have arrived here before the weather broke. I'm not sure I'd have enjoyed being in the open in this kind of weather."

Dale grinned. "Perfect timing really. The rain will obscure our tracks. A good heavy downpour should wash away most of the traces we left behind on our way here."

"Doubly lucky then." Trystin threw Dale a mocking look. "More benevolence from the gods protecting our footsteps again?"

"Perhaps. I'd certainly like to think so. If the gods are on our side then we should be able to bring our charges in there" - he nodded towards where the three young royals lay sleeping - "to a place of safety."

"May the gods continue to protect us then." Trystin remarked but Dale could tell that he didn't believe. He wanted to, the big man guessed, but try as he might, he couldn't make his well-educated mind let go of learning and logic for long enough to allow the spiritual side of life to have a place as well. For one brief moment, Dale almost felt pity for the man. No gods walked in Trystin's world, to offer him comfort or protection. The slender, pale-eyed man was alone in the world in a way that Dale would never be.

Dale rose early the following morning, by which time the storm had passed and the dawn air was clean and fresh. The forest was alive with the sound of nature making its typical early morning din but somehow the cacophony was reassuring so Dale stood the door to the cottage open to allow the commotion and light of the morning to filter into the cottage. As quietly as he could, to avoid waking any of the other occupants of the little house, he brought in more wood and stoked up the fire, setting a pot of Brew on the hearth to heat. In one corner of the main living area of the cottage was a door which led through to a small extra room which served as a pantry and, having been dug out when the cottage had been built, led to a cellar. The big man looked through the dry goods, picking out a few items which might make up some kind of breakfast for them all and then moved on to a pair of large oaken chests in which he kept clothing and other supplies. He'd been here in the spring to put up his winter-wear, and had taken the opportunity to sort through the trunk in which he kept his own effects, so it didn't take him long to find the things he was looking for. Within ten minutes he had extracted and changed into a simple tunic and hose and an old pair of comfortable boots, also sorting out similar attire for Trystin and Cori. Then he moved on to the second chest, in which he kept the clothes which had belonged to his late wife and children. He'd never expected to need them again but somehow had never felt quite able to dispose of them, unable to break that last link with them after they had died. His wife had been thrifty and had carefully stored the clothes that their children outgrew so that they might be used for the next child. With a fondness and another sense of fate touching him across time, Dale recalled how she had always teased that she intended to match Queen Isolde for children one day. They needed to continue to keep everything, Delan had insisted, so that their last child should have as much to wear as their first. As a result there was a good range of children's clothing of all sizes which would do for Allin and Joss.

When Dale returned to the main area, Allin was standing in the middle of the room. He was wearing only his undershirt, the rest of his clothes bundled up in his arms and he had a lost expression on his face which was heartrending. Dale looked at him silently for a moment or two before speaking, softly so as not to wake the others.

"Good morning. Looks like I'm not the only early riser."

Allin looked almost surprised at being spoken to but then he nodded his head slowly.

"Well, why don't you come and sit by the fire and get yourself dressed?" Dale suggested encouragingly. He didn't like the beaten look in the boy's eyes and feared that reality had finally caught up with the child.

Allin obeyed automatically but when he had seated himself he just looked down at the rolled ball of clothing in his arms as if he had no idea what to do with them.

"I was thinking that those are getting a bit grubby," Dale nodded at the clothes in Allin's arm, "and they aren't all that practical for wearing out here. I've got some other things which might be more suitable if you want to try them."

Still no reply but Allin numbly allowed Dale to take the bundle of clothes from him and hand over the plain woollen tunic and hose that had previously been worn by Dale's son. The boy dressed slowly and then seated himself in the wooden armchair once more.

Dale watched him carefully, the dark head bowed as the child stared blankly at the floor. Despite the warmth of the fire and the clement weather Allin was shivering. Dale added another log to the fire to try and warm him up.

"Are you cold Allin?" He asked solicitously as he did so, but the boy shook his head.

There was a long silence and then for the first time Allin spoke. "Can I go outside?"

Dale studied the child for a few moments, considering the masked expression and the dropping shoulders. Allin had asked with no degree of eagerness or interest at the temptations outdoors, just a flat monotone, and Dale was troubled by what they boy might be intending. He could hardly keep the lad a prisoner inside however, so he nodded. "As long as you don't leave the clearing, please Allin. It can be all too easy to get lost in the forest if you aren't familiar with it."

The dark head inclined slightly to show his acknowledgement and then, after a short pause, Allin got to his feet and walked outside into the sunlight. Dale watched him thoughtfully through the doorway for a few minutes as the boy wandered about the clearing somewhat aimlessly and then he went back to the fireplace to continue with the preparations for the day.

Cori and Joss surfaced half an hour later, Joss bright-eyed and smiling while Cori looked more irritable. Both, like Allin, were still in underclothes, with Cori carrying the clothes they had been wearing the day before.

"Joss decided it was time to wake up so she crawled all over me," he explained somewhat crossly. "I thought the least we could do was not wake Trystin as well." He gestured towards the bundle of clothes in his arm to explain the state of relative undress of himself and his sister.

"Very considerate," was Dale's only comment and then, just as he had with Allin he suggested that they might prefer to exchange the grimy garments in Cori's arms with those that he had sorted out from the cellar. Cori gave him a curious look, not fooled by the suggestion that Dale was planning on cleaning the fine woven clothes which made them distinctive but he obeyed without argument and ensured that Joss too was dressed in the peasant outfits.

"You'll find your brother outside," Dale suggested. "He wanted to take a look around a bit and he might welcome a bit of company."

Cori nodded and took Joss's hand to lead her out with him. As they left Dale issued the same warning that they shouldn't leave the clearing and then he returned once more to work, pouring water and oats into a small pot to make up a thin porridge for breakfast.

Within a few minutes, Cori was back at a run. "I can't find Allin!" he exclaimed in alarm. "I've walked all round the cottage and he's nowhere."

Dale cursed silently to himself that he hadn't kept a closer eye on the boy, and then followed Cori outside to join the hunt.

"Where is he?" The older boy said frantically, running his hands fretfully through his hair. "He should know better than to just go wandering off like this. And if he's walked into more soldiers…."

"Let's not panic just yet," Dale replied firmly. "He can't have gone very far, and the chances of him coming across anyone else way out here is very small. He's probably just seen something that interested him in the trees and gone to take a look."

"If he has I'll…" Cori began angrily and then stopped. "Oh, God. Please let him be all right."

Without thinking Dale slid an arm about the worried youth's shoulders. "It's all right Cori. I'm sure he's fine. Now let's keep calm and see if we can find him. With all this long grass and dew, we should be able to see his tracks and follow his path into the forest."

It didn't take them long to find Allin. As soon as Dale had followed his tracks to the point at which the boy had left the clearing he knew instinctively where their quarry had gone and led Cori and Joss, who insisted on accompanying them, along a short path to a side clearing, unkempt and almost hip high with meadow grass. Mixed among the grasses was an array of wild flowers in reds, purples and golds making splashes of colour all across the little space. Upon sight of the freely scattered blossoms Joss immediately began to wander about to gather the delicate blooms. The sun was breaking through the trees glinting on the dew-fall and scattering light about the clearing, as she criss-crossed the grassy dell. Dale gazed about it with the same sense of peace and security he felt on every visit. It was a beautiful place.

Kneeling in the middle of the little glade, staring down at something he had found among the tall vegetation, was Allin, his face bowed and facing away from them.

Cori, on seeing him, began to demand angrily where his brother had been but as he took a step or two forward he saw what Allin was looking at and stopped in his tracks. It was a grave marker, a small stone cairn carefully constructed to support a carved wooden charm, and now Cori could see that it wasn't the only one in that little spot. He turned and looked back at Dale in question.

"My family," he said quietly but with deep regret. There among the tall grasses lay his wife and children as well as both his parents and grandparents, all buried in the small meadow close to his home.

"We should leave here Allin," Cori said gently. "It's not right to disturb the resting place of other people. Why don't we go back to the cottage?" Silence. "Come on Pup, what do you say?"

Without looking up, Allin spoke in a dull voice. "They're all dead, aren't they?" He wasn't talking about the graves, Dale knew and as he saw this, Cori swung round to look at the big man with a helpless expression on his face. He too knew the question was not directed at the long gone Ronas family and he was at least as afraid of the answer as his younger brother. What they both needed now was hope and some reassurance that it was going to be made right. But all Dale could offer them was honesty.

"I don't know Allin. We have no way of knowing for a while."

"But you think so, don't you?" Allin persisted, sounding angry. "Everyone does. That's why we left the castle, why we had to split up, why those soldiers attacked us and why we're hiding here like this"

"Son, I wish I could give you a better answer. Both of you," he added taking in Cori with his glance, "but you're right; it doesn't look too promising. We must assume the worst for now and then, when there's been time for things to quieten down a little we can find out what's really happened. But don't give up hope just yet."

"People only say that when they want you to carry on as if it's all right," Allin declared bitterly. "But there's no point. They're all gone and there's nothing left. We're alone."

"Not alone Allin," Dale corrected quickly. "There's me and Trystin. We'll be with you for as long as you need."

At that moment Joss came padding over. In her clenched fist was a collection of the wild flowers she had gathered. Solemnly she offered them to Allin.

"What are these for?" he asked as he took them from her.

"To make you happy. Mamma told me. Don't be sad Allin."

It was too much. The little girl's innocent gesture of generosity and kindness finally broke through the resentful exterior that Allin had been so determinedly trying to offer to the world. In a voice wavering with despair he wailed, "They didn't even say goodbye," and he began to cry.

As the boy started to sob Cori hurried to his brother's side. Ignoring the sopping grass he knelt by Allin's side and put two strong arms about him. At the same time Joss, not understanding why her flowers had failed to have the desired effect, also put her arms about his neck.

"Don't cry Allin," she suggested sympathetically as Cori said, more usefully.

"It's all right Pup. We'll be all right." But his voice was also wavering, his brother's grief beginning to bring out his own.

50

Dale watched them for a second or two and then decided that his presence was an intrusion here. Not wanting to desert them, he put a single hand on Cori's shoulder, asking quietly, "Can I help?"

Cori looked at him, his eyes full of tears, and shook his head blindly. "We're all right, thanks Dale."

The big man nodded and, as the three children clung together and wept, he left them.

Dale returned to the cottage, still feeling uncertain that he should leave the children alone, his heart aching for the grief and pain they were now beginning to face.

Trystin had arisen in his absence and was eyeing the rough tunic and hose that Dale had brought out for him with obvious distaste. Before the scholar could even open his mouth to voice his objections Dale said wearily,

"Just wear them Trystin. If this place is to look ordinary, then we need to dress accordingly and I'm not prepared to argue about it. I suppose it must be a big come down for one such as you to have to dress like a peasant but frankly, I'm not all that interested in how you feel, about this, or anything else. I have orders to keep the royal family safe and protected and I intend to do that. It's easier if you are willing to help and support me but if you're not, then I'll do it without. Right now, I'm not in the mood to argue you with you about every last thing so just grit your teeth against whatever objections you may have and get changed." Then he turned and vanished in to the pantry to bring up more supplies, leaving Trystin standing in the middle of the cottage, blinking in astonishment.

The next few days were hard for everyone. After that first grief-stricken recognition of their circumstances the two boys seemed to lose all of the courage and determination they had shown on the journey to the cottage. Now they seemed lost and unless directed could only drift about the clearing miserably. Dale did everything he could to keep them occupied and Trystin, to the big man's surprise, seemed to follow his lead for once and support the efforts to help the children through the difficult days but it was an uphill struggle to keep them motivated. At first the brothers kept close to each other, as though each other's company was all they could cling to but after a day or two this changed and they covered up their misery by bickering and sniping at one another.

This wasn't helped by the fact they were both tired and finding the work they were being set more and more unappealing. There was a lot to do in the clearing to make it look inhabited and Dale co-ordinated the work of everyone. He wanted everyone and everything about the place to look as if it had been there for ever and he was ruthless in his determination to make this so, so he laid out the work like a battle plan and assigned everyone tasks.

Trystin, Allin and Joss were responsible for making the cottage and the clearing look lived in, Dale decreed. They found themselves sweeping, scrubbing and cleaning inside the cottage, cutting the long grass about the clearing with a sickle, removing the tall weeds from about the window, and uncovering the firepit outside the cottage from the moons and years of debris which had smothered it.

"Why build a fire out here if there's a fireplace in doors?" Allin had argued at this, "Why have two fires?"

"The fire outdoors is a working fire. When you fell a tree anything that can't be used for wood gets burned and that can't be done from the cottage - there's too much of it. And before you ask, there's a fire indoors because it gets cold here in winter and its impossible to cook outdoors in the rain!"

It took them two or three days of hard work to get everything looking as Dale wanted and then, as they stood back to admire their handiwork, the big man had merely said grudgingly, "It'll pass. Now what about the garden?"

"What garden?" Trystin had asked suspiciously.

"The one behind the cottage. That large area you seem to have so carefully ignored in all your efforts."

"That's a *garden*?" was the indignant response, for indeed the plot was a terrible mess. Trystin had deliberately avoided any attempt at doing anything with the area, about thirty foot square, which looked like a wasteland. There was a good mix of tall grasses, various weeds and other unidentified plants, in thick clumps and the scholar had assumed it was nothing more than scrub, so now to find he was expected to turn it in to something respectable filled him with dismay. He argued but Dale was adamant. He wanted the weeds and grasses cleared so that the plot would once more look like the cottage garden it had once been.

So the next two days were spent working the plot, pulling out weeds by the handful and freeing what was left of the range of herbs and fruit bushes which had been left to grow wild. As luck would have it, as soon as they started working in the garden the weather changed for the worse again and it began to rain steadily. This made the ground softer and therefore easier to work but it also made it a lot muddier and Trystin and Allin were soon covered in grime from their efforts.

Joss proved to be a great asset in this chore. She was fascinated by the garden and seemed to enjoy helping Trystin and a very reluctant Allin in grubbing out the unwanted vegetation. At first she was indiscriminate in her weeding, unearthing several tuber plants before Trystin showed her what to pull up and what to leave. After that she had a whale of a time wandering about the muddy patch tugging up grasses and weeds.

By the end of the second day of back breaking and dirty work, all accompanied by a steady fall of rain, the cottage garden was looking like a cultivated patch once more, there was a huge pile of wilting greenery in the firepit and Allin, Trystin and Joss were all tired and mud splattered from head to toe.

While Trystin and the younger children were working on tidying up the cottage and clearing, Dale, with Cori to help him, worked on making the place look like a woodcutter's home once more. To Allin's complete disgust, Dale took Cori a little way in to the forest, where they felled a tree and then cut it up to bring it back in pieces to the clearing where they worked to hone it into a number of long logs which could be sold as well as plenty of firewood and kindling for their own use. It was hard work and Cori found it very tough going indeed, hauling the heavy wood about the forest, even though Dale had not taken them very far from the clearing. At the end of every day he all but collapsed in to bed, aching all over, and woke the next morning still tired and wishing he could simply stay where he was. Dale was a hard task master too. He didn't let his young assistant shirk for a moment and every time the lad finished one task, Dale was waiting with another.

Once they had hauled the sections of tree trunk back to the clearing, Cori found that, as well as Dale's tough guidance, he also had to face a barrage of complaints from his brother who was bitterly resentful that, despite Dale's promise on the first evening, Cori had been shown how to use an axe first. Cori was ignorant of the reason for Allin's resentment and was too tired and fed up to bother to get to the bottom of it. Allin too, was tired, dirty - which he found he hated - and feeling betrayed that Dale had made him a promise which in his young eyes, the man was not going to keep. Both lads were also fighting to keep going against the fear and grief that they had lost their family and it made the last vestiges of control over temper ebb away. As a result, whenever they were near each other, they squabbled almost constantly.

The constant edgy bad temper the boys were showing was very wearing to Dale and Trystin who found themselves frequently called upon to referee over some petty dispute or another. They did their best to ease the tension between the brothers but it was hard to do when there was nothing they could do to resolve the real reason for their poor disposition.

During this challenging time, Dale made sure that, if nothing else, there was always plenty to eat. After dark each night he would head out in to the forest to bag a rabbit or a game bird for the next day's fare. From this, the dry store of things Dale had had the foresight to hold at the cottage and the vegetables which were amazingly abundant in the long neglected garden, they were able to eat remarkably well. It was a small consolation but it did help a little.

Things came boiling to a head between the brothers after they had been living at the cottage for about a week. Joss, who was seemingly better able to cope with the sudden change in her circumstances, was contentedly sitting on the grass by the firepit, watching the flames burning through a pile of damp leafy branches cut from the carcass of the second tree Dale and Cori had just brought in. Allin was sitting listlessly beside her, attempting to get the perpetual grime from under his fingernails, and trying to ignore the fine drizzle that was still falling.

Exhausted from yet another day of miserable hard labour, Cori sank down beside them on to a log that Dale had placed there to act as a seat, thankful of a few minutes rest before Dale spotted him and pulled him off to do something else that he wouldn't enjoy. He sat in silence for a short while until Joss lifted her head and, with a piercing look, asked

"When's Mamma coming?"

It was something she had been asking every day or so and had usually been getting some non-committal answer in response but Cori was too tired to be patient with the little girl any longer. "For goodness sake, Joss," he snarled, "will you stop asking that? We don't know when she's coming - so just stop going on about it."

For a second the child stared at him horror-struck and then her pretty face began to dissolve into tears at his harsh words.

Allin glared at his brother. Since his mother had set him the task of looking after Joss, it was something he had taken very seriously. It had become something of a mission for him and to see her reduced to tears so unnecessarily infuriated him "Leave her alone," he snapped at Cori. "She's only a baby. She doesn't know what's going on."

Cori, already feeling guilty for having upset his sister, was certainly not prepared to be admonished by Allin and his temper flared. "Don't you start telling me what to do. I'm sick and tired of her going on about it and even sicker of you pretending you're in charge."

Things went downhill rapidly from here and after a few more moments of hurling insults at each other Allin's restraint left him and he hurled himself bodily at the bigger lad. Head down he ran full tilt in to Cori's stomach and knocked them both to the ground.

By this time, already alerted by the raised voices, Dale was almost with them so the fight was short-lived. He waded in, grabbed the first wrestling body he came across - which happened to be Allin - and hauled, bringing the struggling boy up and away from his opponent.

"Enough!" He barked fiercely, in a tone so threatening that it silenced both Allin and Cori and produced a fresh wail from Joss, now sobbing freely at the sight of all the upset. Dale swung round and dumped Allin none too gently on the ground in front of Trystin who had also hurried over to see what the trouble was. "Right," Dale ordered the boy, still glowering at his brother. "Inside! Trystin find something for him to do to keep him out of trouble. You," he swung round on Cori who was climbing back to his feet, "should know better. Since you can't manage to behave yourself you can get that cord of wood stacked before supper."

"But he started it..." Cori began with some heat, to which Allin spun round and began to protest his innocence.

"Not interested," came the blunt reply. "Now both of you do as you're told." He spoke with such fearsome authority that it stopped any further argument stone dead and both boys went in their own directions to follow Dale's orders, Trystin following on behind Allin.

All that was left by the fire was a sobbing Joss. Dale swallowed his irritation and squatted down beside her with as warm a smile as he could muster. "So my little flower, what's got you so upset then?"

Dale whiled away about half an hour with Joss, comforting her and reassuring her that everything was all right. From her indistinct mutterings he managed to piece together a little of what had occurred between the brothers and - when the little girl once more expressed a desire for her mother - what had irritated Cori so much. Having managed to get the small child smiling once more he left her to watch the fire again and with a slightly weary sigh went to confront Cori.

As he approached the side of the cottage where Cori was, he could see the youth working as he had been directed. His shoulders were drooping and everything about the way he was moving suggested that he was no longer angry over the fight, just plain miserable. Dale watched him thoughtfully for a minute or two and then, just as he was about to step forward and say something, from the far side of the cottage, Allin appeared.

"Do you want a hand with that?" he enquired diffidently.

Cori looked up at him, his face turned so that Dale couldn't see his expression. After a moment or two the lad nodded without a word. Silently Allin joined his brother and together they stacked the rest of the wood into a neat pile. Dale watched, saw Cori put a single hand on his brother's shoulder, Allin's sideways, apologetic grin in return, and then walked quietly away to let the two boys mend bridges by themselves.

Somehow the spat between the brothers seemed to clear the air for them and they entered their second week in a far better frame of mind. Now that the worst of the hard graft to make things look presentable had been done Dale finally eased up the pressure on everyone and the boys felt able to relax a little more. Not that it was all easy going as the big man continued to insist that everyone did their fair share of work but the pressure seemed to be off and both boys enjoyed some opportunity to linger and have time to themselves. As if in response to this, the rain finally let up as well and they were rewarded by glorious sunshine.

After a day or two, Dale introduced a new task for them, one which he knew would entertain them but which would also be useful. He cut a long sapling from the edge of the forest, brought up some twine from the cellar and with a sly smile at the two boys asked innocently, "Anyone fancy fish for supper?"

That day was spent quite contentedly fishing, a hobby that both boys had previously learned from their elder brother, Richol, who was a keen angler. In truth Cori had never much cared for it as a sport but since he was likely to find himself hauling wood as an alternative, he was willing to give it his full attention for the day.

It was one of those hot, dreamy days, which characterised the height of the Bremmand summer and Dale and the two princes spent more of their time drowsing by the river bank than actively seeking fish. As the sun set and it began to get cooler Dale surveyed their haul a little ruefully. They had only managed to catch two decent fish between them, the rest being too small to eat and thus only fit to throw back.

"Oh well," he said with a wry smile. "Maybe we can bag a rabbit on the way home, or it's going to be more tuber than fish tonight."

Allin looked a little crestfallen. "I'm getting bored with tubers. Isn't there anything else?"

"Tubers are all right," Cori corrected, trying to discourage his brother's complaints.

"But getting a bit dull all the same," Dale agreed with a sympathetic smile at Allin. "I think I'm with you on this one Allin. They bore me pretty quickly too. Let me think about it and I'll see what I can do."

Allin beamed at him, pleased to have someone agreeing with him even if only on such a minor matter, and then, around Dale's back, pulled a face at Cori for his attempt to contradict him. Cori scowled but kept his mouth shut, not prepared to make a complaint for something so trivial. Dale wasn't born yesterday, however, and said smoothly, "Well volunteered, Allin."

"Volunteered?" the boy asked suspiciously, "For what?"

"For cleaning the fish."

"I didn't..." He had very little idea of what cleaning fish entailed but there was something about the way Dale said it that made him sure it was worth protesting.

"Well, if you don't have the grace to allow someone else an opinion on a small thing like tubers, I can't think of a better job than gutting fish to teach you a little humility."

"But..." he stammered trying to think up a good excuse, as Cori suddenly began to laugh. It was a neat ploy on Dale's part and there wasn't a lot Allin could do to get out of the unfavourable task, without lying outright and saying that he'd done nothing wrong which he wasn't likely to do. Dale knew the boys well enough by now to know that neither one was deceitful, so Allin was unlikely to deny his guilt.

Allin sighed deeply at the injustices of the world, and sulkily followed the others back to the little clearing. His head was down, as he stared moodily at the ground just before him, so he didn't notice Dale and Cori come to an abrupt halt and crashed in to the back of his brother as a result.

"Hey!" He began irritably. "What...?" but then he too saw what had made them both stop and fell silent.

They were perhaps twenty feet from the main path that led to the cottage and from there they could see, just about to enter the clearing the unmistakable flash of the red cloth which adorned all Empire troops. They had been discovered.

"Oh no," Cori murmured faintly and threw a helpless look at Dale. The Captain had been wrong that no-one would find them here, and now they were in mortal danger once again. Almost instinctively, Cori turned to Allin and said in a low tone, "Get away from here Allin. Run into the forest and hide."

Like a flash, Dale's arm shot out and locked on to the younger boy. "No. I want you to stay by me, son." He looked at Cori and said calmly. "They don't know who we are and we've a perfect right to be here. Our best chance is to brazen this out, all right? We're going to walk right in there, just like we would any other day, because it's our home and there's no reason for us not to. When they ask who we are you are going to let me do all the talking, all right? If they try to talk to you, say as little as possible to answer their questions and make out that you're just two woodcutter's boys, who are not used to strangers." Both boys stared at him nervously but nodded. "Good. Trust me. I'm not going to let anything happen to you but we all need to keep our nerve, all right?" Then without a further word he handed the fish to Cori, drew Allin in to his right side and put his other hand lightly over the sword which constantly hung at his left.

"Relax," he said easily. "This is going to be fine."

No Longer the Enemy

The three of them strode confidently in to the clearing, although Dale could feel that Allin was trembling faintly, and he could hear that Cori's breathing was getting quicker. There were five soldiers in the clearing when they arrived, as well as Trystin standing apprehensively at the doorway to the cottage.

"Something you wanted?" Dale asked from behind them. The soldiers all jumped and wheeled around, unnerved by the sudden appearance of another man. One of them, wearing the marks of an officer pushed his way forward.

"And who are you?" he asked belligerently.

"Ronas," came the truthful answer. "This is my home. What is it you want?"

"And them?" the soldier pointed with his sword at the two boys.

"They're my children," he said, a fraction of irritation in his voice, "and there's no need to wave that thing at them is there?"

The officer sneered at him. "What about that man? Who's he?"

"My wife's brother. What is this? Why all these questions?" Then tiring of the soldier's refusal to answer him he looked past the officer and spoke directly to Trystin. "What's going on, brother? And where's the little one?"

Trystin looked at him nervously but managed to answer, "She's all right. She's inside."

"Good." As though everything was as normal as could be Dale took the fish from Cori, handed them to Allin and said, "Why don't you take them indoors son, and make sure your sister is all right?"

Allin nodded and then, with a courage that made Dale proud, walked between the red clad soldiers on his way to the cottage.

One of the soldiers reached out and took a hold of the fish but, unsure of what to do, Allin clung on to them. The man gave him a shove and wrenched the fish away, pushing the boy to the ground as he did so. Cori tensed behind Allin and was about to move forward when Dale called across, "Let them have them Allin. If they're here to steal fish from children, then there's no point in making it difficult for them."

The officer's eyes narrowed, understanding the subtly contemptuous suggestion that his men were nothing more than common thieves and turned swiftly on his small troop. He barked out a sharp command to the soldier holding the fish, instructing him to return them to the boy. One of the other men instinctively leaned down and pulled Allin to his feet, dusted him down roughly, restored his fish to him with some humorous remark and sent the boy on his way with a friendly slap to the rear.

"We represent the Empire," the officer said coldly to Dale. "You'd do well to remember that, woodcutter."

"The Empire?" Dale looked puzzled and asked innocently "What happened to the King then? Did they make him Emperor too?"

"Insolent Dog! Your King is no more. These lands are now under the rule of Darvett, Emperor of the Kostinian Empire. You serve him now, woodcutter."

Dale shrugged and said indifferently, "So the King has changed. It makes no difference to me. Every King requires the services of men like me and I'll serve this new one just as loyally as I did the last."

The red clad Captain seemed mollified by this, not realising that Dale had just sworn his fealty to Jorvis's successor - not to Darvett. Cori hadn't missed it though and Dale felt the young man shift slightly, suddenly seeming more confident in their current circumstances.

"So," Dale repeated, "if you represent this Empire, what brings you out here. I can't believe that you've come all this way just to tell one simple woodcutter and his family that they serve a new King."

"Not King; Emperor," one of the soldiers muttered irritably but Dale took no notice of this.

"We're on patrol," the officer said, as though it was none of Dale's business but he looked faintly uncomfortable about it and the big man suddenly realised exactly why these men were here.

They were lost! The Empire troops may well be a formidable fighting force but they weren't at all familiar with this kind of terrain and unsurprisingly they had become confused in the acre upon acre of tall trees obscuring a clear route for them. The constant rain of the past week had robbed them of even the sun to navigate by and by now they must be a very long way off course. Dale felt himself relax - these soldiers were not looking for the royal children and probably had no idea that anyone was seeking them. The only thing on their minds was getting back to some kind of civilisation, and soon. They certainly posed very little threat to Dale Ronas and his so-called family.

The big man, raised in these forests and so familiar with them as to be able to find his way about them on the blackest of nights, suddenly saw the humour in the situation. He kept his face straight however. "Well, this must be the first time I've ever known anyone to patrol in this area. It's a lonely place at the best of times. It's a good thing you know the forest though - men have been lost in these parts for weeks, moons sometimes, before anyone comes across their bodies..." A couple of the troops shifted uneasily at this - confirming Dale's suspicions and giving him the opportunity to twist the knife a little more "...if they were found at all - there's plenty that have been taken by the ghosts."

"Ghosts!" someone squeaked, before he could stop himself.

"Oh, aye. There's parts of the Bremmand Forest where no sane man would dare to go. Thick with Spirits they are. But as long as you know where you're going and don't wander anywhere you shouldn't, you'll be all right." He threw them a lopsided smile, as if he was trying to be friendly but he knew exactly what his words would have done to these southern soldiers, used to open lands and most unfamiliar with the closeness and strange noises that a forest must provide for them. "So where've you all come from then?" he asked casually, sounding disinterested and as if he was making idle conversation.

"We've got an encampment at Novoris," the Officer admitted, looking hesitant.

By Brem, you are lost! Dale thought almost gleefully but he merely nodded and said in an offhand way, "Oh, aye. That's a good two days walk from here. You'll be looking for a place to stop for the night then?"

There was another stirring in the ranks and someone said in relief, "Only two days - we must have come round in a big circle!"

The Captain, determined not to ask outright for directions, but just as relieved as his men, nodded, "We are. Is there somewhere near that you'd recommend Woodcutter? Somewhere we can reach by sundown?"

Dale nodded. "If you're heading back to Novoris then you'll be wanting to take that path." He pointed the way he and the boys had just come. "If you follow that for a while you'll come to a fork in the road. Take the left fork, then follow the path and you'll come to a nice little spot - it's about an hour's walk from here, maybe less. It's by the river so there's plenty of fresh water and there's good hunting there too."

"That sounds suitable. Well, I thank you woodcutter." Then the Captain turned to his men. "Prepare to move out. We'll make for this place by the river and stop there for the night," he barked and the soldiers somewhat wearily fell in to line to follow the Officer out of the clearing along the route that Dale had indicated.

Dale, Trystin and Cori watched in silence as the soldiers left. Once they were gone Cori opened his mouth to say something but Dale interrupted him. "Right. We've got work to do. Cori, there's still a cord of wood that needs chopping. I want that done before supper."

Cori gaped at him, as if he couldn't believe the man was going to make him start work after all this but Trystin, after a moment of puzzlement, suddenly understood and took up the big man's lead. "I'll go and get the cooking started. Though I don't think it'll be much of a meal - those two fish won't go very far; especially not now Allin has dragged them along the ground. Come on Cori, the sooner we get started the sooner we'll be done." He put an arm about the boy's shoulder and murmured in an undertone, "Sound travels. We must carry on as if we were a normal family until Dale tells us otherwise."

Dale, relieved that Trystin understood him, gave an approving little nod of his head to acknowledge that this was indeed what he was doing and then said out loud, "I think you're right. That fish isn't going to be enough, Trystin. I'll go and check the traps and see if we've caught anything else to make it into a decent meal."

Trystin nodded back, knowing that Dale was planning on checking that the soldiers had really left, and hadn't left anyone behind to watch them. With a casual wave of his hand, Dale vanished in to the forest.

It didn't take long for Dale to track the five soldiers and check that they were all on the path as directed by the big man and having done this he retraced his steps, did a thorough check of the area around the cottage to ensure there was no-one else about before returning to the clearing.

Cori was the only one visible, steadfastly chopping wood as he'd been instructed. He stopped when he saw Dale, however.

"All clear," the big man smiled. "They're well away from here and probably looking forward to a pleasant night by the river. Are you all right?"

Cori nodded. "Just… a bit nervous. Trystin said we should all act as if they're still here; that they might be watching us."

"And you can feel a thousand eyes on you as a result." Dale nodded wisely. "Not the most comfortable experience, is it?"

The lad flashed him a rueful smile. "I guess I'm not as brave as I'd like to pretend to be."

"Oh I don't know. You do all right, son. You kept your head, which makes it easier for the little ones and makes sure you're still here, safe and sound. That's the most important thing after all."

Cori sighed. "I know. But if the kingdom's fallen to Kostain, like they said, shouldn't I be fighting for it, instead of hiding out here?"

Dale gave him a long thoughtful look and then merely said, "You already know the answer to that one, Cori, don't you?"

"Yes," Cori, probable King of Bremmand, answered slowly. "I think I'm more scared of what that means, than of a thousand of Darvett's men."

Dale laughed lightly and slapped him on the back. "As would I be. All that politics to deal with? Give me something I can stick a sword in any day, even if it does fight back sometimes."

"I suppose it serves me right for not choosing my parents with more care," was the sober reply and for a second Dale stared at the lad in astonishment before he worked out the absurdity of the remark. Then, seeing a twinkle of humour in Cori's blue eyes he smiled slowly and then they both burst out laughing.

The sound of laughter brought Trystin out from the cottage, with Allin and Joss close on his heels. Trystin looked at the two sniggering men in front of him and asked acerbically, "I take it that the danger is passed then, gentlemen, and we can stop cowering inside the cottage?" He'd been very unsettled by the arrival of the Empire soldiers and, while he'd done his best to follow Dale's lead and provide a brave front for the sake of the children, he was very anxious about the sudden arrival of the enemy in this place he had believed to be safe. So to find Dale in fits of giggles outside the door, as if nothing untoward had happened, while he and the two children were still fearful of their immediate future angered him.

Trying to gain control of himself once more Dale nodded weakly, leaning against Cori to keep himself upright, "They're gone. Sorry, Trystin, we just..."

"...couldn't be bothered to come and let us know. It's not as if any one of us was likely to be worried." He spoke with such venom that it stopped Dale and Cori's laughter in a trice.

Dale looked at the little group soberly. "I apologise, my friends. I've not been long back, and I was about to come and let you know it's all clear. Cori just come up with the most half-witted remark I've ever heard and it rather distracted us." He tried a smile. "I'm sorry. They're all on their way south, following the route I suggested and there's no-one else anywhere near us now, as far as I can tell."

Trystin didn't reply, but Allin, still standing rather close to Trystin, asked timidly, "They're really gone?"

Almost unconsciously Cori crossed and slid an arm about his brother's shoulders, "They're gone, Pup. There's nothing at all for you to be worried about anymore."

Allin nodded, tried to look unconcerned but then, like a reflex action, turned and buried his face in his brother's chest, clinging to Cori as if his life depended upon it. Cori hugged his little brother tightly, neither of them saying anything but it was clear to Dale how afraid both boys had been. Dale put a comforting hand on the younger boy's shoulder.

"I was impressed by the way you acted, son. You handled having all those soldiers about you very well."

"Better than I would," Cori admitted. "I don't know what I'd have done if they'd wanted to take something from me. Run a mile probably."

"And you even managed to hang on to supper. I've been looking forward to fish all day."

Allin, buoyed by all this praise, released his crushing grip on Cori but he looked at Dale and asked the question that was on everyone's mind. "What if they come back?"

"They won't son. They're only interested in getting back to their base by now I should think. They've got no interest in us except as someone who could provide them with directions." Dale spoke with absolute certainty.

"Do you know," Trystin said, a questioning look in his eye, "I had no idea we were so close to Novoris. If you'd asked me I'd have said we were far further East than that."

Suddenly Dale flashed him a wicked grin. "We are. Much." At the puzzled look on Trystin's face he explained, "They didn't want to admit it, but those soldiers were lost - very lost. I'd guess they've been wandering about in these forests for the best part of a week, looking for any sign of civilisation and probably very unsure that they were ever going to get home. So I offered them a bit of false hope," he paused and then added with malice, "and a totally incorrect direction to follow. If they were lost before, that's nothing to what they are now."

The evening passed with everyone in high spirits, the relief of having escaped Darvett's troops again and Dale's heartless misdirection lifting the mood once more. The change in diet, if only for a meagre share of the two fish helped, the fresh-caught perch being delicious. Allin hopefully suggested that they should go fishing again the following day to see if they could get more but Dale had merely laughed and suggested that they'd get bored quite quickly if they had to eat fish every day. Besides, he said to the boy with a twinkle in his eye, surely he'd prefer to stay here in the clearing, stacking wood and helping tend the garden, rather than lying by a river bank waiting for fish to bite.

After the children had been sent to bed, Trystin asked Dale again if he was certain the soldiers would not return. He had never been certain in his own mind that they were anything like as safe here as the Captain seemed to think but Dale had replied confidently.

"Quite sure. Trust me on this one. Those men are a long way from home, in unknown territory and lost in the woods. They'll already have all but forgotten the simple woodcutter and his family whose path they crossed briefly and all they'll be thinking about is finding their way out of the forest. They'll not trouble us again."

Somehow, Trystin couldn't quite believe that they were safe, but he could do little else but believe Dale's conviction that all was well and to retire to sleep.

Trystin roused himself with a start, unsure why he was now awake but somehow uneasy with the stillness of the night. It was still dark but instinct told him it was probably somewhere towards dawn. He lay in bed for a while, in the hope that he might simply go back to sleep but he soon realised that that was not to be. He was wide awake and likely to remain that way. As he lay there, he listened to the sounds of the night to try and hear whatever it was that had disturbed him in the first place but, other than the breathing of the three children in the other bed, there was nothing.

It took him a full ten minutes to realise that *all* he could hear was the three children - Dale wasn't there! Now, beginning to feel troubled, Trystin rose as quietly as he could. He didn't know what it was that was alarming him - Dale frequently slept in the chair in the main living room and seemed to function on far less sleep than the rest of them anyway, so for him to have risen during the night wasn't so unusual - but there was something not right about the night and Trystin wanted to know what it was.

Dale wasn't in the cottage, so Trystin lifted the latch softly and stepped outside. There was no moon tonight, and the fire was all but burned out so the clearing was dark. Trystin stood and listened into the darkness for a few minutes, trying to see if he could make out the sounds of the big man moving about but nothing much seemed to be moving

He can't have gone far Trystin assured himself, trying to quell the nervous fluttering in his stomach. *He'd never have left us on our own here.* His words of reassurance didn't help and the feelings of anxiety increased. Trystin turned and went back in to the cottage, picked up the knife he used for cooking from the mantelpiece over the fire and, thus armed, went back outside. By now his mind was back with the Empire soldiers that had visited them the previous day. What if they hadn't been fooled? What if they had pretended to follow Dale's advice to lull the occupants of the cottage into a false sense of security and were now back, to kill them all in their beds?

There was the faintest stirring of a branch along the pathway to the stream. Someone was coming! Trystin gripped the knife blade a little tighter, ready to fight for the life of the three precious children now under his sole protection.

It was all he could do to prevent crying out in relief when he realised that the figure who loomed out of the trees was Dale. The big man, on seeing him crossed the clearing rapidly, coming straight to him. "What is it? What's happened?"

Trystin leaned up against the wooden wall of the cottage, suddenly weak with relief. "Nothing. Something woke me and when you weren't here I thought…."

"I see," Dale replied dryly. He looked at the knife in Trystin's hands silently and then said almost in amusement, "And what were you planning to do with that thing? Scratch me to death?"

Trystin looked helplessly at the small and obviously ineffective weapon in his hand. "Yes, I know. I just…" then suddenly realising that he was being made to feel foolish when he'd done nothing wrong, he hissed angrily, "Where the *hell* have you been? I woke up and you were gone. It's all very well for you to be rude about my combat abilities but if they're so poor, you've got no business leaving us here undefended. Those children's lives depend on us and you suddenly take it upon yourself to wander off and leave us in the middle of the night."

Dale regarded the man gravely then, with a jerk of his head, led the way to the log at the edge of the fire. He took up a few of the off cuts from the tree he had felled with Cori and tossed them in to the burning embers. The leaves started to smoulder almost at once, giving off light and warmth in the darkness. Trystin sat himself beside the big man, wondering what was coming next.

Carefully Dale spoke, without looking at the former tutor. "I went to check up on our visitors of yesterday."

"Then you weren't as sure as you said earlier that they wouldn't be back?"

"Oh no. I was sure. I *am* sure."

"But..." Trystin stopped and a terrible thought ran through his mind. "*Dale.* How can you be so sure? What have you done?"

The flames began to rise up out of the branches in the fire, making Dale's red hair glow and lighting his face with orange light. It threw light on to the front of his tunic too and Trystin could see several dark patches, as if the fabric was wet, marking his chest. "I've made sure." He said so simply it was chilling to the scholar. "They won't trouble us, or anyone else, again."

"You... you killed them?" Trystin was horrified. Then more harshly, "You *murdered* five men in cold blood?"

"I eliminated five enemies who posed a threat to us," Dale retorted angrily. "We're at war, Trystin, and war is a dirty business. I promised Verdin that I would keep the Royal children in my care safe, whatever it took, and that's what I'll do. If those men made it back to their camp and mentioned that they'd seen us, then there's a chance that more soldiers, soldiers actually *looking* for any trace of the Marchand family, would come to find us. Well now that can't happen. The only Empire men who've seen us are dead and their bodies in the river, being carried to the ocean. The chances are they'll never be found and even if they are, it will be so far from here that no-one would ever make the connection with us. We're safe and that's all that matters."

"But, but...." The scholar couldn't speak he was so appalled by what he was hearing. This man he thought he was beginning to know, whom he was coming to trust, was nothing more than an assassin. It was inconceivable. It was... "There's nothing I can say," Trystin said coldly, getting to his feet. "Their blood is on your hands, yours alone, and your soul is stained with their murder. I just hope you can sleep at night." It was a bitter condemnation and Dale was stung by it.

"The *King of Bremmand* sleeps in the bed next to me, Trystin, and he sleeps safely. That's all I need to make sure *my* nights are undisturbed."

"Well, don't get too excited about having a royal presence here, Dale Ronas. I'll do everything in my power to ensure that the King and his family are removed from your influence as soon as it is possible. At the first opportunity I shall see them delivered to the safety of their Grandfather."

"That's all I ask, Trystin. Did you ever think I wanted anything else?" Dale said sadly as the slim man stalked away in to the night.

When the children rose the following morning, Trystin was alone in the cottage, preparing a simple breakfast of oatmeal.

"I thought it was about time we put some thought into your studies," the tutor said when they had finished eating. "We can start this morning."

"Why?" Allin scowled, not pleased to have to be concentrating on schoolwork once more. Then, since the big man had been giving all the instructions so far, he added, "Where's Dale?"

Trystin didn't answer at once and Cori pounced on the hesitation. "What's the matter. Where is he?"

"Right here." Came a calm answer from the man himself, standing in the doorway. He'd changed since the night before, the bloodstained tunic now gone to be replaced with another which bore no trace of his actions. "Why?" His face was bland and he deliberately avoided meeting Trystin's eye.

"You promised me that you'd teach me to use the axe," Allin declared, reminding the man in the hope that it would rescue him from Trystin's much less desirable suggestion.

"I did," Dale agreed, "and I will. But I didn't say when."

Allin gaped at the soldier, unable to believe that the promise was to be broken on a technicality. "But...." He began, already visibly annoyed by this betrayal.

"Other things are more important - one of which is your schooling. So, you concentrate on what Trystin has to teach you and when he's satisfied, I'll teach you to use the axe."

"You *promised*," Allin cried angrily. "It isn't *fair.*"

"No," came the flat reply. "Life isn't, and," he glanced briefly at Trystin, "neither, it seems, am I. But I'm bigger than you, so you don't have a lot of choice but to do as you're told. Trystin says you study, so that's what you do."

Allin glared at him rebelliously for a second or two, seeking a way to win this battle but he found none. So, eventually he nodded. "If you say so," he managed, but without much grace, "though I don't know why. *You* get by all right without all this boring learning. If *you* don't need to read and write, why should I?"

66

For a few seconds Dale regarded the boy and then said coldly "Just because I was raised out here in the middle of the forest, doesn't mean I'm totally ignorant. For your information I can read and write quite well and I'm well versed in several other subjects as well. I'm an officer of the Royal Army, not just some simpleton woodcutter and I'd thank you to remember that."

"Of course not, Captain Ronas," Cori jumped in hurriedly, not missing the slight edge to Dale's voice. "I'm sure Allin didn't mean to be impertinent. Did you Allin?"

The boy was staring at Dale, his mouth hanging open. Dale could be gruff and unequivocal but this was the first show of temper or impatience he'd shown toward any of them since the day that Verdin had put the Captain in charge of the three royal children. Allin couldn't hide his surprise at the seemingly unprovoked irritation from the man but he responded, almost automatically, to his brother's prompting, using the same formal address as Cori. "No. I'm sorry, Captain. I didn't mean to be rude."

Dale cursed himself inwardly. Trystin's condemnation of him had been like a knife in his guts and he was still smarting from it but letting his hurt spill over to poison his relationship with the children was wrong and he knew it. He sighed and said earnestly, "I know - and you weren't - I'm just... not quite myself this morning. Would you excuse me?" And he turned on his heel and left.

"Dale? Captain Ronas?" Cori had followed the big man out in to the sunshine, where he was splitting logs with some force.

"If we're insisting Allin should study, then it wouldn't be fair to excuse you," Dale said, his tone bland. He continued to place logs on the chopping block and splitting each one with a single stroke of the axe.

"Well, as you just pointed out, life isn't fair. Is everything all right Captain?"

Can you turn back the clock? Dale asked silently to himself. *Can you make it so I never told Trystin what I did?* That was the hardest part of all this. Dale didn't regret what he had done for a second. Yes, it had been brutal and he would far rather it hadn't been necessary but he was entirely convinced that it had been his only choice and he wouldn't hesitate to do so again if the need arose. It was the censure and enmity that Trystin had shown that was gnawing at him and he fervently wished he had not told the man, keeping their uneasy relationship in some semblance of order. The next few moon-cycles would be difficult and if Trystin despised him it would make everything a great deal harder for them all. He stopped chopping and looked severely at Cori. "Call me Dale," was all he said. "Don't get in to the habit of using my rank and title. You might use it when it isn't safe."

Cori ignored this. "There's something wrong. Both you and Trystin know about something you don't want us to know, don't you?"

"No," Dale sighed. "There's nothing wrong. You're worrying yourself unnecessarily."

"But you and Trystin…" Cori began to insist, but Dale interrupted him.

"… have had a difference of opinion, that's all. My view on some things differs from his and we can't agree, but it doesn't affect you and it won't prevent either him, or me from carrying out our duty towards you or your brother and sister. It's a private matter and it's something we will have to resolve for ourselves."

"I … see," Cori said slowly. "Is there anything I can do to help…?" He was still young, a mere boy, but that simple offer of assistance was both manly and regal and Dale was momentarily uplifted by the gesture.

"It's kind of you, Cori, but no, you can't help I'm afraid. As I said, it's something Trystin and I need to work out between us." He turned back to the pile of wood and continued to split logs as if they were made of butter.

"Very well. But we, my family, owe you our lives, Dale - you and Trystin - and we know that you two are all that stands between us and Darvett's men now. It pains me to see either of you unhappy and I'll do anything in my power to make this right."

Dale put another log on the block and swung the axe upward. Down it came but it missed the log and buried its head in to the chopping block. Dale swore under his breath irritated at having made such a clumsy swing. He straightened and looked at Cori. "There's nothing you can do, son. Trystin and I just see the world differently and I'm not sure it's something that will ever change. But I don't want you to worry about it. We'll get by."

"Cori?" Trystin came round the corner of the cottage.

The boy turned his brown head, sunlight catching the occasional strand and making it flash gold. "Yes, coming. There was just something I wanted to ask Dale." He turned and headed back in to the cottage but Trystin stayed where he was. He stood in silence for a moment or two and, when it became clear he wasn't about to say anything, Dale turned and went back to chopping firewood.

As he steadily split logs he waited, dreading what he knew was about to come. Trystin had made it clear last night he thought Dale was a corrupting influence on the children, so it was no great leap to suppose the scholar would do everything in his power to keep the Captain away from them. It was mainly for this reason that the big man had told Allin he would only teach him to use the axe when Trystin agreed. The last thing he wanted was for the dispute to become apparent by Trystin refusing to allow such a contact and Allin would be unlikely to be pleased by what he would doubtless see as the scholar's interference in his desire to learn this new skill. So now he worked, holding his breath, waiting for the relegation of his role to that of bodyguard and nothing more. Until now he hadn't realised how much he wanted to be a part of the lives of the royal children living under his roof, so the fact that he was to be denied that privilege was almost physically painful to him.

It took so long for Trystin to speak that Dale began to think he may have returned, unheard, to the cottage. So he almost jumped when the scholar spoke.

"I think I should make my position clear," the tutor began formally.

Dale swung his axe in one last swing, a round powerful swing which ended with the axe head embedded deep in the chopping block. With deliberate care and with a face precisely schooled to be neutral he turned and regarded the thin man.

The impassive expression was somehow so hostile that Trystin was momentarily unnerved but then he cleared his throat and continued with the speech which he had spent most of the night running over and over in his head. "I cannot accept or forgive your actions of last night. You killed five men in cold blood, and you claim to have done it in the name of the King. You may convince yourself that it is patriotism but I consider it to be murder and I will not condone it, whatever you may believe. If I had any choice in the matter, I would take the members of the Royal Family and I would remove them from your influence, so that you could not corrupt them with such barbarism.

"If I do that, however, it puts them at risk, so they must remain and, to prevent your influence holding sway over them, I will remain as well. I will continue to co-operate for their protection but that is all I will do. I do it for them and for no other reason.

"The men you killed last night were not casualties of war and your actions were not in the name of the King, or those of the royal children. Nor, I may add, was it done in my name. If you kill anyone else, Captain Ronas, I want you to be under no illusion that it is on your head and no-one else's. I will not have the royal name tainted with your brutality."

"Their names are not touched with this, Master Trystin, and nor is yours." Dale replied equally formally. "I never consulted with you on my decision. You may consider your conscience clear and their innocence unsullied. You have made your views abundantly clear. I trust you will do me the courtesy of allowing me to express mine."

Trystin looked as if this was the last thing he wanted but Dale's request had been made according to an old Bremmandish custom for settling disputes so the scholar was rather obliged to hear him out.

Dale paused for a moment to order his thoughts and then said, calmly and without emotion, "I was given orders by the Lord Protector to keep the royal children in my care safe. I was instructed to do whatever was necessary to protect them. I will act according to my own judgement to achieve that and as such I accept that the responsibility for the deaths of those enemy soldiers was mine. I do not regret my actions for a moment. They were the enemy and now they are not.

"I intend to continue to follow the orders given to me by the Earl of Langate until such time as they are superseded by another with a higher authority. I do not ask that you like it, or that you support it, and if you wish to deny yourself a part of it, I will not condemn you for it. However, you must accept it, for that is the way things will be from now until the Royal family is safe."

"I see," Trystin said slowly, when he had digested Dale's statement.

"There is one thing we do have in common, Master Trystin," the big man continued, still in frostily formal tones, "Our methods may differ but our goal is the same - the protection of what may well be the last of the royal line. Neither one of us would wish to see them harmed, or have their lives made even more difficult than it must already be. Am I right?"

"Well," Trystin admitted slowly, not sure what the big man was about to suggest. "Yes, I suppose so."

"Then I think it would be best for their sake if we can manage to remain civil with one another. Cori is already aware that we don't see eye to eye"

"Don't see eye to eye? That's an understatement," Trystin muttered.

Dale flicked a look at the man but continued nonetheless. "If we are seen to be hostile and angry toward one another, the younger ones will become aware of it also. They need to be able to trust us both and have faith in our ability to deliver them to safety."

Trystin looked at the man, a strange expression on his face, one that Dale couldn't read, but then he nodded. "Very well. I will endeavour to continue to behave as a gentleman."

The comment was barbed and Dale knew it but all he said in reply was, "Thank you. Upon my honour as an officer of the Palace Guard, I will endeavour to act in like fashion."

Trystin turned on his heel and left, the deep resentment and indignation he felt apparent in the tight pull of his shoulders and his ramrod straight back.

Dale watched him go in silence, knowing there was now no chance of finding a working friendship with Trystin, and then, "Damn!" he muttered fretfully to himself.

The rest of the day passed quietly enough, the children being occupied with Trystin, and Dale took the opportunity to fell another tree ready to bring back to the cottage. He would need Cori's help to haul the main trunk through the woods but he spent the day cutting free the limbs from the main trunk, bringing them in to the clearing and cutting the trunk in to ten foot sections which would be portable and could be split lengthways to make building materials. It was hard work and Dale reflected that, if they were to remain here for any length of time, he was going to have to re-equip himself with the proper tools to allow him to work more effectively. It had been nearly six years since he'd abandoned the life of a woodcutter and returned to the army, so the cradle and sled used, in conjunction with a mule, to haul lumber was long since gone - he'd burned it, as far as he recalled, before he had left, as a gesture of the end of his life as a family man and honest tradesman. Not that it would have been in working order after six years standing out among the elements, so he'd still have had to make a new one but it might have been helpful to have the frame to allow him to use it as a pattern, guiding him as he crafted the new tool.

Making the cradle was no great problem, he reflected, but he was going to need a beast of burden to haul it as well and that was not something he could make of wood. He was going to have to go to Chelland, the small town a day's walk from here, where he could buy a mule and replace the supplies that were now beginning to run down. He idled with the idea of a cow as well - fresh milk would be nice - but he knew that what little he had that could be sold wouldn't raise the money for both a cow and a mule. He might manage to scrape up enough for a chicken or two if he could drive a hard enough bargain and that would give them eggs but that was probably the best he could hope for.

Despite the mean circumstances in which he found himself, and the gloomy start to the day, there was something deeply satisfying about the idea of stocking the cottage with livestock once more and Dale felt a sense of contentment as he worked. He spent the day toiling steadily, thinking only of chickens, the mule and, even more pleasingly, the youngsters he was already beginning to consider as a part of his family. Even the growing rift between himself and Trystin didn't seem as insurmountable as it had that morning.

Although he knew the goal was to get to Hast as soon as possible, somewhere in the back of his mind was the feeling that they would be here for a while. The fact that there were already soldiers setting up camps as far into Bremmand as Novoris told him that the Empire invasion was happening very quickly. That meant that the risks in them all getting safely to Hast when the whole country was being flooded with soldiers were far too high to take the chance. Verdin had told him to do whatever he felt was necessary and now he was beginning to understand what that might truly mean. They were going to have to lie low here for as long as it took for things to calm down once more and only then would it be possible to risk an attempt to get them out of the country.

With these thoughts in his mind, Dale worked steadily, using the long familiar tasks as a way to clear his mind and catalogue all the things that he now needed to do in order to prepare the cottage for long term occupancy.

As the day drew to a close and the light began to change, Dale headed back to the cottage for the final time, with a last load of wood to stack ready for chopping to firewood. The door stood open now, a sign that Trystin had finished with his two scholars for the day. He dumped the logs by the pile of all the others, and went in. Cori was kneeling on the floor playing with his sister but Allin was still seated at the table, scowling deeply and working at some problem written in charcoal on a flat piece of wood. Dale smiled to himself, partly at the ingenuity of the tutor in finding an alternative to parchment and ink but mainly because Allin was still stuck at his studies long after Trystin had released his brother and the look on the boy's face made him want to laugh. It was no great surprise to see proof that Allin was not blessed with the soul of a scholar.

Trystin was just coming out of the store cupboard with a bowl of oats in his hand.

"How are we for supplies?" Dale asked, the sight of the grain reminding him.

Trystin gave him an icy look but then, remembering his agreement of the morning, said in more normal tone "I was going to ask you about that. We seem to be getting low on some things."

"I'll need to go over to Chelland to get more then. Nothing lasts long when there's five of us eating it."

"Perhaps I should go instead? It would seem to make more sense." The scholar was polite about it but he clearly wasn't happy. *What does he think is going to happen*, the big man thought irritably to himself. *I'll go out and kill someone else as soon as I'm out of his sight?* The lack of faith the man showed in him was insulting.

Biting back his annoyance, Dale shook his head and explained as reasonably as he could.

"I'm known there. They'd rook a stranger and they'd never let you have anything without seeing your money first."

Still Trystin looked sceptical but then something else Dale said struck home. It was the first time that the soldier had mentioned money but this reference reminded Trystin that they had very little in the way of gold. He pulled his money pouch off his belt and opened it. "I've got about sixteen florins here. How much do we need for more grain?"

"Just for grain, about four florins a stone, but that isn't all we need. It's off season too, which always pushes the grain prices up. Your sixteen and my five isn't going to make much of a dent in everything we need."

Trystin sighed at this gloomy news. The cottage had seemed a good enough idea at the outset, but now he wasn't so sure. It was clearly nothing like as safe as Dale had originally suggested - less than two weeks and already Empire troops were in their midst - and now it seemed they were going to have to struggle to survive. The prospect of more hard work and deprivation for the three royal children depressed him. They weren't used to such harsh circumstances and, although they were doing their best, it was going to be rough on them.

Cori, listening in on the conversation, got to his feet. From around his neck he pulled a gold chain, on which hung a beautiful crystal droplet, the symbol of faith in God and the tie with Holy Brem, God's prophet. It would have been given to him, Dale knew, at his 'presentation ceremony' something all Bremmand children went through at the age of about eight, when they were presented to the faith and took their first oaths to follow the teachings of Brem. It was customary for the child to be given a 'drop' representing water from the Holy Source at this time, most usually carved in wood or perhaps cast from iron, but for the wealthy the drop might be in gold or, as in this case, a gemstone. It lay on Cori's outstretched hand as he offered it to the big man. "Here Dale," he said. "Take this. You should be able to sell it for a good price so that should help."

Before Dale could say a thing, Allin was on his feet as well. He also removed a similar chain and stone which he handed over without a word. He didn't do so well at hiding how much he hated parting with the pendant as his brother but Dale was overwhelmed by the sacrifice they were both making in giving up one of the most personal ties they had with their family. He'd not want to part with his own wooden version for anything.

There was a small silence and then Dale said slowly. "I can't possibly take these. I wouldn't dream of asking you to give them up."

Somewhat to his surprise, both boys looked disappointed, hurt even, by his refusal.

"Please Dale," Cori begged. "We all have to work together don't we? And this is something that Allin and I can do to help. Won't you let us?"

"Please," Allin added. "We want to; truly we do."

Dale gazed at the beseeching faces for a moment, then threw a helpless look at Trystin who merely shrugged and offered him no help whatsoever. Finally he sighed inwardly and made his decision. Briskly he took the chain from Cori unhooked it and unthreaded the stone from the gold links.

"Chelland's only a small place. I don't think I'd be able to find a buyer for the stones and they're good enough to be remembered but the chains are gold and they're bound to fetch me a good price."

"Will it be enough?" Cori asked a little anxiously, as Allin also removed the crystal pendant from its chain and handed the gold to Dale. The big man hesitated. Gold sold easily and at a reasonable rate even in Chelland, but probably not enough for everything they needed. Cori saw the doubt and instantly pulled the gold signet ring off his index finger. "This is gold too and it's not a family one or anything." A little sadly he added, "Mother said we shouldn't take anything which marked us as royal when we left the castle. It's just as well isn't it, otherwise you'd not be able to sell it."

Allin didn't have a ring to offer but now that he was in the swing of giving up his worldly possessions he pulled his knife from his belt. "What about this?" He asked eagerly. "I think it's a good one, and I'm sure you'd get a good price for it."

Watching this sudden flurry of giving, and determined not to be outdone by her brothers, Joss too came up to Dale. With the fingers of one hand in her mouth, she offered up the contents of her other to the big man. No gold or jewels in this donation however, just a wooden pony which Dale had given her to play with.

Dale couldn't help but laugh at this sudden deluge of valuables on all sides. "I'm not out to beggar you all, you know." He took the carved animal, crouched down and offered it back to Joss. "I think this would be better off in your company, don't you my flower?"

Slowly, the little girl nodded, and retrieved her toy with a smile, clearly glad that she didn't have to part with it.

"You're a good girl for offering though," he added and got a beaming smile in return. Having dealt with Joss, Dale now turned back to her brothers. "Allin, you keep that. Everyone needs a knife."

"But you could sell this one and get an ordinary one instead. That would be cheaper wouldn't it and then you could use what was left? I don't mind, really. Not if it helps."

Still Dale didn't take the proffered blade. "Thank you then, but hang on to it for now. I won't go for a day or two and you need to have something to use until then."

Allin nodded and slid the knife back in to his sheath. "Don't forget to take it when you go though, will you?"

"I won't." He looked at the youngsters fondly, proud of the sacrifice they were making. "I thank you both for these," he said. "I'll be able to put them to good use and as soon as we get established here, I'll find a way to repay you."

"We're alive and safe, Dale," Cori replied, dropping a hand on his brother's shoulder. "The debt is one we owe you, not the other way around. This only goes some of the way to repay what is due to you for what you have done and will continue to do for us. To both of you," he added, widening his gaze to include Trystin.

"It is an honour and a pleasure to serve you, Your Highness" Trystin said gently to the lad. "You and your family. I seek no reward but to see you safe and well and eventually returned to your rightful place. Until then, let's not talk of the debts owed, for there are none. Everything I do between now and then is done out of love and loyalty and that's the only reward needed."

There was silence for a moment after this rather grand statement until Trystin himself added a little thoughtfully "My! That came out far more pompous than it sounded in my head!" He smiled a little sheepishly at them all. "You know what I mean though."

"I do," Cori smiled. "You mean we should avoid driving ourselves to a complete standstill with flowery speeches of mutual gratitude and praise and just get on with the job in hand."

Dale laughed, heartened by this sudden indication that Trystin might be human after all and said with warmth. "I can agree to that. I don't think I could compete with either of you if we get in to a competition of courtly language and I've been in the royal escort far too many times to want to stand around listening to you yammering along trading 'thees' and 'thous' and using fifty words when five would do."

"Deadly dull," Trystin agreed with a faint smile and then changed the subject. "So Allin, have you finished that problem yet?"

Allin pulled a face. "I don't see the point of mathematics," he grumbled.

"That would be a no then," Cori said with a smile. "C'mon Pup, the sooner you get down to it the sooner it will be done."

"And the sooner we can all eat," Dale added. "I suppose people are hungry, are they?"

When, eventually, they were all seated around the table eating Cori raised the subject of Chelland once more. "How far is it?" he asked conversationally.

"As the crow flies, about twelve miles," Dale shrugged, "but there's no decent road that leads directly there, so it's a bit further unless you can fly. I can be there and back in a day."

"A long day though," Cori murmured. "Rather you than me."

Dale was about to reply to this when Allin spoke up, "Can I come too?"

Everyone around the table looked at the boy, surprised by the request. Dale glanced at Cori and, before the older brother could open his mouth to rebuke the youngster, quelled him with glance. Cori, he noted, had a tendency to be scathing of his younger brother and it did lead to Allin insisting on things that he might otherwise have been quite happy to forgo. Gently Dale said, "It's a long old walk Allin and there's not a lot to see in Chelland. To make it in a day means there won't be much time for you to do anything except trail around after me."

"I still want to go," the boy insisted stubbornly.

Dale considered this. There was look about Allin's face that suggested this was more than a mere whim so to refuse him out of hand would be unfair. "Let me think about it, son," he said eventually.

Allin scowled. "That just means no without saying it," he said sullenly.

"He hasn't said 'no' already, has he?" Cori chided him, but not too severely. "Dale's said he'll think about it. I think you can trust him to keep his word." Allin nodded and Cori then went on, "I can't think why you'd want to go myself. All that walking!" He shuddered but with a humorous smile grin. "After last week I think I've had more than enough of that to last me a lifetime. Staying here and letting someone else do all that tramping about all over the place sounds far nicer."

"Thank you." Dale smiled ironically but then looked at Allin again who still looked mulish. "It's not just a sop, Allin. I *will* think about it and I *will* give you an answer. You have my word on that."

"You said that about the axe," Allin mumbled, but in a low voice, so that the others didn't hear him.

That evening, when the royal children had gone to bed, Trystin again voiced his concerns about Dale's trip to Chelland and suggested he go in the big man's stead.

"Everyone wants to go to Chelland," Dale accused him. Then less irritably he added, "I'll only be gone a day, Trystin, and this place is perfectly safe. I wish you would take my word on that."

"Those soldiers yesterday rather prove otherwise," Trystin replied. Suddenly, the disapproval was gone from his voice and, gazing into the fire, he admitted, "You've no idea what it was like when they showed up. All that was going through my head was the realisation that I had absolutely no way to defend Joss from harm if they decided to get ugly. I don't even know how to hold a sword, let alone use one."

The anxiety in the thin scholar's face was easy enough to read and Dale felt momentarily sympathetic. It didn't last long, however as a malicious idea came leaping in to his mind. "Well, we can soon fix that. I can teach you how to fight. We can start tomorrow. It wouldn't take all that long to give you the basics of how to defend yourself."

Trystin looked at him a little astonished and then his eyes narrowed. "You'd like that wouldn't you? Get me in a situation where you can better me?"

There was no point in lying. "Yes. If the situation were reversed, no doubt you'd feel the same."

Silence and then, "No doubt. However, your personal enjoyment in humiliating me in a field of combat aside, I doubt even you can teach me quickly enough to be able to manage if we get another visit while you're in Chelland."

"That's what's bothering you, is it?" Dale said, realisation suddenly dawning. It wasn't about the man not trusting him - he was afraid! "You don't need to worry you know. Those men stumbled upon us by accident and it's a million to one chance that anyone else will ever do the same." Trystin didn't look convinced so Dale went on a little impatiently. "I lived here half my life, all told, and I can't *think* of the last time anyone came here unless they'd been invited or told how to find it. I spent my entire childhood convinced it was the most remote place on earth and most of the world doesn't even know it exists."

"I'm sure Lord Petin does," Trystin challenged. Petin was the Overlord of the region and was reputed to be most rigorous in knowing every last labourer who worked his region to ensure that they paid their taxes. "I can't suppose you've missed visits from his tax gatherers. If they know where you are, you'll be on the records so anyone could find us."

Dale grinned. "That's where you're wrong. Petin's father owed a debt to my granda and my family are exempt from tithing to him unless we start to extend the lands we work. There are fifty acres of land here that as good as belong to my family and no-one ever bothers us. We might appear in tax records of fifty years ago but nothing more recent. This place really is safe, my friend, I'm sure of it."

Trystin shook his head, still not convinced. He heaved another heavy sigh. "If anyone does come, Dale, if that million to one chance happens while you're not here, we're all but defenceless."

"Cori knows how to fight," the big man disagreed. "He's untested but he's skilful enough. He'd be able to hold them off long enough for you and the children to get under cover of the trees and once you're there you stand a good chance of losing anyone out to attack you."

"We're supposed to be protecting him, not the other way around."

"I know, but this is the best we can do for now." Dale sighed. "Look, it *has* to be me who goes to Chelland. They don't know you and they wouldn't trade with you. Especially not at the moment when things are so uncertain. The only alternative to that would be for us all to go together and that's hardly a better solution."

"And yet you are willing to take Allin with you?"

"I am considering it, Trystin. I haven't said I am willing."

"That you would even consider it astounds me. What if Chelland is full of enemy troops? What kind of risk would that put the boy in?"

"Chelland is a small woodsman trading town. There's nothing there. It isn't of military importance or *any* kind of importance to anyone but the people who trade there. If Darvett has reached so far, then his men will be looking for royalty, well dressed and wealthy. A woodcutter and a boy? They won't even notice us, especially not when it is clear that some of the local folk know me. I tell you Trystin, we are already fading into the trees by what we have done here. As far as enemy soldiers are concerned, we're invisible."

"I see. And while you're in Chelland 'being invisible' I remain here and do what? Keep house?"

"It serves a purpose."

"Why thank you," came the bitter reply. Then, as if determined to prove he served another purpose, Trystin fixed the woodman with his grey eyes and said firmly. "Well at least I can keep the children's education going. I trust you have no objections?" The question was more of a challenge than anything else.

Almost in a deliberate attempt to foil this attempt to annoy, Dale replied mildly, "None at all. Did you think I would mind?"

"You've been determined to have us all living like woodcutters, blending in to the background and such. That's hardly consistent with three literate children."

Dale looked unconcerned. "Not so strange as you might think. Woodsmen take the teachings of Brem very seriously. Something to do with making a home of the forest, I suppose. There's something very spiritual about living in such a scattered community and among trees, some of which have been here for hundreds of years. As a result woodsmen follow the three tenets of Brem rather more seriously than other folk."

"Faith, family and learning," Trystin murmured softly repeating those three tenets.

"Right. As a rule half a day a week is given over to faith and the same to learning, so most woodsmen can read and write at least to a basic level." A wicked glint came in to Dale's eyes. "Then we spend the rest of the time extending the family." He put a vaguely saucy emphasis on the last word and added, "One needs to have something to do on a dark night in the woods!"

Trystin ignored the innuendo and said stiffly, "I was planning to do more than half a day a week."

"There's going to be plenty to do to keep this place going and that means work for everyone" Dale replied, thinking of Allin's face as he had been forced to study. Trystin opened his mouth to argue, when Dale said flatly, "You can have the mornings. After that, everyone will have to pitch in and do what work is needed."

Trystin knew it was generous, that it was far more than he would have expected from the blunt soldier, so he found it in him to be gracious. "Thank you. That will be more than sufficient. I know it is necessary to blend in to the background and make these into ordinary children but when we do get them to Hast I would like them to have a little royal polish left."

Dale didn't follow up his threat to teach Trystin to fight the next day. Instead, when the two boys were released from their time with their tutor, he took Cori with him in to the woods to help move the sections of tree he had previously felled back to the cottage. However, when they reached the site, Dale gestured to the young man to sit on one of the lengths of trunk and raised the subject of Allin's request to go to Chelland.

"I wanted your views on whether he should go."

"My views?" Cori looked surprised.

Dale nodded and explained. "You're the oldest member of the family present, so I'd like your consent to take him."

"Oh!" The young man looked disconcerted and ran his fingers through his light brown hair a trifle fretfully. "I'm surprised that you're even considering taking him. He'll just be a nuisance to you if you take him along."

Dale smiled, recognising the natural impatience of the fifteen-year-old with his ten-year-old brother, said mildly. "He's not so much trouble and I don't mind his company. If I'm willing to take him along, are you prepared to allow me?"

"You don't know him like I do," Cori said gloomily. "He's impossibly stubborn and he can play merry hell if he gets it in to his head to do something. If he starts playing you up, he can be an absolute menace. He's quite capable of simply doing what he pleases, regardless of what anyone's told him."

Dale thought momentarily of his first encounter with the young prince, when he absconded from the nursery, and smiled to himself. The boy had, after all, returned to the care of his nurse when faced with a bit of authority. "Well, I'm going to make it clear to him that, if he's to come with me, he's going to have to do as he's told without argument. He has to be prepared to do that for his own safety, if for no other reason."

Cori didn't look convinced by this. "He's only saying he wants to go because he thinks it will be better than doing lessons. He made an awful fuss this morning when Trystin said he'd be teaching us every day. I don't think he's even considered how far fifteen miles really is. He'll never make the distance without slowing you down."

"I'll put that to him - make sure he really understands how tough this will be and if you think this is an attempt to evade his studies then I'll tell him he's supposed to make up for any time lost, in advance. If he's really determined then he'll have to earn the right to go with me. How does that sound?" Still Cori looked unconvinced so Dale added, "I'll also make sure he knows that there will be other times, when I won't have to make the trip so quickly."

"That might work." Cori looked hopeful. "He might be willing to give up this idea if he knows he can go some other time."

"I get the impression," Dale said gently, "that you don't want him to go. You're putting a lot of obstacles in the way of my taking him."

"I know," Cori admitted and then sighed. "Did you have to make it my decision?"

"Sorry son, but he's your brother and I must ask you. But don't let it worry you. If you don't want him to go, then I'll not take him. It's as simple as that."

"He'll be furious with me if I say he can't go, though," Cori said miserably. "He hates not getting his own way and he can be a real horror when he gets told no. You saw what he was like about the axe."

"Don't let that deter you. Make the right decision, and worry about the tantrums later. Besides, I don't have to tell him why I'm not taking him, so he can see me as the villain of the piece."

"That's not fair," Cori said swiftly and then, as Dale opened his mouth to speak, added, "and I know - life isn't - but to allow an injustice when it can be prevented isn't right. If it's my say so that makes the difference then I should take any anger from Allin that results from it. The problem is," he went on more uncertainly, "I don't really have a good reason to say no. I just… when he asked to go, my first impulse was to keep him here, and that's all. Just an instinctive wish that he shouldn't go. The fact that you're willing to take him just makes it harder. I was rather hoping you'd decide it was ridiculous and then I wouldn't have to worry about any of this."

"He'll be perfectly safe with me, son. You know I'll do everything in my power to protect him." Dale gave this assurance wondering if it was this that was worrying the young man.

"I know that. It isn't a question of not trusting you, or that there is any danger in him going. I just…." Cori sighed heavily and said miserably, "I don't *know* what it is."

"Well think on it. I don't have to go for a few more days, so you've got a little time. I'll talk to Allin in the meantime and give him some of the conditions to him coming along without giving him a final answer. You've got a little time to think it through and let me know your wishes."

"My wishes?" Cori mused looking thoughtful. "I think I rather wish you'd not asked my views at all. It would have been a great deal easier if you'd made a decision without me."

"That's not going to happen," Dale stated flatly. "Allin and Joss are your family and you have the right to express an opinion. You should expect that I'll defer to you in matters that affect them."

"Oh!" Cori considered this in silence for a while, realising the burden of responsibility that was being placed upon him. It didn't take long for his sense of humour to find potential in the situation, however, and a sly look came over his face. "What if I wanted something that you thought was wrong? A really bad decision?"

Dale could see that he was being teased slightly, the pressure having been lifted from Cori by being given more time to think about Allin's request and his humorous side showing through instantly as a result. So the big man smiled and said mildly, "That does rather depend. If it were a matter of either his safety or yours...."

"No, no," Cori amended promptly. "Nothing like that. As if I'd do something that put him in danger anyway! Just something you didn't agree with like, oh I don't know, staying up all night, or getting his own way when he didn't deserve it."

"In that case I'd respectfully attempt to advise you otherwise, making my views known as clearly as possible and if that didn't work and I still didn't agree," Dale grinned, "I'd just pull rank."

Cori's eyebrows shot up. "*Pull rank*? Do tell me *Captain* Ronas, what rank you would intend to pull over me?"

"Well, Your Highness" Dale made a point of using Cori's title since the lad had used his Captaincy to emphasise the difference in their respective stations, "I'll agree that I, a mere soldier who earned his rank by hard work and heroism, doesn't reach your exalted levels so richly earned by extreme effort of being born into the right family but I would remind you that I am bigger than you."

"Oh I see," Cori laughed, "It's a question of *might* over *right?*"

"But of course," was the smooth reply. "All this talk about authority by right sounds very proper but might is infinitely more fun." Dale grinned then and slapped the lad on the shoulder. "And don't think," he said with, spirit, "that I can't tell when someone is stalling for time. These logs still need to be moved and trying to distract me with conversation won't work."

Cori groaned as he pulled himself to his feet. "I wonder how long it's been since someone in my family had to haul lumber for a living."

"You're probably in revered company," Dale laughed. "It could well have been Brem himself. Still, it's good for the common man to know that princes can do a bit of honest work from time to time."

True to his word, Dale took Allin aside as the day drew to a close and questioned his request to accompany the big man once again. Sitting on one of the prone logs now lying around the firepit making seating, the boy bowed his dark head and insisted that he still wanted to come along.

"I'll not slow you down," he insisted at Dale's description of hard the trip would be and mutely accepted the conditions placed upon him. He was quite determined and nothing Dale said could deter him in least. But his earnest attempts to sway the lad did have one effect.

"You don't want me to come?" The boy hung his head and sounded so forlorn that Dale was troubled by it. He hurried to correct this view.

"I don't want you to think this is your only chance. This trip will be such a hard one and I'll be pushed for time, so it isn't a particularly good opportunity for you to come along. I can and will take you another time instead when you'd have time to look around Chelland properly. Why not come then and stay here with your brother and sister this time?"

Allin didn't look at him. "I like it better with you," he admitted in a small voice.

Dale considered this carefully and then put a hand on Allin's arm. "You know that you're quite safe here, don't you son?" he said gently, "Cori and Trystin would never allow anything to happen to you"

Allin nodded, still staring at the ground as if ashamed. "I'm not afraid. It's not that, it's just..." he stopped, struggling to find the words and then repeated helplessly, "I just like it better with you."

"Allin." Cori's voice came from behind them, flat and emotionless. "Trystin said you were to come in and wash up for supper."

Obediently Allin rose to his feet, looking a little embarrassed at the thought that his brother might have heard him and looked at Dale. With the big man still seated on the log, it brought them almost exactly to eye level. "So, can I come with you? If I do everything you said?"

"I thought we'd agreed you'd not pester Dale about this," Cori chided his younger brother but in a gentle tone. "He'll tell you when he's decided and I'm quite sure he'll not forget, so you don't need to keep nagging him."

"I wasn't." Allin defended himself a little indignantly. "*He* asked *me* so were talking about it. I..." then he met his brother's eye and admitted defeat. "All right," he sighed and turned to Dale. "I'm sorry."

Dale just grinned and sent him in the direction of the cottage with a jerk of his head. "Tell Trystin I'll be along in a while," was his only remark.

Cori stood watching his brother head for the cottage and murmured, half to himself, "He likes it better with you."

"Don't be offended by that, son," Dale advised, anxious to reassure. "He didn't know he was being overheard or he'd not have been quite so undiplomatic. I'm sure he doesn't mean it quite as it might sound, either. He's still young so he probably doesn't express himself all that well."

"No, he expressed himself perfectly well."

"Cori…" but the young man held up a hand to stop Dale carrying on.

"And in truth, I think I rather agree with him."

Dale's eyebrow's shot up into his fringe. "Oh? Don't tell me you've now decided you want to come along as well?"

"No," Cori said, with a grimace. "I'm quite content not to walk for the best part of a day, just to end up back here. But you're our rock Dale, something for us all to cling to while we weather the storm. It's you that keeps us going and makes us all feel that there's going to be an end to all this."

"I see" Dale replied slowly. "That's… interesting."

Cori looked a little embarrassed. "I didn't mean to make you feel…" he began, worried that the big man might be uncomfortable with such an onerous role placed upon him but Dale shook his head.

"Would it interest you to know that my rock is you - you three? The strength you've all shown - even Joss who barely understands what's going on - and the way you've adapted to everything that's happened with courage and an affection for each other. That's what keeps me going and makes me hope in the future. My inspiration, if you will."

Cori thought about this for a moment or two and then said thoughtfully, "That means that while we all cling to you for support, you're clinging to us. There isn't actually anything keeping us going."

The lad's face was blank as he said this, so Dale wasn't entirely sure what he was trying to say. "So?" he prompted cautiously.

"Well, only that we'd probably better not let the others know the only thing that's *actually* keeping us going is sheer willpower," and suddenly he smirked, the absurdity of it all showing through. "I'm not sure they'd be all that impressed to find out that the whole thing is just so much smoke and mirrors and if they realised it, we might all come crashing down in a heap."

Dale laughed and slapped the boy on the back. "I won't tell if you don't," he grinned.

"We have a bargain!" Cori returned. Then more thoughtfully he added, "and if you really don't mind having Allin tagging along after you all the way to Chelland and back, I've got no objections. Not real ones anyway. Just" - he pulled a face - "don't let him be utterly unbearable on account of having got his own way."

Allin was remarkably well behaved, however, on hearing the good news and over the next few days he firmly set his teeth and concentrated on meeting all the requirements Dale had imposed upon him. He quickly got ahead on his studies - proving, Trystin had remarked to the boy dryly, that he was more than able if only he'd put his mind to it - and rose early each morning to complete extra chores so that he'd not be leaving additional work for Cori while he was absent. He also did everything he could to ensure that no-one would have any cause to complain of his general behaviour and thus oblige Dale to stop him going as a result. In fact he was an altogether different boy, polite, studious and very controlled - so much so that it raised a complaint of an altogether different nature from his brother.

"He's just so... so... *good*," Cori complained to Dale one afternoon as they worked together in the forest, cutting and moving logs back to the cottage.

Dale shrugged. "He wants to go, so he's making sure nothing gets in the way of that. I thought that was what you wanted, for him to behave himself. You were complaining that he was a nuisance a few days ago."

"I know, and he can be, but," he sighed, and leaned against the back of the prone trunk as he tried to explain, "he's usually really full of life and energy, even when he's throwing the worst fit of temper. He's strong - strong of spirit that is - much stronger than me - and so sure of himself. But now, he's none of that. He's just....good. I don't like him half so much when he's being so pious." Cori sighed again and shrugged. "I don't think I'm explaining very well."

"You are," Dale assured him with a smile. "I think you like your brother rather more than you let on."

The young man grinned to himself and nodded his head. "Don't go telling him that, though. There are certain standards one has to maintain as an older brother you know but actually, yes, I've always rather liked him. We all do... did." For a second a trace of grief crossed his face as he corrected himself. "Even Pold had time for him, when he'd do almost anything to avoid the rest of us." He thought for a second before adding, "Though Richol always said Allin'd probably manage to out-do even Pold for outrage when he got old enough."

"Well now, there's something to look forward to," Dale remarked dryly.

Cori looked suddenly a little embarrassed, the royal habit of keeping their private lives very private suddenly reminding him that this little piece of family scandal was not something to be gossiped about. "I suppose you must have heard about that," he said carefully.

"I did. Members of the Palace Guard went with your brother to Hast."

Cori looked suddenly amused, in memory of something he knew of that trip. Without thinking he recounted, "I can remember Pold telling us when he came back that the escort Father arranged for the journey was commanded by some kind of a mad man. Every time Pold so much as complained, this captain'd knock him off his horse. Apparently the man was a total tyrant."

"That sounds like a fair description," Dale said dryly, but with a smile. "I was lieutenant, not a Captain, though."

"You? You led the party?" Cori was embarrassed. "I didn't think... I didn't know it was you, Dale or I'd never have said that. I'm sorry if…"

"I'm not offended" Dale remarked mildly, seemingly unconcerned at the lack of tact. "The King gave me very precise orders that I was to get your brother to the palace at Hast, and to use any means at my disposal to do so, just so long as I didn't cause him permanent injury. I always take my job very seriously, especially when commanded by a King. Your father made it clear that Prince Perrold had no rank or status on that journey to ensure that there was no difficulty for me or my men should he try to give orders. I got the distinct impression that His Majesty was very concerned that something should be done to correct His Highness's manners before it was too late."

"He isn't so bad," Cori said trying to defend his brother. "I know he can be a little difficult to get along with…"

Dale smiled a wintry smile. "Difficult," he agreed. "Not to mention rude, aggressive, disobedient…." Then more thoughtfully, "I rather liked him once I got to know him, though. Just a bit wayward, I suppose. Stuck in the middle, not quite a man and not really a boy either and overshadowed by any number of brothers who excelled where he was just ordinary."

"Ordinary?" Cori questioned. "I don't know what you mean."

"You wouldn't," Dale smiled. "But think about it for a moment. Prince Herest was heir to the throne and well respected, from a young age. Richol was good natured, intelligent and handsome and positively loved by most of the court and Jorvis was always destined to be a great warrior. They were all viewed by the whole court as showing the signs of being great men in one way or another. Prince Perrold didn't have any of the qualities that they had. He was all right to look at but not wonderful, he had a reasonable brain but was no great genius and his fighting skills were reasonable but not brilliant, no matter how hard he worked at it. Then, as if all that wasn't bad enough, you were starting to better him too. Even back then when you were still a boy the gossip around the court was along the lines that you too were another of a great line."

Cori looked embarrassed at that, "I don't know that that's particularly true…"

"But from Prince Perrold's perspective whether the court gossips were right or not was irrelevant. As far as he was concerned they all looked at his brothers, older and younger, and then at him, shook their heads and said *what a pity he doesn't measure up*. How would you have felt?

"Then he fell in with that idiot Tonnat who was determined to make as much trouble as he could possibly manage and fed your brother a whole load of stupid ideas about him being superior and free to do exactly as he pleased. He was really bad seed, that one was."

Cori looked wistful. "I suppose..." he started and then stopped. His face said it all - the troublesome brother they were now discussing was almost certainly dead, along with all his older siblings and, for all Cori hadn't found Perrold easy to get along with, the sense of loss was profound.

He tilted his head upwards and squinted at the sun beating down through the opening in the tree. More briskly he said, "That's not what we were talking about, anyway."

Dale nodded. It was reasonable that Cori wouldn't want to dwell on such things. The grief was still too recent for him to remember his brothers with fondness rather than pain.

"I was trying to explain about Allin," Cori said pulling the subject back to the original topic, "I know I said he was a nuisance but he makes me laugh sometimes too and I like him as he is. When he's like this - trying too hard - it's like it isn't really him and I don't think I like what I get in his place."

Allin's immaculate behaviour continued, however, even despite Cori's gentle remark to the boy that he didn't have to be perfect and thus it was as the second week drew to a close he earned his right to accompany Dale on the walk to Chelland.

It was before dawn when they set off, the air cold enough to make their breath visible and the woods almost silent as the night creatures gave up their prowling and sought sleep but before the early song birds began their calls to welcome in the dawn. Dale set off at a brisk pace, expecting to have to slow for the sake of his young companion but wanting to cover as much ground as possible before this happened. Allin matched his speed but spoke little, except to answer politely, "Yes, thank you," every time Dale asked if he was all right.

In the end, anxious that the lad was not admitting that he was struggling with the pace, Dale questioned him more closely. "I want to be sure you're managing to keep up all right, not just feeling you can't admit it's hard going," he explained but when Allin assured him simply that he was fine, Dale felt obliged to add with an affectionate smile, "You've been very quiet. It's not like you."

"Oh," Allin said thoughtfully and then explained "It just doesn't seem polite to make lots of noise. It seems rather" - he hesitated before finishing rather bashfully - "rude to the forest."

Dale grinned into the darkness. "I see."

"I know that's a bit silly..."

"To be aware of the spirits in the forest? Not at all. I've lived here all my life and the forest is almost a person to me. A rich and beautiful lady, with a long dress of greens and golds. She's my friend, my ally and a place of safety to me."

"Is that why you brought us here - to your cottage? Because you feel safe?"

Dale nodded. "Because I know it is safe. So deep in the forest I can't help but be sure that she'll not let any harm come to us. But you have to treat her with respect," Dale warned his young charge, not wanting to create a false impression of his home. "The lady of the forest has a temper if you don't treat her carefully, so you have to stick to your appointed place and not venture out expecting her to protect you over her other children. As far as she's concerned, wolves are equal to men and if one of them sees you, he's perfectly entitled to his lunch."

The light was beginning to lift from black to grey so Dale could see Allin's smile as he said with spirit, "Or his breakfast!"

Dale didn't miss the hint and smiled. "Are you thinking about breakfast already? It's not even daylight. You can't be hungry yet."

"I can," Allin advised him with a grin. "I can be hungry any time. Rana says I'm the only person she knows who can eat a meal and be hungry ten minutes later." There was a little pause before he added, "Rana's one of the nurses. She went with Dav and Andred."

"I know. I'm acquainted with Rana," Dale said mildly. Allin squinted up at the big man saying nothing but studying the red bearded face. Then suddenly he smirked, but returned his gaze to the road ahead and said nothing. Dale idled with the idea of making further comment but he figured that the boy had already made up his mind about his 'acquaintance' with Rana and any attempt to deny or defend this would confirm the fact in the boy's mind, so he sighed, reflected on how boys seemed to be more aware of some things than was quite seemly at such an early age and said no more on the subject.

Chelland

The dawn began to creep across the sky, fingers of pale blue and yellow against the dark of the night, and gradually they found that they were no longer walking in blackness but in a half light where the trees became visible, first in shape and then colour. As the day warmed, mist rose from the ground - tendrils of white floating across the landscape. It wasn't dense enough to envelop everything, instead rising like a blanket, a sharp edge visible between the mist layer and the ground beneath. The division was so sharp that the mist looked like a real thing and Dale smiled as he noticed his young companion reach out at one point as they passed through a dense patch, just in front of them, to see if he could touch the ephemeral cloth of the forest. The mist eddied away slowly at his fingers' touch and then broke and wavered as they walked through it. The vapours distorted the view ahead and played tricks with the light, bringing an eeriness to the forest.

Allin was even more silent in this curious half light until, after a little while, he asked somewhat breathlessly, "Did you mean what you said to those soldiers the other day - about ghosts?"

Dale smiled to himself but answered securely, "In a forest of this age and size, there are bound to be spirits but they only trouble those who have reason to fear them. I find that as long as I respect the forest and treat her with respect, the ghosts don't disturb me; and you can be sure that this place can mean no harm to you. These forests have been here since Brem himself lived among the trees and the woods have a long memory. No-one of his bloodline need ever fear the woodland spirits."

It was fully light before they shared a brief meal on the road. They didn't stop to eat, consuming the simple supplies as they walked, and as the morning continued they progressed along the pathway that wound through the forest towards Chelland.

They talked more as the sun warmed the day, about idle topics. Dale pointed out a few things along the way that he thought would be of interest to the boy and Allin made the most of the freedom from his brother's watchful eye by asking Dale a whole range of questions which, Dale was sure, would be deemed highly inappropriate by Cori. It was interesting, he reflected, that Allin was quite fascinated by the whole business of soldiering and war craft and he wondered if the boy had yet realised that, if things were as was feared with the rest of his family, the chances of him ever taking up arms himself were quite unlikely.

Allin had been silent for a while when he suddenly asked, "Do you like Trystin?"

Dale's stride faltered for a second at the unexpectedness of the questions, but he answered easily enough. "Why?"

"I just… wondered." Dale didn't reply, so Allin prompted, "Well? Do you?"

This was awkward. The last thing Dale wanted was for the boy to feel that all was not well between the two men, so he ventured cautiously, "We're very different sorts of people."

"I knew it!" came Allin's relieved reply. "I said so to Cori but he just said I was talking rot, like he usually does when he wants me to drop something."

"You've been discussing this?" Dale looked disapprovingly at the boy. "Since when have we become a source of entertainment to you?"

"Not entertainment. We weren't laughing at it or anything. I just thought you didn't like him, so I asked Cori about it. If it makes you feel better," the boy added earnestly, "I don't like him much, either."

"You don't like the fact that he makes you study, more like," Dale observed.

"No. Well, yes, a bit, but it isn't that. He keeps acting like he's in charge. Like he knows better than anyone else, and he doesn't, does he? I mean he doesn't know any more about living in the woods than me or Cori and he can't fight or anything. Even I know more about using a sword than he does and I'm only ten. He can't do anything useful but he walks about with his nose in the air and insists that he knows better than us. And he argues with everything that everyone else wants to do, as if they're stupid and he's the only one who isn't. It just gets on my nerves."

For all Dale knew it would be quite wrong to agree with his young companion there was suddenly something immensely comforting about having all his own grievances about the scholar laid out neatly like this. At least it wasn't just him who felt this way. "We are all going to have to get along Allin. It's a small cottage for us all to have to live in and if we all fall out then it will seem even smaller. Trystin is doing his best but this is a very different life to the one he's used to."

"It's different for me too," Allin protested indignantly.

"Yes, it is, but not everyone is as willing to put up with things as you and your brother seem to be and as we get older it gets harder and harder to get on with life when there is a big change. It takes longer to adapt because you have more years of remembering what it used to be like. I suspect our friend Trystin is struggling to get used to this new way of living. We must be patient with him and help him all we can."

"All right," Allin agreed amiably. Then he added, "I still don't like him though."

"No," - and after a little pause - "I don't either."

The walk to Chelland took them a little over five hours in all and the day was well advanced by the time they reached the outskirts of the small town. Allin had managed the whole journey without a word of complaint but his eyes were wide with exhaustion, Dale noted, and he knew it had been hard going for the boy. Allin seemed unwilling to admit it, however, and merely asked Dale where they should go first in the small settlement.

"Tavern," said Dale succinctly, nodding to a building about halfway down the length of the main road which made up Chelland's main street. "We can sit down and get a bite to eat before we do anything else."

"We don't need to stop on my account," Allin insisted, sounding offended. "I'm not a bit tired."

"Lucky old you, then," Dale replied dryly. "I trust you don't mind if *I* have a bit of a rest do you? I'm older than you and I don't have your inexhaustible supplies of energy."

Allin flashed him an impudent grin, his offence instantly gone. "Of course, venerable sir, if you need to stop, we shall. Are you sure you don't need me to help you drag your poor old bones all the way to the tavern? Here," he offered his shoulder to the big man, "lean on me and I'll help you."

"Cheeky brat," Dale smiled. "I'd box your ears for that if I wasn't so weary."

As soon as they reached the tavern Dale led Allin to one of the tables which were scattered in the open area at the front of the wood and plaster building. None of the other tables were occupied so the big man was able to choose one which gave them the best view of town. Allin sank on to one of the wooden benches that lined the table with a deep sigh and dropped his head on to the table top with a weary thud.

"Hard going, wasn't it?" Dale remarked as he seated himself with a little more finesse opposite the boy. Allin's brown head came up with a jerk.

"I'm all right," he insisted. "Just give me a minute or two and I'll be fine."

"You know," Dale said slowly, "it is perfectly all right to find a journey as long as that one tiring. This constant insistence that you're not the slightest bit tired and refusing to admit that you're feeling the effect might be considered prideful by some."

Allin's eyes widened. "I don't mean to be," he said anxiously. "I just don't want you to think it was a mistake to bring me, or that I'm going to slow you down."

"I know," Dale said, smiling gently, "but you've already proved your ability to keep up with me. You made it here, after all, so you don't need to pretend that you could do it again twice over if needed. Apart from anything else, all this show of energy is making me feel terribly old!"

There were no signs of life from the Tavern, although the door to the building stood open but the ill-matched pair were content to rest their aching legs while they waited for some service. As they sat in the warm sunshine of the morning, Allin took the opportunity to look about the small town a little more. The tavern where Dale and Allin were seated was situated on a crossroads, between the main road which led down to the river and two narrower streets along which stood a hugger mugger collection of buildings.

To call Chelland a town was perhaps a bit of an exaggeration. It was made up of a loose collection of buildings scattered along both sides of the road, mostly constructed from a mixture of wood and mud-coloured plaster, many of them open fronted so that the tradesmen working inside could be seen and approached. At the far end, where the road ran down to the bank of the river Cirran, stood a simple wooden jetty which, Dale explained, was where supplies came in from other bigger towns and was also the crossing point for the river to the towns and lands which lay to the north. On the opposite side to the tavern, at one of the other corners of the crossroads was an open space on which were a gaggle of people with carts and animals, all milling about as they laid out wares and tethered the livestock so that it could be seen to best advantage.

"Is it market day?" asked Allin with interest.

"Not exactly. Chelland's a bit small to have a proper organised market but if you come at this time of the week you'll usually find people have gathered to trade."

"So why is that different from a proper market?" Allin frowned, not seeing the distinction.

"A market is organised. The leaders of a market town set a day aside and sell space on the square to trade. This is unofficial so no-one has to pay for the right to trade."

"Then why would anyone want to go to a market? Surely if they have to pay, no-one would bother."

"Because Chelland is too small and much too remote for any serious trader to want to trek all the way out here just to avoid paying a paltry trading fee. All that happens here is the people who live locally get together to exchange their wares."

"But with a proper market couldn't people just sell their things in the town anyway, and not pay the fees?"

"They could," Dale smiled "Except that a market town is funded by the payment of trade tariffs. It's in their interests to make sure everyone pays so they impose fines if you try and set up a stall, or trade elsewhere or on any other day."

"Then why couldn't someone just set up outside the town and sell there?"

"No reason, as long as it wasn't right outside the town walls, in which case he might find himself chased off, but he'd not get the customers."

Allin still looked puzzled by the concept of commerce so Dale tried to explain it more simply for the boy. "Look at it this way: if you know for sure that on one day a week you'll be able to set up a stall and have the whole of a district coming in to town who might be interested in buying from you, it would be worth the market charge to do it. Especially since one thing the market charges pay for is the town guard to keep the peace so you know you'll be free from trouble and protected while you trade. It's well worth the small levy you have to pay to be worth using one of the market towns like Novoris or Kemsley."

"Or Castle Bremmand?"

"Ah, well, Castle Bremmand is different again. It's a city rather than a market town and it's the royal seat as well. People who trade there do so at the grace of the King and there aren't charges for them to do so. You'll find that the way things are done in Castle Bremmand is very different from either a market town or here."

"You'll also find that everything is overpriced and the food isn't as good!" a dry voice said. Dale and Allin looked up to see that a wiry man with mousy hair and grey eyes had approached their table. He was wearing an apron, which might once have been white had it not been so grubby and which marked him out as the landlord. In his hand he was carrying an earthenware pitcher and cup. He placed the cup on the table without another word and filled it with wine from the pitcher. "Langate Red," he said without a trace of a smile. "I believe the instruction was that it should be served as soon as I saw you, wasn't it?"

Dale's face broke in to a smile. "It was, Iestan. I'm amazed you remember."

"I never forget an order," the innkeeper returned. "Though I almost thought I was seeing things when I looked out and found you sitting out here. I wasn't expecting to have your custom again. The rumours floating up from the south suggest that things haven't gone so well in the war against the empire and I know you are in the military..."

"Not any more," Dale lied smoothly. "I was invalided out a while back. I'm back at the cottage again now."

"Oh," Iestan looked disappointed. "That's a pity. I was rather hoping you'd have some news for me of the campaign to ward off Darvett. The boatmen coming up from Novoris are telling of the place swarming with Empire troops but there's very little else getting through to us here. The little that has reached us doesn't sound good. All the reliable sources have dried up so most of what I'm hearing has been pretty wild and hysterical and probably containing very little in the way of truth." He looked glum as he went on, "The only consistent thing is that I'm hearing nothing good. It's beginning to sound as though the king has fallen and Bremmand's in the hands of Darvett's invaders. If any of what I'm hearing is true, they slaughtered just about any man who stood up with the King and walked in like they owned the place."

Dale unconsciously slid a hand over Allin's arm, seeing the boy's head droop at the reference to his father's defeat and probable death. Dale had warned Allin that there might be rumours about the invasion floating about in Chelland, so he knew the boy wasn't entirely unprepared for such discussion but Dale knew it couldn't be easy for him to hear more gloomy suggestions of his family's fate from the mouth of a stranger.

Iestan didn't miss the gesture of comfort made towards the boy.

"And who's this then Dale? Not your boy, surely? Didn't he..?" he frowned and Dale could see he was remembering the fate of the big man's family.

"Not mine, Iestan. This lad's father went off to answer the call to battle so I've been caring for him. Allin, this is Iestan," he said as he turned to the boy to perform introductions. "He owns the tavern here and is also the source of all information in the district. There isn't a thing he doesn't know and he seldom forgets anything he sees or hears." He made these description with a genial smile, laying out the man's attributes with a show of affection. "Iestan Honrad, may I present Allin of Lech."

Allin rose to his feet a little shyly. "I'm pleased to meet you, sir."

"And I you, young man. He's got nice manners," Iestan observed to Dale.

"He gets it from his mother, I think. She was at the Castle and she was particular about how she raised him."

"Probably had ideas of getting him work as a page or something," Iestan speculated. "You'd have to have pretty manners for that."

"Possibly," Dale agreed, a little warily. He was being obliged to lie more than he liked about Allin's background and, unwilling to allow the conversation to remain in this line to make the lie even more complex, he decided to cut the matter dead. He shrugged his shoulders and said a little regretfully, "But it wasn't to be. So now he's staying with me until such time as I can return him to his father." The implication that Allin's mother was dead was subtle but Dale knew the quick-witted man wouldn't have missed it. Iestan gave a sympathetic glance at Allin and from it, Dale could tell, he had also realised that if the boy's father had gone into battle, with the news as it was, the child was almost certainly an orphan. The pessimistic rumours that Iestan had been hearing would not be mentioned in the boy's presence again.

"So Allin of Lech," the innkeeper said briskly, changing the subject, "seeing as how I've already satisfied your companion's thirst, what can I get you? Do you care for wine, or would you prefer something else?"

Allin looked momentarily confused, uncertain of what one should order in a tavern such as this. Dale saw the hesitation and said easily, "Bring him some brew, would you Iestan? We had an early start this morning and I think he could do with something to perk him up a bit. Me too for that matter. I'm feeling in need of a bit of sparkle and I don't think Langate Red is going to help me there at all."

Iestan grinned at this but didn't comment, merely asking professionally, "And what about a bite to eat? If you've come all the way from that cottage of yours then you must be ready for a good meal, I'll be bound."

Dale didn't even need to look at Allin to know the answer to this question. "Name me one boy of his age you know who isn't *permanently* ready for a good meal. I think we could probably manage some bread and cheese if you've got any to spare."

"I've got plenty to *sell* friend Ronas," the wiry man grinned. "I've got some meat left over from last night's spit as well, if you want some of that, too."

"Why not?" Dale agreed amiably and with that the mousy-haired innkeeper returned inside the building.

"Think you can remember all that?" Dale said to Allin in a low voice. "All those things I had to make up about you for Iestan, that is?"

Allin nodded and then said thoughtfully, "Although you didn't actually lie all that much when you think about it. My father did go to fight Darvett and my mother is from the Castle, so it wasn't all that untrue."

"The secret of a good lie," Dale advised sagely, "is to keep it simple. Only lie where you have to, don't embellish or get creative when you don't need to and stay as close to the truth as possible. That way you stand a better chance of not making mistakes when you have to use the same lie again. You're more likely to remember what I told Iestan just now, because it's almost true, than if I'd told him something really different about who you are. And it's important that, if anyone else asks us anything while we're in Chelland, we stick to the same story."

"I suppose," Allin said slowly, "that if Iestan knows everything and forgets nothing, if we did get it wrong, he'd know we'd lied."

Dale nodded, mildly impressed that his young companion had taken his veiled warning about Iestan so well. "We need to be careful, son. What we build as a story today is going to have to be the story we use any time we meet with people in the future, so that we're not found out." Allin nodded. "We also need to make sure we don't contradict each other, so if you're obliged to make anything up and I'm not there..."

"...I shall have to make sure I tell you what I've made up, so that you can tell the same story."

"That's it. Good lad!" Dale smiled.

Iestan reappeared then, bringing a wooden tray bearing two earthenware mugs of steaming brew, a loaf of bread and a generous serving of cheese and cold cuts of meat. Allin couldn't quite suppress a little moan of hunger as the smell of the just baked bread wafted in his direction and Iestan beamed at him, delighted to have such an easily satisfied customer. He laid the table out and bustled about, seeing that his customers had everything they needed before departing back inside, leaving them to their breakfast. For a while all either man or boy were interested in was the bread, still warm from the oven, and the cheese and meats, piled high on a wooden platter, so they ate in silence working their way through the generous fare the innkeeper had delivered.

"Why Lech?" Allin asked a little while later, when he had consumed enough of the food to feel it was no longer necessary to devote his entire attention to it.

"What do you mean?"

"Well, you could have picked anywhere for me to have come from so why did you say I was from Lech rather than anywhere else?"

"Because I had to tell Iestan that you're from in or around Castle Bremmand. You speak like a southerner," Dale explained, seeing that Allin still didn't understand, "and if I'd said you were from around here, for example, he'd have been suspicious, so I picked somewhere that was near to where you really come from."

"Why not Meiringe or Tobest then? They're closer than Lech."

"I've led Iestan to believe that your father was a soldier and your mother in service at the Castle. People like that don't live in Meiringe or Tobest. Courtiers and senior royal staff live in Meiringe and Tobest is the financial district. You'll only find money lenders and bankers there. Neither of those types of people would be likely to ask a man like me to care for their son. And as a matter of fact," Dale smiled, "Meiringe and Tobest may be closer to the main gates of the Castle but Lech sits at the edge of the cliff right in the shadow of the castle walls, so it's actually closer than either of them. You, my young friend, were born and bred not fifty feet from Lech." Then, with a grin, he added, "although you spent most of your time quite some way above it."

There was a silence for a while and then Allin asked, very tentatively, "Iestan thought I was your son at first, didn't he?"

"Not really." Dale replied distantly, the regret transparent in his face. "He knows my son died, some time back. He remembered that as soon as he mentioned him."

"He's in that meadow, isn't he?" Allin's head was drooping a little, the memory of that beautiful place and the sorrow that went with it, reminding him of his own loss.

Dale nodded, a little cautiously. He didn't really want to make too much of the death of his family, for fear that be too painful for the boy. To his surprise, however, Allin seemed content with Dale's answer, and didn't mention it again. Instead he changed the subject, asking about what could be found up the narrow side streets leading off from the crossroads.

When finally man and boy had had their fill of the simple breakfast, they sat in silent contentment watching the people moving about in the small town. After a while, Allin eyed the remains of the bread thoughtfully. There was perhaps a quarter of a loaf remaining.

"Are we allowed to keep that?" he asked Dale after a little while. "I mean, if we'd eaten it all, it would have been ours wouldn't it?"

"I suppose so," Dale was a little puzzled by the question. "Why? Not still hungry are you?"

Allin shook his nut-brown head. "It's just, it's the first time I've had bread in ages. Since... you know."

"I know. So?" Dale prompted.

"I wouldn't have thought I could miss bread - normally it seems so dull - but if I missed it then I thought... couldn't we..." he hesitated, as if uncertain of what he was suggesting. "It wouldn't be stealing if we took it back with us, would it?"

Dale's face cleared now that he understood what the boy wanted to do. "It wouldn't be stealing, son. But it wouldn't be all that fresh by the time we got it home. It's already going stale here, see," and he tapped the side of the loaf, where slices had been cut and the white heart of the loaf was exposed and drying in the warmth of the day. "There's a bakery down there," he pointed to the winding side street over his shoulder. "I was thinking we could get fresh bread from there before we leave town. It'll keep longer if it's uncut. Does that sound like a better idea?"

Allin nodded, pleased that Cori and Joss would be able to share in the variety to their diet. He looked like he was about to say more but Iestan appeared again, to clear the remains of their meal and offer more brew. Dale declined the latter offer, instead asking, "Does that apothecary fellow still trade in gold - the one who had a place down near the river?"

"Gossan you mean?" Iestan pulled a face as he cleared the table. "He does. Making a pretty penny right now he is, too, trading on bad news. He's been telling everyone how they need to buy raw gold since the king's fallen and florins won't be worth anything once Darvett takes hold."

"And charging through the nose for everyone to do it, no doubt!" Dale commented dryly.

"Aye. He's a villain, that one, making money out of people's fears. He'll have a shock though," the wiry man said, with sudden intense feeling, "when this kingdom doesn't fall as easily as men like him are expecting. He's Arronite, so he doesn't really understand how strong the faith is between the people and the land. Darvett isn't going to keep a hold on Bremmand just because he's managed to take it once, and he's going to find the Bremmand people are far harder to subjugate than he thinks." There was a light of battle in his eyes all of a sudden and Dale could see that Allin was staring at the man with a mixture of surprise and admiration for this declaration of his defiance.

"If he's making such a profit I suppose Gossan will be willing to buy gold as well, will he?" was all Dale said, wanting to avoid getting in to any conversation which, if there was a change in their masters would be considered to be dangerously seditious. For all he agreed with Iestan he couldn't afford to link himself with any trouble while he was responsible for members of the royal family. Fighting back would have to wait until the bloodline was in a place of safety.

"What? Oh!" Iestan dragged himself back to the point. "He must be. Trades in most things, does Gossan. He'll buy or sell *anything* if the price is right."

There was something about the way Iestan spoke this last sentence, a heavy, condemning emphasis on the word 'anything' as though the innkeeper was trying to warn his customer. Dale took heed - he knew Iestan well enough to know that what he knew about Gossan was probably worth listening to.

"When you say anything...?" Dale asked cautiously.

"I mean *anything*," Iestan confirmed heavily. The message was pretty clear. Gossan wasn't to be trusted. He bought and sold anything - including people - and the wiry innkeeper was definitely warning Dale that he should deal with the man with care.

Dale sat in silence for a moment or two, thinking fast. Iestan's implication that the apothecary might betray him was meant only as a warning, the big man was sure, but with Allin at his side, he wasn't prepared to take even this risk. He could leave the boy here while he converted the valuables in to cash but even that...

Briskly, making a decision he got to his feet, looking the innkeeper squarely in the eye. "Look Iestan, if Gossan's that tricky, it would take me time to get a good price for what I've got to sell. But you know him, and could put the time and effort in to making sure he doesn't make too much of a profit from what gold he has to buy. So why don't I sell you the gold I've got, and then you can sell it on to him - rook him, if you like, the way he rooks others - and make a bit of money for yourself in to the bargain."

The moment Dale made the suggestion, the innkeeper pulled a reluctant face and began to back away. Dale, having anticipated this reaction, planted himself firmly in the way of Iestan's path forcing him to answer.

"I don't trade in gold, Dale, and I *definitely* don't trade with people I know. You *know* that. If I buy your gold and then make a good profit on it with Gossan, you'll be out after my blood for cheating you."

"No I won't," Dale insisted. "All I want's a fair price, with a minimum of fuss. I need to get on and bring in all the supplies for the cottage today so I don't have time to play games with the likes of Gossan. I've been living hand to mouth for a while," he added, to explain why he needed to buy so many supplies when he had claimed to be in the cottage for some time, "but now I've got the boy with me I need to rebuild my stocks and make deals. I need to work the land properly again so that we can survive out there for as long as we need to and we need to be on our way back well before the sun sets or we'll not make it home in a day. If you want to make an outrageous profit out of Gossan and pay him out for the way he robs others then that's fine by me - consider it your commission for saving me the trouble of having to deal with him."

"I don't..." Iestan protested again, but Dale pressed home his advantage with determination. "Besides that, it'll be moons before I even see you again, so I'm not going to know if you make a pile out of my haste, am I? C'mon Iestan," he added appealingly. "Help out an old friend here."

"And how long will you still be a friend, if I do this?" the wiry man grumbled. "*Never do business with friends,*" he stated, as if it was a long-held rule.

Sensing that the innkeeper was weakening, Dale allowed himself a small smile. "*And never make friends of the people you do business with,*" he completed the adage. "I know. But you're enough of a friend that I know you'd not try to trick me and *I'm* enough of a friend that I don't begrudge you any profits you can wrangle out of a crook like Gossan. Especially not when it saves me so much trouble, and a walk home with the wolves."

"Oh, all *right!*" The man gave in, but clearly with some reluctance. "You'd best come inside then so I can see what you want me to buy."

At Iestan's suggestion Dale left Allin sitting outside while he and the innkeeper vanished in to the tavern to talk business. Leaving his young charge outside wouldn't have been the big man's first choice but to insist the boy came with him would have looked odd and Iestan was far too sharp for Dale to want to risk his interest. So with a cheery instruction that Allin should behave himself, accompanied by a murmured reassurance that the boy was safe, the soldier departed in to the dark interior of the wooden building.

Allin sat in the sun waiting, watching the world passing by on the dusty road. More people were beginning to move about now, wandering along the main street carrying baskets and pushing hand wagons. The market area opposite was getting busier now, people threading through the irregular arrangement of stalls, looking and prodding the goods on display and arguing about price. At one point a slow wagon pulled by an exhausted looking mule made its way down the main thoroughfare and Allin could see that the wagon was loaded with wood. He watched it as it made its journey from the forest, past the tavern where the boy sat and down towards the river, where it was lost from sight.

Allin was young and slightly nervous at having been left on his own in such a public place and it felt like a lifetime before he saw the broad form of his protector emerge once again from the Tavern.

Dale smiled at him, his own discomfort at leaving Allin alone lifting when he saw that all was well. "That didn't take too long then, did it?" he smiled as the boy got to his feet.

Allin shook his head but then added a little curiously, "But longer than I'd have expected. Why does it take so long just to sell a bit of gold?"

They gathered up their things together and began to walk slowly along the road towards the river. As they strolled along, Dale continued to explain his absence.

"Iestan was doing me a favour by buying it, so it was only fair to return that favour by giving him a bit of news."

"About the war?"

"That and other things. He knows that I must have better word from Bremmand if I've been in contact with your father."

"With...?" for a moment Allin looked lost and then his face cleared as he understood. It was his "soldier" father, who had left him in Dale's care when he went to battle to whom Dale was referring, not his father the King. "Oh, yes." He nodded and looked a bit ashamed of having forgotten so soon.

Dale seemed unconcerned, however, and went on, "So we traded what we knew for a while. It was worth taking the time, as well. Iestan knows everyone in this place and all the traders that travel in so he's been able to suggest who will be the best people for me to talk with and strike a deal for wood. I think he feels that if he helps me out with that, when he makes a profit on the gold I won't be so likely to come after him with an axe."

Dale grinned but Allin's mind was now on to something else. "Did you get a good price? For the gold I mean?"

"I did, but it's probably safer not to talk about such things in public, son. We have to get home safely tonight and I'd not like to be followed by some ambitious fellow that sees us as a chance for some easy cash."

Allin hung his head. "I'm sorry. I just wanted to know...."

He tailed off here, looking a little embarrassed so Dale prompted him gently "To know what?"

"Whose chain fetched the most."

For a second Dale stared at the boy and then he burst out laughing. "You're a rascal aren't you, boy?" he said scrubbing the top of the lad's head with some spirit. "You were hoping to store that up and use it against Cori some time when you want to get the last word in some squabble, weren't you?"

"No... I" Allin began and then admitted, "Well maybe. But you don't know what he's like," he protested, sounding a bit hurt that Dale should see it as so comical. "He always thinks he knows better than me about everything and I just thought that if my chain was better than his..."

"I see," Dale rubbed his beard, still amused. "Well I'm sorry to disappoint you, son but gold is sold by weight and from that perspective they were identical. You'll have to find some other way to compete with him."

"I suppose," Allin agreed gloomily, "and you had his ring too, so...." then suddenly an awful look came over his face as he remembered. "My knife! You were supposed to take that too." He pulled it out hurriedly. "You promised you'd not let me forget. Can you go back to Iestan and ask him to buy this too?"

The lad looked agitated and was waving the blade about so Dale put a firm hand on the boy's arm. "Put it away please Allin. It's not polite to draw weapons in public unless you're planning to do battle." The lad complied unwillingly as Dale went on, "and I haven't forgotten but Iestan wouldn't buy something like that. Gold is one thing - he can sell that on easily but the knife would be harder to trade. We'd have to take that to the smith - he might be interested."

"Is that where we're going now?" Allin asked almost eagerly, anxious that his gesture to supplement their funds should not be forgotten.

"We can if you like but actually I think we may be able to avoid having to sell it at all. We've got all we need for today so you could keep it if you'd rather."

"I don't mind selling it," Allin said. "If it helps."

"Right now it probably helps more for you to keep it. Unless you know what you're looking at you'd not know that your knife is of any great worth - most people wouldn't expect a lad of your age to have anything so fine - whereas gold is obvious and easily stolen. Besides, we never know when we're next going to need something to trade - perhaps with someone who has no use for gold. If it were my choice I'd keep it until such time as we really need to use it."

"All right," Allin agreed but he looked disappointed. "If you're sure I can't help."

Dale stopped and turned to look at his young companion. The boy's face was earnest, almost entreating Dale to allow him to contribute to the household effort. It must be hard, Dale decided, to be old enough to understand the extremity of their current circumstances and yet too young to be able to do anything about it. He put a comforting hand on Allin's shoulder. "You do help, Allin, but it may not be quite as you expect."

"I don't understand."

"Well, the way you help out around the cottage and caring for your sister, for example..."

"That's not the same," the boy argued scornfully. "That's just doing things."

"Ah!" Dale rubbed his beard. "Looking to make some grand gesture are you? A sacrifice that will have people falling at your feet in admiration?"

Allin looked suddenly embarrassed as Dale pointed out his less than selfless motives. Then he sighed, shrugged and muttered, "You don't understand," rather irritably.

"Or perhaps I understand a little better than you'd like." Dale smiled, but he didn't pursue the matter further. "Now, we have a lot to do, so let's get busy."

The next few hours were fully occupied laying in supplies for the cottage. Iestan had given Dale a generous price for the ring and three gold chains - the two from the boys plus the one from Verdin's medallion, still in Dale's possession until he could pass it on to the Earl's young son - so the big man was able to buy all that they needed to last them for quite some time.

Allin had followed in Dale's wake, standing by as he bought wheat and oats, seed for the garden plot and livestock - a clutch of chickens, a nanny goat and a sturdy-looking mule to help with the heavy work at the cottage. In all of these bargains, as he struck them, he arranged to leave his purchases with the vendor until they were ready to leave, so they were able to wander unhampered about the town. Not that, Dale explained, there wasn't a risk that they might come back and find something they'd bought had since been sold on to a higher bidder but if they had to spend the day accompanied by everything they had bought it would be very tiresome.

Having seen to all the immediate supplies they needed from the market traders, Dale began to think about trade agreements. He led Allin down to the river and met with a shrewd-looking fellow who, the big man explained, transported wood from Chelland to elsewhere in the country.

Dale seemed to know the fellow and instead of discussing prices and wood supplies he began by chatting idly about his occupation since they'd last met, the man's family, Dale's family and the rumours floating up from the south.

To Allin they didn't seem to be saying anything of great interest and after watching the ferryman on the river pole his flat raft across to the opposite bank and back again a few times he became restless.

Despite the fact that Dale was here to trade he still hadn't managed to get around to the subject of timber at all, preferring now to discuss weather, the prospects of the harvest and the chances of a good winter. The two men had been talking for some twenty minutes and Dale was starting to move the tradesman towards the subject of the wood industry when he heard Allin sigh restlessly and realised that this was about the fourth time he'd heard such a sound. Absorbed in the careful business of building a relationship before trying to sell his wares, and therefore not really thinking, he thrust a hand in to his money belt, pulled out a tarnished silver coin and thrust it at the boy.

"Do me a favour, son. Run down to the tanner - he's down at the end of the lane there," Dale pointed, "and get me ten foot of leather bootlace - thinnest he's got - and three dozen candles. See how good a bargain you can strike with him," the big man smirked at the other tradesman - the tanner would hardly haggle for such small items, so both men enjoyed the small joke - "and I'll come and join you there shortly. All right?"

Allin looked startled. Up until now, Dale had been quite careful to keep his young charge close by and now, all of a sudden he was being sent off on his own. But he nodded obediently and, with his hand closed tightly over the coin, began to walk in the direction Dale had pointed.

No-one took the slightest notice of a small boy off on an errand but to Allin, alone in a strange town, he could feel every eye upon him. At first he made frequent glances backward to ensure he still had Dale in his sights but then, fearfully, wondered if this would draw attention to him, so fixed his eyes to the front and tried to look nonchalant as he went to find the tanner. His heart was thumping as he walked, trying to look as if he did this every day, but at the same time worried that he looked like someone who was trying to avoid being noticed. How did one look if sent on an errand to buy bootlaces? Having never done such a thing, Allin didn't know. And what if there was someone who recognised him here? He was the son of the king after all and someone might have seen him as he rode out with his family in Castle Bremmand some time. By now, as he rounded the corner by the tavern and headed up the lane where the tanner was said to be, he was sure that his heritage must be screaming at everyone in the town and he couldn't help but glance over his shoulder to see if anyone was staring at him. He gritted his teeth firmly as he moved up the lane and out of Dale's eyesight and determined that, if anyone stopped him, he would have to pretend they were mistaken and that he was just a peasant boy on his way to buy candles. Nothing, he told himself, with grim resolve, would induce him to confirm his identity and thus betray his brother and infant sister hiding in safety in the forest.

So, with a squaring of his shoulders, Allin made his way along the side lane in search of the tannery. Off the main road, the street was narrow and grubby. There were a number of open-fronted cottages scattered along its length where different wares were being bought and sold. Towards the end stood a butchery, the floor laid with blood-spattered straw, with a side of venison and a brace of pheasant hanging from the rafters. Allin, fascinated despite himself, stood and gazed at the stocky man inside as he cut sections off a large joint of meat with single, easy strokes from a cleaver. The butcher glanced up and saw him. "Are you here to buy, or just to gawp?" he asked coldly, clearly not entertained by his young spectator.

Allin started. "Sorry. I was just looking. Excuse me," and he hurried past, still in search of the tanner. He was now feeling even more uncertain of his surroundings and began to fear he might have take a wrong turn somewhere and would never find his destination.

In fact his nose found his goal first. A little way past the butcher there came an unsavoury smell of hot tallow and there behind a wicker pen containing animals destined for slaughter stood a large open fire with a huge cauldron on top of it. Boiling in this pot was a thick dark slurry of animal fat. Standing over it was a tall dark-headed man, who was carefully skimming a layer from the top of the unappealing mixture with a ladle, and tipping it in to a bucket on the ground.

Beyond the fire and its foul smelling mixture was an open space in which stood a sloping table. Pegged out on the work surface was an animal hide, which was being unenthusiastically scraped clean of congealed meat and fat by a dull-witted looking lad of around Cori's age. Past this stood two piles of hide, one ready for curing and the other, swarming with flies and emanating the most dreadful smell, yet to be laid out and cleaned.

Allin stood transfixed for a few moments, both repelled and fascinated by the grisly scene. As he stood and watched the dark headed man at the fire looked up. "Something you wanted?" he asked mildly.

"I was looking for the tanner," he said somewhat stupidly. That he had found his man was patent and to have uttered such an idiotic remark provoked a rude response from the boy at the skins.

The tanner rebuked the lad sharply, stood the ladle up carefully in the soupy concoction on the fire and wiped his hands along the back of his tunic. "That's me. What can I do for you, young sir?" The tanner called everyone who came to him 'sir' be they rich lord or pauper child. Long ago, when he had been an apprentice to the previous tanner, he'd been taught the practice of considering everyone as a potential customer whoever they were and he wasn't about to chase away a sale on the grounds of ill manners.

The boy before him explained his errand, after which the man nodded and led the way to the stall front of his cottage where he displayed his wares.

Allin gazed around in some interest. Hanging on the walls and even from the ceiling were finely crafted leather items. Harnesses for animals of all shapes and sizes, leather caps, jerkins, other clothing items and a whole range of other things. Lying along the table were mostly shoes and sandals but also smaller items, some of which Allin couldn't guess a purpose for. To one side of the table, on a metal frame with hooks hung long straight tallow candles. They came in pairs, each two sharing a single wick, still joined from when they were made. Allin couldn't help but gaze at them in interest. As far as he was concerned, candles only came in candlesticks, mysteriously placed there whenever they burned down by some servant or other. To see them in their original form was a new experience.

"What was it? Ten foot of bootlace?" the tanner asked.

Allin nodded in reply "And three dozen candles," he added a little shyly.

The tanner nodded and counted off the long white sticks from the hooks and then laid them out on the table top. With a flourish he scooped up a few more and added them to the others. "Three dozen," he said. "Fifty six."

Allin frowned. "Three dozen's not fifty six. It's..." he stopped. His mental arithmetic was not the most wonderful so he had to think for a second before he offered, "Thirty six."

"I know that," the tanner replied a little irritably. "I *want* fifty six." seeing Allin's still puzzled look he explained, as though to an idiot, "two shill a pair for the candles, two shill per foot of bootlace. That's fifty six shill in all."

"Oh!" Allin exclaimed suddenly understanding. Fifty six shill was the price! Rather hurriedly he handed over the silver coin still clenched in his fist. The tanner took it without comment, bit it, mostly out of custom, and then delved in to the pouch at the front of his leather apron. The silver coin was soon replaced by a collection of copper ones, which the tanner glanced over in his hand and then selected a few.

"Four tenths, four shill," he commented as he handed them over to the boy. "And thank you for your custom."

"Thank you," Allin replied, and then, with the tanner looking on, began to gather up the candles.

The tanner had been able to scoop up the tallow sticks with his two great hands but Allin struggled to do the same, and every attempt he made resulted in some of the candles falling back on to the table. They were only saved from rolling along the flat surface and on to the floor by the tanner who kindly stopped them before they got too far. He watched the boy's struggles in kindly amusement for a few moments and then, when Allin also managed to drop two of the copper coins he still held in his hand and had to dive under the table to retrieve them from the dusty floor below, the tradesman decided to help. "Don't usually do this by yourself, do you lad?" He asked and Allin rose, brushing the dust from his knees.

"Yes," Allin replied hastily, not wanting to show himself up as helpless. But then he remembered Dale's warning that he shouldn't attempt to lie for the sake of it added more truthfully, "I mean...."

"I know, " the tanner grinned. "First time your Da's sent you on an errand alone and you want to prove you can do it all by yourself. Am I right?"

Allin nodded. It was the first time Dale had sent him on an errand, after all, and he did want to carry it out properly. "Except..." he began to explain that Dale wasn't his father but the tanner had seen the nod and that was all he needed to hear.

"Let me show you a trick then," he said helpfully, taking up the length of bootlace, and wrapping it deftly around the fat bundle of candles. He tied the length off and handed the whole parcel to the boy. "It's never a bad thing to get help from others. It doesn't show that you are too stupid to manage - just that you have the wisdom to ask. See?"

Allin looked at the man's smiling face and thanked him with a shy smile of his own. "I'll remember that," he said. The kindliness of the man was reassuring and his nervousness faded a little.

As he turned to leave, planning to head back down the lane and meet Dale as he came this way, one of the small leather items hanging from the wall suddenly caught his eye. It was a flower, each petal made from a separate piece of leather and pinned together at the centre with a single round heart. The petals and the heart were worked in several different colours, red, green and gold, and the whole thing was hanging on a length of bootlace looped so that it could be hung from a wall. "Oh!" Allin forgot all his fears and cried out before he could stop himself. "What's that for?"

The tanner followed his gaze. "Just a decoration. I make them from the off cuts. To brighten up a harness or decorate your home. Why? Do you want it?"

"Oh, yes," Allin said wistfully, without thinking. "My sister would love it."

The tanner plucked the little ornament off the wall. "Here you are then. Five shill."

Only then did Allin realise that he'd actually entered in to a bargain. "I can't," he said in some alarm. "It's not my money."

The tanner shrugged. "Well, say that the bootlaces cost more. Five shill per two foot, instead of four. Then no-one'll be any the wiser and your sister can have her flower. I'll not let on."

It seemed like an ideal solution and Allin almost nodded but then he hesitated. He knew full well that it was wrong and money was certainly something they had to use sparingly at the moment, so he stamped on his temptation and shook his head regretfully . "I can't," he repeated. "It wouldn't be right. Thank you all the same."

"Surely your Da wouldn't mind you buying a present for your sister, would he?" the tanner said persuasively. "That's what a good brother should do after all, isn't it?"

Beginning to feel very uncomfortable at the predicament he had got himself in to, Allin shook his head once more but could find no words to excuse himself. He was now too intimidated by the turn of events to try once more to clarify that it wasn't his father who had sent him on his errand. His upbringing told him that to turn and leave would be rude but he was beginning to think it might be a better option than staying here and continuing to be coerced by the tanner.

"I could do it for you for four shill if you like." The man was putting all his effort into the sale, for all the world as if it was a five hundred florin bargain instead of a meagre five shill and Allin found himself taking an involuntary half-step backwards, ashamed and miserable at the pressure to buy that was being placed upon him. But then a warm hand in his neck brought his rescue.

"Push him to three and it'll be a good deal," Dale's soft voice said in his ear.

The boy felt a sudden wave of relief at the return to his side of his protector and Dale, through his hand at Allin's neck could feel tension dropping away. Dale hadn't been thinking when he'd sent his young charge off on his own and when it had occurred to him what he'd done he'd finished his bargaining in a hurry - and somewhat to his detriment in the deal he had struck - and come to find the youngster. It wasn't so much that he was concerned for Allin's safety - he knew that Chelland was safe enough and, as he had already satisfied himself, as yet free of Empire troops - as it was an anxiety for the boy's lack of experience. Despite the level of familiarity that had grown between the man and boy, Dale reminded himself that Allin was a prince and as such had probably never been anywhere on his own before. In the castle and grounds there would have been nurses and servants and, had he ever ventured out in to Castle Bremmand itself it would have been with a full royal escort. So for Dale to leave him alone in a new town full of strangers would have been disconcerting for the boy and it was this concern for Allin that had sped the big man on his way to find him. The feeling of relief that passed between the boy and man in that single touch told Dale that he had been right in his guess and he cursed himself for such a careless lapse in his care for the child.

His first feeling of relief passed, Allin swung round stammering an explanation for the attempt to buy the unneeded flower.

"It's all right, son," Dale smiled, to reassure the boy that he wasn't in any trouble. "I know Faljon well enough to know that if once you give him a chance he'll do everything but throw his mother in to the bargain. If once you let him see your interest, you might just as well give up and hand over your money."

Faljon the tanner smiled at the new arrival, no longer a professional smile from salesman to customer but one of friendship to a man he knew. "Well, here's a face I've not seen in a while. This lad yours then is he?"

"Not my own, but he's in my care," Dale smiled, explaining easily where Allin had failed. "So I'll thank you not to encourage him to rook me. Five shill for two foot of bootlace indeed!" he added with a snort, to show he'd heard the devious suggestion. "If he'd told me that you'd have had me back like a shot complaining about you taking advantage of a child."

"He wasn't having any of it though," Faljon smiled. "Honest as well as a good brother. At least now I know it's you, I know you wouldn't object to a small thing like this." He picked up the leather flower from the table, and passed it to

Dale. "It's a nice piece and if the lad thinks his sister would like it, I'm sure even you'd not deny it for the sake of six shill."

"You said four," Allin corrected in some surprise. Surely the man hadn't forgotten the price already.

Faljon met Dale's eye, not in the least abashed by this attempt to push the price up. Dale didn't even look at the object of the deal, saying easily, "I'd have thought that, since I'm about to buy a good harness, you should throw it in for nothing."

Slowly Faljon smiled, "I'd forgotten what a wily sort you were," and passed the flower to Allin. "Always happy to oblige a long standing customer," he said, ruffling Allin's hair genially.

Allin was so pleased to have the flower which he knew would delight Joss, that he barely noticed his hair being messed up - something he usually hated. "Oh, thank you," he said in delight and slid the leather item carefully in to the pouch which hung from his belt so that he shouldn't lose it.

Faljon grinned at him and looked again at Dale. "Nice lad. Not your own though, you say?" The inquiry was mild, merely a friendly interest, and Dale answered in the same easy tone.

"No. He's fostered with me while his father's away."

"Ah." Faljon said wisely. "And how old are you then, young sir? Twelve? Thirteen?"

Allin looked pleased. "Ten"

"Ten? You look older. And what's your tree?"

Dale felt himself go cold at this question, for all he should have been expecting it. It was an old woodsman superstition that when you were born determined which tree you were likened to and thus your nature. For the tanner to have asked was a perfectly natural inquiry and for any ordinary lad not to know would be very unusual. For those few moments, even Dale couldn't think under what tree Allin had been born.

But, somewhat to the big man's surprise, Allin was able to answer the question for himself.

"Walnut," he said and then added with a grin. "My father always says that I couldn't be anything else - as stubborn as a wall and as hard as a nut!"

Faljon and Dale both laughed. "Fits him well," Dale added affectionately.

"You're in for a hard time then, if he's true to his tree. Especially up against yours." Then with a final smile at the dark-headed boy, the tanner got down to business. "Now, what can I do for you in the way of a harness?"

"I wouldn't have expected you to know an old woodsman superstition like the birth trees, Allin," Dale commented as they walked away some time later, the big man having examined and finally decided upon a harness which suited his purpose.

"When I was born, I was given a walnut tree. The leader of the woodsman guild, or whatever it is, gives one to the... to my father," he corrected himself from mentioning the king's name, "every time someone is born in our family. All the trees are planted in the castle grove. It's always been done, ever since Brem first came here. Some of the trees are hundreds of years old."

"I didn't know that," Dale looked interested. "That means there are trees there for your brother and sister too then?"

Allin nodded. "Joss is a hazelnut - I helped plant it - and Cori's got a beech. What did the tanner mean when he said you'd be in for a hard time with me up against you?"

Dale laughed. "You're a walnut - which means you can be inflexible, difficult and uncompromising." Allin nodded to show he knew the characteristics that could be attributed to him. "And my tree makes me unrelenting and strong-minded."

"So which tree is that?"

"I was born on the spring equinox," Dale smiled, but could see that Allin didn't know what this mean so he added dryly, "I'm under the oak."

They were almost done in Chelland, Dale having been able to buy or bargain for everything he needed for the cottage. They even had a few florins to spare so before they collected their possessions for the long journey home, they stopped off at the Tavern once more. The open courtyard was busy this time, other traders now stopping in to get something to eat or drink before heading back to their respective homes. Two serving women weaved their way between the tables, delivering drinks and foods and gathering up used crockery on the return journey inside the building.

Allin seemed somehow intimidated by the crowds, keeping himself seated close to Dale and saying little as the big man ordered food for them both. Now that the courtyard was so busy, it wasn't possible for them to get a table to themselves and they had to share with two woodsmen, one of whom was angrily complaining about the price he'd had to pay for an axe head

"Two florin, he charged me," the elderly man was saying to his younger companion. "Two florin for a plain axe head. I paid no more than fifty shill last year and he just stood there, pleased as you like, and told me it was the war that made the prices go up."

"Well, I suppose a lot of the iron has gone to making swords this summer. It must push the prices up," the other man said mildly.

"It doesn't increase them threefold. I've been working these forests for nearly fifty years and there have always been wars being fought, but it's never been used to twist every last penny out of the foresters before. If you ask me, the King would be better served by fighting less wars for other people and spending more time in ensuring his own people aren't cheated."

"Don't be a fool," the younger man retorted, annoyed but also wary of the disloyalty being shown to their king in such a public place.

"A fool am I?" came back the angry reply. "Maybe if you had to earn your own keep instead of living off me, you might find paying three times the price for things something worth complaining about." The young man opened his mouth to reply to this but before he could his older companion had swung round on Dale, seeking confirmation of his opinion. "Tell me," he demanded, "have you ever heard of anything so outrageous?"

"As what?" Dale replied mildly, even though he had been listening to every word. It wouldn't have been polite to admit he had been eavesdropping.

"Two florin for an axe head" the old man repeated in scandalised tones, "and blaming the war for the rise in prices."

"Seems a bit expensive," Dale agreed, but added evenly, "though this is the first time I've ever known Beltan rise prices since I first started coming here with my Da, so it's not as if it isn't time. I've seen the prices in Castle Bremmand and you'd be lucky to get a head for less than three florin there."

The old man scowled. "Beltan died last winter," he informed Dale coldly, "and now his son's taken up his father's trade. He knows there's nowhere else for us to go, so he's pushed the prices up since we've no choice."

"There's always choice," Dale replied. "Some artful trader will start bringing them up river from Novoris or elsewhere, and sell them at half the price. Or there are a couple of woodsmen who know how to cast iron and they'll start making for others. You'll see - if this fellow's being greedy, he'll soon learn when he loses his custom."

"That's true," the younger man said brightly, encouraged by someone else's less than pessimistic view of the smith's exorbitant charges.

"Besides," Dale went on, "if the price rise is because the iron's gone for swords then I for one am happy to pay that price for our freedom. I don't much care for the alternative."

"You believe the rumours then?" the younger man asked, looking eager at the chance to discuss the news that was floating up from elsewhere. "Do you think the Kostain empire is really looking to Bremmand's borders?"

The older man snorted derisively. "They'll find slim pickings if they try. Bremmand won't bow to anyone but the blood royal."

"And if they're given no choice? If the king has fallen, like Brophy was saying earlier?"

This was clearly some kind of long running argument, for the older man began to look annoyed. "How many times do I have to tell you? If this Empire tries to take control here, none of the people will serve them. These foreigners don't understand how things are here. Woodsmen have lived in these lands for longer than anyone can remember and they were the first of the peoples who Holy Brem made faith with. He came here and he lived among our people, right in these very forests. We taught him and he taught us and the ties that were made then won't ever be broken, no matter what. So it doesn't matter if this Darvett fellow claims he has some right by conquest of these lands. The woodsmen will continue to live and work in the forest and provide their service to the descendants of Brem, none other, just as they've always done. It isn't a question of who sits on the throne, or who killed who, it's a matter of the bond between the people and the holy blood. They won't bow to another unless God himself decrees it." There was a ferocious light in his eyes, that of a man so utterly convinced of the rightness of his position that he was almost evangelical with it.

"Well said," Dale murmured, looking satisfied. "Service to the one true King is the only service"

"Ay," agreed the old man. He glanced at his companion with a condemning air "Some would do well to remember it!" Then, as if he was determined not to be diverted from his original complaint he added, "Doesn't help me today though, does it?" he grumbled. "I've still had to pay two florin for a single axe head." But then, having had the last word on the price of axe heads and as if seeing Dale for the first time, he changed the subject. "I've not seen you about Chelland before. Where do you hail from?"

Dale entered into an easy conversation with the two woodsmen then, trading information about each other, swapping stories of forest life and discussing the latest news that was to be had. As they talked, Allin sat silent, at first listening to the conversation and then letting the chatter of voices drift over his head, the early start and long day finally catching up with him. He didn't allow himself to fall asleep but he was in a world of his own as Dale sat and talked, at first with the two woodsmen and then, when they left with others visiting the small town.

From time to time Allin would hear something that would pull him up out of his reverie - usually related to the battle between the Bremmand army and the Kostinian Empire. Someone had news that Darvett had made a fast incursion in to Bremmand but then fallen back and been defeated, although others seemed to be more pessimistic. Different voices gave different snippets of information. There were locations where troops had been seen, some word of battles and skirmishes and rumours - dozens of rumours of differing shapes and sizes -

telling of what had happened in the south. Iestan was there too, Allin realised, serving and sometimes stopping to talk, passing information he had heard back and forth and picking out new tales from his customers. He was building a picture, the boy realised, from all the scraps of information so that he could use it to gain a complete knowledge of the changes in the south. Allin tried to do the same but he was too tired to be able to pay attention and to sift through all the things he was hearing to determine what might have happened to his father. The fact that Dale, with his easy conversation, was doing the same never even occurred to the boy.

Eventually Dale gave him a gentle nudge to the shoulder and, with a few words, guided them both away from the tavern to make the long trip back to the seclusion and safety of the cottage in the woods.

The journey home took longer than the outbound walk. It was light for a large proportion of the journey, mid-summer not being far off, and when night did eventually fall, their journey was accompanied by the clean light of the full moon. Despite the assistance that this gave them, the addition of the livestock and all their other purchases slowed things down considerably. The mule had been pressed in to immediate service and loaded with sacks and boxes. Suspended either side of its neck by a rope hung a pair of slatted crates containing the half dozen chickens which squawked and flustered and took the whole business of being transported in very bad part. Having been thus laden, the mule proved itself to be true to his nature and had to be cajoled and bullied in to moving, forcing Dale to focus all his efforts on getting the wilful beast to keep going. He handed the lead rope for the goat over to Allin but as soon as she sensed herself under a weaker master the young beast took advantage of the less determined hand. She grabbed every opportunity to investigate the verges, almost dragging Allin off his feet after her in her determination to explore. It was very wearing for the lad but he gritted his teeth, persistently hauled his charge back on to the path and struggled on behind Dale. With the additional effort demanded by their livestock, it was heading towards midnight before they finally made it home.

"We're *living* here!"

When Dale came in to the Cottage clearing, some nineteen hours after first setting out, tired, towing two weary animals behind him and with Allin asleep on his shoulder, he was expecting all to be silent and calm. He was first alerted to the fact that this might not be the case when he caught glimpses of light through the trees long after the fire in the clearing should have burned down. A trifle anxiously he quickened his pace, now eager to reach home. Caution always with him he was careful to make no sound. As he came to the edge of the clearing, he loosed his hold on the two animals to give him a free hand as he peered through the tree line and took in the sight which greeted him.

There were no uninvited guests or signs of violence in the clearing. Just Trystin and Cori sitting on the log seat by the blaze, talking in low voices as they passed the night. Curled up in Trystin's lap, Joss was drowsing. For all it was late, the scene was normal and Dale allowed himself to relax. He retrieved the mule and the goat and took the last few steps that completed his journey home.

"Hello," he said softly, not wishing to wake the two sleeping children. "Everything all right here?"

"Dale!" the tutor exclaimed as Cori rose to his feet and crossed the distance between the fire and the big man.

The golden-haired youth gazed at his sleeping brother and remarked regretfully, "So it was too much for him, after all"

"He did damned well" Dale retorted defensively, not wanting to allow Cori to condemn the younger lad out of hand. "I've not had a scrap of trouble from him all day and he only allowed me help him even this last part when I forced him." He would have said more but he could see it wasn't necessary. Even in the dim light of the moon he could see that Cori was speaking with affection rather than criticism and didn't need telling.

"I'm glad to hear it," Cori murmured, as he reached over and rubbed his brother's back gently to wake him. "Hey, there Pup," he called softly. "Time you were in bed, I think."

Allin lifted his head from Dale's shoulder blearily, trying to make sense of what was being said to him. Then, as he focussed on where he was, he shot an accusing look at Dale. "You said you'd wake me before we got home."

Dale couldn't deny it. Allin had been so reluctant to give in to his obvious fatigue that the big man had only been able to convince him to agree to be carried on the promise that he would be woken in good time to walk the last few steps and thus disguise his need for assistance from his brother. "I did," Dale apologised, "but I wasn't expecting us to have such a reception awaiting us. I thought it would be enough just to wake you once we reached the clearing."

112

"It doesn't matter anyway, does it Pup?" Cori smiled, helping Allin to slide to the ground. "You've had a long day, so who's to mind if you needed a bit of help? I'm sleepy myself." He glanced at the laden animals, now standing with drooping heads in the clearing. "You seem to have brought back quite a haul for us, too. Did you have a good time?"

With an arm about his brother's shoulder he led him away, listening with interest to Allin's eager description of Chelland, pausing only to lift Joss from Trystin's lap, bearing both youngsters away to bed.

"You had a good trip I see," Trystin commented mildly as he watched the three children vanish in to the cottage, also eying the livestock standing wearily at Dale's side.

"Not bad," Dale agreed, as he towed the goat and the mule to the side of the cottage and tethered them there.

"Was there any... news?" Trystin had followed him and was looking on in tense expectation.

The big man shook his head, lifting the two crates of chickens to the ground. They grumbled briefly and then settled back in to sleep. "Rumours by the barrel load, but that's all. Chelland is too small and isolated to get news so quickly and by the time anything reaches them it's been through so many people that it is a long way from the truth."

"It was big enough to provide you with plenty of supplies," the scholar commented, once again taking in the vast array of things Dale had brought back. "All this is excessive just to provide a bit of background colour, isn't it? I'm sure the money could have been better spent."

"Give me a hand here, will you Trystin," the big man said abruptly, as he lifted one of the sacks off the mule's back. "These need to go indoors, or they'll get damp. Don't worry about putting anything away properly, though. Dump it in the store. We can sort it all through in the morning."

Trystin glared at the soldier for a moment. He'd been shut down. Whatever reason Dale had for bringing such a wide array of supplies and livestock, he wasn't going to share it with the scholar, or even allow the slender man to ask about it.

Trystin was getting tired of the fact that Dale was the only one who seemed to have an idea of what was going on and was not prepared to share his plans with anyone else. It was as if the big man didn't trust him or didn't think him capable of understanding what was intended .The resentment Trystin felt at being so belittled was growing by the day. He was a highly educated, intelligent man and he was perfectly capable of understanding whatever simple-minded plans the soldier might have in store. His opinions were at least worthy of consideration, only the woodsman disregarded Trystin as if he were worthless. He took the sack which Dale had passed casually to him, staggered slightly under the weight, which was far more than he had expected, and hauled the load into the cottage as directed, seething to himself at the appalling way he was being treated by the arrogant soldier.

When he returned, Dale, not aware of the slim man's antipathy, moved the conversation on to a topic that had been puzzling him. "How have things been here, today? Is everything all right?" he asked.

"Yes, everything's fine. Why shouldn't it be?" Trystin assured him frostily.

"Only that I wasn't expecting to see you still up and waiting for us like that. You knew we would be late. I expected you all to have long since gone to bed."

Trystin considered this for a few seconds. In truth, the day at the cottage had been a hard one. However little Trystin cared for Dale, he couldn't deny the role the man played as their protector and, without him, both he and Cori had been far less confident. Being alone in the deserted clearing, they had done their best to keep busy but even that hadn't helped. They had felt tense and nervous all day, constantly on the lookout for Dale's return or a stranger's arrival. When the long day was finally over, neither one of them was in the least bit willing to sleep so, without even the need to discuss it, they had sat together by the fire, until Dale and Allin came home.

The last thing Trystin wanted to admit, however, was that they were there because they were afraid. Dale clearly thought him useless enough as it was and the tutor wasn't about to give him evidence of the fact. He had to tell the man something though, so he chose to reveal the reaction of the third member of the party who was left behind. "We none of us remember that Joss, small as she is, sees and hears as well as anyone. When she woke to find you and Allin gone this morning she was inconsolable. We couldn't convince her that you would be coming back and kept insisting that you were going to be gone forever 'like the others.' It's unsurprising that she should not believe us, when she's been getting evasive answers to every question she's asked about her mother. Our telling her that you and Allin would be back 'soon' wasn't in the least bit helpful. Nothing we could do or say would made her settle and in the end she was wandering about like a lost soul trying to see where you might have gone. Getting her to go to bed was impossible and she insisted that, if you were coming back as we'd promised, she should stay up and wait for you. So we all sat here, keeping the girl company, while we waited. She had not long dropped off to sleep when you came back."

"Poor little mite," Dale murmured, thinking of how distressed the little girl must have been. "With most of her family going and not coming back..."

"Exactly. It's been a bit trying," Trystin sighed.

"And catching, no doubt," the big man remarked sagely.

"Meaning?" Trystin tried to sound as if he had no idea what Dale meant.

"Having Joss insisting you were never going to see us again must have been difficult for Cori as well. Even when you know something isn't so, her distress must have affected him too."

"Perhaps a little," Trystin agreed, reluctant to allow Dale to think ill of the Prince. "He's coped with her very well."

"He's a good lad." Then he grinned reassuringly at Trystin, "but I imagine our little girl is going to be very pleased to see Allin when she wakes in the morning."

"Indeed she will," Trystin nodded and then unthinkingly allowed his guard to slip slightly as he admitted, "I don't think any of us have particularly enjoyed today."

Allin would have liked to have slept late the following morning, after such a long day but even the exhaustion that seemed to seep in to his very bones and which had finally forced him to give in to Dale's insistence that he have help on the journey home was not enough to keep him asleep against the persistent braying of the mule at the onset of dawn.

He fought against it for a while, pulling the blankets over his head in an effort to shut out the noise but when the animal's song also woke Joss his hope of remaining asleep were dashed for good and all. On seeing her brother in the bed beside her the little girl squealed with delight and crawled all over him in excitement. Allin pushed her off grumpily but nothing could diminish her pleasure at his return, or convince her that allowing him to get back to sleep would be a more kindly way of showing her affection for him than attempting to play a game with him.

Finally giving up, Allin rose crossly, dressed himself, helped Joss to do likewise at her demand and then led the way in to the main living area of the cottage with his sister clinging to his arm like bindweed. Cori and Trystin were both seated at the table, just finishing off their breakfast, while Dale stood at the small fireplace.

"Good morning," the tutor greeted them cheerily. "We wondered if you'd manage to sleep through the morning song of our new arrivals but it would seem not."

Allin scowled. "Joss woke me. She screamed in my ear, crawled all over me and now she won't leave me alone. Why can't you" - he gave the little girl a shove to get her to give him more space - "go somewhere else?"

Cori studied his brother's stormy face, his little sister's plaintive one and, rising to his feet, executed a rapid rescue to avoid bloodshed. "C'mon Joss, why don't we go and say good morning to the donkey. We can see if he wants any breakfast." And without giving the child a chance to argue he swept her briskly out of the cottage and in to the sunshine.

"I think you'll find it's a mule," Trystin corrected as he followed them both outside, shooting Dale an unsympathetic glance which clearly said, 'Enjoy your temperamental breakfast companion,' before escaping the sour atmosphere in the cottage.

Allin seated himself at the table irritably. "I don't know what's the matter with her," he complained. "She won't leave me alone. I almost fell over her at least twice when I was trying to get up."

"Well," Dale said thoughtfully, putting a bowl of hot porridge in front of the boy, "maybe she missed you and was glad to see you back."

"We were only gone for a day," came the indignant reply. "She doesn't need to crawl all over me and all but drag my arm off. It's not as if we were gone long."

"True, but things are different for Joss now, just as they are for you." Dale sat down beside him and pointed out gently, "In the last few weeks everyone around her has been going away and so far, none of them has managed to come back. She's not old enough to understand *why* things have been changing but she knows that they have, so it's not surprising that she should feel upset when someone else she cares about isn't there when she wakes up. Especially since no-one thought to tell her that we were going and explain that we were coming back again. According to Trystin she was pretty upset yesterday and wasn't prepared to believe we'd be back just because he or Cori told her so."

Allin gazed at Dale in horror. "I didn't think..." he began and then got to his feet. "And then I was rotten to her. I should go and talk to her - say I'm sorry."

Dale put a restraining hand on his arm. "It can wait until you've eaten, son. She's seen you now so she knows it's all right. Once you've had breakfast, you can go and join her and Cori, and give her a bit of reassurance."

Allin nodded and resumed his seat. Suddenly a pleased look came over his face. "I've got that flower thing for her too. She'll like that."

"I imagine she will, judging by the collection of dead weeds we seem to be acquiring in here." He gestured with his head towards a corner of the room where Joss would sit and play, and in which she stored the flowers she liked to pick whenever she was able. They didn't last of course and the result was a sorry-looking pile of dried blooms, which were beginning to be scattered around the cottage as the air was stirred by the movements of its occupants and the summer breezes that wandered in when the door was left standing open.

Allin grinned across at the pile. "Maybe I should explain to her about keeping flowers in water. Then they might last a bit longer."

That was a full day for the little community at the cottage. In the morning Trystin set Cori and Allin to their lessons, while Dale worked outside, chopping, quartering and hewing timbers so that they would be ready to haul to Chelland to begin the agreed supply to Kurop, the wood trader. Then in the afternoon, when he had the two boys to help him, they worked together to build the accommodation for the livestock.

First was a chicken run, woven out of willow saplings about a frame of poplar branches. Dale hammered the narrow stakes in to a rectangle about fifteen feet long and five feet wide, and then showed Cori and Allin how to weave the flexible willow boughs in between, to make a solid wall. Even Joss got in on the task, helping by carrying the saplings from the pile where Dale had placed them and handing them to Cori and Allin as they needed a fresh one to feed in to the weave. Then she became eager to help further, weaving a sapling or two herself in to the wall. She didn't make a particularly good job of it, not having the strength to work the wider end of the saplings or turn them back on themselves at the end of each row and unable to push it down hard on to the weave below, as Dale had shown the boys. However, Cori observed, as he pushed her weave down and tidied the ends, it seemed only fair that she too should help with the building of the run, making its construction a family affair.

One of the narrow ends of the run was left open and, as the children built up the sides, Dale planted another quartet of stakes in to the ground a little way off and wove them skilfully in to another wall. When he had finished, he pulled the complete hurdle up from the ground, trimmed the end and then fixed in to the open end with supple leather straps to make hinges. This made a door so that, he explained, they would be able to get in and out of the run to feed the chickens and fetch eggs.

Allin worked alongside his brother as he was bidden, but he was tired and fractious and there were several squabbles between him and Cori during the day. He was equally difficult with Dale and while he did as he was asked, raised objections irritably where he could. In particular he couldn't see the point of the chicken run. At the palace, he pointed out crossly, the chickens had always been left loose in the castle farmyard and they had never wandered off. Why they had to spend all this time making a pen for them, he couldn't understand and made his objection known to the big man.

"It would take a fairly bold fox to have stolen a chicken from inside the castle walls," Dale had observed with a patient smile. "Hereabouts they are more likely to come past at night and help themselves to our chickens." He then explained further that chickens would scratch anywhere they thought there might be food and that would mean they would need to be penned to prevent them eating every last seed from the garden. "Much as I want the chickens to be well fed, I'd rather it wasn't at the expense of our harvest." With a grumbling acknowledgement that this made sense, Allin returned to the building up of the wicker walls.

Once the run was complete it was time to build the hen house so that the chickens would have seclusion and safety to lay eggs.

Under Dale's guidance, Cori and Allin learned how to build a hen house by first hammering stakes in to the ground to make corners and then nailing rough-hewn planks against them to make solid walls, with a bag of nails that the soldier had thoughtfully purchased the day before. Then, when Dale decreed that the walls were tall enough they placed a row of shallow boxes inside, which Dale had made up from short lengths of planking, and laid dried grass in the boxes so that the hens could make nests. Then finally, they fitted a flat plank roof to the top. This was made in two pieces, one section lying over the top of the other and fixed with more leather hinges so that it could be folded back to allow access to the house. From here the eggs could be retrieved each morning.

"Assuming our ladies decide to lay," Dale remarked sounding a trifle doubtful.

"Any reason why they shouldn't?" asked Cori. He peered dubiously at the five hens and the cockerel still confined in the slatted cases in which they had been transported the previous day. They were huddled in the corners of the boxes, looking thoroughly disconsolate.

"They're full grown," came the reply from the big man. "The fellow that sold them to me assured me that they were still laying, but they're past their prime and they were suspiciously cheap. To be sure of good layers, I'd have had to buy pullets - young birds only hatched this last season - but they would have cost too much."

"Hmm." Cori rubbed his finger under his nose thoughtfully, not noticing the stripe of grime he was leaving across his face. "I suppose if they don't lay, we can eat them?"

Dale nodded. "We can, though it's an expensive way of buying meat. Still, while we fatten them up for the pot they serve nicely to make us look like a normal woodsman family, complete with livestock." Then he picked up the two crates and carried them over to the newly-made run.

Allin and Joss were standing side by side outside the chicken run as Dale approached, looking absurdly excited at the prospect of their own construction being put to use. Neither of them had ever made something like this before - carpentry and building being skills that princes were never expected to require. Even Cori was feeling very proud of that afternoon's work and as Dale put the boxes in to the run, pulled the side away from them and shooed the birds out in to the wider space, the youth said, somewhat grandly, "I think we should mark this construction as the first of many acts of collaboration between the five of us. May our friendship be long and fruitful."

Allin groaned loudly at this, never particularly patient with the pomposity of his fifteen-year-old brother, especially not today, and said scornfully, "It's a chicken run. Anyone would think you'd just founded a kingdom."

There was a frozen pause at this rather unfortunate choice of words and then seeing Cori about to respond to his brother with some regrettable remark, Dale said hurriedly, "So, these chickens need feeding every day. Who's going to volunteer to do that?"

He was planning to pick on one of the arguing boys to assign to this task but before he could, Joss grabbed his hand eagerly. "Me, me," she begged. Oblivious to the tension between her two brothers and fascinated by the new additions to the homestead she could only think that she would be able to visit the chickens every day. "And the donkey, please Dale. And the goat."

"All right," Dale agreed amiably. "And you Allin," he added, "can help her and gather any eggs we get. With both of you looking after the animals we should stand a good chance of them not being forgotten too often." Allin scowled but he didn't argue - for all he'd been crotchety all day, he'd been careful not to do anything to further upset his sister. Dale could see the lad wasn't keen, however, so he added, by way of compensation, "And since you two are going to take charge of our little farm you can come up with names for the animals. Think you can do that?"

Allin's face brightened a little at this prospect and Joss clapped her hands in delight. "We should call the donkey 'Noisy'," she declared instantly and even Allin laughed at this wonderfully appropriate name.

He took his sister's hand and led her towards the goat "Only if we can call the goat 'Stubborn.' She had to look behind every bush all the way home."

"Then we should call her 'Nosey'," Joss argued.

"We can't have 'Nosey' *and* 'Noisy.' They wouldn't know which one you were calling," Allin retorted, but with a laugh, as they began to debate the names in earnest.

"I don't see that it would make much difference," Dale muttered. "I can't see either one of those wretched animals ever coming if somebody called them!"

He turned, smiling, to see Trystin standing a few feet away. He'd come out to look at the craftsmanship of his three students but now he was looking at Dale with a furious expression on his face.

"Cori," Dale said, without even looking at the lad, "go and wash your face. You've got dirt and sawdust all over it."

"But…" he began to protest, then he too saw the expression on Trystin's face and nodded. "Yes. All right," and he was gone.

There was a long silence, the two men just standing and facing each other but then, finally Trystin spoke. His voice was heavy with venom, and his anger was barely under control. "We are not going to use this place as a temporary stopping point, are we?"

"Of course we are," Dale replied, deliberately misunderstanding. "We're here aren't we? It's as I said. We sit it out here for a while and then…"

"I've just looked over what you brought in to the store yesterday and it isn't just short term supplies. Oh, there's grain and food all right but there are also seeds and a work harness. Not to mention the livestock. You don't buy things like that for a short stay. You have no intention of following Lord Verdin's orders of getting the royal children to Hast, have you?"

"Of course I have," the big man retorted, knowing full well that other options and possibilities were already presenting themselves to him but not wishing to share them with the scholar who, he had now learned, could not deal with the harsh realities of what it was going to take to survive. It was better for Trystin and easier for Dale to keep the man in the dark and get on with the job in hand regardless.

"Then why waste money on the kinds of supplies that are going to allow us to live here forever. We aren't waiting here until it's safe. We're *living* here."

Dale shrugged. "Contingencies. That's all. You're making too much of it."

"Am I? Am I *really*? Well tell me this then, Master Ronas…."

"We've decided to call the mule 'Shout'," Allin said abruptly from behind them in a voice that was a little too high and loud. The two men wheeled round and stared at him in surprise, both wondering how long he had been there and how much he'd heard. Joss, Dale noted thankfully, was not with him so she at least had not seen the sight of the two men in dispute. The big man swallowed down his irritation and, finding a smile for the boy, said easily.

"Shout, eh? That sounds… descriptive. Why did you decide against Noisy in the end?" He wandered up to him and began to lead him away, back to where the animals were tethered.

"Because he isn't really noisy. I mean he's quiet now. It's just that, when he does make a noise, he's really loud. Joss said it was like no-one had ever taught him not to shout…"

Trystin watched them walking away, not quite believing that that big man had dismissed their conversation in favour of a trivial discussion with Allin. Having got to a point where he could actually challenge Dale with something more solid than a sense of being left in the dark, when he actually had evidence of the man's deceit, all the soldier had done was find a diversion and walk away. For a brief moment Trystin contemplated going after them and insisting that Dale justify his ever more arrogant behaviour but then he realised how futile it would be and so, once more seething with frustration, he went back inside the cottage.

With Dale's return from the supply run to Chelland there was now plenty to keep the children occupied. As well as looking after the animals there were seeds to plant in order to try and reap a harvest of vegetables. It was late in the season for planting and it meant that Allin and Cori were tasked with the additional chore of bringing up water from the little brook which wound its way through the trees nearby, in order to keep the delicate seedlings watered.

Dale also had an order of wood to fulfil and he put both boys to work helping him prepare the first batch for delivery. He had finally shown Allin how to use an axe although it didn't work out quite as the boy had hoped. Instead of being able to wield the same tree axe which Dale used, he found himself presented with a small hand axe instead, with a T-shaped head. Even before he saw the scowl, Dale knew that Allin would want to protest but he diverted the complaint by repeating his promise that he would teach the boy to use a long-handled axe as well. "But right now you'll be more use to me if you can master that. It's used for cutting off the rough edges and making the logs true so that they can be put to more use. There's quite an art to doing a good job, so don't be in too much of a hurry to look down your nose at it."

Having been issued something akin to a challenge in mastering the T-axe and buoyed by the fact that Dale was prepared to spend time with him helping him perfect the technique of hewing the lengths of wood to a smooth finish, Allin soon proved himself to be quite content to concentrate his efforts on the smaller alternative to his main wish.

While Cori and Allin began to spend more of their days with Dale, Trystin was left to tend to the cottage and look after Joss. Having always preferred to serve himself while living at the castle, the scholar was proving to be a good cook and thus even he had to admit that being set to provide for the domestic needs of the little household made sense but even in this Dale had assumed that housework and drudgery would fall to Trystin while he spent his time wandering the forest with the boys. The bitterness at this further relegation of himself simply added to the offence the thin man was already feeling.

It was inevitable, therefore, that matters between Dale and Trystin would eventually come to a raging head.

It all started innocently enough one afternoon, perhaps a week or so after Dale had returned from Chelland. The big man was nearly ready to haul the first load of wood down to the main forest path, where it would be met by one of the wood haulers that worked the forest and delivered to Kurop, the trader from Chelland. He bound up the logs and harnessed the mule to the sled the big man had built for the purpose. There was an air of satisfaction about him, as if his plans were all slotting in to place, and Trystin tried once again to get at the truth of what the soldier had planned.

The scholar opened with a few idle-sounding questions about the deal that had been struck between the big man and the trader, asking about frequency and the details of what they could expect to get in return. When Dale explained that they would receive regular supplies of food Trystin asked if it might not have made more sense to get gold instead. "We'll need it on our journey north."

"We need to not starve as well," the soldier replied, a little brusquely.

Once again, biting back his irritation at being spoken to like a halfwit, Trystin tried to find out how long Dale was planning for them to stay at the cottage and once again Dale turned the question aside with an evasive response and a muttered remark that he needed to get on. But, as the big man tried to walk away, Trystin stopped him.

"Not this time," Trystin declared. "You'll stay and answer my questions for once. How long are you planning that we stay here?'

"This doesn't serve any purpose..." Dale began, sighing with exasperation at the man's stubbornness.

"You mean it's too much trouble to you to bother to explain anything to others? Or is it that you know I won't agree with your plans to hold these children here?"

"Don't be a fool Trystin. There's work to be done and I don't have time to stand about arguing with you."

There was something shifty about the way Dale was trying to evade him, Trystin decided, and then, in a flash of inspiration, he realised why. "That's it, isn't it?"

"What is?" Dale growled, but he tried once again to turn and leave. But Trystin wasn't giving up this time and put himself directly in the big man's path.

"You're going to keep the children here. You lost your family so now you've seen this as a chance to take over someone else's."

"Now that really *is* ridiculous!" Dale said, trying to sidestep the man.

"That's why you killed those men, isn't it? Because if they were able to report back, we'd have had to continue the journey to Hast. With them dead, with no-one any the wiser, it will be all right for us to stay here indefinitely." Another thought struck him. "How long before you slit my throat as well Dale? How long before you decide that I'm in the way for your attempt to usurp the royal family? How close am I to being removed by you?"

"You're getting quite close to my knocking your teeth in," Dale snarled, his temper rising in response to the accusations being hurled at him.

"I'm sure. I must be quite an inconvenience to your plans, mustn't I?"

"Now look," Dale said heavily. "I have no intention of keeping the royal family, or to try and pass them off as my own and I never have. I am following the orders that the Lord Protector gave me; that I should get the children to Hast, but above all else to keep them safe. He told me to do whatever it takes and that's exactly what I am doing."

"I don't believe you."

"That's up to you. But I'm going to carry on following those orders until I'm told otherwise and if you try to get in my way I'll walk right over you. Their safety is my responsibility and everything I do is for their protection. Nothing more and nothing less."

"Prove it then!" Trystin cried. "Prove that you intend for them to be brought to Hast."

"I don't need to prove anything to you, Master Scholar." He used the title with derision, clearly showing what he thought about the fussy and troublesome man.

"Yes you do. Because if I'm not satisfied, I leave here today and head for Hast by myself. If King Perrold hears that you have his grandchildren held captive here, you can be sure he'll send some of his men to retrieve them from you." Trystin was boiling now, his face pinched with rage, and his voice was raised in fury as he declared his intent. "Tell me when we will be heading for Hast, tell me how you plan that we should get there and tell me why we are waiting here when we could be on the road right now."

Dale looked at the man, and seeing the determination in the slim face, decided he'd have to give on the point. So, in clipped tones, he rapped out, "I don't know when we can leave, or how we're going to get to Hast, and we're waiting here until I can get the information I need to work those things out."

"Meaning?"

"Meaning that we are safe here - as I have told you at least a dozen times, except that you are too damned full of yourself to hear it - and it means that I can leave the children here, knowing they won't come to any harm, while I try to find out exactly how much of a grip the Empire has on the Kingdom."

"You were in Chelland...." Trystin began to argue, but Dale cut across him sharply.

"Which is too far out of the way to get the kind of information I need. If we want to know what's really going on then Chelland isn't the place to get it."

"Then...?"

"I have to go to Castle Bremmand."

Trystin stared at him, momentarily too astonished by this revelation to speak. Finally, he found his voice. "Are you mad?" He glared at the big man in furious indignation. "You're planning to leave us here, alone in the middle of the forest, where anything could befall us, and head straight back to Castle Bremmand?"

"That's right. That's where the information I need will be."

"That's where Darvett will be! You're planning to walk straight in to what is likely to be his most well-defended holding point. What if you're taken? Then

Darvett will know exactly where to look to find the royal children and we'll be sitting ducks."

"I won't get caught and, even if I did, do you think for a second I'd give the location of this place away?" Dale felt his anger rising at the suggestion that he might betray his charges and at Trystin's continued interference in his decisions.

The scholar reacted to Dale's assertions with insulting scorn. "Then you're not just a fool, you're arrogant as well. You are so full of conceit and determined to do what you want, that you don't even consider the possibility that anything might go wrong. You act as if you are in charge and yet you fail to anticipate even the most simple of possibilities or allow anyone else to have a say - even to know what it is you are planning. You're not a leader, you're a liability, and you have been since the first day."

"Oh, really? And how far would we have got under your control, Master Scholar? Not too damned far, I'd guess. If you spent less time whining and picking faults with what others do and concentrated more on being useful instead of dead weight, then maybe I'd be inclined to share a few thoughts with you. As it is, *I* am in charge and I don't have time to waste on arguing with you and having to explain my every action to a milk-fed gentleman who has no idea of what it takes to stay alive and who wants to bury his head in his apron every time something he doesn't like comes along."

"And who has us hiding out in a forest?" Trystin hurled back at him, his blood thoroughly up by now. "Who murders men in their sleep like a filthy assassin? Who...?"

"*Enough!*" Cori was there, a furious look on his face. The tone of his voice was enough to render both men silent for a moment and then they turned on him, both speaking at once to state their position. Once again, the young man cut across them. "I said *enough*! I don't care what you are arguing about, or who has what to say. I can't think that there is any excuse for this kind of display. You are behaving like a pair of children and I want it to stop."

"It would never have started if Dale didn't constantly act as if he's the only one with an opinion, or a thought worth hearing," Trystin snarled.

"Perhaps if you remembered from time to time that I'm in charge and didn't argue at every turn...." Dale fired back but then remembering the presence of the younger man he snapped out, unthinking, "and in any case Cori, this has nothing to do with you."

The golden head come up, as Cori pushed his chin higher. With calm but frosty tones he replied, "Am I to be obliged to remind you who I am, *Captain* Ronas?" He swung round and threw his glare on to Trystin "Or to you, Master Scholar?"

Both men were stopped dead in their tracks by the remembrance that the young man standing before them was a royal prince and outranked them both by a significant degree.

Dale was the first to recover himself and, swallowing down his anger, he replied in formal tones, "No Your Highness, that won't be necessary. I meant no disrespect." Trystin added his own apology and then Dale went on "This is merely a..."

"...a difference of opinion?" Cori finished for him, smoothly. "Yes. Last time there was a 'difference of opinion' you assured me that it would not trouble me or my family. Well, they look pretty damned troubled to me." With a gesture of his head he indicated to where Allin and Joss were standing, holding one another's hand and Joss with her fingers in her mouth. Both looked worried and distressed by the ferocious argument they had witnessed.

Dale stared at them for a second and then swore under his breath. How could he have allowed his temper to get the better of him and risk the confidence of the children as a result?

"How long have they been there?" Trystin was asking worriedly.

"Longer than I have," Cori replied. "I am not pleased."

"No, Sire, I can imagine," Dale replied contritely. "I'm sorry. It wasn't intended that they should have to see this."

"If I thought it was intentional Dale, I'd..." He paused for a moment, trying to work out what he could do to the man who was several inches taller than him and could probably swat him like a fly. He decided not to bother with an idle threat and instead said, "This is hard enough for them as it is. I hardly need to remind you that we are stuck together for the foreseeable future and that they rely on you for support. Seeing you hurling abuse at one another and behaving like bad-tempered brats is not going to help them."

"I know," Dale agreed, and he took a step towards the two youngsters. "Perhaps I should..."

"I'd rather you didn't," Cori stated crisply. "I'll attend to my family. You would better serve by doing whatever it was you were doing before this absurd display began - both of you. And by keeping away from one another, since you are clearly incapable of behaving civilly towards one another."

And, with this last rebuke leaving both men thoroughly chastened, Cori turned and walked over to where his brother and sister were standing, spoke a few words to them and then led them away from the clearing.

Dale took Cori's suggestion to heart and headed out in to the forest, working alone among the trees, all the while cursing himself for a fool. He'd allowed Trystin's petulant insults and idiotic behaviour get to him and as a result had given the young royals cause to doubt his ability to protect them. He needed them to trust him and to follow his lead so that, should real danger arise, they'd obey him without question. Now, thanks to that wretched scholar he could find himself back at the beginning again, having to build a friendship with these lost and frightened children.

That Trystin was the cause of the problems was clear in his mind and while he was annoyed with himself for losing his temper, not once did it occur to him that Trystin might have a good cause for complaint.

He remained away from the clearing for the rest of the day. It irked him a little that his prolonged absence allowed the scholar the opportunity to attempt to sway Cori and the children to his way of thinking but he wanted to avoid a further confrontation with Trystin and felt sure that this wouldn't be possible should their paths cross. He worked in the forest until the light faded and he was forced to stop, walking slowly back to the cottage in the darkness. The sun set late at that time of year, so he expected the rest of the household to be asleep by the time he returned. He was wrong however. Sitting by the fire in the clearing was Cori.

"I would have thought you'd be in bed."

"I wanted to talk to you," the youngster said. "To both you and Trystin. About earlier"

"I see." Dale kept his voice even, but he felt his temper start to rise. "May I ask what he's been saying?"

Cori gave him a cool look. "We've not spoken today. I've been occupied with Allin and Joss and I don't especially wish to hear a one-sided argument anyway. If I ask him to come out so that we can talk are you prepared to be civil?"

"I am always prepared to be civil, if others are civil to me," Dale said with great dignity.

"Good!" Cori got to his feet and, with a stern glance that momentarily made Dale feel like a naughty child being rebuked, vanished into the cottage.

When the young man returned, he had Trystin at his side. The scholar's thin face was bland but there was a look about his mouth that suggested his neutrality was being maintained only at the cost of some considerable self-control. Dale had remained standing while he waited for the return and it was only at Cori's instruction that he took a seat on one of the log sections, keeping his distance from Trystin in some hazy reasoning that by being further away from him, there would be less opportunity for disagreement.

"There cannot be a repeat of today," Cori stated firmly. "We cannot continue if you both treat one another as enemies. If we lose sight of the true enemy then we are lost." Dale nodded at this, for the moment hoping that Cori would now put Trystin in his place and allow him to get on with the job in hand. "If matters are to be settled between you, then it would strike me that a good starting point would be for each of you to state your grievance and then..."

"I hardly think..." Trystin began, looking uncomfortable but Cori cut him short crisply.

"I am still talking, Trystin. Kindly do me the courtesy of allowing me to finish." The scholar was so astonished by the sharp rebuke that he subsided at once. "As I was saying," Cori went on, "once each of you has stated your cause for complaint, without squabbling like children and being determined to force your own view upon the other, we might be able to find a way to resolve matters."

"Now," he glanced at both of them briefly. "Who would like to go first?"

There was a pause as both men eyed one another suspiciously then, coolly, Dale said, "Trystin should. I have no particular complaint against him but I'd be interested to hear what it is that he finds so objectionable about me."

Trystin opened his mouth to protest to the implication of fault that Dale had made, but Cori was quicker. "I should make it clear now that I have no patience for sly attempts at insult or snide remarks. Try it again Dale and I'm going to lose my temper. That goes for you too, Trystin. I expect you both to behave like gentlemen." He threw out a disgusted glance. "I trust you both know how to do that, despite recent evidence to the contrary?" He got a nod from both men. "Good. Trystin then, since Dale has laid the floor open to you - what is your case against him?"

"I wouldn't consider it to be a 'case' against him exactly," Trystin began slowly, "but I am concerned at the level of authority he seems to have assumed since we came here. He has made a number of decisions of not insignificant consequence without any consultation, or indeed any belief that consultation would be necessary."

"With whom would you expect him to consult?" Cori asked. "When it comes to deciding how to live out here, neither you nor I would be particularly useful as a guide to him."

"It's not a question of domestic matters - although he does seem to make all the decisions there as well - it is on far more important matters that he is taking a high-handed approach."

"Such as?" Cori prompted. "Give me an example."

"Well..." Trystin hesitated, thinking fast and then, because he was feeling sufficient malice toward Dale to want to spread it around, he said, "I would have thought that the decision to commit murder - multiple murder, I should say - in our name should have involved a little more thought of those whom he was claiming to kill for."

Dale drew his breath in sharply. Even in the darkness he could see that Cori looked shocked and it made the big man boil that Trystin had used such low methods to make his own case. Cori swivelled his head to look at Dale for a moment and then turned back. "How so?" Cori asked. "Tell me about this claim of murder."

Trystin described the incident of the five Empire soldiers in some detail, to his credit being truthful in his description but he couldn't disguise his own feelings of revulsion at what had happened. As a result, the impression was clearly given to Cori that Dale was a brutal killer who hadn't hesitated for a second in wiping out the men who, he had decided, were a threat to them and had probably relished the experience. "And this is the man whom you have taking your young brother away for days at a time to Chelland," Trystin finished with some anger.

"Yes," Cori said slowly. "I see." He paused, took a steadying breath and then prompted, "Is this your only concern, or is there more?"

"Cori. Sire." Dale protested. Was he to be allowed no opportunity to put forward his side of the story?

"You'll have your turn, Dale," Cori assured him. "You have my word that this will be equitable."

The big man subsided, not satisfied but prepared to let matters proceed for now, allowing Trystin to put forward more complaints against the big soldier.

Now that Trystin had begun to hit his stride and feel that, finally, his point of view was being heard, he began to pour out his complaints about the way he was being treated. How Dale seemed to exclude him, to consider him incapable of doing more than drudge work, to deride him and to generally treat him as if he had nothing to contribute. What was more, Dale seemed to have taken steps to act in direct contradiction of their goal. The cottage was being made into their home - all the evidence pointed to the fact that they were to remain in Bremmand, when they had specifically been instructed to make their way to Hast. "And today," Trystin finished in bitter resentment "I learn that he has decided that not only will we remain here but that he will leave us here alone while he goes back to Castle Bremmand where he's well-known and would be easily recognised. He's of the palace guard and he isn't exactly unremarkable.

"What's more, he is the only trained soldier standing between us and harm if someone were to come upon us here. I'm not concerned for myself particularly, but for you brother and sister and, of course, yourself. If he leaves us here, we'd be all but defenceless. I know you know how to fight," he looked at Cori, "but you're unproven and I don't even have the most basic of abilities with a sword, and yet he has decided to leave us all unprotected."

"Hmmm," was all Cori said and then, seeing that Trystin seemed to be running out of things to complain about he turned to the soldier. "What about you, then Dale? You said you had no complaint of Trystin but I imagine you have a few observations to make on his concerns."

"One or two," he said dryly.

"Don't you always," Trystin muttered bitterly causing Cori to give him a sharp look.

Dale decided to ignore this and instead got straight to the point. "I have a job to do. Your safety is my first concern - my *only* concern. Everything I do is driven by that."

"Including murder?" Trystin couldn't help himself from saying.

"It's war. They were Empire soldiers. They are the enemy and they could not be allowed to get back to their barracks to let anyone else know about us. I explained that to you once already but you seem incapable of accepting it."

"Gentlemen, please," Cori remonstrated, at the voices beginning to be raised in anger. "Apart from anything else, if you start bawling at one another, you'll wake Allin. Trystin, Dale heard you out; please show him similar courtesy. Go on, please, Dale. You were saying you have a job to do."

"Yes. I do. And I'll do it. I have no particular complaint against Trystin, as I said, although I do find having my every decision and action questioned and argued against irritating. It's a waste of time and pointless. I'm sure Master Trystin is a good and worthy scholar, and presumably a good teacher but this isn't a schoolroom. It's the real world and out here we're in the middle of war. He's out of his element but I'm not. This is *my* world, it's what I do and I'm getting a little tired of being challenged by someone who probably only sees the light of day once a year, let alone understands what it takes to survive out here.

"Yes, I killed those men because they were a threat. Yes, I'm establishing us here and have enough supplies to keep us here for as long as we need, because I don't know when it will be safe for us to travel and I won't take us back on the road unless I can be sure you will be safe. And yes, I intended to go to Castle Bremmand. We have to know how the land lies before we leave here; to know how strong a hold Darvett has on the lands; if travel is going to be difficult or easy; what Hast is doing; how much trouble Darvett's having establishing his rule. All those things are important and the best place to find them is Castle Bremmand.

"This idea of consulting on everything is absurd. Can you imagine what it would be like if I asked the men under my command every time I gave an order? I'd get dozens of different views and everyone would be so busy arguing that the enemy would be on us and we'd be cut to pieces before we could even get fallen in.

"So I make decisions. If I consulted, as Trystin seems to think is necessary, then apart from the fact that his opinion is hardly going to add a great deal to my decisions, I'd spent most of my days debating every last damned thing I do and nothing would ever get done."

He stopped abruptly and shrugged. "That's all really."

"Yes," Cori said sounding thoughtful. He rose to his feet and walked a few paces off from them. After a few moments he came back.

"Things cannot continue as they are, I'm sure you both agree with that, even if you can agree on nothing else." Both men nodded if a little reluctantly. "Good. You have something in common at least! Only you can find some way by which you can get along. I could command you, and I will if it becomes necessary but I suspect that would be a very inefficient way of working this out. So instead I'll tell you what I think, and then I'll leave it to you to establish a working basis.

"Dale, you are a soldier - as you rightly point out. You are used to giving commands and expect to have them obeyed. However, Trystin is not a soldier and he certainly isn't a subordinate, so you cannot treat him as such. Furthermore, his revered scholastic abilities of which you are so derisory happen to include military history, so he does have some idea of warfare and what it takes to live in the real world, as you call it.

"You may think it is easier to make the decisions and force them through but the evidence seems to suggest otherwise, if today is anything to go by. And yes, perhaps discussing your plans might lead to debate before the fact but it surely can't hurt to try it once in a while. You might even find that, if you explain your reasoning well enough, Trystin may agree with you. He is a scholar after all, which means he's more than intelligent enough to understand your decisions.

"As for you Trystin, you seem to want things both ways. On the one hand Dale is some kind of barbarian assassin who is a danger to myself and my family and on the other, he's the only protection that we have and his skills as a warrior are far too important to us for him to be allowed to leave here. You need to ask yourself which of those it is?"

He paused and then said, "For the record, I happen to think it is the latter. He's a soldier and by all accounts he's a rather good one. I know Lord Langate thinks highly of him and trusts his judgement. If he feels that killing those soldiers was necessary then I think we must accept that and get past our own squeamishness of the necessities of war. They are the enemy - they are invading our homeland and killing our people - so they are better off dead. We may not like the means of their death but it's necessity can't be questioned.

"What it also means is that I agree with you that Dale should not go to Castle Bremmand. If your responsibility here is to protect us, Dale, then you have to be here to do so."

"Cori, I must..."

Cori held up his hand to stop the man "... know what is really happening, yes. But it needn't be you that gets the information, need it? It seems perfectly simple to me. Trystin should go."

"But..."

"But...."

They both started to protest at once, Cori's declaration taking them both by surprise. "There," the young man almost smiled, "it would seem you have something else in common."

"Cori, I'm not sure it's such a good idea," Dale ignored the young man's jibe at their joint protests "Trystin doesn't have any fighting skills. If there were to be trouble he'd be defenceless."

"Then you'll have to teach him won't you? I'm sure it wouldn't take him long to pick up the basics."

"Do you know what you're suggesting?" Trystin was still looking staggered by the prospect of going to Castle Bremmand and said somewhat helplessly, "I don't even know the way from here."

"I expect Dale could draw you a map."

"Or what information he's looking for."

"Then he'll have to tell you. You, gentlemen, are actually going to have to work together to make sure this journey works. And now," he yawned abruptly, "I'm tired and I'm going to bed. Good night." And he was gone.

After Cori had left them, both Dale and Trystin sat in silence for quite sometime. Then, finally, into the darkness Trystin said dryly "There's nothing quite like being ticked off by a boy for making one feel ridiculous."

Dale snorted. "Just what I was thinking. But not a boy, Trystin, not any more." As he said it a number of thoughts and observations about Cori which had been occurring to him over the past few weeks crystallised into a realisation which made his spirit soar. "He's a man and by Brem's beard, he's going to make some kind of a King!"

Trystin looked at first surprised and then, almost reluctantly, a faint smile sketched across his face. "Something else we have in common, then," he remarked. After a short pause he continued, thoughtfully, "He's quite impressive, isn't he? He didn't hesitate or falter for a second in telling us who was in charge. I know his upbringing prepared him from leadership but I can't imagine that any of his brothers would have taken up the mantle so well at his age. I can't wait to see him back in a position where he has real power and authority at his command."

"You realise that it's up to us to see that he lives long enough to do that?" Dale looked at Trystin, suddenly sober. "Whatever you may think of my methods, Trystin, don't doubt that my goal is - and has always been - to protect those of the royal family who are in my care."

Another silence and then Trystin said slowly, "Cori was right to seek out those things that we have in common."

Dale understood him at once, "We both want to see them safe."

Trystin nodded and sighed, "Which means that we *have* to find a way to work together. If we fight amongst ourselves then it takes us further away from the goal we both claim to seek."

Neither one of them said anything more on the subject that night and after a short period of silence, Trystin took himself off to bed.

Dale fully intended to follow Trystin's example but he pondered a while longer at the fireside reflecting on how he and the scholar could find a way to tolerate one another. It wouldn't be easy – they were clearly very different sorts of people and their views on life were at opposite ends of the scale. However, the intent was there now to get along and find the means to work in some kind of harmony. It was a start and, to Dale's mind, as good a start as any.

Just as the big soldier came to this conclusion and decided it was time to turn in, a faint stirring from the side of the cottage made the hairs on his neck prickle. Something was moving along the shadowy gap between the woodpile and the chicken run.

After the first instinctive anxiety, Dale wasn't overly alarmed by this. It was probably some fox feeling bold enough to investigate the chicken coop, hopeful of a way in and an easy meal. It didn't do to ignore it, however, since foxes learned quickly where they could hunt undisturbed. If Dale scared him off now and kept an eye out to do the same for the next few nights, the beast would soon change his patrol route to exclude the clearing. So the big man rose to his feet and padded softly towards to corner of the cottage, planning to give the animal as much of a fright as possible to impress upon it the dangerous nature of the place.

As Dale closed in on the woodpile, however, the sound he had heard came again and this time the woodsman realised that it came from no animal. This was a man, doing his best not to be heard. Dale's pulse quickened. No-one had any right to be creeping about round here and he wasn't taking any chances, so he loosened his sword in his scabbard and, with his hand resting gently on it, ready to bring it out and in to use if he had need of it he turned the corner to see who was creeping about in the shadows.

"Cori!" for it was he, seated on the pile of logs waiting for splitting, his back against the cottage wall. The lad jumped at Dale's voice and he shot a guilty look at the man who had discovered him. "What's the matter?"

The young man shook his head, "Nothing."

Dale looked at him keenly. "Rubbish!" he replied decisively after a short examination. Cori wasn't hard to read, even in the poor light, and the hunched shoulders and hanging head gave the lad away. "Something's bothering you. Tell me."

Again a shake of the head. "I'm all right. You don't need to trouble yourself."

Dale considered this. Whatever had kept Cori awake and brought him out here, away from the others, he clearly didn't want to admit to it. It was particularly puzzling to see this reticence and uncertainty in one who had been so surprisingly confident and imposing that same day when adjudicating on the difficulties between Trystin and himself.

With a sudden burst of intuition Dale guessed what might be on the lad's mind. "Come by the fire," he suggested. "It's chilly back here and you might as well be warm if you plan to sit up all night agonising over exercising your authority for the first time."

Cori's eyes widened in surprise but from his expression Dale could see that he had hit the target full square. He said no more, standing and waiting until the lad was compelled to rise and head out in to the open space of the clearing and the warmth of the fire.

Dale chucked another log onto the dying embers in the firepit and gestured to Cori to sit. "Want to talk about it?" he inquired, "or would you prefer me to bugger off and leave you to it?" Still Cori looked uncertain so Dale decided to choose for him. "Well, I'm to bed then. If you need anything, you know where to find me." He turned to go, but then swung back. "Oh, and one thing to bear in mind. You command by right and tonight you did rather a good job of it."

He got no more than five paces before Cori's voice reached him. "I was supposed to take up my position in court at mid-winter – to manage some part of the kingdom's affairs. I was looking forward to it. A chance to prove myself and show how I was the perfect leader – just like the rest of my family. I'd have been a disaster."

"What on earth makes you say that?" Dale was indignant.

"I had no idea what I was doing today."

"So?"

"I was just copying what I've watched my father do. If people fall out at court he forces them to talk to each other – to hear one another out and then gives his own opinion before guiding them to reach an agreement themselves. All that telling you to behave like gentlemen and the other things – that's just what I've heard him say." Cori sighed. "He always made it look so easy."

"He's had a lot of practice. The more you do it, the more you get used to it and the easier it becomes. Besides, you did the right thing in pulling us up short today, so the fact that it feels strange to have done so isn't something to be unhappy about. You should be proud that you did it, despite how it feels."

"I wish I hadn't had to. You and Trystin…"

Dale cut across him frankly, "… are old enough to know better. As you pointed out yourself, us behaving like a pair of spoiled brats was getting in the way of the job at hand. We needed to have someone else point that out to us, or it could have gone on forever. As it is, we are now at least thinking about how to work together, instead of constantly trying to score points over one another."

"That's something, at least," Cori said, sounding forlorn.

Dale regarded him closely and then remarked, "Neither one of us resents you for having taken the matter in hand, as you did. Is that what's on your mind?"

"I don't know," Cori mumbled. "Maybe."

"Son, both Trystin and I have spent enough of our lives around Kings, Princes and other noblemen to be able to accept that they rule and we serve. It's how it is. Neither one of us has ever been in doubt that we serve you, not the other way around."

"When I owe you so much... when you've been friends to me and mine..."

"Put all that from your mind," Dale said firmly. "What happened today was nothing to do with friendships and the bond that has grown up between us." Cori looked blankly at him, so Dale went on. "Think of it being like military service. You'll often see different ranks mix and get on well together in social situations but when they are on duty there is a recognised line of command and that is always observed. I've served with officers who I could go drinking with and abuse to their face but if I'd done it when we were in uniform I'd have quite reasonably expected to find myself in very hot water. This is no different. We get along as friends, you and I, but when it comes down to it, you are Marchand and I serve the line, just as any good Bremmand man would. In a strange way, it was rather nice to have you show us that you know how to use your rank when you need to, even though you did make us both feel like idiots in the process. Now," Dale clapped him on the back, "stop tormenting yourself for something that you had to do and can't change anyway and get to bed."

Stinkworm

After this life at the cottage settled down to a more easy rhythm. Now that he felt his opinion had been given and heard and having taken Cori's observations to heart, Trystin was more able to accept his role as domestic servant to the cottage occupants. Dale similarly saw that he had perhaps been uncharitable in his opinion of Trystin and did his best to be less autocratic towards the scholar.

The matter of the five Empire soldiers was not discussed again and Dale knew that this, unlike other disagreements, was unlikely to be resolved. Trystin, he surmised, simply couldn't accept the harsh realities of war and the death of those men was, to him, a cold-blooded murder. It made Dale uneasy to know that he was thought of this way by the scholar, like most men not believing himself to be an evil person, but he was reasonably sure that this was a matter that would never be resolved through words. Trystin did seem to be taking Cori's advice, however, and allowing that Dale had superior experience in military matters which meant that his decision had to be accepted as correct - however unpalatable - and to allow the topic to rest.

Other matters, however, they did discuss, in particular Dale's method of taking decisions without thought for others.

"I think you'd find I objected to them less if I understood them," Trystin had explained one evening, when the youngsters had gone to bed and there was time to talk. "I'm not some foot soldier who has been drilled in to doing as he's told and not to ask questions and I don't think I shall ever be able to adapt to that. I don't respond well to surprises or having to guess what you'll come up with next and even less so to seeing evidence that you've already made the decision without bothering to mention it to anyone else."

"Meaning the cottage I suppose?"

"Yes, that particularly, although there are other things as well. I'm getting a little tired of being treated as if you can't trust me and my opinion isn't worth a shill. It isn't too good a feeling to know you are seen as dead weight most of the time."

"Oh, I don't see you as that," Dale said thoughtfully, "Not for a moment. In fact," he paused and then decided to take a risk - a big one - and share all of his plans with the slender scholar, "I think you may end up being essential to our goal." Then, in reply to Trystin's quizzical look, Dale outlined his thoughts about what he thought the future was going to bring. It wasn't a fully considered scheme as yet but there were some things he knew would have to happen to give them all the best chance of survival and these he now shared with Trystin along with all his other thoughts and ideas.

Trystin listened, questioned and sometimes argued but mostly he came to agree that Dale's approach was probably right. On some points he probed deeply, challenging Dale's reasoning and exploring other possibilities, on others he merely nodded and agreed that the approach made sense. They debated possible outcomes of Darvett's battle, what each possibility might mean and how that would affect the decisions they took going forward.

They talked through the night and it was only when Trystin noticed with a start that the birds were beginning to give voice in the trees that he realised that dawn was almost with them. As if the realisation of the hour had reminded him, he gave a huge yawn. "It's been some time since I sat up all night talking," he smiled.

"I wouldn't have thought you were much of a night animal," Dale replied. "You don't strike me as the type."

"Well, I don't spend many nights going in to Castle Bremmand carousing," Trystin smiled thinly, "but when you get a group of academics together with differing viewpoints, the conversation can get quite lively and has been known to last the night."

"I see," Dale replied, not quite able to hide his view that this was hardly his idea of an exciting lifestyle but Trystin merely smiled and remarked without rancour that it was each to his own.

It was this all night discussion, as much as Cori's forceful insistence that they both grow up, which began to break down the barriers between the two men. From the detailed discussions, at first entered into grudgingly but, as time passed, with more willingness, they were each able to start to understand the abilities and gifts of the other and in particular where their own skills could complement those of the other man. Trystin began to be impressed with Dale's talent for foresight and planning, having already considered many options and the actions that would be required in each case. Dale meanwhile found that he was able to discuss his thoughts intelligently with the scholar and found him to be not in the least bit timorous or squeamish on matters of war. Slowly, over the next weeks that they spent together, preparing for the right time to seek more information from Castle Bremmand, the two men found that not only could they work together but they were beginning to respect and even like one another.

Within a day or so of the big argument, Dale began to teach Trystin the basics of swordsmanship concentrating primarily on what would be needed to survive an attack. To do this he broke a number of rules in what would normally be considered to be the correct teaching methods. Doing this wouldn't provide the man with full command of the weapon but Dale knew there were only a matter of weeks to deliver what training he could, so he knew that he had to impart the bare essentials and worry about technique and finer points some other time.

Cori quickly offered to help Trystin's education, training with him to free Dale to continue work in the forest. It gave the lad a chance to practice too, he remarked and Dale, taking the hint, began to spend a bit of time putting Cori through his paces. This, he had to admit, kept them both in shape.

Cori was skilful, years of training with the Weapons Master having prepared him well. He was also young and healthy so Dale's superior experience and strength were well countered by Cori's agility and speed. They would frequently have practice bouts which would last some time as each tried different approaches to defeat one another and these sessions became something that both looked forward to and enjoyed enormously.

Often, watching the combat training from the sidelines, would sit Allin, keeping an eye on Joss as the weapons were wielded in the clearing. It was clear that he viewed the short cuts which Dale was using for Trystin with some envy for, as with most noblemen's sons, his military training followed a formal route which saw the majority of his training to date being focussed on defensive and attacking forms and exercises to build balance and strength. Very little of it involved the type of fighting that a boy would consider to be exciting so seeing this opportunity to do something less tedious with a sword the youngster soon requested that Dale also resume teaching him to fight as well.

Unfortunately, he made the mistake of making his request within earshot of his brother and Cori, expressing the view that Dale had to much to do already, insisted that he continue Allin's training instead. To the boy's utter disgust Cori took it upon himself to carry on where his previous instruction had left off. Instead of allowing Allin to have a fast route to fighting he maintained the same practices of rigour and precision as the Weapons Master.

Allin complained bitterly at first to Cori and then, when this got him nowhere, to Dale who, suspecting that Cori was being overzealous in insistence on the tight discipline of their previous teachings, tried to get the older lad to relent. Cori had proved to be stubborn on the point, however, expressing the opinion that Allin was being allowed to get away with far too much already.

"He's only a youngster," Dale tried to argue, "and he's said before that he finds swordsmanship dull, so what's the harm in making it a bit more interesting to him?"

"Not everything in life is going to be interesting to him," Cori remarked sententiously. "He has to learn that there are expectations upon him to do what is required, even if it doesn't interest him much."

There was no moving the young man and since Dale himself had made it clear that Cori had the final say over his brother and sister - something the young man pointed out to Dale with some irritation when he wouldn't let the matter drop - there was very little Dale could do. The one concession he did manage to obtain was that he could take on some of Allin's teaching to relieve the sibling resentment that must be irking the boy as much as the need for rigorous training.

Respecting Cori's wishes Dale took Allin through the formal steps and exercises that were used for teaching principles of the sword, despite the fixed scowl on Allin's face throughout. It wasn't a particularly harmonious hour, and when, towards the end of it, Cori arrived to watch, Allin's expression became even blacker.

On seeing the youth, Dale broke off the training and turned to him. "I see what you were so picky about now," he said frankly. "He's going to be good, isn't he?"

Cori looked a trifle disconcerted that Dale was expressing this view within Allin's hearing but he nodded. "Master Grise thought so. I overheard him saying something to my Father once about him being the best of all of us."

"Me?" Allin said sounding surprised. He looked questioningly at Dale, "Am I good then?"

"Maybe, if you apply yourself," Cori said crushingly. "But only if you work hard, and stop trying to cut corners."

"I don't..." Allin began to argue but Cori ignored him, talking over his protests and acting as if the boy wasn't there at all. "Allin never seems to want to work at anything and I think Master Grise was beginning to think he didn't have the discipline to go with the talent. It's not as if the Master didn't try to make sure he had a proper training and didn't learn any bad habits but I think he's found it difficult to get Allin to work at it like he's supposed to."

"Master Grise hates me," Allin muttered sulkily. "I never do anything right as far as he's concerned."

"Master Grise is a good teacher and if you worked at it, you'd probably find he was less critical."

"Well, perhaps," Dale said, adding candidly to Cori, "but Grise has never been as good at lavishing praise, as he has complaint. I can see why he might want to keep to a strict line of training with the boy but all he seems to have succeeded in doing is make swordplay seem deadly dull. Perhaps if Allin knew *why* he was being made to get every last exercise perfect before he could move on to the next, then he might be more willing to persevere with it."

Allin was tiring of being talked over so he nudged impatiently at Dale. "Why did he then?"

"Because it matters," Dale turned to the boy with a gentle smile. "You have a gift, but it needs to be shaped and worked at. If you were just ordinary, an average swordsman, then the odd short cut to a movement or a stroke would matter little, but you've got the potential to be really good at this, so it is worth the effort now to try and get it absolutely right. That's what Grise was trying to do but I suspect he didn't realise that he was taking every last bit of fun out of it as he did so."

Allin pondered this for a while, for the first time looking pleased about the tedious, if essential, exercises he'd been obliged to complete. Never before had he understood the need for the discipline which the Weapons Master had applied and his family had insisted he follow, despite his protests. Finally, sounding almost hopeful, he looked at Dale. "Will you keep teaching me? Properly, I mean, like Master Grise thought I should?"

"Well…" Dale pondered, but with a wink at Allin's older brother.

"Please," Allin begged. "I'll work at it, really I will."

"I thought you thought it was boring," Cori countered, but he too was teasing, amused by the sudden change of heart in his brother.

Allin shook his head but then, rather more honestly, said, "It is a bit, but I don't mind now. It was different before. I always thought I was useless, so there didn't seem to be a lot of point but if I'm going to be good at it then I can stick at it. I won't complain or anything."

"I'll believe that when I see it," was all Cori said but Allin could already see that his brother was on his side. He beamed at Dale, who also relented and agreed to continue the boy's training, much to Allin's delight.

"Are you sure it was a good idea to let Allin know that he's got talent?" Cori asked later. "He may think he can cut even more corners now that he knows he's good at it."

Dale raised an enquiring eyebrow, "Did he look like he wanted to shirk?"

"Not really," Cori conceded, "but he's not usually dedicated to something for very long."

"He's ten years old," was Dale's reply. "You can't expect him to have the discipline of a man just yet but he clearly wasn't enjoying the work that was being demanded of him before. Perhaps if he understands why; if he thinks there is something there for him to work towards, it might make a little more sense to him and he'll start to get something from it."

"I hope you're right," Cori said doubtfully. "If he decided that he can take it easy now that he's found out he has a gift for fighting, there'll be no way to get him to work at it."

"You know," Dale said with a pained expression "I begin to get the impression that you don't trust my judgement."

Cori's eyes narrowed but then he saw the warmth in Dale's face so he replied in similar vein. "In military matters, you have my complete and utter trust but Allin is more trouble than even the full allied forces when he puts his mind to it and I suspect that you have yet to understand the nature of your enemy in this case. Still," he shrugged, "your confidence that you know what you are doing is amusing and I'm looking forward to seeing the expression on your face when he outsmarts you, just as he does everyone else."

In the weeks that followed, as life at the cottage became more and more settled, routines began to be established. Mornings were spent in education and training of all types. Trystin worked with Cori and Allin on their book learning and even a little with Joss teaching her her letters and numbers and a little reading while Dale adopted the role of weapons master, continuing to develop Trystin's skills, keeping Cori in trim and, of most interest to him, seeing the undoubted abilities of young Allin start to take shape.

The afternoons were for work, as Cori and Dale departed for the forest, to haul lumber leaving Trystin, Allin and Joss behind to care for the cottage, the garden and the livestock. Now that he had been shown how, Allin also helped with the timbers as they came in, using the hand axe to remove small branches and smooth the edges of timbers fit for hewing in to saleable logs. Then, when Dale had a load ready, he would accompany the big man, steering the head of Shout, the mule and keeping him on the narrow pathways through the forest, as Dale guided the sled from behind, taking some of the weight and preventing it from snagging on roots and branches. Their loads would be left at the roadside, ready for collection by one of the wood haulers who worked the forest. Each load was marked with two basic symbols, one to show who had provided it and the other where it was going. That way, Dale had explained to Allin, the haulers knew where to deliver and to whom the returning payments in kind were destined . Allin also accompanied Dale when he went to check the drop point in the woods the day after each load had been delivered to collect the supplies that had been provided in payment for their labours. The boy especially seemed to enjoy returning to the cottage with Shout, laden with some sack or box, and teasing Joss into guessing the contents.

Evenings, as the light began to fade, were when the occupants of the cottage were able to turn to matters of their own interest. To everyone's surprise this was when Trystin came in to his own. For while Dale had considered him a scholar and knew he taught history and politics he had no idea that the man's true field of research was in ancient history, most of which had been handed down through myth and fable rather than the writings of official recorders. As a result, Trystin knew every last tale of the old times when Holy Brem and those that served with him strove to create the kingdom and, even more surprising, he proved to be an excellent story teller. Most evenings they would all sit outside by the fire, Joss sitting on Cori's lap, or snuggled up along side Allin with sparkling eyes, mouth open, and listen as Trystin regaled them with some exploit of Brem, Langilia or their loyal and trusted subjects.

The stories of the old times also seemed to inspire Allin who, it now appeared, could draw. His task of preparing timber for sale put him in the position to set aside bark stripped from the logs in large enough pieces to use and dry them flat in the sun. He also took to rising early and poking about in the remains of the fire to retrieve what charcoal he could. Thus armed with everything he needed he would spend what free time he could in drawing pictures of whatever came to mind. Sometimes he drew from imagination, scenes from the tales the Trystin told, and sometimes he sketched something of their surroundings, the cottage in the clearing, the animals or, especially for Joss, some of the flowers.

Cori seemed most interested in extending his education in all things military, taking from the stories that Trystin told what he could in terms of battle tactics and engines of war. Here Dale was also able to extend his interest, telling the lad what he knew of methods he'd seen used in his years as a soldier. Cori, it appeared, was not just curious about method but also means of delivering war, which meant that both Trystin and Dale struggled to assist him with the way certain weapons were built and engineered, although between the three of them there was usually enough book learning and practical experience to allow them to work most things out.

Through this time bonds were formed between the five occupants of the little cottage which deepened and shaped every one of them, bringing them together in friendship that they would never forget. Allin no longer seemed to resent or avoid Trystin (although his attitude to book learning was never all that positive) and Dale and Trystin ceased to be at daggers drawn over the way Dale chose to guide the little group. The three youngsters drew closer to one another through this period as well. The most likely possibility for the rest of their family was never discussed, nor did either of the boys allude to the uncertainty of their future but in their hearts all three royal offspring knew that their future was to be considerably less clear and safe than their past.

One afternoon when Dale and Cori were in the forest, the big man was instructing Cori how to get better yield from the axe. Cori hadn't found himself able to master the single sweep of the tool that Dale was trying to explain to him and the lad's patience was beginning to give way so, seeing that the he was losing his temper, Dale decided that he should give it up. He took the axe from the lad, drew it back over his shoulder with an easy swing, trying to prove how easy a manoeuvre it was and, thanks to sweaty palms and his own conceited attempt to prove a point, the axe handle slid effortlessly out of his grip and flew, without elegance, to land on the opposite side of the clearing, landing handle-down in a patch of mud.

Cori, to his credit, said nothing, although Dale could see his young companion was struggling not to laugh but that evening, during dinner, the lad had made a single, sly dig at the skills as a woodsman the big man was teaching him. Almost without thinking Dale shot back a cheerful if fiery retort, highly inappropriate for a crown prince but, despite Trystin's somewhat surprised expression, Cori clearly considered it to be amusing.

That was the start of it. From then on, the two of them traded insults on a regular basis, with good spirit and jocularity that in no way disguised the mutual affection that was developing between them. Where Dale had once seemed affronted at Allin's suggestion of his lack of book learning, he was now quite prepared to allow Cori to suggest he was merely an ignorant peasant, replying to this with retorts about the sissy up-bringing of the royal youth.

Allin had watched during the early exchanges between his brother and the big soldier and then he had taken the opportunity to seek clarification on this new and unfamiliar form of humour. "You like Cori, don't you? I can tell you do?"

"Of course," Dale had replied.

"But you say horrible things to him. If I said things like that he'd knock me flat."

"He knows I don't mean it. It's always a little different with brothers anyhow. After all, I can say things to you that would have you frothing at the mouth if it was him, can't I?"

Allin had nodded and from then on had watched this curious 'game' of trading insults between the two men with some amusement and from time to time even assisted one or the other of them in the sport by providing ammunition of previous follies Cori had committed when they had lived at the palace, or sharing something he had observed Dale doing when his brother was elsewhere. He had the good sense, however, not to enter the game, understanding that this was only something that could be played between equals.

After some six weeks had passed since they arrived at the cottage and begun their life of isolation in the forest, Dale announced to Trystin late in the evening that he would be heading to Chelland once more the next day to get supplies and a bit of news.

"To see if the time is right for me to go to Castle Bremmand?" the scholar suggested, licking his lips nervously.

The big man nodded. Encounters with the wood haulers along the forest paths had already confirmed what they had feared - that the Kingdom had fallen to Darvett - but other than that news was scant. "Iestan keeps his ear to the ground and if we're lucky I may learn enough from him to save you the trip."

"You don't look convinced." Dale merely shrugged. "Why wait until now to mention that you are going? The idea can't have just occurred to you."

An air of the old hostility was back in Trystin's tone and Dale hurried to reassure the man. "Allin would want to come again if he knew. If there is news of the last battle or of his family, I don't want him to hear it without first having a chance to soften it a bit for him. Besides, he still has work to do here and I don't want him getting the idea that he can dip out whenever something else happens."

This much made sense and Trystin said so, adding, "How long will you be gone?"

"Only the day. There's not much I need to do: talk to Iestan, get a few things, talk to the wood merchant to see if he's happy with supplies and that's it. I'll be back before you know it."

Dale's trip to Chelland was, as he had promised, brief. It was also uninformative. News was slow to travel in these parts at the best of times but travellers were few and far between at the moment, making it even harder to get information. Iestan bemoaned both facts to the big man, putting the same emphasis on the lack of news as in the loss of custom for his tavern as if they were of similar importance. Thus, apart from a few supplies that were needed he could bring nothing of much use back to the cottage.

He arrived home in daylight, the mid-summer sun of the evenings lighting his way home, in time for supper. Joss, Allin and Cori were all outdoors, Cori chopping wood for the fire and Allin playing absently with his sister. The little girl was the first to see Dale and came running towards him to greet him. He swung her cheerily in to his arms, pleased by the welcome and glad to be home with the youngsters he was becoming so fond of. Cori waved at him, finished splitting the log on the block and then he too strolled over.

"Enjoyed your day off, did you?" he enquired, with a good-humoured edge to his voice.

"Anything to avoid a bit of hard work," Dale retorted with a grin. "What about you then? Had a good day?"

"Not bad," Cori replied although he couldn't keep his eyes from flicking briefly in his brother's direction.

Allin had glanced up when Dale had entered the clearing but then had rather pointedly turned his back and was now scratching at the dry earth by the side of the fire with a stick. There was an air of injury projecting from him and Dale could almost see the scowl on the boy's face reflected in his shoulders.

Dale met Cori's eye and raised his eyebrows. The youth returned his look and shrugged slightly but couldn't quite keep the look of amusement out of his eyes. He'd said he would enjoy seeing Dale coming up against Allin at his worst and it looked as if he thought now was going to be one of those occasions. The big man handed Joss in to her brother's arms and then walked over to where the younger lad was sitting and braced himself for the full force of the ten-year-old's temper.

"Allin?" No reply. Dale sat on the log beside the boy but even this provoked no response. Never one to evade a problem, the big man suggested, "You're angry with me?"

"You went to Chelland without me."

"Yes."

"You didn't tell me you were going because you knew I'd want to come."

"Yes."

Allin swung round. He hadn't expected quite such a brutally honest response. There was hurt in his eyes. "You didn't want me to come with you?"

Dale wasn't about to lie to the boy. "It isn't always going to be possible for me to take you with me." The scowl was back proving that Allin didn't much care for this answer. "I hope," Dale went on with deliberate care, "that you've been behaving yourself today."

"What's that supposed to mean?" came the challenging reply.

"That I wouldn't like to hear that you've been making life a misery for everyone else, just because you didn't get your own way. It would have been very tiresome of you if you had."

The flicker of guilt on the boy's face gave Dale the answer to that, as if he hadn't already guessed, but he waited for the boy to say something. "Why didn't you want me with you?"

"I never said 'didn't want' Allin. I said 'not possible.' I don't want you exposed to anything nasty and that means it is sometimes better to leave you behind. Besides, you have work to do here. That has to be attended to as well."

He didn't look pleased but all he said, rather plaintively, was, "You could have told me that. You didn't need to go sneaking off that way."

"Probably," Dale conceded, "but I can't believe that you would have accepted it without argument. I don't have a great deal of patience for long debates."

"I can attest to that." Trystin had come out from the cottage alerted by Cori and Joss that the soldier had returned. He was smiling faintly, glad to see the big man back or perhaps amused that it wasn't just himself who found Dale's autocratic style annoying.

Dale met the scholar's eye, heaved an elaborately dramatic sigh at the dig and then turned back to Allin. "If it helps at all, I rather missed having your company."

"Really?" the boy looked hopeful.

"Really. It's a lonely old walk without someone to talk to and it isn't as if there's all that much to do in Chelland. Oh, by the way, Iestan sends his regards."

"You found *something* to do then." Allin managed a grin, knowing that if Dale had spoken to Iestan he must have spent time at the tavern.

"Only to while away the boredom. Here" - this last he added as he passed a package to the boy - "why don't you take that in and see if your brother and sister and you can think of something to do with those."

"What are they?" Allin looked at the wrapped bundle with some eagerness.

"Take them inside and find out," the big man replied with a smile. "And see that the others get a look in. No making out that it's just for you. I brought those for us all to share."

Allin was on his feet before Dale had finished but when he got perhaps halfway to the cottage he turned and asked, "Can I go with you next time you go to Chelland?"

"Perhaps," was the non-committal reply and then, seeing the boy open his mouth to complain, he added, "I won't make a promise I can't keep and I may not be able to take you on my next visit. But I will remember that you want to come. You don't need to worry, you know. I imagine you'll be making a few runs to Chelland before we leave here."

Satisfied, Allin headed in to the cottage with the parcel leaving Trystin and Dale alone in the clearing.

Even before he spoke, Dale knew what Trystin was going to ask, "Any news?"

The big man shook his head. "Nothing of consequence. News travels slowly around these parts."

"Then I still need to go to Castle Bremmand?" Trystin looked nervous, an air of worry behind his grey eyes.

"Let's talk about it tonight, when there aren't little ears to hear," was all Dale said.

Back in the cottage, a small dispute had broken out over the package that Dale had brought from Chelland. "He didn't say we couldn't open it," Allin was complaining as the two men entered.

"If it was for us all, we should wait until we are all here," Cori retorted, putting emphasis on the word *all.* "It would be rude not to."

"We're supposed to decide what to do with them," the younger boy continued heatedly. "Dale said so. How can we do that if you won't let us look at them?"

Cori had a look on his face which expressed clearly what he thought of little brothers and was about to open his mouth to exert his authority but Dale intervened. Letting out a sigh of deep feeling he placed himself between the two bickering lads and said wearily, "Must you two argue over *everything?*"

Both Allin and Cori replied to this by trying to explain themselves and, more particularly, prove why his brother was wrong and his own view perfectly justified.

"I think we can take that as a 'yes'," Trystin remarked, with a thin smile.

"I won't bother to bring anything next time, if this is the fuss it causes." Dale reached over and took the unopened parcel from the table. "Shall I chuck these on the fire? That should solve the problem." He met Trystin's eye and the scholar smiled faintly at this solution.

"I think that's an excellent idea," the slender man replied gravely. "In fact I'm a little surprised you bothered in the first place."

Both princes changed protests of the other's wrongs to persuading Dale not to carry out his threat. Hasty assurances were made that there was no need to dispose of the package and that the argument was already forgotten. It was clear that the dispute went deeper than the immediate argument, however, when Cori found it necessary to remark, "Allin was just being too eager, that's all. I'm sure he won't do it again, will you Allin?"

It was a petty dig and made it clear that Cori was laying the blame firmly at his brother's door. Nor, Dale could see, was Allin about to let the remark by, as the youngster opened his mouth to give some retort to this unfair attack on him.

Dale was quicker, however, and, meeting Cori's eyes, said dryly, "You, of course, are quite without fault."

"I..." the lad began but then stopped. He could see two things: one was that Allin looked satisfied that the big man had come to his defence and would now let the squabble subside; the other was that Dale was genuinely irritated at the mean snipe at the younger boy. He could almost hear the man lecturing him - *he's only a child, but you are quite old enough not to need to win every quarrel.* What he knew for sure was that he didn't want to get ticked off in front of everyone else. He was in a losing position so retreat was his only option. He dipped his head to acknowledge Dale's point and then, with as much dignity as he could muster, replied, "I always do my utmost to emulate you, Sir."

As a riposte, it was perfect. Trystin stifled a smile and, for a brief moment, Dale was rendered speechless. Then, knowing that Allin had probably been insufferable all day, and had most likely taken his irritation out on his brother first, Dale decided that allowing Cori to come away from his own ill-behaviour with his dignity in tact was fair enough. The annoyance evaporated from the big man's face and Cori saw a twinkle of amusement play in his brown eyes. "You're a villain," Dale remarked. "Don't expect to get away with it every time.

"Now" he thrust the parcel at Joss who hadn't taken her eyes off it for a second, the squabble between her brothers seemingly of no interest to her compared to the importance of what was inside the package. "Why don't you open this up, Little Flower, so we can see what all the fighting was about."

Late that evening, when the three youngsters were in bed, Trystin and Dale wandered outside to sit by the fire and discuss Trystin's trip to Castle Bremmand in more detail. With so little news around Dale wasn't sure it would be safe in the city as yet, but he knew they had to get news before the invaders managed to close all the routes north and across the Hastian borders. Thus, he explained, Trystin was going to have to go soon. If Castle Bremmand was still in turmoil then the scholar would have to turn around and come back.

Trystin nodded but he couldn't keep the apprehension from showing in his face.

"You'll be all right," Dale assured him. "If you keep your head down, are careful about who you talk to and what you tell them, then there's no reason for you to draw any attention. And, if you do run into trouble you know how to defend yourself now." This much was true. The few weeks of intensive and rather unorthodox training had brought Trystin to a point where he could stave off an attack from Dale and, by some rather foul play and the element of surprise, even stand a chance of defeating an attacker.

"When do I go?"

"Soon. It should take you no more than a week to get to Castle Bremmand but you want to arrive on Market Day. Even if the city has been taken there'll be plenty of people travelling in who will be wanting to trade and won't know how the land lies. So, if you set out the day after tomorrow, that should time it for you nicely."

Together, they sketched through the details of Trystin's trip: where he should go, what sort of information to seek, the best places to get it without drawing attention to himself and how to blend in with the rest of the people so that he could move about unnoticed. They discussed the matter at some length, debating options and the relative advantages and weaknesses of each and made sure that Trystin knew where in the city would be the most likely places to find those who could safely tell him what he wanted to know, as well as what route he should take to reach the city without incident.

Finally, in the small hours of the morning, Dale nodded and said, "You'll do. Think on what we've talked about over the next day or so and you can ask me anything else which crosses your mind before you set off."

"There is one thing," Trystin said quietly. "I need you to tell me how best I can kill myself."

Dale stared at the slender man aghast. "What for?"

"I'm no soldier, Dale. However much I like to believe it, I'm not a hero. If I were to be taken - if the Empire troops knew who I was and wanted me to tell them where you all are - I don't know how well I would be able to withstand whatever means of torture they would use to find out. While I may lack courage to face that kind of pain, I am prepared to give my life to protect the royal family. If the worst should happen, I need to be able to take my life, quickly and in such a way that they can't stop me, so that you won't be betrayed by my weakness."

The cool and calculating way that the scholar said this left Dale lost for words for a moment. He was briefly reminded of the same calm dignity with which Queen Isolde had faced a similar choice and, for the first time, felt a burst of real respect for the tutor. "There is a herb that can be distilled to make a poison. It's quick, painless and needs only a small amount to do what you need. I'll see that you have some."

"Thank you."

"I don't think it will come to that Trystin. Castle Bremmand is a big place and you'd be very unlucky to come across anyone who would betray you to the Empire troops."

"I know - and I'm not being as overdramatic as you might currently think."

Dale nodded but didn't look convinced. "Just so long as you only use it if you really need to. Neither one of us would admit to our being the best of friends but I want you back. I can't get our young friends to safety without you."

"I assure you I'm not going to panic at the first sign of military interest, and then poison myself," Trystin remarked, smiling thinly. "I don't actually *want* to die in the service of my king, even if I am prepared to do so. This is merely a precaution in case my connection to the Princes becomes known but it will put my mind at rest to know that I have a way of protecting your location."

"Then we're settled. You go the day after tomorrow."

Trystin nodded. "Do we tell the children?"

"Hmm." Dale rubbed his beard thoughtfully. "I'm not sure. Allin for one doesn't seem to like it when we make decisions without consulting him."

Trystin pulled a face. "That might be a good argument for not saying anything. He has to learn some time that he can't have it all his own way. I think I might enjoy the prospect of him coming up against your will. I suspect it might be even more intractable than his."

"Oddly enough, Cori said something similar recently but in the hope that his temper might humble *me*. It would seem that he thinks I'm far more likely to fall foul of Allin than him meeting his match in me."

"I think it would be fair to say we would both watch a confrontation between you with considerable interest but neither of us would be willing to take bets on who would win."

In the end, they did let the young royals know that Trystin was soon to set off on his trip to Castle Bremmand and, two days later, at first light, the scholar had a royal send off - quite literally - when the whole family got up early to see him off and wish him a safe trip.

Trystin was gone for over three weeks, in which time everyone in the little clearing found his absence left more of a hole than they might otherwise have expected. Even Allin, who had previously professed himself not fond of the scholar's superior attitude, seemed lost without him. Apart from anything else, the care of his young sister fell almost entirely to him now that Trystin was not there to watch over her and this was a demanding burden for the lad. However, it wasn't just this, or the weighty list of study assignments that had been left for him to work on in the man's absence that seemed to trouble him. Somehow the fact that there was one less person at the cottage had unbalanced things for him and he was less than happy with the change.

Cori too proved himself ill at ease now that the slender man was gone. He, of all of them, had been most inclined to seek out Trystin's company and, Dale suspected, had shared with the man some of the fears and concerns which he kept well-hidden from the rest of them.

With both boys showing themselves to be brooding at Trystin's departure, Dale braced himself for several weeks of ill-temper and arguments, but in fact they both showed great restraint. There were still a few minor squabbles but the most serious argument that disturbed the peace in that time was a heated dispute between Allin and his sister over which chicken was which.

Apparently, having named the mule and the goat, Joss went on to give every one of the chickens a name as well but sadly, since they were all very similar, it was sometimes hard to remember which bird bore which name. Allin, having quickly found that Joss was very insistent about getting the names right when feeding them and looking for eggs (so far without success), made a point of working out who was who: the cockerel was Digger, the hen with the darker band on her leg was Poppy, the one with a few missing tail feathers was Ruffle and so on. Unfortunately, his memory and ability to find differences by which to remember the names was better than Joss's and there was a loud and somewhat tearful dispute between them when he insisted that Peg was the one with the lighter feathers on her head, *not* the one with the black spot on her beak. Matters were made even worse when an exasperated Allin picked a hen at random and declared that he didn't like the name Joss had chosen and from now on the bird should be called Stinkworm.

The wail of distress from Joss was so piercing and prolonged that it brought Dale and Cori at a run to see what terrible disaster had befallen the little girl. Once it was established that she wasn't seriously injured, Cori had gathered her up and carried her indoors, while Dale tried to find out from Allin what all the fuss was about.

The boy had been mulish and bad-tempered about the matter, especially when Dale didn't seem to understand his point of view.

"Joss is *wrong!*" he protested angrily.

"Yes," Dale agreed, "but Joss is three."

"That's not fair. Everyone always takes her side because she's little and because she cries when she doesn't get her own way. No-one ever sticks up for me."

Cori had returned, having heard Joss's side of the story and was intended to do battle with his brother but on hearing this he checked himself and instead said, quite reasonably. "They're only chickens, Pup. Does it matter so much what they are called?"

"Yes!" the boy declared angrily, rounding on his brother. Then he corrected himself. "No. I don't care."

"Then why...?"

"Because she keeps insisting that I get the names right and she gets cross with me if I don't but I'm *never* going to please her if she keeps changing her mind about which one is which."

"Oh dear," Dale said, taking in Allin's agitated expression and doing his best not to laugh. "They didn't include this in military training." He saw Cori meet his eye and could see that the youth was also amused but, in deference to the younger boy's obvious distress, Dale swallowed down his laughter and said sympathetically, "I don't think you'll ever win this one, son. It doesn't seem that she can tell one from another but she wants to think she can - so just let her. Pretend she's right, even if she isn't. You've said yourself that it doesn't matter."

"But.." Allin protested but then he stopped. "Oh, *all right!* They're only stupid chickens, anyway."

"Good for you," Cori said encouragingly, adding dryly, "So perhaps you could now go and reassure Joss that she isn't obliged to call one of her Chickens *Stinkworm* for evermore."

And that was the end of the matter, except that, despite Joss's initial dismay, the name Stinkworm somehow remained, even after Cori pointed out that it wasn't a very nice name for a girl. What was more, a few days later, it was Stinkworm who finally settled down to lay the first eggs for the cottage.

The King is Dead, Long live the King!

The sun had set and the moon was new so it was dark in the forest. Dale was sitting outside the cottage. The fire was still burning but dying down so the light didn't spread too far through the clearing. The youngsters had been in bed for a while now, Cori the last to go perhaps half an hour back, so Dale was able to enjoy the peace and solitude of the darkness to collect his thoughts and consider what the next day would bring.

Some slight disturbance in the trees made him lift his head sharply as somewhere deep in the forest, a pheasant was roused from its sleep, giving a loud scolding cry. A fox barked roughly in reply to the disturbance while Dale sat, not breathing as he waited for anything out of the ordinary to give him more clues as to whether something untoward was closing in on him. Just as he was deciding that he must only have heard some animal circling the clearing, another rustle of undergrowth sent him flying to his feet, bringing his sword out from its sheath in up in front of him ready to defend against the threat he was now sure was coming towards him up the narrow footpath.

"Dale?"

In some relief, the big man let his blade fall away sideway at the familiar voice, calling softly from the shelter of the trees.

"Trystin? Come in to the light man. What are you doing hanging about in the bushes like that, making me jump."

"I wanted to be sure the children were abed," the scholar replied softly, as he came into the clearing.

Dale looked at him keenly. Even in the dim light, Dale could see that he looked weary and careworn, as if he was weighed down by some load too heavy to bear. His hair was unkempt and wayward and there was a smudge of grime running along one cheek. "You look worn out man. Come by the fire and I'll go and get you some wine."

"No!" Trystin caught hold of his arm. "You might wake them."

"That matters?"

A dismal nod. "I wanted to tell you - tell you it all of it. Then we can decide what we should tell *them*."

"The news isn't good then?"

Trystin's head dropped momentarily as he nodded and then, staring in to the dying embers of the fire, he told his tale.

I had an easy enough journey *Trystin told him* and found the main road to Castle Bremmand just like you'd said I would. It took me perhaps three days to reach the city but the last day of it, the roads were just full of Empire troops. They were *everywhere*! So many of them too. Hundreds of troops, marching out along every road, going to all parts of Bremmand. At first I tried to hide from them, heading off in to the undergrowth whenever I heard them coming but then I began to worry that if I was found trying to hide it would draw more attention to me than if I tried to brazen it out. So next time a patrol came by, I just stood aside and let them past. They weren't interested in me. In fact, they took no notice of me, or anyone else on the roads, just so long as everyone kept out of their way. If you didn't have sense to stand in the verges when they came past, they just pushed you off the road anyway, so you soon learned to stand aside for them. They certainly weren't interested in a simple traveller on his way to the city. I think I would never have manages the last few miles to the city at all, if I hadn't walked on the verge. There were enemy troops on the road almost non-stop. It was unbelievable that there should be so many of them and they should be marching about as if they owned the place already.

In one way, the presence of so many Empire troops was a good thing. Out there in the forest, it was natural to feel intimidated by these huge numbers of armed men marching past, but the closer I got to the city and the more of them I saw, the more I became used to the sight. By the time I reached the castle walls I could let them by me without looking like a frightened rabbit all the time. I felt quite proud of myself for being so blasé about the presence of the enemy so close to me, without my even flinching!

Everything changed when I came within sight of the city walls, however. Even before I was at the foot of the rise which leads to the main gates I could tell that this wasn't the same city I had lived in and left only a scant two cycles before. The whole forest which sits at the foot of the city approach was hung about with a pall of smoke and there was a sort of eerie stillness about the place which wasn't at all natural. But, even as this un-naturalness began to un-nerve me, I laid eyes on the main gate and felt as if someone had reached out, taken a hold of my heart and was squeezing it even while it still beat in my chest. The gates, the gatehouses and the walls that line the city, that mighty barrier which always seemed so inviolate, were all gone. Instead there lay piles of rubble and charred wood, where the army must have thrown down the defences as they stormed the city. The Divided Castle still stood but you could see how badly it had been damaged by fire. The walls were smeared with black streaking out from every window and arrow-slit and parts of the towers were cracked and falling. Empire troops were watching the main road from along the battlements, standing in their arrogant conquest so that they could overlook our city - our home.

When I travelled before, coming home had always been with a sense of pride, even from an early age, to see those strong, impenetrable walls and the men on sentry duty at the gate keeping watch over the comings and goings of the city. It was my home, and it was the heart of everything I had been raised to believe. Now, I was standing in that same place looking at what I knew was only the first of many signs of devastation. My home was gone, Castle Bremmand itself was gone and my heart had been torn out and destroyed, just as the city itself had been.

I don't know how long I stood there - it felt like forever; it was as if time had stopped and I was going to spend the rest of eternity just standing there, unable to move, looking at the remains of my home - but then another of those accursed legions came out and I had to move or be marched right over. I don't think I've ever hated myself more than I did at that moment, when I just stepped aside and let those invaders pass me by without doing anything to pay them back for what they had done. Or for making so many objections to the royal children being left without their main source of protection which meant that it was I who had to go and witness what the glorious city had become. If I'd just kept my mouth shut I could have remained in ignorance and continued to remember Castle Bremmand as it had been before Darvett and his hordes swept into it and laid it waste.

I don't think I really took in what I saw in the first part of my journey inside the city walls; my eyes were open but my mind was closed to it. Somehow I couldn't bear to walk the Royal road. I knew it would be full of *them* - Darvett's men - holding all the points that I used to frequent when this was my home. I headed through the Outer District towards the East Side, which I guessed would be of less interest to the troops in their first plunder of the city. At first it seemed that the more I walked, the worse it got.

I have hazy impressions but there was so little left there of the buildings that had stood there, that I did my best not to look. There had been fire - I remember that much! I could smell it as much as I could see the charred remains and smoke still rising from place to place. There were people too. Not many - a solitary soul picking through the rubble from place to place and once a few children, huddled together, not doing anything, just sitting in amongst the debris. I saw them - I think I even stopped to look at them, but - may God forgive me - I turned and left them there. I just kept going. I couldn't feel pity for them, or sorrow for their losses, whatever they may be; indeed I was beyond feeling anything anymore. I just knew I had to keep going, to get away from this devastation and find a place to stop and rest and collect my thoughts. I would never have believed it of myself but after walking through the devastation for a while I began to blot out the desperate plight of those people. I actually became immune to their poverty and helplessness. It was as if my heart had turned to stone and I knew it and I loathed myself for it but somehow I couldn't prevent myself either.

It had been late in the day when I entered the city and it was almost dark when I finally reached a part of the city that was less badly damaged and I found a tavern to stop for the night. There were plenty of people there but the atmosphere was tense and suspicious so I didn't try to talk to anyone or find out what had happened. It wasn't hard to guess that any outsider was going to be seen as a possible threat and it was clear that there had been enough violence towards these people already that they weren't about to risk saying anything to a stranger. No-one asked me my business, not even the landlord, and I didn't offer anything. It was a good enough place I suppose - clean and the food was edible - but I can't say I felt comfortable staying there, or slept well that night. I didn't stay more than that one night - it was too uncomfortable having all those suspicious eyes on me.

I turned and headed north the next morning, making my way through the East Side until I came in to Dracia. That was where I was born and as absurd as it sounded I was aiming for the Library. I don't even know why, but some time during that sleepless night I had becomes convinced that I had to ensure the sum of all our learnings over the centuries had not been destroyed. It became like an obsession - a desperate urge to get there as fast as I could manage to be sure that it was safe. I think in my fevered panic I had some idea of taking up residence to guard it; that it was more important to do that than to carry out the mission I had come for. I think that day I must have been temporarily insane, that I should put learning above the bloodline but unless you'd been there, unless you'd seen what it was like in that place, you couldn't possibly understand what it would do to a man.

In the end I never reached the library. Something else happened instead, which made me change my mind. I wasn't walking fast, you'll understand, since I didn't want to look like a man in a hurry and draw attention to myself. I just took up the same pace as most of the people I'd seen moving about - of which there weren't all that many - and ambled, with my eyes fixed to the ground, doing everything I could to seem invisible. So, it was mid-morning, and I had reached the heart of Dracia when I came across Dostain.

I didn't know that was his name when I first came across him, of course. He was lying by the side of the road, close up against the wall of a house which had been abandoned and he was badly wounded. By this time I had seen plenty of destitute people lying by the roadside so I didn't take much notice at first but he called out to me and begged for help and it stopped me for long enough to see that he was not just homeless but hurt as well. I may have learned to harden my heart to the poor and the dispossessed in my day and night in Castle Bremmand but I couldn't ignore this man, so I stopped and tried to help him. His face was covered in blood which had long dried and was crusted in his hair line and in his side was the broken-off shaft of an arrow. It was clear that he needed more aid than I could offer in the street, so I knew I would need to move him to somewhere where his ills could be attended.

As luck would have it, a few minutes later someone passed by. He was doing his best not to take any notice of us, for which I cannot blame him for this was just what I had done but I called out to him to gain his attention. His eyes flicked over in our direction but then turned away again and he continued on his way.

"Good neighbour," I tried again. "This man is hurt. Can you not stop and help him?"

"If he's been foolish enough to put himself in the way of the soldiers, then that's his own lookout. I for one am not going to throw suspicion on myself as being still loyal by helping him."

I couldn't believe it. He was prepared to walk away and not give his aid to a dying man. "Has the invasion changed the Bremmandish so much that they would forget even the most basic of Brem's teachings?" I cried out in indignation.

"Brem's gone," he declared, whirling round on us with a wild look in his eyes. "The kingdom has fallen and the bloodline with it. Everything we learned from Brem is lost to us and the best we can do now is survive. I intend to do that *neighbour*" – his tone was laced with such irony it was clear that I was most certainly not a neighbour to him - "by not allying myself with those foolish enough to cling to what is past and not bringing the Empire's gaze upon me."

With that he hurried on his way and was soon lost from sight.

The injured man laughed vaguely at this, a spit of blood coming on to his lips as he did so. "He's right," he wheezed. "If that is how people really see it, then Bremmand is most assuredly lost."

"Don't give up yet," I declared. "One frightened and ignorant man doesn't speak for all." I looked into his face, troubled by his pallor and the distant look in his eyes. If he didn't get help soon then he wasn't long for this world. "Will you be all right here if I leave you to go and get help?"

He nodded but I could see he thought that I too was abandoning him. "There is an inn a few streets away," I told him. "I'll go there and get the landlord to help me take you there. I *will* be coming back, friend and I expect you to be still here when I return. *Do you hear me?*" I spoke fiercely, somehow affronted by his belief that I, too, would turn my back on him and determined to make him see that not all men had forgotten the teachings. He nodded but I wasn't sure he believed me even then.

Still, there was no time to lose so I turned and hurried away from him to find help. I must admit I was a little fearful that the inn might not be open for business and I knew it was a risk for me to go there, where I was known, but the man needed help and I was so indignant that that scoundrel of a passer-by had refused to assist that I didn't much care about that. I would prove that Bremmand wasn't yet lost - that most of us were still good people. That I was bringing myself in to danger and putting myself in the way of those who knew I had held a position at the Castle was no longer important. They knew me from when I grew up in Dracia, so I could be reasonably sure that they would not betray me. What I did not expect was that they would turn me away.

No, not just turn me away, but drive me away. At first the landlord had listened, uninterested when I told him of the injured man and his plight but then I saw his eyes narrow as he took in my face and he realised that, despite my shabby clothes and weary look, he recognised me. Then his expression changed and his look became hostile.

"I know you, don't I? You were at the Castle." I nodded. I could hardly deny it. "And yet you come here, to bring danger to all those who live here. To your friends and family?" I didn't know what to say to this; I didn't really know what he was talking about. I was bringing no danger to them. If anything it was the other way round and I had a secret to protect that was more precious than life itself. And yet here was someone I had known all my life acting as if I was carrying disease to his door. "Get away from here," he ordered and, to my disbelief, he turned and picked up the cudgel he kept behind the door in case of trouble. "Go, and don't come back! You're not welcome here. You'd be best off getting right out of Castle Bremmand so that no more of the innocent are tainted by their association with you and your kind."

My kind? Was he mad?

"You loyalists have brought down trouble on us all and I'll not put myself and mine at risk by having it known that I've had anything to do with you. Now get out of here before I set the dogs on you."

That was an empty threat, I knew. "You have no dogs," I said, scornful and angry, "but I'll go and I'll take my loyalty with me. I'd not stay here where a man's service of our King is viewed with such revulsion. You stay here, safe, mired in your own cowardice and maybe, one day, you'll remember what it was to be a man of honour and faith who was prepared to die for his King and country. It's no wonder Bremmand has fallen if its people are so craven as to act as you do."

It was foolish of me to declare myself so openly, I know, and it could have brought disaster down on me but I was burning up. The day before I had grieved for the city, so brutalised by Empire troops and for the loss of life that was only too evident, but now I was beginning to feel that it was deserved. How could people have allowed themselves to give up everything they had believed in in such a short space of time and for so base a reason as fear? Such was my anger that it brought with it a resolve that, if no-one else would, I would see to the hurt of the wounded man and prove to him, even if he didn't live to know it, that not all of Castle Bremmand had turned its face away from Brem Marchand and his line.

Before I went back to my new-found friend, I walked a few streets looking for somewhere that I might take him where he could be safe. It wasn't hard - there were plenty of houses which were no longer occupied and as soon as I had discovered one that had not been too badly damaged or looted and was free of the bodies of its occupants, I returned to bring the injured man to it. It took me a while, for he was badly hurt and couldn't move very fast but eventually we made it and I was able to do something to make him more comfortable. The short journey exhausted him and he passed out almost as soon as I brought him over the threshold of the house in which we were now squatting. In some ways that made my job easier for I was able to tend to his injuries and remove the arrow from his side while he was still unconscious and by the time he awoke once more, his wounds were treated and bound as best I knew how.

That was how we stayed for the next few days and we struck up a friendship as a result of mutual refusal to give in to Empire will. It was here that he told me his name - Dostain of Saphir - and how he was a craftsman, making a good living with his brother from weaving. He had been out of Castle Bremmand when the city fell, trading in Norris, so he didn't know much of how the attack came but had hurried home when he had heard the news to see what had become of his brother who had remained here in the city. He'd been here a little over a week before he was injured and had learned enough to tell me much of what had been going on and why the people were so afraid.

Since the occupying force had taken hold they had begun to purge the city, going to great lengths to root out and kill anyone who could be deemed to be loyal to the king. What was more, their definition of loyalty seemed to be very tenuous indeed. Not just the declared loyalists, such as soldiers, were being tracked down, but their women and children too. Anyone who could be connected to the royal family or his court, even indirectly, was being butchered by the Empire troops. Even merchants who traded at the castle (just as Dostain and his brother had done) were considered an enemy of the state and by the time Dostain returned to the city his brother had gone and a friend from previous times had taken up possession of their business.

"It was probably him who sold my brother out," Dostain had guessed gloomily. "People are proving their loyalty to the new regime by selling out neighbours. I am almost certain that he betrayed me."

Dostain had been back in Castle Bremmand for nearly a week and had taken rooms in a nearby tavern while he tried to resolve matters with the man who had taken over his business, when soldiers had come for him during the night. Fortunately the tavern owner was a good man and had given him warning so he had managed to flee the tavern but not without being fired upon by the troops and taking two hits from their arrows. He had managed to keep running, even despite the injuries but eventually he had fallen, unable to continue and remained where I had found him that morning.

Since he'd been among friends for that week before he was betrayed he had been able to find out what had occurred in Bremmand since we left. News of the King's final battle is scant. People only know what the Empire troops are telling them - that the Alliance failed and was defeated and that thousands lost their lives. From what Dostain had heard and then told me, I think we must have been defeated by sheer weight of numbers. Darvett and his army came sweeping in to Bremmand like a plague, destroying everything that stood in their path.

The King fell in battle, as did his sons - all four of them. To prove it, Darvett brought their bodies back to the city and put them on display so that any who desired proof could come and see for themselves. They were still there. After Dostain told me about it, I had to go, in spite of myself, to be sure that it was true.

They were there, just as Dostain told me, stripped naked and nailed to the castle walls. Their bodies had begun to decompose but I could still tell that it was them. They weren't alone. Darvett had put some of the King's most loyal commanders there with him - all in the same manner - like some hideous version of the Oath of Fealty. The Queen and Lord Verdin were there as well - they must have been caught on the road north.

Dostain had been told that, at first, the people had tried to take the bodies down - to give them a decent burial - but Darvett's men had punished any who tried to defy the Emperor's wish to display them in this way. Retribution was swift and savage and it was from this that the campaign was started to punish anyone who showed loyalty to the old order with death.

When I stood there myself, and looked upon my King, his Queen and the sons that I had taught and known, it was as much as I could do to stop myself from doing something about this abomination myself. To be defeated in battle was one thing but to humiliate my King in such a way as this was as much as I could bear. I had to keep reminding myself that the royal line still had need of me and I must remain unnoticed and unknown until I had completed my mission to see them to safety. It was just as well for, as I stood there, I noticed a woman also standing and looking upon the bodies. She was weeping, grieving for her King as was right. Then, suddenly there were Empire soldiers there and, without so much as a second's thought, they cut her down where she stood, making some declaration that all other loyalists would suffer the same fate. Even if anyone had been inclined to go to her aid, they would have had no time to do a thing, except perhaps die alongside her.

I saw very little of the atrocities myself – the woman at the castle walls was the worst of it. I spent most of my days tending to Dostain, only venturing out to get food, but from what he had told me of the slaughter going on daily - as Darvett had his men hunt for anyone they saw as still loyal to the King - I began to understand why I had been so harshly rejected by the innkeeper and the passer-by in Dracia. The reign of terror which Darvett had applied to the city was so complete that one could hardly blame men if they cared more to protect their own families than show concern for a stranger. What I found harder to forgive was the loss of faith in the Bremmand line - they had given up so quickly and turned away from all that Brem represented and that I still feel unable to comprehend. Bremmand isn't lost because the King is dead. Bremmand is lost because the people have given it away.

Most of the rest of what Dostain was able to tell me was just news of how people were getting by through the occupation, although there were more tales of atrocities and snatches of how Castle Bremmand fell to the Empire.

According to some that Dostain spoke to, there were Empire troops inside the walls before the siege even began and there are rumours that we must have been betrayed. It wasn't something I could get proof of, and of course there are always rumours of betrayal after a defeat, just as there are rumours of poison when a King dies suddenly. There was one thing that Dostain told me that I knew to be a lie, however.

When Darvett took the Castle he took a number of the officials hostage. Very little is known of what has become of most of them but one was brought out in front of the people and forced to bear witness to a number of things in order to corroborate the fact that defeat of Bremmand was complete. As luck would have it, Dostain remembered the name of this official: Staval.

I don't know if you knew him. Staval was a junior administrator in the King's advisory staff. Bright, ambitious and loyal but not all that courageous - or so I thought. Apparently he had been put on display to tell the people of Castle Bremmand that Kostinian custom forbade them from displaying the bodies of children so, as a member of the King's court, he was there to bear witness to the deaths of the other five royal children. It is true about the way Kostinians view children - I happen to know that for a fact. They have no compunction about killing the children of their enemies but they do believe strongly that even enemy offspring should be given a proper burial. That was why they had brought Staval forward - so they said. But, of course, I knew that Staval had lied to them. He hadn't seen all five royal children because three of them are still alive and well in the forest. I don't know who he bore witness to, what poor innocents had been presented to him, for him to have been able to lie, or whether he had told Darvett's men that he had seen them when it wasn't true. But either way, the Empire believes that it has eliminated the whole bloodline. Which means that they won't be looking for us for as long as they believe what Staval has told them.

Dostain and I stayed in that house for three days but then, on the fourth night, I woke to hear him calling me. At first I thought he needed a drink, or some other minor thing but when I reached him and saw his face I knew that something had changed. It had come on him suddenly. Over the past three days he had been rallying, and I thought he might recover - in fact the previous evening we had been talking of leaving Castle Bremmand together, and travelling north to friends of his in Norris - but now suddenly he had worsened and it was clear from his pallor that his time had come.

He knew it too and he said as much. "I don't fear dying, Trystin," he told me breathlessly, "but I'd rather not face it alone. Will you sit with me and talk. I should be glad of your company."

I sat at his bedside, took his hand and then, as he waited for death to come to him, I said impulsively, "I lied to you, Dostain. There is something I want to tell you."

When Dostain and I had exchanged tales on the first night in the house, I had concocted a plausible lie about how I spent the time since the fall and how I had come in to the city to return home. Now I wanted him to know who I really was. So, I told that dying man the truth. How I wasn't a humble librarian who had been visiting friends but a tutor to the Royal family and how I knew for certain of the survival of some of the King's brood. I didn't go so far as to say where they were now but he knew that they were in my care and that I would never rest until they were back on the throne. It felt wrong to break my vow to keep them a secret but at the same time, their survival is worthless if no-one knows of it. Anyway, it isn't as if Dostain was ever going to tell anyone, for I buried him myself the next morning.

Before he died, he gripped my hand a little tighter and said to me hoarsely, "I can give you nothing now, to thank you for your kindness to me, a dying man, or to the hope you have brought me in my last hours that this is not yet finished but what little I can, I give you. When I am gone, take my bag and inside it you will find a seal. It is the guild seal of the master weavers. Use it to become Dostain the weaver of Saphir. A travelling weaver with apprentices won't raise any questions and you can travel safely to Hast. Use my name to protect our King.

Dostain drifted in to sleep shortly after this but I remained at his bedside until he died, shortly before dawn.

When Trystin had finished his tale with the death of Dostain, he fell silent and both men sat, staring in to the fire as they came to terms with what Trystin had learned.

"You realise," Dale said eventually, "that Staval may be the one who betrayed the city."

Trystin turned and stared at him stupidly. "Staval?"

"Betrayal makes sense, Trystin. The city fell too fast, from what you have told me, for it to have been anything else. Someone let the troops in to the city and Staval has the power and influence to see that that happened. Then he pretends to be a hostage and under duress, but we know he was lying. Why not say the children are dead to get the people to believe the bloodline is gone and make them more co-operative to the enemy? Darvett knows he still has a threat in the shape of the younger children but he might as well pretend that his victory is complete."

Trystin thought this through and then nodded. "It is possible. It is certainly wiser to believe that and that Darvett is still looking for us, than to believe ourselves safe."

Dale put a hand on Trystin's shoulder. "But your friend Dostain has given us something that makes our job a little easier. By granting you his identity and the chattels that go with it, it solves a problem for us."

"Yes." Trystin lifted his head. "I owe Dostain a lot - the information he gave me, the friendship, the hope that not everyone had given up, and in the end, his very name - I won't forget him."

"Did you..?" Dale hesitated. Was it right to ask this now? It was so much less important than the main thrust of what Trystin had told him but still, he had to know. "Were you able to get in to Ventis?" Ventis was the district in the West of the City where Verdin's mistress lived. Before Trystin had left, Dale had asked him to go there and see if he could get a message to the woman. He didn't dare try to bring the lord's son to the cottage, so had not given Trystin the token Verdin had given him, but at least if the seamstress knew someone was coming for them, she might be reassured of her safety. This was now more important if Verdin's death was being so publicly confirmed. The last thing he needed was for Sela to panic and give up the child to his enemies in an attempt to protect herself or to try and move to somewhere more secluded and thus bring danger down on herself or the child.

Trystin's head drooped as he nodded in answer to Dale's question and at the need to deliver still more bad news. "I tried, but Ventis is gone."

"Gone? What do you mean gone?"

"So many who lived in Ventis worked in the Castle. Anyone who worked in the Castle needs must be loyal to the King, so they purged the whole district. About two weeks after the city fell, soldiers rode in to Ventis during the night and razed it to the ground. Then, during the confusion of the fire, they cut down anyone who was still alive. It is thought that no-one survived the butchery of that night." Dale couldn't find the words to express his rage at this latest atrocity and Trystin, misunderstanding his silence said expressively, "I'm so sorry Dale. I know you didn't say it but I guessed the boy must have been your son. I wish there was some easier way to have told you of their loss."

"*My* son?" Dale said a little blankly. Then he pulled himself together. "No, Trystin. Not mine. I knew him but he wasn't my boy. The Earl of Langate had an association with the woman and he left Lord Willan with her, rather than in the care of anyone at the Castle. He had asked me to come back, when I had completed my mission to get the princes to safety and take Lord Willan to join them."

"I see." Trystin let out a long, drawn-out sigh. "If Lord Willan didn't survive then the Langate line has been ended. Darvett has taken so much of Bremmand from us."

"Yes. But not all of it," Dale said with sudden resolve, "and not all of the people have given in, just yet. For every innkeeper who turns away a man in need, like that fellow in Dracia, there is someone like Dostain who will stay loyal despite everything. This isn't over yet, no matter how many districts they burn and innocents they butcher. In the end, even the most fearful will see that they have nothing left to lose by defying these invaders so they may as well make their stand with us."

"Yes," Trystin agreed, sounding more certain. "I do know that, Dale. Forgive me if I seem to doubt it."

"There's nothing to forgive, my friend. It would take a man with a heart of pure stone not to be profoundly affected by what you've had to witness over the last few weeks and a man with no heart at all not to fear and doubt what the future will bring us. But, Master Trystin, there is a future and it is right here, in our protection. The bloodline lives on, as does the hope that people need to rally them once again, just as soon as we have brought them to a place of safety. The King is dead, Trystin. Long live the King!"

"Dale?" As if on cue, the door to the little wooden cottage swung open and Cori came outside. He had pulled on his tunic and boots but was barelegged and unbelted. "I thought I heard you talking and I wondered if..." then he saw the slender figure of the scholar who had risen to his feet on hearing Cori's voice and was now walking towards the youth. "Trystin. Welcome home." Cori looked delighted to see the man back but as the two met halfway across the clearing everything changed and it changed forever.

It was hardly surprising, Dale reflected later, that Trystin should act as he did, considering all he had seen and all he knew and, in particular, the faith he needed to restore but it was an unfortunate way for a young man to learn that he had lost both his parents and all his elder brothers. For, as Trystin came face to face with Cori, he went down on one knee, bowed his head and to his new King, said formally, "Your Majesty."

For a frozen heartbeat Cori stared down at the man and then with a despairing wail of "No!" he began to back away. He only retreated a few feet before he sank to his knees, buried his face in his hands and sobbed like a child. As if by instinct Trystin rose, crossed to him and, kneeling once more, drew the lad in to his shoulder as he wept, holding him as the loss of his family poured out of him in waves of grief.

"It isn't true," Cori cried, heartbreakingly. "It can't be just us." Trystin didn't attempt to correct the lad or give him more. He just kept his arms about the boy.

Dale stood and watched, but did nothing. There was nothing he could do - not yet. Cori had to face this reality and become a King but not tonight. Tonight he needed to grieve the loss of his family and Trystin could help him in that just as well as Dale - better probably. The lad had always confided in Trystin more easily than in Dale, for all the strength of the friendship between the woodsman and the prince, so it made sense for them to take this journey together. It wouldn't be the last, after all.

Eventually, the sobbing subsided and slowly Cori released his hold on the Scholar. He was shivering so Trystin gently coaxed him back to his feet and brought him to sit beside Dale at the fire. Trystin seated himself on the other side of the lad and the two guardians of the Royal line waited until the King of Bremmand found himself enough to speak to them.

It didn't take too long. Cori let out a deep sigh and then said numbly, "What happens now?"

"We do everything that is necessary to protect you, son," Dale said with calm certainty. "The kingdom is in the hands of invaders and they hold the land at the moment. From what Trystin has told me of what is going on in Castle Bremmand the people are losing heart. They need to know that there is still hope. It's a hard thing to have to take on, Cori but you must ask yourself, are you ready to be King? For your subjects have never needed their King more than they do now."

There was a long silence, as the flames danced about, throwing reflections of gold on to Cori's face and the only sound was the crackle of sticks on the fire. "If I'm to be King," Cori said slowly, "then my first command is that I have you by my side to guide me."

"That doesn't need to be a command. Cori," Trystin said instantly, "It's our duty and honour to serve the true King of Bremmand, always."

Dale said nothing, thinking deeply, but Cori hadn't missed the absence of a similar protestation of loyalty from the soldier. "Dale? Is there something wrong?"

"No," he replied, "but my duty has first to be fulfilled to another. My final duty to the Lord Protector.

"I swore to him that I would see you and the others to safety and the more I think about it, the more I realise that Verdin's approach was the right one."

"I don't know what you mean," Cori said puzzled. "What approach? All he did was split the party up..." his voice trailed off as he realised what Dale was saying. "You want to split us up. You want to take Allin and Joss away from me." He leapt to his feet and started to pace away.

"Cori," Dale called softly after him, getting to his feet to follow.

"NO!!" The boy swung back on him, his face twisted in fury. "I won't let you break us apart. We're all that's left, and we're going to stay together." Then all the anger left his face leaving only pain. "You can't make me do this, Dale. They're my only family; all I have left."

"I know son." Dale came close and put his broad hands on to Cori's arms, in a gesture of support. "But if you're the King, we *have* to get you to safety and the risk is much greater if we all travel together. It makes most sense for you and Trystin to travel together - no-one will pay all that much attention to a travelling trader and his apprentice - and for myself and the children to stay here, in safety until we get word from you. "

"They're all I've got left," Cori repeated numbly, his head drooping against the idea of more separation.

"And I will protect them and keep them safe for you, Sire; and when the time is right, I will deliver them back to you."

It took a few more minutes of assurances before Cori could be persuaded to return to his seat by the fire and more minutes still before he agreed that rending the remains of his family asunder was the best course but finally he bowed his head and admitted to the wisdom of Dale's suggestion. "A King can't be driven by his own wishes, but by what is best for his Kingdom. My father taught me that much about Kingship." He said it numbly as if it was too much to bear. "The least I can do to honour his memory is to accept that. If this is the best course for the Kingdom, then I must do the right thing. But tell me, Dale, why must I leave? We are safe here. Why can I not remain here, with the others, where no-one will ever to think to look for me?"

"You are King," Dale said with feeling, "and this is your Kingdom. You cannot allow it to remain in enemy hands while you hide among the trees, unknown and unacknowledged. Go to Hast. Be recognised as King of Bremmand and Heir Presumptive to Hast. Get the support of the rest of the Alliance and rebuild the army. Bremmand should not be subject to an invader's rule for a second longer than it has to."

Cori stared at him, surprised by the vehemence of the man's statement. Dale's attitude to the Kingdom had always been one of duty. This was the first time Cori had seen a sign of the man's own feelings towards his king and country. In a way he had not expected, the youthful King was buoyed by such determined patriotism. With a final resignation of his obligations, he pulled his golden head upright and looked Dale square in the face. "Very well, Dale. If this is how it has to be, then I put myself in your hands. What do you want us to do?"

The three men sat and talked through the rest of the night, Trystin giving Cori a few more details of his parents' death (although not the humiliation they had since suffered at the hands of their enemy) and Dale outlining the plan to get Cori and Trystin to safety. The gift of Dostain's token of identity, as well as fabric samples in the bag he had bequeathed to Trystin, made matters a little simpler, since it would be perfectly natural for a weaver to be travelling the land to trade his wares. Cori could pose as his apprentice and it was unlikely that they would be interfered with by soldiers on their journey in to the north. They would follow some of the quieter roads, crossing the river at Novoris rather than following the North Road, which was likely to be busy with Empire troops and then travel through the forest heading for Langate. From there, they could easily pick up the Kesh road and find a way across the border in to Hast where, hopefully, passage would be allowed for an honest trader and his apprentice. From there they could journey in relative safety to the King.

It was Trystin who suggested that, even at the Hastian castle, Cori should keep his identity secret from general knowledge. Darvett would have good reason to want Cori dead and with the force of army at his back he might decide to continue his rampage north to invade Hast as well, in order to complete his conquest of Bremmand's royal line. After a little thought, Dale agreed. "We'll leave it to King Perrold's advisors to decide how best to let word escape that Bremmand still has a true King. It goes without saying that no-one must know that you are not the only survivor. While Allin and Joss are still within Bremmand's borders, their anonymity is their greatest protection."

"I can't help feeling a little relieved that there will still be a representative of the bloodline within the borders of the land," Cori said, but then shrugged, "although I think the prophesy is already fulfilled, so perhaps it is a moot point." He was referring to an ancient piece of the legend of Holy Brem in which God made a bargain with his ancestor. It was said that while direct descendents of Brem and Langilia remained within the borders, Bremmand would always belong to his people. If ever they should depart from its borders then Bremmand would be lost to them.

"I don't think we can keep the children here indefinitely just to satisfy an old superstition," Trystin observed. "Their safety must come first."

"It's hardly just a superstition, Trystin," Cori retorted. "The covenant between God and Brem forms the basis of the faith. I am supposed to lead the people in the following of that faith. I should at least try to remember it."

"There's time enough to worry about that later," Dale pointed out. "By the time you have established yourself outside the borders and secured some support from the alliance, it will be heading into winter. There is no way that I can transport two young children in the heart of winter, so it will be next spring before we will be able to remove them from Bremmand and who knows what will have happened by then."

"Next spring," Cori said gloomily. "That's almost a year."

"I know, son. It seems a long time, but this is the best chance for all of you. If I could see another way, you know I would suggest it." As Cori nodded, Dale turned to Trystin "And speaking of superstition, if you are going to be travelling through the Forest you'll need to be familiar with some of the Woodsmen's ways or you'll draw suspicion on to yourselves. I know Cori knows his but what's your tree Trystin?"

"My tree?" the scholar looked astonished. "I've no idea. It's hardly something I've ever needed to know and I don't believe in the old ways."

"Well you need to start learning them now. The tree dressing is less than two moons away and if you are still in the forest then you will be expected to know. When were you born - which season?"

"Spring. In the third moon, ten days after full."

"Chestnut then. Yes, I suppose that makes sense."

"Meaning?" Trystin asked heavily.

When Dale didn't answer Cori allowed himself a sly smile and told him, "Chestnut's irritate easily and act as if they are superior to others."

"I see. Thank you"

"It's a good thing that you don't believe in it, isn't it?" Dale remarked. "Though Chestnut also stands for honesty and a sense of justice, so it isn't all bad."

"You're an oak, aren't you Dale?" Cori smiled.

"I am. I suppose Allin told you that."

"Yes, but it isn't a hard one to guess, is it? Oak's are unrelenting. I can't think of a word that described you better." Then he smiled, "Or a trait that you will need more, with my walnut of a brother!"

They were still talking when dawn came, none of them feeling able to go to sleep and instead spending the time talking over the journey that Cori and Trystin were about to make, and other considerations for the next few mooncycles until Cori's safety was established. The young man spoke openly of his concerns at the responsibility now falling upon him for which he felt so ill prepared but even as they talked Dale and Trystin could see the mantle of monarchy beginning to settle upon his shoulders, and there in the dark, on a summer's night, the three of them worked together to make a King.

Shortly after first light, a new challenge came to Cori, one not related to monarchy. Perhaps disturbed by the sound of talking, or by some sixth sense, Allin awoke and came out, already dressed, to cross the dew-drenched grass of the little clearing.

Dale took in Cori's troubled face in an instant and put a warm hand on his arm. "Do you want me to talk to him?"

166

For a second Cori looked as if he wanted to say yes, but then he squared his shoulders and pushed his chin up. "No, thank you Dale. He's my brother. This is my responsibility now. Would you both excuse me?" With that he rose to his feet and crossed the distance between himself and the boy with the courage and dignity of a man twice his age. The King of Bremmand put an arm about his brother's shoulder, turned him gently and together they crossed the clearing and vanished into the trees.

Dale never knew what passed between the Marchands that day. Cori and Allin were gone for perhaps an hour and then they returned briefly. Allin had vanished in to the cottage and returned leading Joss by the hand. Then all three had again left the clearing and were gone for the rest of the morning.

When they returned, together, Allin still holding one of Joss' hands, they were all solemn-faced but showing very little in the way of emotion. Even Joss who could have been expected to have less self-control than the others was grave but dry-eyed. Both Trystin and Dale were there to see them return but neither man knew quite what to say. The children seemed as little inclined to discussion so it was Cori who spoke for them all and, when he did, it was the words of a King.

"I name my brother Prince Allinaias, heir to the throne of Bremmand and, by right of that title, the Duke of Raz. I have explained to him, and to Joss, why we must be parted while I travel out of Bremmand and they remain here. In my absence he stands in my stead as representative of the crown in Bremmand. He speaks for me on behalf of the Kingdom and also for my family." Allin didn't look at them, or speak. Instead he kept his eyes fixed firmly on the ground. Cori was still speaking but now he had moved on to other matters. "I have very little in the way of a court, while my Kingdom is in the hands of a usurper, so I must make appointments with what means I have. Trystin, since we will travel together, you will be my first advisor and Lord Chancellor of Bremmand. In the next few cycles I trust you to help me make the decisions that will be necessary to regain Bremmand and free the people from the invaders." Trystin bowed his head, but said nothing. "As for you, Captain Ronas. I leave you here with the protection of my family in your hands. To do that, I can do no better than to appoint you Lord Protector. It is one of the few ranks that gives authority over royal personages, in order to ensure their safety and I believe that it is a right that will ease the task ahead of you. I'm sure Lord Verdin would forgive me taking the honour of this title away from his line but it serves me better in your hands."

At some point, Dale reflected, Cori would need to be told that the Langate line was no more, but he had heard as much bad news as he could manage for one day and he didn't need to know that Lord Willan had died in the massacre at Castle Bremmand. Trystin would doubtless tell him when they were on the road towards Hast. Right now, however, there was something else from which Dale needed to divert the new King. For now, Cori had drawn his sword and was advancing on Dale. "Kneel before me, Dale Ronas," he commanded, but the big man shook his head.

"Not for me, Cori. I'm a soldier, not a courtier. Knighthood isn't for me. I couldn't serve you well in such a guise."

"But…" Cori began to argue.

With a sigh and a rapid diversion into the disrespectful teasing that he and Cori had adopted over the last few week Dale met his eye and said, "Do you *really* see me in coloured hose, and silks?"

It was a comical image and, with a smile, the King relented. "No. I suppose not. Not really the kind of thing that might suit you. All right, I'll leave you a commoner but if you ever change your mind, let me know and I'll make the appropriate arrangements. However, I will promote you to the rank of Commander. I'd put you in charge of my armies but at the moment I'm not sure I have any."

"That will come with time," Dale assured him and Cori nodded.

Then the young man took them all in with his gaze and said soberly, "To make the customary oaths towards my kingdom and people seem futile at such a time, so I will not attempt to make them but I will promise this much. Bremmand is still the birthright of my family and I will do all in my power to resume my rightful place on the throne at Castle Bremmand. My family have sworn to aid me in that accordingly. Bremmand is ours and we want it back!"

Having made this first speech as King of Bremmand, Cori suddenly seemed lost for words and he gazed somewhat helplessly at Trystin for direction.

Only then, in to the silence, in a small voice Joss said, "I forgot to feed the chickens."

In other circumstances it might have been comical but there was something forlorn in her tone that removed the urge for anyone to laugh. Gently Dale came and took her other hand. "Come and get something to eat for yourself, Little Flower - there's rabbit stew waiting for you - then we can see to the animals."

"Allin too," Joss suggested, keeping her grip on his hand. "He didn't have breakfast either."

"I'm not hungry," the boy said dismally but then, with an effort, added, "but I'll come and keep you company Joss. We can feed the animals together."

When Dale had led the youngsters away, Cori finally allowed his head to drop and he admitted to Trystin with a heavy heart, "They are braver than I am, Trystin. They accept that we are all that is left and that we have to be separated far better than I have done. I wish I felt worthy of them - worthy of a Kingdom that needs me so badly."

"I think you will prove yourself more than worthy for the needs of both your family and your subjects: besides to have doubt only proves that you have the qualities you need. If you didn't question your abilities, if you thought it would be easy, then I might wonder whether you were well equipped to take on such a role but I look at you, Your Majesty, and I see the qualities that it takes to be a man and a leader. I follow you with the love and loyalty that you deserve, not just that which your birth demands."

"Then I shall lead, just so long as you and the others are there to guide and aid me. Together, we five will take back what is ours."

Heir to the Throne

At first light the next morning, Cori and Trystin left the cottage in the forest. They carried very little with them, other than a few supplies for the journey, Dostain's bag and enough gold to buy provisions along the way. It was some two hundred and fifty miles from the Cottage to Hast, Dale had estimated, so they were expecting it to take them the best part of a moon-cycle to get there, allowing for diversions and rest days. They weren't going to hurry. Instead they would make out that they were taking their time to reach each destination and thus disguise the need for urgency in their travel.

Before he left, Cori had one more thing to say to Dale. He'd spent the evening thinking about what he could give to the man to whom he was entrusting his family and how he could show his trust and respect. It had come to him in the early hours of the morning and there, in the cottage clearing, he made a gesture that was of special significance to a soldier. Without warning he drew his sword and once again began to advance upon the big man.

Seeing him coming, and thinking his intentions were the same as the previous day, Dale opened his mouth to argue, but before he could protest, Cori said simply, "Will you honour me by exchanging swords with me, Dale?"

Dale gaped at him. Exchanging swords was something that soldiers did from time to time, to indicate close bonds of friendship or deep obligation. Usually it would be done before a battle and then the weapons exchanged back again if both men survived. A soldier carrying the blade of a friend would have the spirit of that friend by his side and the duty to honour the weapon of another as well as that which was required towards the officers. The companionship and trust the sword exchange represented provided an extra incentive to a man going into battle. If one man fell, then the other had the consolation of knowing that his own sword was lying in the field with his companion and he would return his fallen friend's blade to the man's family. Thus exchanges were only done with the closest of friends and the meaning of it in men of equal rank was highly significant. Exchanges between men of different ranks was extremely rare and for Dale to be offered the chance to exchange swords with his King was unheard of. While he was still searching for something to say in reply to the vastness of this offer Cori added, "I can think of no man more worthy of holding my sword and using it within the lands of Bremmand to defend the kingdom and protect my family and I can think of nothing I would like better than to hold your sword until we meet again, to remind me of the honour I owe you for your actions towards me. Please Dale, do this for me."

That settled it, and Dale drew his own sword, offering it gravely to his King, hilt first. "I cannot refuse you this, Sire. You are my King and nothing would honour me more. I trust that it won't be too long before I can return your own blade to you."

"Amen to that," Trystin murmured softly.

Allin and Joss had risen with their brother to see him and the scholar off and now the time had come for them to say their final goodbyes. It was a difficult parting. At first they had all tried to be brave but then, just as Cori was about to turn and go, he couldn't control himself any longer. He reached out and grabbed his brother and sister pulling them in to a tight embrace and hiding his face in their heads. The three of them clung together in silent sorrow at the separation that they all knew they must suffer. Then, finally, Cori loosened his grip slightly, kissed them both and murmured with deep feeling, "Be happy. *Please*. Be happy until we are together again. I couldn't bear to think of you any other way." Then, as abruptly as he had taken hold of them, he released them, turned and left the clearing without another backward glance.

The two youngster watched him go, Joss with her eyes brimming with tears and her fist in her mouth to stop herself crying out. After a few seconds Allin suddenly took a few steps forward as if he wanted to run after his brother but, at Dale's gentle word, stopped again and instead turned and headed off in to the woods in the other direction.

In the first few weeks after Cori and Trystin had gone, their presence haunted the clearing like ghosts. Every time Dale picked up his axe to work in the forest he found himself involuntarily looking out for the young man who had acted as his assistant in their time together. Even while Trystin had been away mornings had been dedicated to education, Cori taking on the tutelage of his younger siblings. Now there was no-one to take that role and there was a huge gap in the youngsters' mornings although both Dale and Allin did put some time in to teaching Joss her letters and numbers. Dale soon filled the empty time for them, by handing over many of the chores that Trystin had fulfilled in caring for the cottage and garden to Allin.

For Allin this was a hard time. He was desperately lonely, missing his brother far more than he would have imagined possible but he did his best to do act as he felt was expected of him as heir to the throne and representative of the King. He should be obedient, so he did as he was told without argument, even in things he hated doing. He should care for his sister, so he steadfastly spent time with her, watching her in her play and allowing her to show him her amusements. He should be a man, so he hid his feelings and pretended that nothing was troubling him.

Despite Allin's manful attempts to keep his feelings hidden, Dale could tell the boy was unhappy. The depression that was with him followed the lad like a black cloud and although he did as he was requested in everything, he took no joy in it. In fact very little seemed to entertain him these days and he went about his duties with the same fixed determination with which he had earned his right to accompany Dale on his first visit to Chelland. It was almost as if he was carved of wood - going through the motions of living, instead of showing any joy in it. It was heartbreaking to watch this spirited and jovial youngster struggling to keep going and Dale began to wish that there was something, anything, he could do to break his young friend out of this rapidly hardening shell of indifference to life.

There is an old Bremmandish saying that goes *Be careful what you wish for* and it soon proved itself to be true for Dale. For Allin, having cocooned himself in a defensive armour, was still festering on the inside and eventually the pressure built up inside him until his neutral veneer came away from him all of a piece.

Even afterwards Dale couldn't quite understand how it all came about. It had seemed like a perfectly normal morning. Allin had been his usual, non-committal self when he rose and brought his sister in for breakfast. When Dale had mentioned in passing that he would be going in to the forest that day, so Allin would need to remain at the cottage and watch over his sister, the lad had seemed at first put out and then offended by the man's instructions.

He had tried to persuade Dale to let him come along but this was out of the question. Joss was too young to be taken in to the trees when there was work being done and equally she could not be left alone. So Allin would have to remain.

"Then don't go," Allin said flatly. "Stay here with us."

"I can't. There's work to be done."

"There's work to be done here. You keep telling me to tend the garden and if you stayed, you could do that instead."

"I could, if I stayed," Dale agreed, "Except that I'm not going to stay."

"Well, I'm not staying here on my own any more. Either I come with you, or you stay here."

"No," Dale stated firmly. "I am going to work in the forest and you are going to stay here and look after your sister. I am not prepared to argue about this Allin."

Allin looked mulishly at him for a minute, trying to find a good response. Then, as if it settled the matter, he stated, "I don't want you to go."

"I'm afraid you have no choice. We can't always do as we want to, you know."

From his seat at the table, Allin's face went from pink to white. "You think I don't know *that?*" he hissed furiously. Then he got to his feet and he declared, "I'm the King's brother and you have to do as I say."

Suddenly Dale understood something Cori had said to him when he left. He had appointed Dale as Lord Protector with the words *I believe that it is a right that will ease the task ahead of you* and it was moments like these that Cori had anticipated. For Allin's brother had several times remarked that Allin could be all but impossible when his temper was up and Dale was now facing it without support but also with the prickly problem of this angry ten-year-old outranking him. The Lord Protector, however, was one of the few roles in the Bremmandish court which had the right to outrank any and all others, up to and including the King himself. In truth it was only applicable to matters of the personal safety of the Royal Family but the precedent was there and Dale could see that he had been granted the right to use it at times just such as this one.

So instead of being forced to retreat, Dale had the confidence and the right to outface the angry boy and say firmly. "I have no intention of bending on this point, Allin. Now sit down and stop making a fuss. It isn't as if I haven't had to leave you here before."

In the next few seconds, what was, to Dale, a minor dispute suddenly exploded in to a major catastrophe. Enraged by this defiance of what he saw as his winning thrust Allin hurled at the big man, "I won't stay here. You've no right to do this to me!" and faster than Dale could react, he was out of the door, across the clearing and had vanished in to the trees.

"Hell's *teeth!*" Dale swore and he pulled the cooking dish of pottage off the fire, snatched up Joss and hurried off after the boy.

To begin with, Dale had expected to find Allin quite quickly and to settle the matter but after half an hour it became clear that Allin's departure was supported by far more determination that just a brief burst of rage. He was gone and Dale was going to have to search for the boy in earnest.

He threw a glance at Joss, in his arms. She hadn't been fully dressed when Allin had run out and he could hardly carry her about the forest in just her tunic and bare feet. She'd get cold and be vulnerable to brambles and nettles if he didn't take the time to dress her. So, teeth clenched in frustration at the lost time in his hunt for the boy, he turned back in order to better equip them both for a proper search of the forest.

For the rest of the day, with Joss in his arms, or at his side when she insisted on walking, Dale scoured the forest. He went down to the river where they had been fishing with Cori the day the soldiers came and he made his way along to the path which led to the Chelland road, in the hope of finding some sign of the boy but it was to no avail. As the day progressed with still no trace of Allin, Dale felt the irritation change to anxiety and from anxiety to horror. He had been entrusted with the care of this young royal and now he was wondering how on *earth* he was going to explain to the King that he, Dale Ronas, had lost the heir to the throne of Bremmand.

As the light began to fade Dale returned to the cottage, his heart weighing heavily in his chest. He wasn't about to give up the search but they'd been in the woods all day and Joss was beginning to complain of hunger and tiredness.

He'd take her back, feed her and put her to bed. Then he could return to the woods and resume his hunt for Allin without having to worry about her for the rest of the night. The prospect of not finding the boy before darkness was filling him with dread. He simply *had* to find Allin.

As he and Joss broke through the tree line into the clearing in front of the cottage the little girl pulled a finger from her mouth and pointed. "Look," was all she needed to say. For there, sitting on one of the logs encircling the firepit was Allin, poking moodily at the smouldering embers with a stick.

The relief Dale felt on seeing the boy safe and well quickly evaporated in a wave of fully justified anger. He dropped Joss on the ground and crossed the distance between himself and the boy in a trice. Hands on hips he demanded, "Where the *hell* have you been?"

Allin glowered at him. "I went for a walk. Not that it's anything to do with you."

"I've told you before, you don't go wandering off in the woods without me. From now on you stay in the clearing and you do as you're told."

Allin boiled to his feet, and yelled furiously, "How *dare* you tell me what to do? I'm a prince - the heir to the throne - and I do as I please. I'm sick and tired of taking orders from… from …" he halted fractionally as he hunted for the most hurtful word he could find before spitting out, "a filthy *peasant* and I'm not going to do it any more."

It was the final straw. Dale knew the words being spat at him were borne out of grief and frustration and in other circumstances he'd have allowed the boy to vent his fury without remark but he was tired, hungry and he'd spent the best part of the day racked with fear over Allin's fate so to now be insulted and abused by the object of so much anxiety was too much and his temper finally snapped.

In an instant he grabbed the boy, swept the small frame effortlessly under one arm, head first and propped his knee up on one of the logs to give himself balance. Then, with the flat of his hand he began to wallop the exposed rear end with a vigour.

Dale was a strong man and his temper was up, so he didn't hold back in communicating his disapproval to his young charge. The speed with which Dale moved came as such a surprise to the boy that he barely had time to react to the swift punishment before he was thrust back on to his feet just as abruptly.

"I have better things to do than chase about after you all day. From now on you don't set one foot out of this clearing without my permission and you do as you're told - first time and without argument. Is that clearly understood?" Dale barked at the lad.

Allin looked absolutely furious and for a second seemed to be considering answering back but then, through clenched teeth, determined that he shouldn't allow the big man to see him cry, he hissed "Yes," and turned and bolted for the cottage. As he reached the door he stopped, however, and with every ounce of spite and venom a ten-year-old can muster spat out, "I *hate* you" before vanishing inside, slamming the door behind him.

The second the small figure was gone, Dale realised with a sinking heart that he had made a terrible mistake. Here was a young boy who had lost his entire family, catapulted from a life of luxury to poverty and deprivation in the space of a few short weeks and who was almost sure to know that his very life was at risk. Yet Dale had lost control and taken his anger out on a boy who had probably never had a finger laid on him in all his young, spoiled life. His fury turned back on himself and he began to swear and berate himself. He aimed a vicious kick at the stick Allin had dropped when Dale had scooped him up, sending it somersaulting in to the low flames, making the charred logs hiss and spit and causing a cloud of embers to fly upwards. Then he sank on to one of the logs, his head in his hands as he wondered yet again how he was ever going to be able to serve his King in the care of these children.

"Is Allin really bad?" Dale lifted his head to see a pair of wide, brown eyes gazing anxiously at him.

He reached out and pulled Joss up on to his lap. "No, Flower, not bad. I was just worried about him and that made me angry. So now he's angry at me too. Don't you worry about it." He hugged her close to give her comfort, and they sat together for a little while, in the stillness of the forest as the sounds of the day began to fade away. Holding the small child was very soothing to the big man so by the time it was beginning to get chill he was feeling much more composed.

"Shall we go in then, little one, and get you something to eat?" he suggested to Joss who nodded contentedly and then wriggled free so that she could walk to the cottage by herself.

The cottage was dark when they went in, the only light coming from the fire which was glowing gently. It was silent too and there was no sign of life coming from the other room. Dale felt a stab of alarm. It hadn't occurred to him until now but Allin could easily have climbed out of the rear window and headed off in to the forest once more and the stillness in the cottage made him wonder if this was exactly what had happened.

Stamping down his anxiety, he quelled the urge to give in to panic and took the taper from the mantle shelf using it to light the candle above the fire. He steadfastly went round the room lighting each candle in turn and only when the last one, the one standing on the table, was burning did he pick it up and walk through to the other room.

To his immense relief, Allin was lying there, face down on the bed, unmoving. Dale crossed the room and, placing the candle on the little wooden table, laid a hand on the boy's arm. "Allin?" he said softly, not wanting to wake him if he was asleep.

He wasn't. Allin reacted like he'd been stung, rolling half on his side and wrenching his arm away from Dale's touch. "Leave me alone," he hissed.

This wasn't good, Dale reflected, but he determinedly kept his voice neutral. "I'm about to make supper for your sister. Do you want to join us?"

"No. I'd rather starve than take anything from you. I don't want anything to do with you, ever again." And he flung himself face down in to the bedding once more.

"As you wish," Dale sighed. "I'll leave you the candle though, in case you need it." With that he returned to the main room and Joss.

The mood in the cottage was glum that evening, Dale still troubled by the rejection of the boy and Joss, who was surprisingly sensitive to the situation, didn't fill the evening with her usual, inane chatter. Instead she retired to the far corner of the cottage and entertained herself with a handful of now-dead flowers she had taken to collecting. When the evening grew late and Dale couldn't delay it any longer he rather cautiously led her in to the back room to put her to bed.

Allin was still face down, the candle burning at his side but he made no sign that he was awake and didn't move or acknowledge their presence at all so Dale assumed that this time he was asleep. As quietly as possible he helped Joss out of her tunic and boots and lifted her in to the bed, tucking the blanket about her. He took the blanket off the other bed, where Cori and Trystin had slept and which Allin still refused to use, and laid it over the top of the boy sleeping at Joss's side.

She watched him with big brown eyes, and then asked in a soft voice, "Is Allin going to be angry forever?"

"No, Flower, I shouldn't think so." He gently urged her to lie down and then stroked her face to soothe her. "You don't need to worry, little one. He's not angry with you anyway. I'm sure when you get up in the morning you'll find he'll be feeling better and ready to play with you again." *Even if he won't speak to me* he added to himself ruefully. He sat with Joss a little while longer, still stroking her cheek gently until her eyes began to grow heavy and then he kissed her, laid a hand gently on Allin's motionless head, picked up the candle and returned to the main room once more.

He sat for some time, in silence, lost in thought. So deep was his mood that it took him some time to hear the new sound and even longer to realise that it wasn't coming from outside the cottage. He listened more carefully now and then it came again. Muffled and uneven but unmistakably the sound of a child's sob. Softly he got to his feet and stood at the partition to the two rooms. Another sob forced its way out just as he reached the doorway.

"Allin?" Dale asked softly. It had to be Allin; Joss never made any attempt to hide her tears, seeking the comfort and attention that inevitably followed. The moment Dale spoke everything in the room went still. Not even the sound of the boy's breathing could be heard as he tried to avoid discovery. Another sob betrayed him, however, forcing its way past his tightly held breath.

"Why don't you come in to the other room, son?" Dale suggested kindly "Let's not wake your sister, eh?" and then he turned and left the boy to come to him.

It took a while, during which time Dale sat in the chair by the fire and waited patiently, but eventually, Allin did appear at the entrance to the main room. He stopped there for a while, his teeth clenched tightly together and his face taut, as though still uncertain of what to do. He wrapped his arms tightly about himself, as though he was desperately trying to hold himself together, and came no further. It was clear that this was as far as he was prepared to come without prompting..

"Come here, Allin," Dale suggested gently and the boy crossed to stand in front of the chair in which Dale sat. He kept himself just out of reach, wary of the big man now that Dale had established himself as prepared to take robust action when annoyed. Dale would have found it amusing had the expression on Allin's face not been so tortured. Instead he leaned forward slowly and put a hand on the boy's arm, tugging him forward so that he was standing against the big man's knees. Allin's was pushing his chin up with an effort but he didn't dare to look at Dale's face. In the light from the fire, Dale could see dirty smudges across the boy's face, where he had hastily wiped away his tears, still determined not to show any emotion.

Then, abruptly, Allin said in a strained voice, "I'm sorry," shuddered slightly and tears began to run down his cheeks again. Without hesitation, Dale lifted him up on to his lap, as if he were a small child and wrapped his arms about the boy. At first Allin sat woodenly in Dale's arms, not resisting, but not welcoming the gesture, then suddenly he turned in to Dale's chest, flung his arms about the man's neck and began to sob bitterly.

Dale sat and held the weeping child, cuddling him as if he were a three-year-old. Only as they sat there did it occur to the big man that, other than the first day they had been at the cottage, this was the only time he'd known Allin to cry. All the grief and misery, fear and loss that he'd gone through had been tucked away, his emotions all hidden behind an outer veneer of flat reserve. Now, however, they had finally found a way out and Dale allowed them to flow, as the boy cried out all his pain in to the man's chest. He didn't attempt to say anything, or try to stem the tide in any way. Instead he kept his arms wrapped securely about the slender frame of his young charge, holding him safely as the storm of emotion ran its course.

Eventually, the sobs began to subside and then died away, the small form still clinging to Dale's neck, the only sound in the cottage the crackling of the fire and his faltering breathing as he recovered himself. Only when Dale felt himself released from the stranglehold and a hand moved down to wipe away the tears with a balled fist, did he finally speak. "All right?" he asked softly. He felt rather than saw the head nod and then rise up slightly out of his chest.

"Sorry," Allin mumbled, and then he pulled himself more upright, suddenly aware of the very childish position he was in. Dale didn't attempt to hold him there and allowed the boy to slide off his lap and back to the floor.

"Why don't you pull up that stool," - Dale pointed to the three-legged seat standing at the edge of the fireplace - "and sit here for a bit?"

Allin nodded and obediently dragged the little stool so that it was beside Dale's chair and then sat on it. He stared in to the fire, occasionally rubbing his eyes with the balls of his hands, sniffing and rubbing his nose. He didn't speak and Dale didn't attempt to prompt him. This needed to be done in Allin's own time and Dale was prepared to let the boy find his own way; he had to if there was to be trust between the two of them.

"I didn't mean it," the boy said eventually.

"What?" Dale asked, slightly puzzled.

"About..." the young voice cracked slightly, the memory bringing up a fresh well of emotion, "about hating you. I don't. I just..."

It was as far as he could get without breaking down again, so he stopped. Dale put his hand on the boy's back in a gesture of comfort. "I know. I understand." Then he smiled. "It's a little difficult to feel any other way to someone who's just tanned your hide."

The boy's head drooped. "I am sorry. About being so much trouble all the time and going off like that and... everything. It won't happen again. I'll not give you any trouble from now on."

The big man couldn't help but smile in to the gloom at this. "I suspect that's a little unlikely," he remarked. "I..."

But Allin broke across him before he could say any more. "I won't. I won't be bad or difficult at all. You can trust me to be good and do my duty and everything. Really you can. You don't need to tell Cori that I failed him. Please give me another chance and I'll prove to you that I can do what's expected of me."

"Allin," Dale said gently, "I already trust you, son and there isn't any question of my giving you *another* chance because you've not squandered the first one; not that it's a question of chances at all." He paused, thinking, for a moment or two. "Perhaps we should make a few things clear here, you and I. I think our paths are going to be linked for some time to come so I don't want you to have any doubts about how things stand. All right?" Allin nodded but didn't look too certain about what was coming next.

"Firstly," Dale went on, "I do not expect you to be perfect. You are allowed to have a life here - not just obey every rule as if duty commands it of you. I'm not judging you on everything you do and I'm not going to report back to Cori at every little misdemeanour. We have to live here and you have a right to be happy. So stop trying so hard to be a paragon. It's not possible and you'll make yourself ill, or mad, or both if you try it."

Allin scuffed his toes in the ground, his gaze fixed on them, and then said, "Cori said I should be good, and not give you any trouble."

"I can assure you he didn't intend for you to take it so seriously." Dale wondered momentarily if he should tell the boy what Cori had said once, when Allin had been determinedly trying to behave so he might join Dale on a trip to Chelland.

I don't like him half so much when he's being so pious…. I know I said he was a nuisance but he makes me laugh sometimes too and I like him as he is. When he's like this - trying too hard - it's like it isn't really him and I don't think I like what I get in his place.

In the end he decided not and said instead, "Secondly, you need to understand that, whatever you do, however foolish you might be or however badly you lose your temper," he cocked an eye at Allin and said jovially, "it's quite an impressive temper you have there, too; you seem to lose all reason," the boy didn't smile at this but Dale could see he knew the remark was said with affection, so he went on, "whatever you might say or do in the throes of anger, however badly we fall out over things, at the end of the day I will be there for you. I am always going to support you and be your friend. Friends fight occasionally but that's as much because they know they can without damaging the friendship. It gives you someone to fly at when you can't fight the real cause of your pain.

"And thirdly," Dale gave him a more serious look, "you need to understand that I also made a promise to your brother. I gave him my word that I would keep you safe and do what I felt was right to raise you until you are back with him." Allin nodded.

"That means," he went on, "that if you ever run off like you did today, or put yourself at risk any other way, or disobey me in matters which are important for your safety and our continued well-being here then you can expect the consequences to be similar."

Allin nodded. "My father…" He stopped.

"Go on. What about him?"

The boy swallowed and then admitted in a small voice, "He always used a switch."

Dale felt a rush of relief. The domestic arrangements of the royal family were not something that was shared with the likes of him, but to discover that the King had clearly administered corporal punishment to his sons made Dale feel a little better about earlier. At least it wasn't the first time the boy had been beaten. He didn't betray this to the boy, however. He needed to establish the ground rules with Allin - agree the terms of engagement - so he didn't want the lad to be misled about what he might expect in the way of consequences if Allin broke the rules.

"I didn't have one to hand," was all he said, flatly.

Allin nodded and then his eyes widened slightly at the implication. It was luck, not a difference in method, that had spared him a bout with the switch. "Oh," he said, then nodded again. "I won't run off again. I won't do anything like that ever again."

"Then I think we can consider the matter closed, don't you?"

Allin nodded, not really sure what that meant but willing to agree with Dale's suggestion. He stared in to the fire again, watching the flames curl around the embers of the wood. Something settled, a hollow of one of the logs finally caving in, and a plume of flames rose in to the chimney.

"Hungry?" Dale asked, interrupting Allin's thoughts.

The boy looked up at him as he thought about the question and then realised the answer with a sudden pang. "Starving," he admitted.

"I thought you might be. I rather suspected that you didn't mean it when you said you'd rather starve," Allin hung his head at the reminder of that extra hurled abuse at the big man, but Dale was smiling. "I put something by in case you changed your mind. It won't take long to heat it, if you'd like me to." Allin didn't need to answer. Dale had already tossed another log on to the fire and was moving, fetching down the iron skillet and a bowl in which was lying a leg of rabbit.

They chatted idly as Dale cooked, not talking about anything particular but simply re-establishing links, putting the trials and tribulations of the day behind them. Then, as Allin ate and Dale watched him, the big man asked curiously, "What made you so angry this morning Allin? I'm still not sure I understand why you flew in to such a temper and went off the way you did. Was it because I refused to acknowledge you as a prince?"

The boy shook his head. "I don't mind about that. I never liked all that bowing and scraping anyway. You can't talk to people who just agree with everything and won't even look at you."

"Then what?"

"I just..." the blue eyes slanted up sideways at him, "I'm fed up with being on my own."

Dale drew his brows down in puzzlement. "Then why go off on your own for the whole day?"

It didn't make much sense, Allin knew, and he didn't answer straight away. Then, after a few moments of struggling to find the words he said, "That was different. I left *you*."

In the pure simplicity of those words Dale suddenly understood the deep sense of abandonment that must be consuming the life of this ten-year-old. Necessity had seen him separated from father and his eldest brothers, then his mother and two more brothers and then, finally, within hours of learning that he was orphaned and one of only three survivors, Cori had been forced to leave him too.

Since his brother had left him he had filled his mind with the concepts of duty in which he had been daily drilled for all of his life and buried his own fear and loneliness, in an effort to carry out what was expected of a royal prince. In the end, however, when Dale, the only sense of continuity remaining, also seemed intent on leaving him, it had become too much and he had given way to a burst of uncontrolled rage.

Dale reached out and put a hand on his arm. "Were you trying to show me what it was like?"

He shook his head. "I just wanted to get away from someone else who..." he faltered, "didn't want to be around me."

"Allin!" Dale looked at him in horror. "No-one left you because they didn't want to be near you, son. Don't *ever* believe that."

"Cori thought I was a pest. He always used to say so. He only started having anything to do with me when he had to. I'll bet he wished that I'd gone with Dav and Andred."

"Then you'd lose that bet," Dale said firmly. "Nothing pained him more than having to be separated from you, Allin, and he would have done anything in his power to have found a way that meant you could have stayed together. In fact," Dale hesitated before admitting, "it was I that forced him into agreeing to being separated from you, because the work to get rid of the Kostinian invaders has to start now and it needs to be done from outside the borders. He would have sacrificed his Kingdom to stay with his family but I wouldn't let him."

Allin gazed at Dale in astonishment. He hadn't expected this. "I'm sorry," the big man admitted. "It was my fault he left."

It was a gamble, for Allin had every right to feel enmity to the man but at least he wouldn't believe himself disliked by his brother. If Dale had to win the boy's trust over again then he was there to do it but an absent Cori had no way to prove his affection.

"Cori said he had to go for the good of the Kingdom," Allin said eventually. "I thought he was glad of it. That it gave him an excuse."

"Well, now you know that isn't true. Don't blame him."

"No." The dark head drooped as he gazed down at the table top.

"Do you remember the last thing Cori said to you, before he left, Allin? What he wanted for you and Joss more than anything else?"

"To be happy?" Allin answered eventually.

"To be happy. That isn't the wish of someone who wants to get away from you. It's the wish of someone who cares and who hates that fact that he has to go."

The boy nodded but he didn't look up

"And I don't go in to the woods to get away from you, either," Dale ventured. "I have very little option while Joss is too small to be allowed close to tree felling. She might get hurt and I don't think either one of us wants that, but she can't be left alone either."

"I understand," Allin agreed drearily.

Still the head remained down. "But, if it really makes you unhappy Allin, if you hate it so much, then we'll find another way. You and I will put our heads together and find some alternative that means I don't have to leave you like that. All right?"

"All right."

"We'll work it out Allin. That's what friends are for, after all."

Finally the head lifted. "Are we really friends?"

"Always, Allin. That's what I said earlier and I meant it. That isn't something that will ever go away. Even when you are back in Castle Bremmand, with your brother, and are busy ruling the Kingdom at his side, I shall be there, one of the captains in your armies, being your friend, ready when you need me again."

It was in the early hours of the morning when Allin finally went to bed, after spending several hours talking to his newly-acknowledged friend. Having admitted to his self-doubt, the boy found it easier to divulge himself of his other concerns and he and Dale talked about some of the matters that had been weighing on the boy's mind since Cori had left them.

He was still grieving the loss of his parents, that much was clear and he had been fond of his elder brothers in that remote, worshipping way that a large age gap usually leads to. Their loss still weighed heavily on his mind.

Being one of only three remaining royals also left him feeling a huge responsibility towards his sister, for whom he was now twice obligated to care. She was so young and so vulnerable and he'd promised his mother and then Cori that he'd look after her. But it was harder than one might imagine. He tried his best to keep her entertained, but it was a tall order and sometimes she simply wouldn't be satisfied by anything. How could he ever live up to the expectations of the dead and absent in Joss's respect.

He was naturally apprehensive about the future as well. His family had fallen in battle or been murdered and he was intelligent enough to know that he too was a target for Darvett's men. At the back of his mind was the memory of the Empire soldiers who had already come once to the clearing. What if they came back? What if there were more next time? What if they knew who he was next time and came for him?

His biggest fear by far, however, was of failing his brother. He had no idea of what was required of an heir to the throne and what he had seen of Prince Herest, his predecessor as Duke of Raz did very little to guide him in the matter. It wasn't something that Dale could help him in adequately so didn't try.

"You know what?" he said, instead, "The most important thing you can do, in the current circumstances, is to bide your time until your brother needs you. The Heir to the Throne, as I see it, is like a Captain in an army. He's there to back up his Commander, to give support, to be loyal and to help carry out his leader's wishes. The last order you were given 'Captain' was to be happy, so I think you should work on that. The King clearly thinks that is important. You'll do that best by not trying too hard to meet everyone else's expectations and be yourself a little more."

Allin considered this and then, with a sly smile said, "I'm happy when I go fishing."

"Oh-ho!" Dale laughed. "Didn't take you long to find a way to exploit that one, did it Your most cheeky Highness? Well, let me think about that, and I'll see what I can do. There's still a lot of work to be done around here."

"We don't have to go every day," Allin replied airily, "but one should always have something to look forward to. It makes the days go quicker."

There was such a sage look on the boy's face that Dale couldn't help but laugh again. "Rascal! I can see you fast talking your way in to us spending the rest of the summer lazing by the river bank living entirely on fish. But," he held up his hand before Allin could say anything more to support this, admittedly, tempting suggestion, "I've said I'll think on it and I will."

Allin nodded in agreement, seeming suddenly cheered by the prospect of a little light relief from the life of drudgery he was now living. Then, abruptly, he yawned deeply and Dale gave him a friendly pat on the back.

"Bed!" he ordered. "You're fit to drop, and so am I. We can talk more in the morning."

Allin got to his feet willingly enough. It was late and he was tired but, just before he turned to go, he impulsively put his arms about the big man's neck and hugged him tightly one more time. "I don't mind so much about fishing," he informed him, "as long as you're my friend." With that he was gone.

Next morning, Allin seemed far less cheery that he'd been as he went to bed the night before but when he spent the whole of breakfast yawning, Dale dismissed it as fatigue, rather than a return of his gloom.

"You know," he said as the two children finished eating, "we need to make another trip to Chelland to stock up on supplies and I thought we should make a proper trip of it this time. If we take Shout with us, Joss will be able to ride him, so it won't be too hard a trip for her and if we stay overnight at the Tavern, we can linger a bit instead of having to rush every last bit of trade."

As Dale outlined the trip Allin's face brightened visibly with every word. "Can we?" he asked eagerly. "You'd like to see Chelland, wouldn't you, Joss? We could explore it together."

The girl nodded, her eyes bright at the prospect. "Let's go now!" she suggested. "I've had my breakfast."

Dale stroked her head affectionately. "And has Shout? It wouldn't be very nice to make him walk all that way on an empty stomach."

She slid out of her chair. "I'll feed him now," she suggested, "and all the others. Can we take them too?"

Allin laughed. "Silly. They'll have to stay here."

"They'll be lonely," the girl protested. "They should come with us as well."

"Well how about this?" Dale suggested, with a wink in Allin's direction. "If we didn't go to Chelland until tomorrow and you were to spend a lot of today keeping them company, then I expect they wouldn't mind being left here for just one day. The chickens don't much like travelling anyway and Nosey could stay behind to watch them."

That seemed to satisfy Joss and obligingly fitted in with Dale's original plan of travelling the following day so it was mid-morning of the next day when the three of them, and a somewhat weary mule, arrived at the Tavern in Chelland. The first thing that caught Dale's eye as they took a seat at one of the tables in the yard by the crossroads was the presence of four very unappealing looking soldiers, all in the crimson tunics of the Empire. On seeing the new customer arriving at the Tavern, one of the soldiers rose and crossed to where Dale was concentrating on seating Joss and Allin.

"Your name?" the soldier growled.

Dale looked a little surprised, but he answered easily enough. "Dale Ronas." Then, as if misunderstanding this questioning as some sort of social opening, he asked in return, "And yours, sir? You're new to these parts I take it?"

He got a sour expression in return but before the crimson-clad man could speak further, Iestan came hurrying out. "Dale!" he exclaimed, as if greeting an old friend. "I wasn't expecting you. Come, take a seat, I'll have food and drink here in a trice."

"You know this man?" the soldier demanded of the sandy-haired landlord.

"Of course. Dale's an old friend of mine. He's a woodsman. Holds acreage south of here. We go back a long way." Iestan didn't even flinch as he added smoothly, "The boy's his foster son, Allin and this" - and here he dropped an affectionate hand on Joss's head and said cheerily directly to her - "well now, I see that you're grown up enough to come and keep your brother company, aren't you my little one? Did you like the flower Allin brought back for you from last time?"

Joss, who had been sitting with her mouth open at the presence of so many strangers, managed a shy smile at this and then dug in to her pocket and brought out the leather ornament he had given her as a gift. "It's a flower," she said, "because I'm a Little Flower."

Dale grinned and gave her a little hug and even the soldier's face softened a bit. "My girls are about the same age," he said, a trifle wistfully.

"You're a long way from home and hearth I take it?" Dale said sympathetically.

The man nodded. "That's a soldier's lot. But service of the Empire has its rewards." Then he pulled himself together and said abruptly, "Chelland is now held by the Kostinian Army, for Emperor Darvett. All lands that you formerly held for your lord now belong to him and your tithing will be going to a new master from now on. You, your family and all your goods and chattels are subject to Empire rule."

"I see," Dale said mildly. "Thank you."

The soldier nodded curtly and then went back to the table with his comrades.

"How long have they been here?" Dale asked as soon as he and Iestan could talk without being overheard.

"A few days. So far they've not been much trouble. They announced themselves, told everyone that we belong to the Empire now, and imposed a trade tax - a small one. Other than that they hang about here, driving most of my best customers away."

"Sounds harmless enough," Dale remarked.

"Yes, but have a care, Dale Ronas. I don't like some of the things I've been hearing from elsewhere. I don't think they'll be so content to leave you to yourself if they knew what you used to do. Soldiers who served the King aren't faring too well, so I hear."

"I'd heard something similar. Is it safe for us to stay here? I'm not worried for myself but the children's father…"

"There's not that many here that know you that well and those that do are sound enough. They'd not betray you. Just be cautious who you talk to and what you tell them."

"You can be sure of that, my friend. And would you be willing to give rooms to us, or are we too much of a liability with our tainted past?" He said it with humour but he knew Iestan might not want to take the risk of association in the current climate.

"You can stay," the wiry man said. Then he grinned slyly. "Business is business after all - and if you're staying, we can talk this evening." With that he turned and hurried away and for the rest of the day, when they saw the man, he treated them as regular customers and nothing more.

"It doesn't look too good," Iestan said to Dale that evening when they were alone. The tavern was quiet and they sat, lit only by the glow of the fire to share news. "There seem to be Empire troops taking up occupation everywhere. Anything south of the Cirran is already in Empire hands and they are starting to move north. One of the fur traders from up Amert way, who comes down through Chelland on his way to Castle Bremmand says he's seen them in several of the villages on the north side on this trip. He's moving fast." Iestan shook his head, "Unbelievably fast. He must have just about emptied all of his southern lands of troops and pushed them all up here, so that he could take the whole Kingdom in one go."

"He didn't like being beaten that time. I suppose he wants to be sure that, having defeated the King on the southern border, he then doesn't let it slip through his fingers by being stretched too thin."

"Well, he's going to have taken all of Bremmand by autumn if he keeps up this pace. And the King?" The innkeeper looked pained. "Did you hear what he did to the King?"

Dale had to be careful now. Thanks to Trystin's visit to Castle Bremmand the big man knew things that he should never know as a woodsman living in an isolated cottage, so he shook his head and then sat and listened for a second time to the outrage that Darvett had perpetrated on his monarch - Allin's father. He got the whole terrible tale again, including the fact that the line was dead and gone.

"The man's a monster," Iestan finished. "He must be insane to do such a thing to a defeated enemy. They say Darvett has given the lunatic Bremmand because he's too much of a threat to the throne in Kostain."

"What lunatic? Who d'you mean?" Dale asked abruptly. "I thought it was Darvett who did this."

"No. Darvett has more respect for the fallen dead of his conquests. It was Sallent, the Emperor's bastard half-brother. Darvett has handed Bremmand over to him, along with control of all the troops that are here. This Sallent's a by-blow of Darvett's father but apparently the old Emperor doted on him as a child and he was well liked around the court. The way I hear it, he's been getting too fond of his position of favourite in the south and starting to have ambitions of his own, so Darvett has pushed him up here to keep him out of the way and busy for a good while to come, in the hope that it will distract him from the idea of taking control of the Empire."

"Sallent?" Dale frowned thoughtfully. "I know the name,"

"Most people do. There was some uprising in Rakish a few years back - the harvest failed and the people protested at the taxes when there wasn't any bread to eat. Darvett sent Sallent to put it down and they say he put half the population to the sword."

"That was it, but that must have been an exaggeration."

"Probably, but he was beyond ruthless. He killed enough of them to cure the famine - I know that much."

"And now he's here?"

"Now he's here," Iestan nodded slowly. "Darvett is supposed to have told him to make sure the Kingdom is converted to loyalty for the Empire."

"Which he's doing by killing anyone who he thinks might be hard to convince?" Dale rubbed his beard. "I wonder what the Alliance are thinking about all this."

Iestan pulled a bitter face. "They're thinking *how fast can I run and protect my own borders.* Kils is already looking like it wants to leave the Alliance so that it isn't caught up in Darvett's next claim on our lands."

Dale nodded at this gloomy news.

"There's something else," Iestan went on depressingly. "I think we were betrayed."

"Because?"

"Darvett got some courtier who'd remained in Castle Bremmand to bear witness to the death of the King and his family, so that everyone would know the royal line was broken. Once that was done, there was no reason for Darvett to keep the courtier alive."

"And he still is?"

"Alive and well and making speeches in favour of the new regime. Dale, when the King fell, they got word to the Queen and she was taken out of Castle Bremmand to flee north in to Hast. She's King Perrold's daughter so they knew he'd give her and her children shelter even if his own borders were at risk as a result but the Empire caught up with her on the way north and that was how the whole line was wiped out. They must have known what route the Queen would take. They must have been told. Darvett knew right from the outset where to look for them and sent a troop to make sure that not one of the King's children survived." The agony on Iestan's face was clear and shadows danced across his face in the glow from the fire as he told what he knew. "Some of them were little more than babies, Dale, and that blackguard betrayed them to an enemy who had every last one of them murdered."

Dale swallowed hard, his own emotions at the news, along with the pain for those orphaned and grieving from this act, making him want to go, find the nearest enemy and cut him down where he stood. But he knew he had a bigger mission than revenge and he must, yet again, keep his own feelings under control, stay in the background and protect the few children that Darvett's murderous hunt had failed to find.

On the walk back to the cottage next day, Dale turned over everything he had heard from Iestan thoughtfully. He considered the news that Bremmand had been made a prize for Sallent and that the Alliance was already abandoning its most influential member to the mercies of the Kostinian invaders. Most of all he pondered on the level of information that seemed to have come the way of a simple innkeeper who kept an out of the way tavern. True, Chelland was a crossing point for the Cirran River, so people did come through there; true Iestan was one of those people who had always seemed remarkably well-informed - just as his father had before him - but still, there was something here; something else, that Dale couldn't quite reconcile with what he would expect of a humble trader in a remote little town like Chelland.

After the trip to Chelland, Allin seemed to settle better in to his life at the cottage. Whether it had been the release of his anger and sorrow at the loss of his brother, Dale's unequivocal establishment of his own authority, his assurance to the boy that he would stand by him, or some other turning point that happened over those few days but when they returned from the village, the lad seemed more at ease and content with his lot as the ordinary foster son of a woodsman.

Dale didn't forget Allin's hint from the night that had sat up together and he made sure that he found time for them to go fishing together once in a while. It was here, Dale noticed, when they sat together staring in to the river and waiting for the fish to bite, that Allin would raise topics which he would not discuss at other times. Here, by the peace of the river bank, the lad felt able to talk to the big man and ask questions about his family and his future. It was as if, at the cottage, he was a normal little boy but when they went away from this and found a place to sit and think, he allowed himself to confide in Dale and consult with him.

If Allin was becoming normal in most ways, there was one way in which he was not and that was in his relationship with his sister. When they had come to the cottage, Dale knew the boy had been charged by his mother to look after the little girl and then this mission was repeated by Cori before he left. However, Dale had not expected this dedication to the young girl to last. The interest of a ten-year-old were a world away from those that diverted a little creature such as Joss and Dale fully expected that Allin's loyalty to her would wane over time. In this, however he was proved wrong. Allin's devotion to the three-year-old was unswerving and he showed only love and endless patience towards her.

Not that it was hard to adore Joss, Dale reflected. As she too settled in to life at the cottage she showed herself to be a delight in everything she did. She was as bright as a button, cheerful and lively, with alert eyes and a pert little face that made you want to break in to a smile the moment you saw her. She had a deep interest in everything that went on about her and was a joy to be with. Dale began to see why the only daughter to bless the late King and Queen had been a blessing indeed. It was almost as if the child carried a light with her that illuminated everyone who fell in to its aura.

So time passed, the three becoming a family, watching the season change and autumn set in, cosy and content in the sturdily build cottage, safe and anonymous among the trees. The only shadows that touched them were the ever-rumbling threat of the Kostinians as they tightened their grip on the Kingdom and, for Allin, the absence of the strength and security of his older brother. He seldom mentioned it but Dale knew that the boy was waiting impatiently for the promised message from Cori to say that he was safe.

Torvik, son of Maes

Matters relating to the Kostinian invasion got progressively worse as the season moved on. By the time Dale next went to Chelland with his two charges, the news Iestan had to give him was considerably worse. Kils, as had seemed likely last time they spoke, had left the Bremmand Alliance. It had only ever been their respect and trade needs with Bremmand itself that had kept them in the Alliance, the innkeeper remarked, so now they were looking towards their own interests and had pulled away from the significantly weakened Alliance in order to better defend their own borders.

"Or be better placed to strike up trade deals with the new masters of Bremmand," Dale reflected, gloomily. "No-one can ever say that Kils looks out for anyone else's best interests."

"Perhaps, but I can't say I blame them so much. The rest of the Alliance is falling apart without Jorvis to keep them together."

Apparently the defeat at Kantora had left the allied nations badly shaken. Sabbant, Ghala and Arron, who had provided the main fighting force, along with Bremmand itself, had suffered terrible losses and were eager now to ensure their own borders were defended against possible retribution from their new, aggressive neighbours. Hast, predictably was arguing for retaliation at the invasion and for all the Alliance members to muster new forces and launch an attack on Darvett to reclaim Bremmand. As for the rest of them, they were wavering wildly as the moment took them, afraid of the threat that Kostain posed to them, anxious to preserve trade agreements but most of all shocked and horrified by the ruthless speed and efficiency that Darvett had employed in his conquest of Bremmand.

"I give it a year," Iestan said gloomily. "It was always Bremmand that kept them together."

"And Darvett knew it. To kill a lion..."

"... all you need to do is cut out its heart," Iestan finished for him. "I know."

Dale stared. That particular saying had been a favourite of the King's, so it was sometimes repeated around the Castle, but it was hardly something that would have been heard in so remote a location as Chelland. He said nothing, but his mild wondering about Iestan was fast becoming a strong interest. There was definitely something about this man that didn't add up.

Iestan, unaware of the curiosity he was invoking in his old friend, had moved on to tell of the latest atrocities being carried out within Bremmand's borders by Sallent, new Governor of Bremmand.

Apparently, the death of the last of Brem's bloodline and especially the dreadful way the bodies had been displayed had caused such consternation that the church felt compelled to make protest. The Abbot of Rurig Abbey had travelled the short distance to Castle Bremmand to petition the new ruler for tolerance of the beliefs of his people. The Marchand line was, after all, a holy line and there was much of the faith of the people tied up in the King and his family. He had requested that the bodies be handed to him, the Abbot, who would see that they were disposed of in an appropriately discreet manner but so that the common people might feel that their royal family had been suitably recognised in their passing.

Sallent had listened and then requested a private audience with the Abbot. The next that was heard was that a troop of soldiers arrived at the gates of the Abbey, broke down the doors, killed anyone they could find easily and then piled the bodies of the monks in the courtyard. On top of this they had placed the already dead body of the Abbot and, finally pulled down off the castle walls, the rotting carcasses of the Royal family. Having created this pile of the dead they proceeded to burn the whole Abbey to the ground.

The message was plain. Any attempt to protest to the Governor would be met with severe punishment and not even men of God were exempt. The church could continue to administer to the people, so much was clear from the fact that the religious orders had been instructed to pay huge tithes to Sallent in exchange for non-interference from the secular rulers of the land but they could do nothing else. Sallent had his own religious advisors, who had travelled from the South of Passant to be with him and he had no fear or respect for what he was calling the peasant beliefs. The people couldn't look to the Church to defend them. Sallent had even robbed them of that.

"He's doing everything he can to break the people's spirit," Iestan sighed. "He wants them to have nothing left to hold on to to remind them of who they were and what Bremmand used to be."

Dale thought about this and then asked, "Is it working? Are we beaten already?"

"I don't know. Not yet, perhaps. I think some of the things he has done have made people angry and that is helping to keep them hanging on to what really matters but they are afraid too. How can you stand up for what you know to be right when you have children to protect? He's already proved he doesn't have any compunction about slaying the innocent. Staying alive and protecting your own is more important than fighting back for most."

"I can't say I blame them," Dale considered, knowing what lengths he would go to to keep his own two charges safe from Sallent's men.

"All the same, if there is any hope for Bremmand, if by some miracle Hast manages to convince the Alliance and brings a force to fight off Sallent, there won't be anything left for them to fight for, if the people have all given up."

"Don't lose faith yet. If we can hold up against this first onslaught, then it should all settle down and give us time to regroup."

"Oh, I'm not about to give up but any hint of loyalty to the King is enough to condemn a man. Sallent is putting more and more effort in to the hunt for the loyal and it is getting dangerous even to talk about the old ways. He is terrifying people into thinking how he wants them to think. Anyway, most people think we've lost already. No Marchand left in Bremmand means God's covenant is broken, so that's that."

Dale knew that Iestan's pessimistic view was probably true but he wasn't ready to lose heart just yet. After all he knew, as no-one else did, that there were still living descendents of Brem within the land, so as far as God's promise went, it wasn't over yet. Once Cori was safe in Hast, it would be time to start working on rebuilding the morale of the people, and preparing them for the return of their true King.

The next morning, Dale spent the morning in the village trading for supplies. He had initially arranged to trade directly with Kurop because he had needed a quick and easy deal but it was always far better to make agreements directly with traders of other goods and then Kurop would act as a broker, for a small commission. Dale would continue to supply to Kurop and use his wood haulers in the forest but would then get credit with the Chelland traders instead of with Kurop himself.

Now he took up a table in the yard and there, in the autumnal sun, he sat drawing up a list of the trades he had agreed to give to Kurop and making an account of the wood he would need to supply to ensure he met his half of the bargain. He was taking on a lot of work, more than one man should really accept, but he wanted to have plenty of credit to make sure that, when the time came, he would have everything he needed to get Allin and Joss to Hast as safely as possible.

As he worked, he couldn't help but feel oppressed and preoccupied by the conversation of the night before. The picture Iestan had painted was of a defeated Bremmand, a crumbling Alliance and no hope of Cori having anything left to fight for by the time he reached his Grandfather in Hast and was able to muster an army.

As he tried for the fourth time to keep his mind off this so that he could add up the column of numbers, Allin and Joss returned after a morning down by the river, having been escorted by Iestan's pot-boy, Zacharus. Together they had whiled away their time by watching the comings and going of the river boatman. Both children were babbling away merrily, talking of what they had seen but Dale let their chatter flow over him as he continued with his figuring. He took no notice, either, at the sound of Iestan's voice being raised to another customer at a table behind them.

Joss and Allin noticed, however, and both turned to look as the wiry innkeeper had a heated exchange with the man sitting at the table. He was young, perhaps only a few years older than Cori, but this was an ill-kempt fellow, his tunic grubby and worn, one of his boots looking as though it was coming apart at the toe and with a threadbare look about everything he wore. His face and hands were dirty, too, and he looked thin, as though he hadn't had a good meal for a while. With a pinched face, his blue eyes and blonde hair, which would otherwise have been handsome, looked only exhausted and pained.

Against Iestan's angry onslaught he was doing his best to defend himself but, after gesturing twice to the few coins spread on the table before him, he seemed to be at a loss as to what to do next. Iestan snarled something down at him and then turned on his heel and headed back in to the tavern buildings.

Joss seemed unable to stop staring at the blonde man, despite Allin tugging at her arm and pointing out firmly that it was impolite to stare. In a few moments Iestan was back but he didn't say anything more to the man, instead walking past and coming to the table where Dale and the children were sitting.

The innkeeper seemed his usual self once more as he cheerily took orders for the two new arrivals and refreshed Dale's goblet of wine. Then, unable to contain herself, Joss demanded,

"Why were you scolding that man?"

"Joss!" Allin remonstrated sharply. "It isn't any of our business. It's not polite to ask questions like that."

"But I like him. He looks nice," Joss protested, her interest in the blonde man, who now sat with his head in his hands, still driving her to keep pushing the point. "And now Iestan's made him all sad. Why?" She asked again, her brown eyes fixed appealing on the face of the innkeeper.

Iestan seemed reluctant to answer but then he said, "Just business, little one but, if you like him, I shall make sure I'm nicer to him in future. Is that better?"

Joss beamed and nodded and Iestan, with a grin at having been defeated, not for the first time, by Joss' charms, said to Dale, "When it comes to this little one, there isn't anything I wouldn't do. How do you ever get past her?"

"I don't," Dale smiled briefly. "It's a lot less trouble to give in straight away. She has a way of curling herself around your heart and there's nothing you can do but submit to her every whim."

Allin grinned, pleased, as always, to hear others praising his little sister and then said, "If she's taking a fancy to that man, we'd better watch out that she doesn't get any ideas about us taking him home with us. She tried that with a fox a few weeks ago and she only gave up when she realised that he'd eat all the chickens."

"What's the problem with that fellow anyway?" Dale hadn't so much as looked at the man, still preoccupied with his own business affairs but the children's interest had got a little of his attention. "Short on his bill?"

Iestan nodded, "Only by a shill or so, but times aren't so good that I can let it by. It's not as if he's a regular who I could allow a little credit until next time."

"Yes," Dale said absently and then dug in to his money pouch at his belt and dropped a few copper coins on to the table. "Will that cover it?"

Iestan began to laugh, his grey eyes twinkling, "She really does have you dancing to her tune, doesn't she? Yes, that'll clear what he owes. Thanks Dale."

The innkeeper headed back in to the tavern once more, and Dale returned to his papers but Joss, encouraged by getting her own way, got to her feet and trotted over to where the blonde man was sitting.

"My name's Joss," she advised him gravely but before he could do more than lift his head and look at her, Allin too had hurried over and grabbed his sister's hand.

"Let's not disturb the gentleman," he said and tugged her back to their own table. When she was back in her own seat he instructed her firmly, "You don't talk to people you don't know. He might not be very nice."

"But I like him, and he looks like he's sad."

"It doesn't matter what he looks like. Sometimes really horrible people *look* nice and we shouldn't like it if he did nasty things to you." Joss looked plaintively at her brother but she seemed unable to find a good answer to this. Allin went on, "Promise that you won't ever talk to people you don't know unless I say it's all right?" She nodded but threw one more wistful glance at the blonde stranger as she did so. Allin also followed her look and then felt a qualm. The blonde man no longer had his head in hands but instead was sitting up and gazing at their table, with a somewhat puzzled look on his face. "Dale," Allin said in a low voice, "he's staring at us."

Dale flicked the boy a sharp look without moving his head and then said calmly in the same low tone, "He's probably just interested because Joss went over to say hello. It won't be anything." Then, finally, he turned and looked the man over. "Well, I'll be damned!" he declared flatly then got to his feet and crossed to the table. "Torvik? It is, isn't it? Torvik, son of Maes?"

The blonde man came rapidly to his feet, his face relaxing at the mutual recognition. "Yes, sir, it is. I thought it might be you, but I wasn't sure if I should…"

"Of course you should," Dale said warmly. "It's good to see you man. How are you? What are you doing in Chelland?"

Torvik looked uneasily at him. "Just… passing through. You know." He gestured to a seat. "Will you join me, Sir?"

The second he had made the invitation Dale saw the younger man's face blanch as he realised that he was offering to buy a drink for another when he couldn't even pay for his own. Dale said diplomatically, "Why don't you join us? We've already ordered food, so it would be easier for you to share ours than for us to cancel and then you have to order." He turned and led the way back to his table and the waiting children who were gazing at the two men with open-mouthed astonishment. "This is Torvik, son of Maes," Dale introduced the man. "Torvik and I used to..." he hesitated briefly and then said with care "be in the same line of work. This is Allin and Joss. They're in my care. Their father was in the same trade too."

"Oh?" said Torvik, catching on. Then guessing the corollary to that added, "Ah!" sympathetically.

"Now, sit," Dale instructed. "You look about ready to fall down anyway. Things have been rough for you these last moons, I'm guessing?"

"Not so bad, sir. I get by. I'm still alive which is more than I can say for most of my..." He stopped. He'd been going to say Legion but this would give him away as a soldier to anyone listening in and that was far too dangerous an occupation to admit to these days. He amended himself "...most of my friends."

"That's true enough," Dale said, understanding. "You know there's no need to be calling me *sir*, don't you Torvik? I'm not in that trade anymore. I was injured so I had to come back to woodcutting. Dale's good enough for me these days. In fact I seem to recall it was good enough for you in the old days, too."

That much was true. Dale had known Torvik, as he had hinted, during his army days. In fact before he had been transferred to the Palace Guard the then Lieutenant Ronas had been in the same Legion, the 5th, as Torvik, a young and talented soldier. Torvik had, Dale had later learned, lied about his age to get in to the army and then distinguished himself on the battlefields in the fight to defend Junao from invasion some three years ago. He'd been barely sixteen at the time but Dale had seen a talent in the young man which he knew would lead to the making of a great officer. Thanks partly to Dale's sponsorship, Torvik had been promoted to Sergeant in Dale's command and later, after Dale had been transferred, was again elevated, this time to Lieutenant. In the time the two had served together they had become friends and remained so when Dale moved on. It had been almost a year, however, since Torvik had been stationed near enough to Castle Bremmand for them to have seen one another. After their last meeting Dale knew that the 5th Legion had been stationed on the southern borders, part of the defensive force placed there after Junao finally fell in to Darvett's hands. Torvik would have been a part of that force and would, without doubt, have fought in the final battle at Kantora. Here then, was someone who could give Dale real information of what happened on the battlefield and the big man was determined not to lose touch with Torvik until that had happened.

"I'm sorry, Dale," Torvik apologised. "A lot has happened since we last met and I wasn't sure if you'd be so pleased to see anyone who could link you to... then. People like me aren't all that popular these days."

"I know, Torv," Dale said. "No more am I, but I was born in these parts and I think we are safe enough here, just so long as we are careful. Besides, I'd never turn my back on a friend and I know I can trust *you*. You know you can trust me too, don't you?"

"Yes, of course," said Torvik but in truth he looked relieved.

"You said you were passing through. Where are you headed? Back north to your father's place?"

Torvik was the son of a farmer south of Amert, so it was a logical assumption but the young man dropped his head and sighed before answering glumly, "I've not long since come from there. He's dead. They found out that his son was an officer so they came for him."

"*Torvik!*" Dale put his hand on the man's arm his sympathy at this personal loss among all the brutal tragedy showing clearly.

Torvik shrugged his shoulders, as though in the face of so much, this last had been too much to take in. "They took his lands. Gave them to the villain who turned evidence against him."

"I trust you took them back?" Dale inquired in a hard voice.

"What would be the point? If the Empire troops had heard about it, they'd just have come after me too. It's done anyway - killing him wouldn't have brought my Da back." Torvik had always been such a positive force that for him to sound so defeated was profoundly shocking to Dale. Had Darvett's troops broken down even the strongest of spirits so quickly?

"I suppose not," was all the big man said. "So what now? Where are you heading for now? What happens next for you?"

"Actually," Torvik dropped his voice slightly, "I'm not the only one who survived the battlefield. There are a few of us - those who can't go home for fear of what it might mean, or, like me, have already lost everything else." He grimaced then. "We're a pretty poor bunch and we've not got much but we're doing what we can to hold together. I came here today to see what this place is like for Empire men, to see if it would be safe for us to use as a trading post."

"They're here," Dale told him, "but not in any great force yet. There are one or two people hereabouts I'd steer clear of though. Most people wouldn't hand you over, even if they knew, but one or two aren't fussy about how they earn their money."

Just as Dale was about to go on, Iestan returned with food. When he saw that his debtor customer had joined them he couldn't help but ask of Allin, with a grin, "Don't tell me. She *has* talked you in to adopting him?"

Allin had to laugh at this reference back to their earlier conversation but shook his head as Dale interjected.

"He's joining us, Iestan. Bring enough for one more, would you?" Iestan rolled his eyes at this, clearly thinking Dale was a soft-hearted fool for letting this man sponge off him but he merely nodded and, having put down the food for Dale and the three children headed off to get the fourth meal.

"It's kind of you Dale," the blonde man began, not quite managing to keep his eyes off the plate of hot stew that Iestan had bought for Dale, "but.."

"Can't a man stand an old friend dinner once in a while?" Dale interrupted firmly, then he pushed his plate in Torvik's direction "Here." Torvik hesitated but Dale said calmly enough, "Don't be a fool man. I can see you're on your uppers. Take it and put it to good use. You'd do the same for me if the situation was reversed."

Torvik didn't take much persuasion and he ate the stew with undisguised enthusiasm. It had been his first good meal in days, he admitted, the few of them who were hiding out in the woods not being very good at making a living from the forest. They managed the odd rabbit, he explained, but that didn't go far among eight of them and bigger quarry was proving to be harder to catch than any of them had expected.

"We're mostly soldiers - or at least we were - and you get used to having a supply line with a constant stock of food. The only one of the camp following who's with us is one of the healing women. She can cook but only if someone catches it for her first. Having to fend for ourselves isn't proving to be all that successful so far."

"Just a matter of knowing where to look and what to look for," Dale said easily and gave the man a few tips on how to improve the results of his hunting. Then he grinned and remembered an old joke they had shared in their days together, "I take it now you aren't so scathing of the wild men of the woods, are you 'farmer boy'?"

For the first time, Torvik laughed, his youth showing in his careworn face for the first time. "I see that they have their uses, but then I think I always said that. I just don't see that your people have to go all precious about how the land belongs to you because you were here first, and for being the only ones who can tell one stupid tree from another. If you can once explain to me why *that* is useful, then I'll not complain about them again."

"You'll soon wish for us when you get lost in the forest," Iestan remarked, returning just in time to hear the last exchange and putting his own view in to the discussion with good humour. "Might have guessed one of you Langatian types wouldn't understand what it is to be a woodsman. All that corn you grow gets between your ears."

"Two against one," Torvik grinned. "I'm not fighting against those odds." He got to his feet.

"You're not leaving, Torv?" Dale was surprised at this sudden departure.

"Need to take a leak," he said succinctly and slapped his former commanding officer on the back. "Don't worry, I'll be back. I know how to exploit an old friendship and you're still in the chair."

"Seems like a nice enough fellow," Iestan remarked as he watched Torvik weave his way between the tables and head off behind the tavern building.

"He is," Dale grinned, knowing Iestan well enough to know he would now be expecting information on the man as a trade for all the information he had shared with Dale in the past.

Dale waited expectantly for another gentle inquiry - the next move in the little dance as Iestan tried to learn what he could. Today, it seemed that Iestan wasn't in the mood for subtlety however.

"Do you trust him?" he asked bluntly, as soon as the blonde officer was out of sight.

"Yes." Dale replied flatly, taken aback by Iestan's directness.

"Loyal to the King, then?"

"Completely."

Iestan nodded, as if satisfied, prompting Dale to ask, "Why? Did you have reason to think he wasn't to be trusted."

"I don't know. I don't know him. I would have been able to decide for myself eventually but it's quicker to ask you. Your word's good enough for me."

Before Dale could think of anything to say to this Iestan seemed to want to change the subject. He took up the empty dish that Torvik had cleared and said, "He finished this fast enough. Want me to bring him another?"

Dale nodded. "Bread as well, please Iestan, and more wine. He's more than just a friend. We saw a few rough moments together, he and I, and to see him hit hard times like this..."

"I get it," Iestan said and Dale could see that he did. It wouldn't be hard for the innkeeper to work out that, if Torvik was a friend of Dale's, then he must be a soldier and if he was a soldier then he probably fought for the King in the last battle.

"He's a good man, Iestan, someone who deserves to be safe from those who might wish him ill."

"Is he going to be around this way for a while then?"

"Maybe. There are a few of them trying to scratch out a living in the forest near here. Can he look to you for help?"

"Well," Iestan said thoughtfully, "I think he may be able to help me, as it happens. As long as you think he's sound."

"Rock solid," Dale assured him. Then he smiled, as he saw Torvik heading back towards him. Already the man was looking less defeated. "Although he' a bit of a rogue. He has an irritating habit of being able to talk his way out of most things."

Torvik hadn't heard the last exchange but he could tell he was the object of the two men's discussion so he said airily as he seated himself, "Talking about me already? Must be my infallible charm and boyish good looks." He winked at the children with a grin but Dale could see a wary look about the man's eyes.

Iestan had seen it too but he didn't comment on it. Instead he merely remarked dryly to Dale, "I think I see what you mean."

"Torvik, this is Iestan Honrad. He's a friend of mine and you can be sure of him. He also knows everyone hereabouts, so he knows the good traders and the bad; who you can get a good deal with and who you should stay away from; that sort of thing."

"That's kind of him," Torvik replied, eyeing the sandy-haired man carefully.

"I do nothing out of kindness," Iestan stated flatly, "but I was loyal to the King and with him gone there's little else to cling to now, except to protect one another from these invaders. While Sallent has his hounds out hunting you, you can be sure that I'll do what I can to keep you hidden from them."

"Then thank you," Torvik said slowly and put out his hand, to show his willingness to trust the man.

"And as it happens, I think there's someone who you might be able to help me protect right now."

Dale looked curiously at the innkeeper. "You said you thought Torvik might be able to help you. What's the problem, Iestan?"

"We had a bit of trouble, last night. Nothing I couldn't handle and not anything that would have disturbed you, Dale, but something that I'm scratching my head over."

"Go on."

"One of the young men from the village is in a similar situation to your friend here. He fought in the battle at Kantora and lived, just, to get back here. He was injured and he's still slowed down by the hurt he suffered but he's been on the mend. His family took him in, of course, but they have to keep him hidden. He's known here and not everyone can be trusted enough not to give in to fear or a bit of greed. So, he's been lying low mostly, taking time to heal up and keeping out of trouble."

"So what's changed?" Torvik wanted to get to the point of this and find out where he came in.

"He comes here from time to time, usually late in the evening, when he can get a drink or two without being noticed. Last night, though, he had too much. Far too much"

"And he was seen by someone who might sell him out?"

"No, but he started getting pretty angry about his lot. He was bellowing on about how no-one was prepared to sully themselves by helping him, that only his own family were willing to take him in and they were at risk as a result."

"I can understand that," the bitterness in Torvik's voice was evident. "It's hard to be understanding when you've lost everything, to find that the people you fought for, who your friends died for, are too afraid to help you."

Iestan nodded and went on. "He went on like this for a bit but in the end he said he was going to do something about it; that everyone was far too willing to sit back and let the invaders take over without doing anything to stop them. He was going to start fighting back. His first idea was that he was going to kill the patrol of soldiers that are here but then his plan got wilder until he was going to march on Castle Bremmand and attack the castle."

"He's out of his mind!" Dale exclaimed. "He'd be dead before he got through the gate."

"He knew that, but he thought being dead was better than hiding in a basement for the rest of his life and if he took a few of their soldiers with him, that would be all to the good. He was drunk but he was deadly serious and we couldn't take a chance that he'd do something that would bring more soldiers in to Chelland. We've been lucky so far that we haven't attracted much attention and frankly we'd like to keep it that way."

"So?" Dale asked "What did you do with him? Where is he now?"

"We, err…" - Iestan looked uncomfortable - "knocked him out and locked him in the stables. He's still there, sleeping it off. He might just wake up and not remember anything of last night but even so…"

"The thoughts are there." Dale rubbed his beard. "Next time he comes up with some cracked idea of martyrdom, he might be sober enough to do it."

"So how can I help?" Torvik asked. "You know this chap better than me, so what makes you think I can do anything that you can't?"

"Dale said there's a few of you out in the forest, in the same predicament. You could have Salvit go with you. He knows the woods, so he'd be of use to you and he'd not be forced to live in hiding anymore. If he had some kind of a life, he'd not be so all-fired determined to bring disaster down on himself and everyone else."

"Or maybe he would," Torvik retorted. "You're asking me to take on a man who's determined to sacrifice himself in some futile gesture and risk the lives of everyone else who is trying to survive out there."

"Yes," Iestan said simply. "Will you help him?"

Torvik blinked, then he swung his gaze over to Dale, who looked as if he wanted to laugh at Iestan's frank reply. Then the blonde man shook his head wearily as if in despair at the folly of these two woodsmen.

Seeing that Torvik had been won over, Dale slapped him heartily on the back. "Good man!"

"Mad man," Torvik corrected him. "I know nothing about this fellow and now I'm taking him to where he could betray a dozen people if the mood takes him."

"Iestan wouldn't have suggested it, if he didn't think this Salvit fellow was safe," Dale assured him, then he glanced at Iestan. "Who is he, anyway? I can't say the name is familiar."

"He's Julyan's eldest."

"Julyan?" Dale frowned for a moment but then his face cleared. "Oh, I know! The butcher who trades up by Faljon."

"That's him."

"Couldn't be better then." Dale grinned at Torvik. "He'll know enough about hunting to get you a few decent meals. Shall we go and take a look at him? See if he's slept off enough of your beer to be ready to travel?"

A close inspection of Salvit showed that he hadn't suffered any lasting damage from Iestan's somewhat rough attempt to save his life. However, the more inevitable side effects of excess alcohol were taking their toll on the unfortunate young soldier. He seemed willing enough to take up Torvik's offer of joining him in the forest, remarking that anything would be better than being cooped up in his father's basement, although Dale wasn't sure his head was clear enough for the decision to be sound.

Dale and the children were about to take their leave of Chelland and Torvik seemed ready to leave as well, having established that Chelland was a safe place to come as well as acquiring an extra member of his small community. It was thus natural for them all to begin their journey together. Torvik's camp was south east of the town so the first part of the journey was along the same road.

For Dale this brought an extra advantage. As well as being a chance to catch up with an old friend it was an opportunity to get more information on what had happened on the battlefield at Kantora and, better still, to get the perspective of those who had fought. Taking care to see that the children were occupied with one another, so couldn't overhear, he asked the blonde lieutenant for more on the last stand of the Bremmand Alliance.

Torvik's assessment was tragically brief. "We were outnumbered. It didn't matter that we had all that advice and expert strategy from the advisors Hast provided. I don't think even the most brilliant military genius could have found us a way to survive against the vast force that Kostain sent against us.

"We had the higher ground to begin with and we had several ranks of archers firing down on to their infantry but they just kept coming. Then they unleashed a great flood of cavalry who came tearing in to us and wiped out most of the archers in the space of a few minutes - it seemed like that, anyway - but I suppose it took longer.

"After that, the high ground didn't seem to be much of an advantage for us. Three legions went forward to meet the Kostinian Infantry but they were met by about five legions of the enemy and it was just a massacre. They put their cavalry in behind our men and if we tried to retreat the Kostinian cavalry would cut them down. I'm not sure that I saw more than a handful of our men break through and get back to our rear guard.

"We tried sending in another legion, to take out some of those mounted butchers but they just turned about and hammered in to our new force instead, until we were forced to retreat back up the hill.

"The 5th Legion were held back to begin with, as a reserve, along with the 8th and the King's. We had Prince Jorvis riding in the vanguard with us and you could see him getting more and more impatient that we were being forced to sit and wait it out while we watched our comrades being butchered like that. In the end, when we could see Darvett's troops starting to advance again, we made our move.

"All three legions set up a huge roar - like you've never heard - and we came pouring down that hill as though we were riding the wind itself. I like to think Darvett must have wondered at all that noise and speed - wondered if there wasn't something he'd missed, that we knew something he didn't and he was about to be defeated.

"In truth, I think we all knew it was probably a lost cause but we were going to show them that we weren't afraid and we knew how to die with courage.

"The King rode into the fray with us. He led the charge. It was something to see, him riding the lines, building us all up for that attack. Madness really for him to risk himself that way, but I think when it came to it, with him there with us, when we made the final charge we actually thought we could win. I know I did.

"I don't remember much else of it, after we charged down the hill. I was taken down quite early and the next thing I remember it was several days later and I was in some village a few miles north of the battle. They told me that they had found me a little way off the day before, injured, raving with fever and trying to get back to my legion on my hands and knees. I suppose I was lucky to survive. Once the battle was won, apparently Darvett ordered that anyone from the Allied armies found alive was to be killed. He wanted - and still wants - every last soldier of the Bremmand Army dead."

"Then you don't know how the King died, or the Princes?" Dale couldn't help himself from asking.

Torvik shook his head. "There's not many that lived to see it. The whole King's legion was lost. According to Fenner - he's one of our number - not one of them survived but not a man among them turned and ran. If the King fell, it wasn't for his men deserting him. They did what they could to protect him but he insisted that he would take to the field. Prince Perrold was with him so he would have fallen with his father. Herest took the lead with the 8th. I don't know about Prince Richol - I think he'd been with the archers, so he'd have been lost to the Kostinian Cavalry."

Dale was about to ask more but at that moment Allin came running over, laughing and demanding to tell them of some minor amusement of his sister's and there was no more opportunity to discuss the battle.

Shortly after this, the two men's paths divided and Torvik headed east, leading Salvit away to his camp, while Dale and the children continued south to the path which took them back to the cottage. Before they parted company Torvik said warmly, "If ever you need help Dale, or if the soldiers get too close to you where you are now, you'll always be welcome to come and join us. Head east from here, and you'll come across a path - not much of one, but it's there if you know what to look for. Follow that - it's quite a way, but keep going - and you'll come to our camp."

Dale nodded. "I know it. There used to be a charcoal burner's place there. He died when I was a youngster and we used to go out to the abandoned cottage from time to time. You're not more than a few hours' walk from me, Torvik."

"Well then, that makes us neighbours," the man grinned. The transformation in him since first meeting with Dale a few hours before was amazing. His confidence had soared at having someone to talk to and having found safe contacts in Chelland. Suddenly he was no longer scratching a living but was starting to establish a community and had friends around him to help him do it.

"It does," Dale returned warmly, "and I'll do my best to be neighbourly. Safe journey then Lieutenant."

"And to you, Captain, and to you!"

The Bremmand Army

The meeting with Torvik seemed to mark a change, Dale reflected. Up until that point they had lived in relative isolation in the cottage but now there were others also hiding out in the woods, refugees in their own lands. News seemed to become more easy to obtain as well. Before this he'd heard very little but now, as if it suddenly became necessary, people began to talk and rumours spread. The infrequent encounters Dale had with the forest haulers or other woodcutters were interspersed with some fresh piece of news of what the invader forces were doing, or some new tale of the battle at Kantora. Stories were told in cautious, hushed voices but they were being told.

Despite the fact that many lived in fear of betrayal it was somehow a comfort to Dale to know that he was not the only one left. While Darvett and his brother Sallent were trying to eliminate any chance of invasion by killing anyone who might pose a threat to them, what they were actually doing was forcing their enemies into hiding where they could remain undiscovered until they were ready to fight back. For now Dale had the protection of Allin and Joss to worry about but perhaps, when he had discharged that duty by escorting the children to their brother, he might be permitted to return and see what could be done to start showing Sallent that it wasn't as easy as it looked to trample over the Bremmandish people. However, that would have to come later. For now he was content to remain at the cottage living life like a normal family but knowing he could some day seek out Torvik and his people again and see what could be made of them.

Time was passing quietly enough, the three of them living life at the cottage in relative harmony. Dale did his best to remain close to the children when he could but if he did need to head in to the forest to bring down another tree, he always made sure it was as close as he could manage to the cottage and that Allin knew where to find him, so that the boy would feel he was within reach.

On one such occasion, Dale had felled a tree and was working on cleaving off the main branches before breaking it in to sections so that Shout could haul it back to the cottage when Allin came haring out of the trees breathlessly and raced over to him.

Dale had been mid-swing when the boy appeared almost right under his nose so he swung wide with the axe, aborting his stroke and burying the blade in to the side of the horizontal trunk. Without thinking, or stopping to ask why, he loosed his hold on the axe handle and boxed Allin soundly about the ears.

"You don't *ever* run about like that when I'm working with an axe," Dale commanded.

"Yes, but..."

"No. No buts. I might have taken your head off. You don't do it. Understood?"

Allin nodded contritely. "Yes, sir." Then, as Dale gave a nod of satisfaction that his instruction had been understood, the boy anxiously went on, "I came to get you. There's something wrong with Joss."

If Dale felt guilty that he'd scolded the boy when something serious might be the matter, he didn't show it. Instead he nodded, pulled the axe from where it was buried in the tree and with a "Right" headed back to the cottage with Allin in tow.

"She was picking flowers," Allin explained, as they stood together looking at the girl grizzling by the firepit in the middle of the clearing. She looked thoroughly miserable, her face flushed and her eyes puffed up from crying. Whatever it was that was wrong, she was certainly unhappy about it. "Then she just started crying. I went to see what was the matter and she said one of the flowers had stung her. At first I just thought she'd grabbed a nettle or something but she wouldn't stop crying and I think it's getting worse. So, I thought I'd better come and fetch you."

"Yes. Quite right," Dale agreed absently, his mind on the girl. "Now then, my little flower, what's the matter here then?" He sat beside her and pulled her comfortingly in to his arms.

"It hurts," Joss explained succinctly. "I feel sick."

"I see. Where does it hurt?"

"Everywhere." Not helpful, but then she added, "My arm feels all funny."

Dale rolled her sleeve up and could see a pinkish rash spreading from her hand and up towards her elbow. "Well, it seems that one of those flowers you are so keen on pulling up didn't want to come with you," he said cheerfully, trying to reassure both her and her brother who was hopping anxiously from one foot to another. "What say you come and have a lie down inside? I can give you a herbal drink that should make you feel better. How does that sound?"

Joss nodded but showed no inclination to move by herself, so Dale carried her in to the cottage and tucked her up in bed.

An hour later, despite Dale dosing the girl with the cure-all herbal remedy his mother had always sworn by, Joss was no better. In fact she seemed to be worsening. She was starting to show signs of fever and then her breathing began to come with difficulty. By mid-afternoon she was barely conscious and was only taking air in tight rasping gasps.

Dale sat at her bedside sponging her face down to try and cool her and beginning to fear for the child, while her brother wandered listlessly about, sometimes outside, sometimes within the cottage, not wanting to go far from his sister but having no useful way of helping her either. Finally, unable to hold his anxiety in any longer, he came up close to Dale and asked in a worried tone,

"She isn't going to die is she?"

That settled it for Dale. He'd been pushing back similar fears for some time now and hoping against hope that things would somehow turn around for the sick little girl. But now, finally, he faced the reality that she was really ill and there was nothing he could do to help her. Decisively he got to his feet.

"She needs proper help from someone who knows more about such things than I do." The boy looked questioningly up at him and Dale went on briskly "Go and feed the animals and shut them up for the night. We'll go to Torvik."

"Torvik?" Allin looked blankly at the man.

"That's right. He said one of his number was a healer. We'll take Joss to her. She'll be able to help."

Once the cottage was shut up and the animals set for the night, Dale wrapped Joss as warmly as he could in a blanket and picked her up in his arms. Then, with Allin at his side, he set off through the afternoon forest at a brisk pace, heading for where he knew Torvik and his friends had set up camp.

The autumn was well upon the forest and the trees were showing their beauty in an array of yellows, golds and browns. Dale usually loved to wander through the woods at this time of year, enjoying the chill in the air and the still determined fall of the sun, while leaves fell slowly about him. Now, however, he barely took in the glorious scenery as he pushed along the narrow pathway, simply anxious to reach his goal.

It took them a little over an hour, almost half the time it would normally take, to reach the clearing which had once been a charcoal burner's home. Now it was just a hollow area, free from trees, at the centre of which was burning a somewhat smoky-looking fire. A number of makeshift structures had been thrown up randomly about the place, not proper buildings like the cottage, but wooden skeletons made from narrow branches with fir and skin thrown over them to provide protection from the weather. They were typical of temporary army shelters and were known as 'pitches' by the soldiers who were adept at throwing them up and pulling them down again as they moved about on campaign, although these ones were ill-kempt and rough looking.

As Dale came to the outskirts of the little community, a gangly woodsman's lad spied him and raised a call to the others. An elderly man approached and, when Dale said he knew Torvik, sent the boy running to find the young man. Dale didn't stop moving, however, and continued to walk in to the settlement.

Torvik arrived shortly after this, at first walking easily but then, when he saw Dale's anxious face and the child in his arms, he quickened his pace. "Dale? What's happened?"

"I had to come Torvik. I didn't know of anyone else who could help. The little one's sick. You said one of the healing women from the army followers was here...?"

"Of course." He swung back to the tall youth. "Here, Nollan, go and fetch Marta." The lad looked unwilling at being continually made to run and fetch people but he did as he was told. As he walked across the encampment Torvik barked after him, "Now, boy, not next week. Go on *run*!"

As Nollan broke in to a trot, Torvik turned back to Dale. "She's this way, come on," and he began to lead the big man and his two young charges in the direction the red-headed youth had already taken. Shortly, hurrying the other way with Nollan at her heels, came a stocky woman of middle years, with alert eyes that were so dark they looked almost as black as her hair. There was something about the way she moved and the tilt of her head that reminded Allin of a blackbird. When she spoke, however, her tone was anything but birdlike.

"So," she demanded, hands on hips, "what's all this? Nollan came and dragged me down here saying you're ill?"

"Not me," Dale said, using his free hand to slide Joss slightly off his shoulder so that the woman could see her better. "The child. At first I thought she'd been poisoned by something in the forest - she's been picking flowers and suchlike - but now, she's burning up and I'm beginning to fear it might be Spring Fever."

Dale couldn't quite disguise the anguish in his voice at the idea of his foster family suffering the same fate as his own children and, after a quick searching look, Marta said less acerbically, "I'd be more inclined to favour your first thought. If she's been picking flowers and now she's sick that's far more likely to be the cause - especially at this time of year. Let's get her to my pitch and then I can take a proper look at her. What's her name?"

Within a few minutes, the brisk woman had brought Dale and Allin to a pitch at the far end of the camp and laid Joss out on a simple cot bed in a rear section of the mean lodging. She instructed Dale and Allin to wait outside, which they did, anxiously, for a few minutes before she came back. "There's a rash all the way up her arm. Did she get that from the flowers?"

Dale glanced down at Allin, who nodded. "I think so," he said in a voice hoarse with anxiety. "Is she going to be all right?"

"We'll see," Marta replied and then asked, "were you with her then? Did you see what it was she picked that did this to her?"

"I... not really" he stammered miserably. "I wasn't really watching. She just started crying and when I got there she said one of the flowers had stung her." He stopped briefly and then went on to explain, "She'd picked a whole load and they were all in a pile beside her. I suppose she dropped them."

"And she didn't say which flower stung?"

"No ma'am." Allin hung his head.

"Were there any flowers that weren't in the bunch, son?" Dale prodded, to try and get him to help identify the poison. "Anything lying elsewhere? Or growing there about that might have been what she picked last?"

Allin shook his head once more. "I didn't really look..." Then he stopped and thought again. "There were some white flowers I think. Growing in the thicket just by where she was. Tall ones."

Marta gave him a searching look. "With the flowers all the way up the stem?" and then, when Allin nodded, more urgently, "and the bloom shaped like a hay-cutter's hat?"

Allin gazed at the woman, confusion overwhelming him. He'd never seen a hay-cutter, let alone the hat such a person might wear, but he couldn't think of a single thing to say that wouldn't give this fact away. For all he knew, not knowing what a hay-cutter looked like might be the thing that gave away who he truly was and put them all in danger. And yet, if he couldn't tell them what it was that had made Joss so ill, his little sister might die. "I don't know," he almost wailed, his voice breaking as he struggled not to cry.

"It's all right Allin. Not to worry," Dale reassured the boy, sliding his arm about the slender lad's shoulder.

Marta gave Allin a searching look. "This boy's exhausted," she declared to Dale in an accusing tone.

"I had to get Joss here as soon as possible so we had to hurry. It was faster than he's used to," Dale agreed, knowing he'd had no choice but to walk Allin off his feet.

"Well, you both go and get some rest and something to eat then. There'll be someone at the fire who'll see to you."

"But..." Allin began to argue, not wishing to leave his sister.

"There's nothing you can do here for now. You may as well get off your feet for a while. I'll come and find you as soon as there's anything to tell."

Dale nodded in agreement. "She's right. We'll just be in Marta's way here. Let's go, Allin," and he led his reluctant young charge out into the fading light.

There were a handful of men seated on the ground around the fire when Dale and Allin arrived, one of whom was Torvik. He rose as soon as he saw them. "How is she?" he asked at once but Dale shook his head.

"We don't know. Marta said she'll let us know."

One of the other men snorted. "Threw you out in other words. No-one's allowed near Marta when she's working." Despite his bitter words there was a rough affection in what he said. This was confirmed when he added, "She's the best healing woman I've ever known though. Your little one's in good hands."

"Thanks for that," Dale said, seating himself beside the man and gesturing to Allin to do that same. The lad slid down to the ground, keeping quite close to Dale. The big man slipped his arm around the boy's shoulder and tugged him gently in to his side, giving him comfort. Then he glanced at the elderly man who had spoken once more. "I'm Dale," he said in a friendly tone, "and this is Allin."

"Fenner." The man introduced himself easily. "Formerly with the 8th. Torvik tells me you're a military man as well."

"Was," Dale corrected. "I didn't see the battle though. Invalided out."

"Wish I had been" one of the others, a young man, replied gloomily. "I'd give a lot not to have any memories of that carnage."

"I'm sure," Dale murmured sympathetically. At his side, Allin's head drooped. Any reference to the battle inevitably upset the lad and Dale tightened his grip around the narrow frame. Almost idly the lad picked up a stick lying on the ground and began to scratch out patterns on the ground. Dale went on talking to the stocky old soldier. "I heard it was bad, that last battle. The boy here lost his father and brothers in it too."

"Oh yes? And what legion did they fight with?" Fenner asked the boy with interest.

Dale kicked himself for not anticipating the question. It was normal for soldiers to want to classify each other by their rank and the legions in which they served so for Fenner to want to know about Allin's father was entirely natural. All the big man had wanted to do was make it clear that talk of the battle was likely to be upsetting for the boy and divert the topic elsewhere and instead he'd invited another need to invent more about Allin's supposed family. Allin just shook his head however. "I don't know" he mumbled and went back to scratching in the dirt.

"King's Legion," Dale said softly, when Fenner looked to him - it was as close to the truth as he could manage. The King's Legion, actually the First Legion but never called so, always fought alongside the King and stood with him in battle. It was also, Dale recalled from Torvik's recount of the battle, one of the legions that had been utterly annihilated with not a man surviving. It meant that there was no risk of coming across anyone who might have served with Allin's fictitious family.

The stocky soldier shook his greying head. "So sad." He too knew the fate of the King's Legion. "You can take comfort in the knowledge that your family died a hero's death. The King's Legion didn't run - not down to the last man. They stood and fought until none were left and the King stood and fought alongside them, showing them that every single man under the Bremmand banner was going to fight to the death to protect our lands. I've never heard of such courage."

"Nor I," Dale murmured. Every tale he heard of the battle, filled him more and more with an admiration for the countless men who had faced the onslaught of the tens of thousands Darvett had brought to destroy them.

Allin's head had also come up. What he'd heard of his father's death so far had only been what Dale had allowed him to learn - that he'd fallen in battle. This was the first time he'd heard anyone speak admiringly of the manner of his death. "My father believed that Bremmand was worth fighting for," he declared, in a flat voice. "He'd never have run - even if there were hundreds of enemies and only him."

"He sounds like he was a fine man," Fenner said gravely. "You have every right to be proud of him."

Allin bowed his head once more and returned to scratching marks on the ground.

"You should eat something, son," Dale suggested kindly but Allin shook his head.

"I'm not hungry." And then, almost in the same sentence, "Will Joss be all right?"

"I don't know," Dale answered honestly, knowing that to try and build false hope would be wrong. "We have to wait and hope that she will be. Now are you sure you don't want anything to eat? We've come a long way and you need to keep your strength up."

Another shake of the head and this time Dale didn't attempt to persuade the boy. Instead he just gave a little squeeze to Allin's shoulders and let him continue to deal with the agonising wait in his own way.

For the next while, time seemed to pass painfully slowly. Dale talked a little with the men who sat around the fire, most of it aimless small talk about nothing in particular. The air of the place was gloomy, which matched his own mood well enough, the majority of the men finding little to enjoy in the tough existence they were now eking out. True, the life of a soldier tended to be bound in discipline and the demands of obedience and courage but there was usually enough to eat and regular leave to compensate for the hard times. The deprivation they were now undergoing was both uncompensated and, it would seem, never-ending.

While Dale talked, Allin continued to scratch about in the ground with the stick. At first Dale had taken no notice but as time went on, the constant grating noise began to get on his nerves. He was about to snap at the boy to stop, when the brown head came up once more. Dale felt a tug on his sleeve and Allin said,

"It looked like that."

The light was fading so it wasn't easy to see the shape drawn out in the ground. Torvik sitting just beyond them also turned to look and, when he couldn't make the drawing out either, reached into the fire, pulled out a burning stick and used it to illuminate the ground by Allin's feet.

He had drawn a flower. It was a little crude but the shape was unmistakable.

"Black Virgin!" Torvik and Dale both exclaimed simultaneously but Allin shook his head impatiently.

"It was white, not black. I told you."

"It's called 'virgin' because it's white," Torvik explained. "The 'black' is because it's poisonous. Have you never come across it before?"

Allin shook his head. Then, once again, he asked "Is Joss going to die?"

"Not if Marta has anything to say about it," Fenner remarked in that same scornful yet affectionate tone. "She considers it a personal insult to find an illness she can't cure. She saves most lives by the patient not daring to die on her!"

Dale patted Allin on the shoulder. "Black Virgin is nasty but it isn't usually fatal. But," he started to get to his feet, "we should let Marta know that that's what it was. Then she'll know how best to treat it."

Torvik as on his feet in a flash. "I'll go. You stay here and rest. You've had a hard day," and, before Dale could argue or protest, the blonde officer was gone.

He was back almost as quickly with a broad grin on his face. "Done," he informed them and added merrily, "and I was told in no uncertain terms to get out of Marta's way and to stop slowing her down. That's always a good sign. The more confident she is of her patient's recovery, the more bad-tempered she is with everyone else."

It was another hour of difficult waiting before Marta finally same down to the fireside to find them. "She's sleeping," the dark featured woman informed them with a satisfied look on her face. "The fever's already coming down." She looked at Allin and offered him her hand as if she'd known him all his life. "Do you want to come along with me and see her?"

Allin got quickly to his feet but hesitated when Dale didn't come too.

"You go," the big man suggested. "Too much of a crowd might wake her up."

The woman and the boy returned after a short while, Allin looking cheerful for the first time that afternoon. "She's snoring," he told Dale happily, which caused a ripple of laughter round the fire.

"The poison hampers the breathing and she's still fighting it a little, so it's making her snore," Marta added. "Leave her with me for a few days, so I can treat it and make sure she's recovered."

"A few days?" Dale sounded scandalised. "We can't just leave her here."

"What were you intending? To carry her back though the forest on a chill night like this? You'd kill her." Marta retorted sharply. "I won't allow you to do it. She'll be quite all right staying here with me."

Allin had listened to this exchange in silence but now his eyes widened as he took in the meaning of what was being said. "We're not going to leave Joss here on her own, are we Dale?"

The big man looked at him, sighed and said glumly, "We may have to, son. If she's still poorly then Marta's right that it would be foolish for me to carry her all that way home, just to get sick again."

"Then why can't we stay too? She's too little to stay here all by herself."

"There's work to be done, Allin. You know that. We have another load of lumber due for Kurop for the end of the week and there's the animals to tend to."

"But..." Allin began to protest but Dale held up his hand.

"Let me be, for a minute Allin. I need to think."

"Why not leave the boy here, too?" Torvik suggested easily. "He can keep his sister company and we can watch them both until the little one is ready to be taken home. They'd be very welcome."

Dale shook his head, "It's kind of you, Torvik, but I won't impose him on you." Not to mention the fact that Dale would then be out of sight of both of his precious charges. The protection of these children was everything to him and there was no way on earth he would leave them both among strangers for days at a time.

"I think," he said slowly to Allin, rubbing his beard as he did so. "I think we'll have to go back to the cottage tonight and..."

What happened next surprised even Dale. Allin, having realised that further argument wasn't working and without waiting for Dale to finish what he had been about to say, suddenly pulled himself up to his full height, squared his

212

shoulders and looked the big man steadily in the face. For the few seconds while he did so, he was no longer a boy, but a man. A man of ten years old it had to be said but a man none the less.

"I'm sorry Dale," he said with calm firmness. "I will not leave my sister here on her own. It is entirely *out of the question.*" Then he turned and headed back to Marta's pitch to sit with the little girl once again, his speed of departure giving away his anxiety at having outfaced the big man.

Dale felt his heart pounding, so astonished by this that he felt sure that everyone else there couldn't fail to notice that this was a royal child.

Torvik, who had been watching raised his eyebrows slightly and his lips twitched in some amusement. He threw a side long grin at Dale and said, "I don't think I'd want to make bets if there was a debate on who rules the roost in your household."

Seeing that the blonde young man was joking and hadn't seen anything but a stubborn and wilful child in front of him, Dale allowed a sly smile in return. "You'd find no-one to take such a bet," he replied with a laugh. "It's absolutely clear who's in charge."

"The boy?" one of the other men laughed.

"No." Dale shook his head. "Who's in charge in any household, if it's not the woman? Joss may be only three years old," he smiled wryly, "but when she tired of our company she had me carry her through the woods in order to find new friends and now won't permit us to leave her. We'll just have to sit, frozen and powerless to move, while we wait for her permission to leave again. Oh no, it's not Allin who commands - it's his little sister!"

Having made light of the affair, Dale strolled casually up the slope in search of his young charge. He wasn't angry, although by the rate at which Allin had retreated, the boy wasn't sure of that fact. What did concern him was the conundrum they now faced. He didn't know what to do for the best and Allin wasn't making things any easier.

When he reached Marta's pitch he walked inside to where Allin was sitting, holding Joss' hand as she slept. The glow from the tallow candle threw long shadows across the room, but Dale could easily make out the apprehension in the boy's face.

"I won't leave her," he repeated but the tremor in his voice was clear.

Dale crossed and squatted down beside the stool where he was seated. "I know how you feel, son, really I do."

"Then we can stay?" he sounded terribly relieved that Dale seemed to be taking his side now.

"It's a bit of a problem, Allin," Dale said evenly. "Joss has to stay, and you don't want to leave her. The animals at the cottage need to be fed and yet you *know* that I cannot leave you both here on your own. What would you do?"

Allin pondered this. "You leave us alone at the cottage," he said eventually.

"But not for days at a time and I'm never very far away. I could hear you calling and be with you within moments"

"And in Chelland?"

"Zacharus is always there."

Allin sighed, and dropped his chin on to his fist thinking hard for a way to make this work.

Finally, Dale relented and said resignedly, "I suppose I could leave you here with Torvik to watch you for a few hours a day," - the brown head came up, hope shining in the blue eyes - "while I walk back to the cottage each morning to feed the animals and then come back."

"Oh, Dale!" The boy flung his arms about the man's neck for finding a solution for him.

"You'll be the death of me," Dale laughed, accepting the affection with pleasure. "Just make sure you don't cause any trouble when I'm not here. I don't want Torvik thinking I mind unruly brats!"

So it was arranged. The next morning at first light, while Allin was still asleep, Dale made the walk back to the cottage, fed and watered the animals and walked back again, bringing with him some eggs and a skin full of the goat's milk. The men of the camp had seen little in the way of fresh food in some time so the gift produced some excitement and not a little disagreement as to who should gain from the dairy produce. It wasn't until Torvik stepped in, exerting his authority as much by the most astonishing verbal dexterity as anything else, that the matter was resolved.

Dale found himself grinning at the sight. He had forgotten the awesome command of language the young officer had when it came to delivering a dressing-down and, while amused, he was also thankful he'd never been in a position to be on the receiving end of one of Torvik's tongue-lashings.

When the blonde man had finished his tirade and commanded one of their number to deliver the dairy goods to Marta for her to disperse them to whoever she felt would gain the most benefit from them, he turned back to Dale with a sunny look on his face as if nothing untoward had occurred. "It's a handsome gift, Dale, and will be much appreciated."

"Consider it payment for providing us with lodging and aid." Then, with expansive warmth he put a big arm about the young man's shoulders. "I've missed your company, Torvik, my young friend. I always promised myself that if I ever had say in appointments I'd send for you and have you under my command again."

Torvik grinned but a look of infinite sadness also flitted across his face. "Another thing of the past, Dale."

There it was again - the air of surrender and crushing defeat. These weren't just men in retreat, waiting to regroup. They were well and truly beaten. They had given up.

It was everywhere in the camp. From the shoddily thrown up pitches, to the dirty attire and slovenly attitudes of men who had once been well drilled and well disciplined the whole place reeked of defeat. It was as if nothing mattered any more and no-one was there to care about it.

Standing there, Dale suddenly realised that he was angry. Not the usual explosive burst of temper but a slow and growing smoulder which had been steadily building in the moons he too had spent in hiding, at the way that the Bremmandish people had all, as one, lain down and allowed Darvett's army to walk all over them.

Dale said nothing of this to anyone at the camp, of course. Instead he spent the day putting himself to good use. He took a bow in to the forest and shot a deer, showing two of the camp men how to track it once the wounded animal had run off in to the forest to die. Killing a deer with a bow was seldom an instant task, he explained, and the trick was to ensure you could find the animal when it had finally bled to death. He also showed them how to snare rabbits, which were smaller fry but a good deal less trouble to catch. But, he grinned down at Allin, he drew the line at wild boar hunting. It was too early in the season and he didn't have the energy for it.

With the aid of Salvit, who seemed more open to him now that he was recovered from the appalling hangover of their last meeting, they then butchered the venison and set it up over a spit on the fire to roast. The smell of cooking meat floated about the camp site throughout the afternoon and spirits began to rise.

That was nothing, however, compared to the soaring mood that came when one of their number came in from Chelland. He was almost bursting with excitement as he told the tale.

According to the innkeeper in the town, there was a rumour about how the king of Hast had received a visitor in the night.

One of the others made a vulgar remark to this but the story teller said irritably, "It was men. One of them was a youth."

Another, even more coarse joke at this, but the man with the news was not to be swayed. "There's some that says the lad was his grandson."

Complete silence. Most of them didn't even really understand what this meant. It was left to Dale to say steadily. "The King of Hast had only one child. A daughter. She was married to King Jorvis and was our Queen. His grandson must be their son."

Now the silence was not from puzzlement. Finally, as if not daring to believe it Fenner said, "One of them survived? One of the Princes?"

"The King," Torvik corrected firmly. "He's not a Prince. He's our King."

"*If* the story is true," Karrec, an elderly soldier said dampeningly. "It's a rumour, just like so many others. It could just be make-believe."

"Why should anyone make up such a thing?" someone else demanded and the group fell in to argument about the likelihood or otherwise of the story.

Dale left them to it and took a few paces away from the debate. Allin was there as well, listening in to the conversation, his eyes alight with what he had heard. Dale put an arm about him and murmured softly, "It sounds like they made it."

Allin nodded, looking almost afraid to say anything. "I wonder what he's doing now."

"Don't you worry about that. If he's safe and with King Perrold, he'll not take long to have me take you to join him."

"Yes," said Allin, but his tone was absent; sad even.

The good news didn't serve to keep moods positive for long, for in a short enough time the deeper implication of the appearance of the surviving royal in Hast began to sink in.

It was Sarian, whom Dale had already singled out as a cynic, who put it in to words. "If he's in Hast, then it's all over," he declared gloomily. "The Holy bloodline has left Bremmand's borders. We're on our own from now on."

Dale was sitting in Marta's pitch with Allin, entertaining a recovering but sleepy Joss when this depressing conclusion was reached or he might have been tempted to contest the fact. As it was, he missed that opportunity and the crushing sense of defeat already pressing down on these injured and dispossessed soldiers grew all the stronger.

By the time the moon had fully risen, and the night chill had wrapped itself about the forest, the departure of the King from Bremmandish soil had more than outweighed the fact that one of the holy line lived on.

Joss settled into sleep and Dale brought Allin down to the fire for something to eat. It was late and the boy was more tired than hungry so, after a few mouthfuls of the well-cooked venison he leaned up against Dale and drowsed in the warmth of the flame.

Dale, however, felt entitled to a celebration. While the soldiers were inept at providing food for themselves they had proved themselves anything but when it came to brewing. It wasn't uncommon for any squad of soldiers to ensure its own comfort when it came to beer and among this group of survivors was one for whom this had been one of his unofficial duties. Thus, from grain which would have been far better suited to making bread, had come beer. It was young yet, so it was sour and cloudy but it was strong and made the head light with relative ease. Dale, knowing that he had managed to see the first third of his mission completed, considered he had earned the right to get a little drunk and allowed himself to be plied generously with the rough beer.

He was on his third (or was it his fourth?) mug of the stuff when Torvik appeared from somewhere with a grin on his face. He was pleased to see his former officer letting go a little for once and settled himself down beside the man with the firm intention of catching him up as swiftly as possible.

Dale returned an uncoordinated smile to the blonde officer. "Here's to the new King!" he toasted, waving his mug at a sideways angle.

Across the fire someone toasted back, "And to the death of Bremmand."

Dale's head snapped up sharply peering across the round firepit to see who had said such a thing. Allin had heard it too and he was also sitting up, more alert at this terrible remark.

"Don't be a fool, Brell," another voice rapped out. "We're not dead yet."

"We might as well be. Even the bloodline itself has abandoned us."

It was the final straw and Dale's smouldering anger erupted. He'd had enough of the defeatist attitude and sour view that everyone seemed to take. It was time someone took this rabble and reminded them of who they were.

"We might as well be dead, if this is the best that men like you can come up with as defence against the enemy," he snarled furiously. "Look at you all. No-one would think you were soldiers. This place is a disgrace. *You* are a disgrace. You wander about like sickly old women, bemoaning how it used to be, and how you've been betrayed and how it's all lost, but not one of you - not a single, spineless, wretch among you - is prepared to do anything to set things to rights."

"Like what?" a scathing voice demanded from the dark.

"Like fighting back," Dale roared. "You're soldiers."

"Were," Sarian corrected him.

"You *still are*. Did any one of you receive discharge from the army?" No-one answered but Dale wasn't asking idle questions so he rapped out, "Well? Did you?"

"Of course not," a thin sour faced fellow replied, clearly thinking this was folly. "There wasn't anyone left to discharge us."

"Then you're still in the army! You answer to the line of command and you follow orders."

"There are no orders - and no commanders, come to that."

Torvik touched his arm, trying to cool the big man's temper. "Come on, Dale, it's just talk. Let's not be foolish."

The big man rounded on him in full fury and barked, "As for you, I expect better of you. You allow this rabble to drag themselves about in this helpless way and think that's acceptable?"

"Well..." Torvik began but Dale was having none of it.

"You're an officer; or have you forgotten what that means?"

For a second Torvik stared but then both the question and the answer began to penetrate his brain, so dulled by weeks of hiding and inactivity. He straightened his back to sit upright and said more smartly than he had done in some time, "No sir. I remember."

"Then start bloody acting like one," Dale snapped and turned back to the rest of them.

"You are soldiers of the Bremmand Army. You fight for the King wherever he may be and you have standing orders, in the absence of any others, to protect the Kingdom and fight the enemy."

Sarian rose slowly to his feet. "For what purpose? Haven't you been listening? The holy bloodline is gone - left the kingdom and abandoned us to Darvett and his mad brother. If the bloodline leaves then the kingdom will fall!"

"So what?" Dale roared with passion, bounding to his feet to tower over Sarian. "The story says what happens if the bloodline leaves but it doesn't say anything about after that. So the kingdom has fallen. Well, by God, let's fight to get it back." No-one looked all that convinced, so Dale went on passionately, "Bremmand isn't what it is because of the bond between God and Brem, it isn't what it is because of the holy bloodline. They stand as our tokens of who we are but Bremmand is what it is because of its people. *We* are Bremmand – the Woodsmen, the Bremmandish and the Langatians - and we are more than some rabble of mixed races who follow the man who sits on the throne in a city a week's walk away. This is *our* kingdom, these are *our* lands and anyone who believes that should be working towards regaining them from these invaders."

No-one answered this, everyone around the fire taken aback by Dale's vehemence. He let the anger subside a little and said more reasonably, "I'll tell you this much; if the King has gone abroad, I can bet it won't be to hide. He'll be doing all he can to muster support and return this kingdom to its rightful owners."

"That's true," Karrec agreed, suddenly. "If he's a son of Jorvis, he'll not be running away. His father stood up to Darvett even when he knew he couldn't win - our new King will do the same."

"Exactly," Dale growled. "If you believe in God and you believe in the bond with Brem then you have to believe that God won't abandon us now. His trust still rests with the holy bloodline and we have a duty to serve that line, just as we have always done. Bremmand isn't lost so long as the people keep faith with their King and their God. We, the soldiers of the Royal Army, keep faith by doing the one thing we have always done; the one thing we are trained to do. Fight!"

Whether it was the words, or the sentiment or the immense power and passion Dale used to deliver it but the men around the fire were drawn to it and rose to its meaning. By the time Dale barked out that call to arms, every man of them was on his feet and uttered a roar of approval which reverberated around the night time forest. In the moon-cycles since the fall, every one of them had been wandering leaderless through life. But now, here was a new leader, a new purpose and with it an energy to start taking back what had been stolen from them.

It was time. Bremmand was about to be reclaimed.

It was cold and the ground was hard. For a moment Dale couldn't think where he was or how he came to be sleeping outdoors in late autumn when he had a perfectly good bed in the cottage. He stirred, meaning to roll over and seek a bit more comfort but he was gripped with a wave of nausea and a throbbing head which gave him a sharp reminder of where he was.

To no-one in particular he muttered, "In Brem's name, what was that stuff I was drinking last night?"

"Good morning," Allin said by way of a reply. Dale forced his eyes open just as the boy moved in to Dale's eye line. He'd clearly been awake for some time for he was fully dressed and looking cheerfully alert.

Dale moaned and shut his eyes, as much to blot out the impudently pleased face of his young charge, as to shield his eyes from the sun which was blazing away in a most unnecessary fashion. "How long have you been up?"

"Oh, ages!" Allin couldn't hide the glee in his voice at Dale's clear suffering. "I was wondering if you were going to sleep all day."

A number of choice replies rose in to Dale's mind but he bit them back. It wasn't often that Allin had a chance to feel superior to the big man and he was only here through his own folly, so he couldn't blame the lad for enjoying it while it lasted. In the end, all he said was, "How's Joss"

"Awake and wanting to go and see the chickens."

"Good." Dale rubbed his face and tried once again to force his eyes open. This was clearly not going to be a pleasant experience, he decided. "So, are you going to stand there grinning at me all morning, or are you going to show a bit of kindness and get me a brew?"

Allin laughed but Dale heard his footsteps move away as he went on his errand of mercy for the big man.

By the time he had returned, still looking immensely pleased with himself, Dale had brought himself in to a sitting position and had pulled on his boots. It didn't do much to improve his head and his memory of last night was still distinctly vague - he remembered a lot of shouting and an awful lot of drink but not a lot else - but he did feel at slightly less of a disadvantage to the ten-year-old. When he was handed the hot mug of brew he even managed to nod his thanks as if nothing was wrong.

Allin sat down beside him. There was an excitement in the boy's face that Dale was beginning to be puzzled by. He was almost bursting with it and Dale wondered what could have happened that was so entertaining the lad.

Be careful what you wish for the saying went and this was clearly one of those occasions. "Everyone's really bucked up after what you said last night," Allin said.

Memory returned in a rush, as sharp and painful as being impaled by a spear. He'd had too much to drink and incited this small band of refugees to start a war against the occupying forces of the Kostain Empire. All his caution and prudence in keeping a low profile had been thrown to the winds because he couldn't keep his temper. Inwardly Dale moaned. If these men took it upon themselves to mount an attack on an Empire outpost it could see the end of them all in Brem knew what kind of retribution. How could he have been so irresponsible?

As if this thought led him to the next he suddenly found himself wondering just how irresponsible he had been. He now recalled a passionate speech about not giving up and them all still being soldiers but he knew that the conversation had turned around the King being in exile and the bloodline being outside the borders too. "I didn't," he asked fearfully of Allin, "Did I mention anything about... well, you?"

"Me?" for a second he looked confused.

Dale dropped his voice. "About the King's brother still being within Bremmand?"

"Oh!" A shake of the head. "Don't you remember?"

"Brem only knows what was in that beer," was his answer. Allin just looked like he wanted to laugh again. "You wait." Dale said with feeling. "One day you'll have too much to drink and then I shall be only too happy to poke fun at you, my young and disgustingly healthy friend!"

When Dale had managed to collect himself enough to face others, he strolled down the slope towards the hollow at the centre of the camp. His expectations of how he would be received were apprehensive enough from his memory of the night before but he wasn't in the least prepared for what was awaiting him.

The few remaining soldiers of the Royal Bremmand Army were waiting for him, fallen in to a well-drilled, if somewhat shabbily-turned-out, line and they greeted him with a smart salute.

"Holy Brem's beard!" Dale muttered explosively.

"Good morning, Captain," Torvik greeted him formally. "The men are ready for your inspection."

Dale gave him a sour look. "I told you before Torvik. I'm not a Captain any more. I was injured and gave up my command."

"I rather thought you'd re-enlisted after last night," Torvik smiled.

"Well you were wrong. I'm a woodsman and that's all."

"But.." a worried look came across Torvik's face. "Last night you said..."

"Last night I was drunk," Dale snapped. "I didn't know half of what I was saying."

"Yes you did," Torvik retorted obstinately. "You knew exactly what you were saying. It's the first bit of sense anyone's talked since the battle. Bremmand is still Bremmand and we are still her army. It's up to us to keep fighting for her."

"Up to you maybe. Not me."

Torvik just stared at him and Dale could see the rest of the men also looking at him with growing dismay in their faces.

"You can't be serious! You can't be suggesting that you are going to walk away from this." Karrec had broken from the line and had approached him. "We need you. These men" - he gestured with a wave of his hand at the line up - "*need* you."

Dale shook his head. "No. They need good leadership and strong direction. Torvik can give them that as well as I can. Better probably. And you, you're a Captain. Between you you've more than enough of what is needed to do what is required."

"We do this in service of our kingdom and her people - of Bremmand," Karrec reminded him. "Where is your loyalty to your King?"

"I am a loyal subject to the King," Dale hissed, stung by this, "but I cannot serve him as you do. I serve in my own way."

Karrec and Torvik gazed at him in disbelief and even Allin, standing at his side was staring at him, his mouth hanging open.

"We've outstayed our welcome," Dale spoke brusquely. "We should go. Allin, go and get Joss."

"But..." he began.

"You said she was better; that she wanted to go home."

"Yes, but..."

"Then don't argue with me, boy. Go and fetch her. We need to be on our way."

Pouting at the curt way Dale spoke to him, Allin turned and headed off to do as he was bidden as Karrec gave the big man one last look and said slowly, "Yes. I think it is time you left. Some of us have work to do." Then he turned on his heel and went back to the line of men, barking instructions to them as he went, getting them assigned to duties to begin to improve the state of the camp.

"I'm grateful for the help you've given to Joss," Dale said to Torvik.

"Don't mention it," the blonde officer returned sounding bitterly insincere. Then, his face twisted in to puzzlement. "You really won't stay?"

"How can I?" Dale asked pleadingly. "I have two children to care for."

"Brell's boy, Nollan, is here. Your two would have a home here too."

"This is no life for children, you know that, and I gave my word that I'd care for them as best I could. If the man who gave them over to me for safety had known I was going to lead them in to a war, he'd never have trusted them to me." Dale shook his head. "I'm sorry Torvik. I have other responsibilities and you don't need me as much as they do."

"No Regrets?"

The walk back to the cottage was more leisurely than the trip from it two days before but the burden that Dale carried with him on the return trip was even heavier than the sickly child had been. For all his protests and stubborn insistence that he wasn't needed, he knew it wasn't so. There were so few of them and the odds were all stacked in the Empire's favour. He felt bitter and ashamed that he had been forced to walk away from this small spark of hope in the ruins of Bremmand. But, he reminded himself, he had other responsibilities, far more important responsibilities, than a fighting force that would barely make a mark in the huge wave of Kostinians sweeping the land.

He gazed down at Allin who was walking in silence beside him, holding Joss's hand as they made their way home. The youngster didn't understand this either, Dale guessed by the frosty reception he was getting. Allin was still a boy and he clearly saw the romance in a heroic if futile fight to get the kingdom back for his family. The fact that he and his sister had to be protected at all costs, the fact that the King himself was relying on Dale to bring them to safety, hadn't occurred to him.

He'd come round, Dale decided with a sigh. The memory of the small band of exiled soldiers would fade and other things would occupy the boy's mind. Then perhaps he'd remember who he was and why he mattered so desperately to this war torn kingdom.

If Allin was to reconcile himself to Dale's seeming retreat from the field of battle it wasn't going to happen quickly. Once they were back at the cottage he seemed to be remote from Dale once more and less settled than he had been before the visit to the camp in the forest.

After a few days, Dale did try to talk to the lad but even as he had attempted to open a dialogue on the subject Allin had merely said, "I was bidden by my brother to do as you asked and to place my trust in you. I will do as my brother asks. If you say we stay here, then I will do as you wish," and he had turned and walked away.

It wasn't as if the boy was isolating himself, Dale reflected, or being difficult. He was doing as he was told, looking after his sister and tending to the cottage and garden. It was just that he seemed unable to find any way to talk to the big man any more. Dale began to wonder a trifle worriedly if he had managed, by walking away from the fight, to destroy the faith the boy had in him.

All in all it was a difficult week. While Allin wasn't prepared to discuss his feelings there was nothing Dale could do so he decided the best course was to carry on as normal. However, he wasn't above trying a few things which might just get the lad to open up to him.

Thus, one morning he announced that he thought it was about time they had a bit of fish for supper. Despite his reserve Allin couldn't keep a gleam out of his eyes. He loved fishing!

"Chores first," Dale reminded him. "And your lessons. Get those done and then we can go down to the river."

Allin pulled a face, but did as he was told. Over the weeks they had spent together, Dale had encouraged Allin to get the less palatable of his day's tasks done as early as possible. The big man was a great believer in getting things over and done with and he encouraged Allin to take the same approach. "Put them off," he had advised, "and you have the thought of them hanging over you all day. Once they're done you can enjoy the rest of your time freely." Thus Dale always saw to it that his young companion attended to the garden and got his studies completed first. Then, this done, they would both spend time in the clearing working at Allin's swordsmanship which fell somewhere between work and pleasure for both of them.

On this day, as had been the case for some few practice sessions, Allin was struggling to master his lessons. He had learned the basic attack and defence positions and knew how to meet each attack with a defence but now Dale was trying to teach him how to use those figures to his advantage. It was always a difficult step for any student and Dale had shown endless patience in taking him again and again through the sequences until he could see how they fitted together. However, it was slow going and after a week of, to Allin, no progress he was becoming frustrated.

"Come on boy, think!" Dale barked as Allin became more ragged and wild in his movements.

"I *am* thinking," the boy shouted back angrily. "You just keep yelling at me."

Over and over, round and round until they were both breathless and Allin was boiling with fury.

Dale was about to tell the boy to give it up for the day, weary of the lack of progress when he heard Joss give a low giggle and he realised she wasn't alone.

When he and Allin trained, Joss always sat on the tall stump of a tree at the edge of the clearing, where she could watch what they were doing but wouldn't be in the way as they worked. As Dale glanced across he saw that, by her side was a tall, blonde figure, one arm about her waist, watching along with her.

"Torvik! How long have you been there?" This was a little awkward. He was supposed to be an invalid, unable to fight, so for him to be coaching Allin belied that fact.

Torvik however, seemed not to notice. "A while. I didn't want to interrupt." He strolled over to Allin. "Can I make a suggestion or two?" Then he glanced at Dale "You don't mind do you?" The big man shook his head. He wasn't getting anywhere with the boy, so another opinion might help.

Torvik smiled easily at Allin, who still bore the scowl on his face from the frustrations of the session with Dale. "Firstly, you need to keep your temper. The easiest way to beat an opponent is to make him angry, which means that if you lose your temper you are a good way towards losing the fight already. Anger is hard to control, and this type of combat is all about control." Allin nodded his understanding. "Good. So take a deep breath and stop scowling like that.

"Secondly," Torvik went on, even as a slightly startled Allin took a moment to compose himself once more, "you are thinking too much."

Dale just said I *wasn't* thinking," Allin complained.

"You weren't *concentrating*," Torvik corrected. "That's because you were too busy being annoyed but I can see in your every movement that you are thinking in steps. Give him another combination Dale, not too quick" and, as the big man offered up a sequence of attack poses Torvik rapped out briskly "Attack six, needs defence four. Attack three, needs defence one..." and so on. When the sequence ended, he took hold of the stick Allin was using as a sword and waved Dale round to face him. "Same combination. Now watch. We're going to do this twice." The first time, at each step he repeated the same litany "...attack one, defence five; attack seven, defence nine...." Then, after a brief pause, they started again but now Torvik was silent, instead answering each blow with a fluidity of movement that had not been there before.

"The positions help you learn," he explained to Allin, "but they aren't a hard and fast rule. Stop thinking of it as question and answer and think of it more like a song. String combinations together to make a tune and you'll find you can dance to it. Understand?"

Allin nodded slowly, his face still clouded with incomprehension but there was the beginnings of a light in his eyes.

Dale wiped his face on his sleeve and slapped the boy gently on the back. "Enough for now, son. Go get your things together."

As they watched him collect Joss and head in to the cottage Torvik murmured, "Looks like he's got potential."

"I'm hoping so. He's young yet."

"Never too early for real talent to show itself."

"Perhaps. We'll have to see. So," Dale deftly turned the subject away from Allin and sword fighting, "what brings you here?"

The blonde soldier shrugged gloomily "It's not working Dale. We've not got what's needed to make an army. I just came to see if you'd consider..?"

"No!" Dale knew what the man was about to ask him. "I can't. I've already explained that. Please, don't ask me again."

Torvik sighed and said regretfully, "I just hoped you might have had second thoughts. You sounded as if you really believed what you said that night and I hoped you might have found the desire to join us."

"It's not a question of desire," Dale replied. "If it were just me, I'd come in a heartbeat but there's the children. I have a promise to keep to their family, and anyway, I left the army for a reason. I can't fight any more."

"It isn't your fighting arm we need, sir. It's your leadership."

Dale was puzzled. Torvik was an excellent officer and a good leader of men and he said so.

"I can lead a squad of soldiers, train them and manage their discipline. But this? This is different. I'm starting from nothing and we've got too many officers for so few men. Right now we're spending as much time arguing about who should be leading as we are getting anything done."

"You shouldn't have too much trouble with that, Torvik. I never knew a more capable man in my life."

"Nice of you to say it but my disadvantages far outweigh my abilities. For all you may think I'm good, I'm still a sapling in the eyes of the likes of Karrec and Sarian.

"Karrec was a Captain and he knows nothing about me. He's a third generation soldier, I think, and he thinks ability is more about experience than anything else so what could I possibly know? Besides which I'm only a lieutenant, so he isn't prepared to respect my authority and," he pulled a face, "I'm not about to defer to him. He'd have us follow every drill there is, waiting for the King to return, but not give anyone a single taste of real combat to keep them sharp.

"As for Sarian, I don't think anything will get that man to stir himself for real action. He's been a lieutenant for ever and that by right of birth rather than ability. I begin to wonder if he survived the battle by not exerting himself enough to engage with the enemy. The only thing he seems able to do with any enthusiasm is find fault with everything and everyone else.

"It was one thing, in an army of thousands of men. They'd see me as young but they'd also see some hulking great brute of Captain standing at my shoulder to slice a few heads off if they refused to listen to me..."

"I can't say that was ever my more favoured means of enforcing discipline," Dale murmured, as a smile flitted across his lips.

"Perhaps, and it wouldn't work here anyway. There aren't enough of us. Make an example of a couple of men and we cut our numbers by a third." At least the young man could still see a joke in this situation. "That's why I came, though."

"To have me fight your battles for you?"

"To stop it being a battle. There's real work we could be doing and we're just wasting time at the moment."

Again Dale shook his head. "It simply isn't possible. I'm sorry. Besides, I'm not sure I'd be so welcome after walking out on you last time."

"Don't believe it. Your name comes up constantly, and even Karrec would defer to you. I'm sure of it. We need someone like you - someone who really believes, not just followers of a dim hope. Come man," Torvik put a tentative hand on his arm in mute appeal. "There must be something that would convince you to change your mind?"

At that moment Allin and Joss came back across the clearing, Allin now back in his tunic and both children with long woollen cloaks pulled about them against the increasingly wintry chills of the forest.

Dale shook his head sorrowfully. "Leave it be, Torv. Nothing you could say or do would make me change my mind."

The blond head shook once more as he said apologetically, "I had to try. You understand that? If you ever change your mind..."

"...then I know where to find you. I know my friend, I know." A thought sprang in to Dale's mind. "We're about to head off for a spot of fishing, if you wanted to join us," Torvik looked doubtful. Fishing had never appealed to him all that much but Dale went on more persuasively, "Half a dozen fish would probably lift a few spirits with your men, and you and I could talk some more. I may not be able to join you, but it doesn't mean I won't help."

The afternoon by the river proved to be profitable both in terms of fish and in advice. So, as they sat on the river bank, Torvik laid his concerns before Dale and the big man offered guidance, suggestion and, sometimes when no solution seemed possible, just a listening ear.

From their discussion it was clear that the disillusioned and ill-disciplined group was making little progress towards becoming an army once more and those who should be leading were doing little to help.

Karrec, elderly but experienced, couldn't accept Torvik's leadership but at the same time very few of the men would accept Karrec's. He'd not fought in the final battle, his age being such that he was no longer fit enough for armed combat. Thus he had served behind the lines, as a tactical advisor. The men, few though they were, wanted to follow someone they felt could stand at their side in a fight, not someone considered too old for the field of battle.

Dale did conclude that Karrec felt that he had something to prove and was too set in his ways to allow that Torvik might have the talent to lead but could see no easy solution. Torvik was going to have to prove himself the hard way. But, while Torvik was able, he was also extremely young and inexperienced and his temperament was such that he was finding the constant challenges hard to bear.

There was also a clear and definite schism in the opinions of what the army should be doing. The doubt of all of them that the King was really alive or that so few of them could make any difference made it even harder for them to take any positive action.

For the big captain it was difficult to give concrete advice. He knew things that meant it was easier to have faith and he was so determined that the people of Bremmand should start to fight back that he cared little how much difference they would make. Torvik, however, seemed to draw strength from being able to consult with someone else, so he kept talking, unaware of the increasing frustration it was causing in his previous commanding officer, who was ever more desirous of joining the fight with them, even though he knew he couldn't.

That evening, after Torvik had gone, Allin seemed especially pensive. Then, suddenly, after sitting in silence for some time, he said, "Why don't we join them?"

"Who?" Dale asked, his mind elsewhere.

"Torvik and the others."

Dale sighed. "You know why, Allin."

"No I don't. You told Torvik that you were just a woodsman, but you're not, are you?"

"I also told him that I have to take care of you and your sister. That's still the case."

"We won't be here for long. Cori's going to send for us and we'll be gone."

"Well, when that happens, maybe I will be able to join them."

"But they need you *now*. *Why* can't you see that?" In frustration he turned and bolted in to the cottage so he shouldn't have to face Dale's implacable expression any longer.

Dale watched him go with a stab of pain in his heart. Not that Allin had yet again lost his temper and turned away from the man in disgust but for the single agonising reminder of the fact that, *We won't be here.* A few moon-cycles and he was so used to having the children about him that the very idea of them being gone was physically painful to him. He'd already lost one family and now here he was faced with the certainty of losing another one.

He shrugged off the idea. This wasn't his family and he'd never had the right to think of it as such, so he didn't deserve to feel sorry for himself at any pain that caused him. Right now, it was more important to talk to Allin and get him to face up to the impossibilities of what he suddenly seemed to want so badly.

In the dimly-lit sleeping room, Allin was sitting on the bed he shared with his sister (he still refused to use the other bed, the one Cori had slept in, as if using it would prevent his brother coming back to claim it), back against the wooden logs of the outer wall, knees tucked up and his head buried deeply into them.

Dale regarded him solemnly for a little while, wondering how best to approach this but Allin, sensing he was there, said in a muffled voice, "You don't want to fight. You just want to stay here."

"No," Dale disagreed, but stamped on his own injured pride at the suggestion that he was some kind of coward. "I do what my King commanded of me and that was to stay here and wait for him to send word."

Allin's head came up, his eyes flashing blue in the candle light. "I'm a Prince," he reminded Dale. "The heir to the throne. I could command you to go and help Torvik." The boy looked defiant but he couldn't quite keep the look of apprehension from flitting across his face. His last attempt at pulling rank had ended up with him getting a sound hiding and he hadn't forgotten it.

"You could, but if you did, as Lord Protector of the Holy Bloodline, I would have to decline. As is my right and duty," he added as he saw Allin's mouth open to protest this. In gentle but firm tones Dale said, "We must remain here, hidden, for a while longer, son, just as the King commanded of us both. Torvik will have to find his way without us. He will too, Allin. He's a good man and a clever one. He'll find a way. And if he falters, well, he can always come and ask advice. I'm always willing to talk," he allowed himself a small smile, "and to fish!"

It was an offer that Dale had made to the blonde lieutenant before he had headed home that night, that he could seek out Dale if he felt the need again, at any time. So after that, Torvik paid frequent visits to the little cottage, sometimes combining the visit with a trip to the river but more often arriving of an evening, just as the children were heading for their beds. Together, late in to the night, the two soldiers would sit and talk, Torvik bringing his concerns and frustrations to Dale. It wasn't much, Dale felt, but at least it was something. His life in the background had to continue but this way he was moving others to take the lead in the real battle.

Allin seemed more and more frustrated on each visit that Dale was only offering advice when, in the ten-year-old's eyes, he should be leading the army. He didn't discuss it again and Dale didn't attempt to make him but it hung about them like a cloud. In truth, Dale's own frustration at the inactivity of his role, when he knew there was work to be done, was beginning to eat at him too much to want anyone else to remind him of it. So, they continued to live their quiet, uninvolved life, not discussing it and pretending that there was nothing wrong.

Dale had once said that no-one ever came to the cottage in the woods unless invited so Torvik finding his own way there had been surprise enough but that was nothing to the surprise he got one grey and drizzly morning when Allin came to find him in the woods to say that Iestan had arrived and he had a stranger with him.

As they walked back to the cottage together, Dale wondered what could possibly have caused Iestan, of all people, to tear himself away from his tavern to walk the five hours to the cottage. He could hardly have the need to see anyone else in these parts and the affairs of woodsmen would hold no interest for him. Perhaps the stranger who had accompanied him would shed more light on the unexpected visit.

They were both sitting by the fire in the clearing, Joss standing a little way off, watching them with interested eyes. Allin immediately crossed to her, automatically removed her fingers from her mouth and took her hand in his. He hadn't liked to leave her alone but Iestan had insisted that they could mind her and he hadn't been able to think of a polite way to refuse them.

Dale noted Allin's taking charge of his sister once more and then turned his attentions on the visitors. The man Iestan had brought with him was unknown to Dale and his nondescript attire gave little away as to his station or purpose. His colouring showed him as being from the far north of Bremmand - only there did one see such pale features and fair, almost white, hair. He was younger than Dale, the big man guessed, but a man grown, judging by his features. No youth or stripling, this. His face was round, almost wider than it was long and it made him look as if his chin was missing but somehow it seemed to fit on the stockily built frame.

Both men rose on Dale's arrival and Iestan said immediately, as if anticipating Dale's questions, "This is Givern, son of Grigis. He came through Chelland and has a message to deliver to you, so I thought I should show him how to find this place. He could spend days wandering about the forest trying to find you on his own."

"That was uncommonly generous of you, Iestan," Dale said evenly, wondering again why the innkeeper would put himself out to such a degree.

"Not at all," Iestan returned graciously. "It made a good excuse for me to get out of the tavern for a day and take a bit of pleasure in the forest." His voice changed then, from his usual contented tone to a more dissatisfied one as he added, "We're seeing more soldiers passing through Chelland, and they all come and drive away paying customers, so it's good to get away from them and their sneering for a while."

Dale nodded, filing away the warning of more troops for future reference. From the sound of it, they were making use of Chelland on their way north, the crossing point in the small town being convenient if you were taking a direct route from south to north.

Having taken the hint from Iestan, his thoughts turned to the other man. He was thinking fast. A messenger, who was clearly from the north? Not long after the rumour of the King reaching the Hastian palace? This could be the news they had been waiting for but there was Iestan to consider. The man was too infernally sharp and far too interested in the acquisition of information for Dale to dare allow him to overhear this. And yet, how could he get rid of the man without arousing suspicion?

"I bring a message from your friend Dostain of Saphir," the messenger, Givern, began.

Dale felt himself relax instantly. Trystin had shown the sense of keeping even this messenger in the dark as to who he was or why he was bringing such a message.

"Since I was passing this way, he asked me to send you his greetings and to say that he enjoyed a safe and uneventful journey through Bremmand, although trade has not been as prosperous as in past trips. It would seem the news of the conquest and the spread of Empire troops is proving to make people more cautious in who they deal with." So they had got through Bremmand without incident but had been treated with suspicion and apprehension wherever they had stopped. That much was to be expected, Dale reflected.

"He is now in the capital of Hast. His apprentice has relatives here and they are staying at his grandfather's house for a few days." The *apprentice* must mean Cori. In other words they had reached King Perrold's castle. They were safe!

Dale allowed himself a brief smile, glad that the rumour had proven itself to be true.

"However," Givern continued, his tone slightly sing-song, as he recited from memory, "the situation in Hast is also a little unsettled at present. His apprentice's grandfather has suggested that they will find better trade if they travel north and east. They are taking this advice, in search of improved business, so he thinks it will be some time longer before he will see you again. He hopes business fares as well for you as it did when he last saw you and trusts you will winter well in the Great Forest." Things in Hast were unsafe for Cori, then and King Perrold wanted them to travel. Where? North and East? Maint, perhaps? or Florus? Both were in the Alliance, so might be able to offer shelter to the exiled King. Either way the message to Dale was clear. Stay put. It wasn't safe to try and bring Joss and Allin out of Bremmand now and they needed to find a safe haven for Cori before sending for them.

"Thank you, friend Givern, son of Grigis," Dale replied formally. "I am obliged to you for having come out of your way to find me and deliver this message."

"Who's Dostain of Saphir?" Allin asked unguardedly, his face a blank.

Dale would have to explain the message to him later, he realised, but for now, with others listening in he merely said, "Someone I knew back in Castle Bremmand. He's a weaver."

"I thought I didn't know the name," Iestan reflected idly, picking a strand of grass and chewing it. "What's he doing so far from home?"

"He travels from time to time," Dale replied, "He takes cloth samples in to the north and further abroad to see if he can make sales. On his last journey he stopped by here, seeing as we had been friends before."

"That apprentice of his is fine young man," Givern remarked. "He's going to work out well."

Dale glanced at him sharply. "Do you know him? Well, I mean?"

"No," was the stocky messenger's reply, adding slowly, "but I know his grandfather." Givern knew then. He knew that he was delivering a message from a King. This was no humble traveller, bringing along a message in passing. He was of the King's messenger service, a part of the army which dedicated itself to communicating between parts of the military forces and the alliance members. Thus he was probably someone who Dale could trust. These men took an oath of loyalty to protect the secrets they carried even under pain of death. Whether this man Givern knew why the King wanted to get word to a humble woodsman in the heart of the forest was not clear but Dale wasn't taking any chances. Unless Givern indicated otherwise, Allin and Joss were going to remain unrelated and anonymous.

Dale smiled and repeated easily, "Well I'm grateful to you for bringing the message. It's always good to hear from friends, especially in such uncertain times. Can I offer you both meat and drink?" He barely turned his head as he said, "Allin, go fetch the tankards. There's brew a plenty," he offered to the men indicating to the pot sitting in the hot embers at the edge of the fire. He always had some of the hot drink ready.

Both men accepted his hospitality gratefully. The walk through the forest was a long one and Dale knew to have reached him so early in the day they must have set off before the sun had risen. It was cold at night at this time of year, the first frosts now touching the forest floor as the naked trees no longer protected the ground and kept it warm. Thus, they drank eagerly of the hot brew and accepted the bread and cold meat he was able to offer them as food.

As they ate, Iestan in his own inimitable way began to share information with the big man, filling him in on the latest developments in and out of Bremmand. "Hast has made protests to Sallent and to Darvett, apparently," he said. "Hardly surprising when the Queen was King Perrold's daughter. The King of Hast has pledged to do all he can to avenge his daughter's death and help the rightful King regain his throne. I don't think the Kostinians were all that impressed by it, Hast being so small."

"Hast had better be careful," Dale warned. "It's one thing to make angry complaint when the enemy is hundreds of miles away but the Empire is right on their doorstep now. It wouldn't take much for Sallent to unleash his armies on Hast as well."

"It may be small but Hast hasn't been defeated in battle in over six hundred years," Givern put in. "Small doesn't always mean defenceless or helpless." There was a pride in his voice that made Dale look at him in surprise and Givern was obliged to say a trifle apologetically, "My wife was Hastian."

On they talked, Iestan telling of new taxes being imposed on the common people and the ousting of the rightful lords and heirs to every estate and castle by Sallent in order to hand them over to his own friends and vassals. "Petin's out," Iestan remarked succinctly. Lord Petin lorded over all the lands from Rurig to the river which included Chelland as well as Dale's cottage. "His three sons all served in the King's army and Sallent decreed him a traitor. He's given the whole lot to Staval." Iestan spat almost instinctively. "So now we serve and tithe to a real traitor. He's done well at feathering his own nest out of all of this."

"Always the way in war," Dale remarked. "Scum makes its way to the surface when the river's stirred up. It sinks back down to the murky bottom in the end."

"There's a whole range of new taxes coming in as well. Sallent is making every over-lord pay for his nice new title and castles, so they are finding the money for it by squeezing the people. All tradesmen now have to give 100 florin - 100, I ask you! - for the right to hold an established trade in Staval's lordship, to be paid on midwinter every year, or the business is forfeit. What's more, anyone who travels in pays a florin for each visit. They've even started charging merchants market fees in Castle Bremmand. Sallent'll squeeze this land dry within a year if he carries on like this."

Dale rubbed his beard thoughtfully. "If he squeezes too hard, he'll have a rebellion on his hands. The people won't stand for being starved to death in their own homes." In the back of his mind, despite the outrage of the harsh tax he was pleased. Sallent was grabbing all he could and doing it clumsily. If the people were discontented with his rule, they might be less afraid to stand up to it and that would be all to the good for Torvik's infant resistance.

There was a gleam in Iestan's eye too. The man clearly had similar thoughts. He made no allusion to it, however and soon moved the discussion on to other, less contentious matters.

After Iestan and Givern had gone, heading back towards Chelland, Dale explained the significance of Dostain, and what the message had really meant. Allin looked relieved that his brother was safe but on hearing that they were to stay longer he asked immediately, "Does that mean you'll be able to go and help Torvik?"

Dale stared at him. "No, of course it doesn't. What would make you think that?"

"Because you said you couldn't because of us - me and Joss. You thought we'd all be leaving soon, so you wouldn't be able to help them." Allin looked at him with those penetrating blue eyes, daring Dale to argue with him. "But we're staying now. The message said we'd be here all winter. So we can go and fight."

"We?" It might have been amusing if it weren't so troubling that the boy was thinking along such dangerous lines. "You think *we* should be fighting? *You* were planning to join this little army were you?"

"Why not?" the boy demanded, his hands on his hips. "You said the King needed everyone to fight for him so that when he came back he'd have an army waiting ready for him. I can fight - everyone says I'm good with a sword - so why shouldn't I help?"

Dale gazed gravely at him. "We've been through this. We have to remain here until we are sent for. Apart from anything else, Torvik is living rough in the heart of the woods. We can hardly expect that fellow Givern to comb the forest in search of us. Now, stop with this. You don't know what you're talking about."

Allin's eyes narrowed and he said bitterly, "I know that Torvik still can't get the others to work together properly. I know that if he could, he'd be able to start fighting back. And," he said in a soft voice but with a weight and agony that took Dale's breath away, "I know that Sallent killed my family and he's still hurting the people of Bremmand. This is my brother's kingdom and I want to help get it back for him. Don't you?"

Dale thought, and searched, trying to find a way to answer this that would change the boy's mind and yet satisfy him at the same time. And yet – yet? Allin had been orphaned by this madman and his brother. He'd lost parents, brothers, friends, everyone to the savage overrun of the land and now, who could blame him if he wanted to fight back. There was no way, through wit or wisdom that Dale could make him feel differently about that, short of diminishing his family in his eyes.

Nor, indeed did Dale want to. He too burned with the anger and grief over the lost. Friends, compatriots, lovers - all had fallen to the sword. All deserved their deaths to count for something and hiding out in the forest, playing the humble woodsman was no way to do that. Slowly, with feeling he spoke.

"I want to fight Allin. I want to fight so badly that sometimes it hurts. I see the people of Bremmand injured and frightened and their pride crushed like a flower under the heel of a boot."

"Then why...?"

"Because this is where the King will send to find us. He needs to know where we are, when he comes. That means, however distasteful it is to either one of us, we must remain here, where he can find us."

Allin was silent and then suddenly his hand slid across the gap between them and rested on Dale's arm. "You hate it as much as I do, don't you?"

"I do, Allin, I do."

"I'm sorry. I didn't understand."

"How could you? I didn't do too good a job of understanding your sudden desire for bloodletting either."

"Well!" The boy sounded suddenly all business — somehow, absurdly comical coming from one so young — "now that we understand one another, we shall have to try to be more tolerant of the other's feelings."

For all it was amusing to hear such words coming from a child and even though it was almost certainly a quote from a nurse or adult escort to the boy, Dale wasn't about to belittle him, so he nodded and offered his hand. "You have my word as a woodsman and an officer."

"And you have mine as a Marchand and a... a," he stumbled to find some other rank by which his oath might have meaning. Finally he found one and, with a sly smile, he finished, "a gardener."

Allin and Joss were alone at the cottage some two weeks later, Dale having left them for a few hours to haul a load of timber to the main pathway. They had fed the animals, looked with interest at the hens, three of whom were now broody, to see if any eggs had hatched yet and had carefully pulled out any weeds from the garden so that the tubers which they had planted could continue to grow without competition.

Now, the daily chores done (except Allin's studies, which somehow slipped his mind) they were sitting on the grass outside the cottage laying out pebbles to make patterns in the ground.

So absorbed were they in picking out patterns in the mud that Allin failed to hear the footfall of someone approaching the cottage. It was only when he got up to pick more stones out of the garden that he finally saw the arrival of a stranger to their home.

Dale had, by now, carefully coached Allin in what to do if someone did come to the cottage. This was their home and there was no reason for anyone, whoever they were, ever to see him and his sister as anything but normal children. All he had to do was to stay calm, show no concern and come to find Dale as soon as possible. It had all seemed very straightforward, but now, faced with a visit from a stranger for the first time, Allin couldn't help but feel a burst of anxiety that he was about to be caught out.

Taking a deep breath to try and steady his nerves he reached down, grabbed his sister's hand and pulled her upright and behind him, so that she should be safe. Then, having made sure of her protection he faced the stranger as bravely as he could manage.

The man was tall, and solidly built, with an unruly shock of dirty, red hair and an unkempt beard which marked him out clearly enough as a woodsman, for all they were matted and plastered down against his head. His clothes were grubby and hanging off him, as if he had lost a lot of weight but had no means of getting something to fit him better. Slung over his shoulder was a leather bag and in his right hand was a stout oak stick. The other arm was tucked in to his waist band as if it was injured and when he moved toward the children Allin could see that he had a curious, sideways way of walking, as if his left leg didn't work properly.

"Can I help you, sir?" Allin asked, a little breathlessly.

"Who are you? What are you doing here?" the man demanded, seemingly surprised to see them there.

Allin ignored the first question and said, "We live here. This is our home. Was there something you wanted?"

"*You* live here?" Allin nodded, wondering why this was being questioned when Dale had assured him that this was the one thing that no-one would even think to doubt. "Well," the man said gruffly, "explain to me how that can be when this is *my* home?"

Allin stared. He couldn't think of a single answer to this. "It can't be," he said a little stupidly, "you must be mistaken. We live here."

"Who's *we*? You and the girl?"

"Yes, and our friend. He's in the woods at the moment but he's expected back any minute." How Allin wished this was true!

"And how long have you been here?"

"I don't know. A while." Allin tried to be vague to make it sound as if they had been here longer than the few moons it had actually been.

"I see. Came across this place did you? Saw it was empty and thought you'd move in, did you?" The man looked down at them, starting to sound aggressive.

Somehow this accusation that they didn't have a right to be here, that they had stolen the cottage made Allin angry and in that anger he found his confidence.

No-one was going to make out that this wasn't his home! Indignantly he flared back, "No, we didn't! This is our home and we have every right to be here. If you think it's yours then you must be wrong. This is the wrong cottage or you're in the wrong woods. You can't come along here, pretend this is yours and hope you can make us leave so that you can steal it away from us. It's *our home and you can't have it.*"

'Now look here, boy!" The man glared, and took one of his oddly twisted steps toward the lad, looking as if he wanted to box the boy's ears but then he was arrested by a stern and familiar voice, ringing across the clearing.

"Lay a hand on him, and you'll answer to me."

"Dale!" Allin cried in some relief.

"Dale!" the man said, simultaneously, astonished to see him there.

Despite his stern tone, Dale was smiling and he came across the clearing in a hurry. Without another word the two men embraced, then as they broke apart breathless and laughing Dale said, "I see you've met Allin and Joss. Children this is Jareth Ronas, my brother. Jareth, meet Allin and Joss of Lech"

Allin blinked in some surprise and Joss simply stared at the stranger from behind her brother's legs.

Jareth nodded his greeting but spoke only to Dale, "I was a little surprised to see them claiming this place as their own but if they're yours…"

"Hardly!" Dale remarked. "Delan's been gone some six years."

"By that woman of yours in Castle Bremmand then," Jareth shrugged. "Rana or what ever her name was."

Allin couldn't help give out a squeak of surprise at this. He and his brothers had suspected something but had never been sure that Rana was seeing one of the officers.

Blithely Dale took no notice, setting his brother straight with the same story he'd told everyone else; that Allin and Joss were fostered on him as a favour to a fellow soldier who went to fight and that he was caring for them until their return.

"But you didn't go to fight?" Jareth looked surprised. "I thought you must surely have been in the final battle. In fact I rather thought you were lost. Lord Petin sent his three sons to fight and not one of them made it back."

"I was injured before the battle," Dale explained, "not fit to fight. That was what brought me back here. I had to make my living the old way. Didn't Iestan tell you that, when you came through Chelland?"

The brothers had seen little of one another since the big man had first left home to join the army at sixteen. Dale had found and secured his lame brother a post at Lord Petin's castle and, from then on, contact had been infrequent and often by chance. Both had made the journey home from time to time when duties allowed but never at the same time. When their father had died and Dale took over his father's business at the cottage, they had been able to see one another more often but then Dale returned to the army and their only link had been via the innkeeper in Chelland. Jareth would sometimes pass through Chelland on some errand for his lord and Iestan would pass on what news he'd heard from Dale. Similarly, Dale would travel to Chelland when he got leave and Iestan would fill him in on his younger brother. But Jareth was shaking his head.

"I didn't come that way. I wasn't about to go anywhere near people. Not when I didn't know what reception I was going to get. What could I do if there *was* trouble?" He sounded bitter. "Run away? So I stayed on the ancient paths. I don't think I saw a soul in the whole journey but I got here all right."

Almost as if he hadn't noticed it up to now, Dale suddenly seemed to see his brother's ragged state. "You look done in, boy. Come, sit by the fire and rest. Here, Allin," this imperiously, as if the boy was little more than his servant, "go fetch him something to eat and a tankard of brew. Make it quick!"

Allin looked first astonished and then annoyed at this high-handed treatment but he went, all the same. By the time he returned, the conversation had turned on to Jareth's affairs.

"… heard about Petin going," Dale was saying. "Though I'm a little surprised it took so long."

Jareth gave a disdainful snort. "Got what he deserved, the old hypocrite. He lasted because he did what he could to keep his own seat warm. When the dust settled from the final battle and it was clear how the land lay, he couldn't wait to send messengers to this new 'Governor,' as he's called, saying how he was a loyal subject and offering funds and the loyalty of his people. You'd think he hadn't remembered that these were the same people that killed his own sons on the battlefield. He even stood by and said nothing when they did…" - he shuddered - "what they did at the Abbey. So, Sallent let him stay there, played him for a fool while he secured the rest of the kingdom and then, when he had the time, he turned his attention to Petin."

"And decided he didn't like what he saw?"

"That, or he saw how rich the lands were and decided to gift them elsewhere, so had to find an excuse. The soldiers who came to oust him said something about Sallent not being able to trust a man who turns so easily. They came, killed Petin in his own hall, his wife with him and then rampaged through the rest of the castle, killing anyone who looked to be a threat, and having their fun with the women." He pulled a disgusted face. "The next morning, our new 'master' rode up and took possession."

"Staval," Dale said flatly.

"Staval!" Jareth agreed in the same flat tone – so similar a tone in fact, that they sounded identical. He squared his shoulders. "Well, I for one won't serve a traitor. I'm loyal, and I'll die that way, if that's what it takes. So, I left and came here."

He said it simply, but Dale knew this was a greater feat for his brother than for another man. Jareth, when born, had been deformed – either within the womb, or during the delivery. His left leg and arm were twisted and misshapen, the knee and shoulder joints facing the wrong way and the foot shrivelled and barely there. The muscles never developed properly and, though he would admit it to no-one else, he was constantly in pain. For most men, the walk from Lord Petin's castle at Rurig took two days at most but for Jareth, even following the main paths, it would have taken the best part of a week. To have avoided the open routes and taken to the forest, without the ability to hunt for himself, it would have been a gruelling time for his younger brother.

But Jareth was proud and hated to be treated as if he was a special case, so Dale didn't attempt to declare himself impressed with the man's achievement. Instead, he said merely, "Well, you're home now and we're glad to see you." Suddenly a thought struck him and he said with more feeling, "Really glad to have you, aren't we Allin?"

Allin didn't look convinced but he nodded politely, saying nothing. He didn't like this sudden intrusion into their lives and rather wished Dale would tell this man that there wasn't room for him. Dale was clearly delighted to see his brother and was devoted to him, judging by the way they spent the rest of the day sitting by the fire in the clearing talking to one another. They talked of the things they had done, the places they had been, stories of their respective lives and then, when they exhausted this line of conversation, moved on to reminiscences of their childhood together. To add insult to injury, Dale had Allin running about after them both, waiting on them like he was a servant. No, it didn't please the boy one little bit to have this newcomer at the cottage and he determinedly sulked and stamped his way through the rest of the day to show his disapproval.

Jareth slept late the next morning, exhausted by his time struggling for survival in the woods. Dale, as always, was up early and when Allin rose he was alone in the clearing, chopping wood and whistling – something Allin had never heard him do before – clearly full of joy at the new turn of events.

"Good morning!" he said sunnily to his young charge, "Beautiful morning, isn't it?" That much was true. It was approaching winter now, and cold, but the sun was out and it was one of those gloriously clear, fresh mornings which made a man feel glad to be alive.

"'S all right," Allin muttered, annoyed at how pleased Dale *still* was to have his brother here.

Dale sunk his axe in to the wood block and put his hands on his hips. "Now, what's the matter with *you?*" he demanded but still with a smile on his face. "You're like a bear that's been woken in winter."

"Nothing's the matter," Allin lied. "Why should anything be the matter?"

"Well, you'll have to tell me that. But something's eating at you and has been since yester.... Ahh!" light dawned. "So that's it."

Allin scowled. "What?"

"Jareth coming put your nose out of joint, has it?"

"No." Another lie, and an even more transparent one than the last. "Why should I care? What difference should it make to me if you spend all your time with him. I don't care if you never do anything but talk to him ever again. It's not as if I have any need for you."

Dale blinked, as always both amused and surprised by the vehemence of this ten-year-old when his temper was stirred. He was also a little taken aback at the jealous way Allin seemed to regard him. Suddenly the boy wasn't willing to share him with another. Mildly, Dale remarked, "It isn't so long ago, my young friend, that you were all but demanding that we go and join Torvik, so that I could lead his little army. If you don't like me spending one afternoon with my brother – who I've not seen in, oh, probably six years – how would you have felt about that? How much time do you suppose I'd have for you then?"

It was a good point and Allin didn't really have an answer for it. He scowled deeply and scuffed at the ground with his foot.

Dale grinned, and then said, almost conspiratorially to the boy, "If the truth be told you should be as pleased as I am at Jareth coming here."

"Why?"

"Well, don't you see? Jareth is the answer to our problem."

Allin frowned. "What problem?" He had no idea what Dale was talking about.

Seeing the lack of comprehension in the boy's face, the big man went on a trifle impatiently, "The problem of having to wait at the cottage for word from…" - he paused and, erring on the side of caution in case Jareth was awake and in hearing – even his brother couldn't know the truth – "Dostain."

Still mystified, Allin said, "I don't know what you mean."

"Come on boy, think about it! If Jareth is at the cottage, he can wait for any message, so…."

Now Allin was beginning to understand. He finished the sentence "… you don't have to be here." Dale could go and help Torvik. That was what he was saying. Slowly, not quite sure he liked the sound of it, Allin said, "You're going to leave me and Joss here with him?"

Dale hadn't considered that but then the children were his responsibility so it hadn't even occurred to him. "No." He waited for Allin to digest this and stood and watched as slowly realization, then joy spread across his face.

In a hushed tone, almost not daring to believe it Allin said, "We can go? We can fight?"

"We can go," Dale agreed. "*I* can fight" He stressed the amendment carefully. "Jareth will stay here; be here in case our friend Givern, or anyone else for that matter, comes looking for us and he can care for the animals and tend the gardens – he's good at both of those jobs – and even do a bit of woodman's work. He'd need help but he could manage quite comfortably. You and I and Joss will go to Torvik's camp and see if they are willing to let me join them and we can start to do something to get ready for when the King comes to reclaim his kingdom."

Allin looked immensely pleased about this but then a shadow of doubt flitted across his face. "Won't Jareth want to come too? Won't he want to fight?"

"He can't, Allin. Much as he may want to, his body won't allow it. You leave him to me. I can make him see that, by staying here, he can be helping fight for the King."

So, later that day, Dale took Jareth aside and said with forced easiness, "Brother, you said yesterday you were loyal. I need that loyalty to help me. There is a small party of men in the woods not far from here. There are few of them but they are mostly soldiers. They think that the King will return and he is going to need every fighting man he can find to help win Bremmand back for the bloodline. They've asked me to join them."

Carefully, Dale explained the problem of having to wait in the cottage because it was the only place Allin's family would know when they came for him. He explained the dilemma of the animals and the wood deal. He stressed his desire, as another loyal man, to serve his King and prepare for battle once more.

Having heard all this Jareth gave his a sideways look and said, "If you are wanting me to suggest I stay here in your stead, as if it was my idea and not yours, then you are wasting your time." He smiled. "Just ask me, Dale, I'll probably say yes. I might even be pleased to help."

First light, two days later. It was cold and overcast, the sky open above, unobstructed by the denuded trees. Dale stepped out from the cottage with a leather pack on his back and his sword – his King's sword – slung easily at his hip. As Allin and Joss came to join him the first flurries of snow began to make their way gently downward from the sky.

"We'll have to hurry," Dale remarked. "If this sets in before we get there, we could have a nasty journey."

"We'll get there," Allin said confidently. He sounded calm, not in the least excited or worried at what they were about to do. In fact he was as contented as Dale had ever known him. "Let's go."

Dale nodded and they began to walk across the clearing together, away from the place that had formed their lives together for the past six moon-cycles. When they reached the tree line, Dale could not help but notice that neither Allin nor Joss made so much as a backward glance at what had been their home.

"No regrets?" he asked, smiling gently.

He looked down on his two charges. Allin turned and looked up to him, their eyes meeting. His face glowed clear and open, framed by the dark hair, now looking over-long and shaggy, and lit by the clear blue eyes that shone in the morning air. He was holding Joss's hand, as she stood beside him, as always held in his protection and linked by his devotion. Dale felt a swell of pride at these two – these *Golden Children* as Trystin had once described them. He thought briefly of the thin scholar and the "apprentice" in his charge and added Cori to his feelings of respect for the Marchand family. By Brem's beard, this was a family worth fighting for!

"No regrets!" Allin agreed. "No more waiting and hiding. Now we start fighting back!"

The legend of Holy Lord Brem

In the ancient times, when Yorin was only made up of a few tribes, Brem Marchand was baron in the west of the continent. He was a fierce warrior and sought power and lands with eagerness and ruthless zeal. The overlords feared his ambition and Brem exploited his position as that of a troublesome minor lord with some relish. He was arrogant and aggressive and not well liked. Even his own people served through fear rather than love or respect. In his pride he saw himself as too mighty to answer even to God and he turned away from his faith.

Then, in one of his many raids on neighbouring lands, his eyes fell upon a woman, Langilia, who was more beautiful than any he had seen before. Her hair was like sunlight and she had eyes of the clearest blue. The moment he saw her, Brem knew he must have her, so he stole her away from her own people like a barbarian. Despite this ruthless act, he loved her with a passion and much to everyone's surprise she returned his affection. Only when he was with Langilia did Brem show any sign of kindness or good nature. To all others he was haughty and proud.

As preparations were being made for their bonding, Langilia was struck down by a terrible fever and nothing anyone could do seemed to be able to save her. In desperation, Brem prayed to God to spare her. God heard Brem and replied to him, offering him a bargain. If God spared Langilia then Brem must turn his ambitious ways aside and instead lead his people in three tenets of righteous living: Faith, Family and Learning.

Proud Brem agreed. He would have agreed to anything. All he wanted was his love to be spared. So God answered Brem's prayers and Langilia recovered on the morning of her planned bonding with her lord.

Now, having got what he wanted, Brem no longer saw the need to keep his bargain with God, so instead of adopting a more devout way of living, he turned his efforts to building an army planning to lay siege to one of the neighbouring overlords and take over his lands.

God was angered by this betrayal of their pact and Brem awoke one morning to find Langilia gone, taken in the night. Bereft without his adored wife, Brem forgot all plans of conquest and instead set all his forces to scour the land and find his lady. But it was all for naught. No trace was found of Langilia, or even any clue as to who might have taken her. In despair and anger, he raised his army once more and attacked and destroyed the overlords of Yorin, one by one. By the time he was done, he held all the settled lands of the continent, but the costs of his conquests were dear. Brem's few friends and most of his armies were gone, the land was in disarray and he still had no wife to serve as his companion in life.

Only now, when he surveyed the wreckage of these once great lands, did Brem turn once more to God.

"Hear me, God," he cried. "Give me comfort in my sorrow."

"Why?" God replied. "You broke faith with me when I helped you before. I have no interest in you."

God did not speak to Brem again, however much he prayed and begged and pleaded but the proud lord finally began to understand that there was no joy in a world where God had forsaken you.

Half out of his mind with grief from the loss of his wife and now the abandonment of his God, Brem travelled across the sea to the lonely west. There he settled in the wooded lands where the weather was inclement and the living hard. His intention was to end his life in this deserted place, away from all the things in which he had once found pride.

For two years he remained, living as a hermit, unkempt and wild, berating himself for his folly at breaking faith with his God. He wandered about the woodlands, eating little and talking only to himself.

Then, in the midst of the dark and wild forests he came upon a people, unlike any he had ever known before. They were little more than savages - big unkempt creatures, with rust-coloured hair and little knowledge in the ways of civilisation. Their language was alien too but despite great strength there was a gentleness in their nature. Seeing this man out of his wits and starving, they befriended him, tending to his basic needs. In return Brem, still raving, urged them not to forsake God and to always think of Faith, Family and Learning. In order to make himself understood with this simple community he began to learn their language and to teach them his. Painstakingly, to save these poor savages from his own fate, Brem provided them with simple rules that would ensure that they kept to God's three tenets - how to observe the faith, how to value the family and how to continue learning.

As they learned to understand this crazy hermit the Woodsmen, as Brem called them, realised that, despite his strange ways, there was something of value in the words of this madman and they began to follow his rules even as they began to consider Brem to be their prophet.

It was some three years later when Brem, while walking in the forest alone, came upon a stream. Brem was puzzled at first. By now he knew these woods well and never before had he come upon water in this place. What was more, the water was pure, clean and fresh. Not even a leaf from the forest was tainting it.

In some curiosity he followed the stream, to see where it led him. For several days he walked, not stopping to eat or sleep, his only sustenance the fresh water that flowed past him. The terrain grew harder with each day, rising from flat land to slope, from slope to hill and from hill to mountain. Finally, on the eighth day, he came to the foot of a cliff, down which was pouring a waterfall. Brem was unable to scale the sheer rock face but now his desire to find the source of the stream was so strong that he was unable to give up his quest. He walked along the edge of the cliff, seeking some way up, until he found a narrow path up the rock face. The route was treacherous but Brem no longer cared. He must find the spring from which this miraculous pure water came.

Tearing his fingers almost to the bone and sustaining many injuries from falling, he scrambled up the rock face. It took him a day and a night but Brem did not give up. Just as dawn was breaking, he finally reached the top. The top of the cliff was a flat table, several miles across, a rich and fertile meadowland. In the distance, Brem could just make out a little spinney, towards the place where the waterfall must have been. He began to run, knowing that the end of his quest was in sight and he would soon find what lay at the source of the water.

As he reached the edge of the trees he stopped. From within the woods, out of his sight, came the sound of a woman's singing - a woman's voice which was familiar to him. Hardly daring to believe it, Brem walked softly in to the coppice and there, sitting on a stone combing her hair by the bubbling spring, sat Langilia just as young and beautiful as she was when he had last seen her, ten years before.

She turned to him and smiled, merely saying, "My dearest one, what a long journey you have taken to find me and yourself once more. Now, come and sit beside me and rest, for God has a task for us both and you must be ready."

Brem sat beside her laying his head in her lap while his wife cupped her hands and helped him drink of the stream at its source. Instantly his injuries fell away, his troubled mind was healed and the ill-health borne of five years of neglect were gone from him.

"You have redeemed yourself." God spoke to him in a voice so quiet that none could hear it, save for those in this holiest of places. "You have raised the woodsmen of this untamed land in my ways and bought for yourself a second chance. I choose you to establish my people here in this land. Everything to the east, west and south that can be seen from here and everything to the north as far as the ocean will be yours. This I promise to you, and to your peoples. Journey across the sea once more and bring your followers here to settle these lands. As long as you and your line dwell here, as long as you continue to have faith in me, thus will these lands be yours."

With much rejoicing and wonder Brem and Langilia journeyed to the east and their home of the past to tell their people of how God had visited his goodness upon them and granted them the right to establish a dynasty in the western woods. Many doubted Brem's word, thinking him mad, and remembered the deceit and betrayal of before. Others, who were beginning to rebuild the lands destroyed by years of war, did not want to leave their homes to start again in the west. But there were some, numbering three thousand from Brem's people and one thousand of the flaxen-haired people from the south west - Langilia's homeland - who believed and followed Brem back to the Great Forest, to join the woodsman and make up the diverse Bremmandish people.

On the high rock where God returned to Brem, there did the people built a great castle, sustained by and at the same time protecting the holy source of the stream. With the help of his followers - Woodsmen, Bremmandish men with the dark hair and stature of their overlord, and the Langatians, blonde and fair of face like the beautiful Langilia - he populated the lands.

By the time Brem died, at the age of 91, his peoples had declared him King. His first son, the first man to be born and raised in the new kingdom of Bremmand took over his *father's role to lead and guide the people in the ways of God and the three tenets of Faith, Family and Learning. From that time on, the pact with God was always maintained and always at least one member of the Marchand line descended directly from Brem and Langilia remained within the Bremmandish borders to ensure that Bremmand continued to belong to her people.*

Printed in the United Kingdom
by Lightning Source UK Ltd.
115360UKS00001B/120